Sinner

Sinner

SHARON CARTER ROGERS

RIVEROAK®
Good News in Fiction

COOK COMMUNICATIONS MINISTRIES
Colorado Springs, Colorado • Paris, Ontario
KINGSWAY COMMUNICATIONS LTD
Eastbourne, England

RiverOak® is an imprint of
Cook Communications Ministries, Colorado Springs, CO 80918
Cook Communications, Paris, Ontario
Kingsway Communications, Eastbourne, England

Cover Design: BMB Design Inc.

First printing, 2007
Printed in the United States of America

1 2 3 4 5 6 7 8 9 10

Unless otherwise indicated, all Scripture quotations are taken from the *Holy Bible, New Living
Translation,* copyright © 1996. Used by permission of Tyndale House Publishers, Inc.,
Wheaton, Illinois 60189. All rights reserved. Scripture quotations marked NIV are taken from
the *Holy Bible, New International Version*®. *NIV*®. Copyright © 1973, 1978, 1984 by
International Bible Society. Used by permission of Zondervan. All rights reserved.

ISBN 978-1-58919-097-9

LCCN 2006932445

For Steve
who captured my imagination decades ago
and has never let go of it since
—SCR

Acknowledgments

First, a grand "thank you" to all the fine people at David C. Cook. Without your enthusiasm and support, this story would still be clattering around in the darkness where the back of my brain resides.

To my agent, Steve Laube … what can I say? You are, without doubt, the best in the business. I'm still a little shocked that you agreed to represent someone like me—but I'm not letting you off the hook, so get used to it.

To my editor, Michael Warden. Thank you for your passion for fiction, and your careful handling of my words.

To Dan Benson, editorial director at David C. Cook. You made this happen. I hope the result is something that will make you proud.

To my killer readers' group—A., N., W., E., K., T., and J.—thanks for your time and impressive feedback. You made this a better book.

And last, but not least, to the one who has always been a friend of sinners. You changed me, and I am forever grateful.

—SCR, 2007

"Life is not what one lived, but what one remembers and how one remembers it in order to recount it."
—GABRIEL GARCIA MARQUEZ, in *Living to Tell the Tale*

"What power would Hell have if those [t]here imprisoned were not able to dream of Heaven?"
—NEIL GAIMAN, in *The Sandman: Preludes and Nocturnes*

"All have sinned and fall short of the glory of God."
—PAUL THE APOSTLE, in Romans 3:23 (NIV)

ONE

FATHER MICHEL RENAULT DIDN'T NOTICE THE VIS-
itor in the chapel of Saint Anthony's Cathedral until he heard
the soft swoosh of the confessional door closing to his left.

He frowned worriedly. "I'm coming," he called. But his
gaze still lingered on the splintered empty drawer protrud-
ing awkwardly from his desk.

The office had looked undisturbed when he entered it
earlier that morning ... until he happened to glance at the
locked drawer of his desk and noticed it had been forcibly
opened. The contents were personal; it contained no weekly
offerings or valuables of the church. Yet it had been completely emptied. The rest of his office remained untouched.

Now the mystery of the empty drawer haunted his tasks, agitating his every thought and distracting him from giving full attention to his duties.

"I'm coming," he called out again as he hurried toward the side of the confessional reserved for priests. He actively pushed his thoughts away from his office and toward the soul inside the booth who needed his services. A moment later, he slid with a practiced ease into the tiny compartment reserved for him. At six foot two and weighing over 220 pounds, the former college linebacker always felt a bit squeezed when inside there. At the same time, it was a familiar constriction, one that was almost comforting. He'd spent many hours alone inside this little room, confessing his own sins before God. In here, at least, was temporary peace and confidence.

He slid open the window between the priest and sinner and caught a filigreed glimpse of a man sitting on the bench across from him.

"Thank you for waiting," he said kindly. "What can I do for you, my son?"

"Bless me, Father, for I have sinned." The voice was even, controlled. Businesslike.

"How long has it been since your last confession, my son?"

A pause. Then, "A lifetime, Father."

Renault nodded knowingly, even though the confessor was looking away. "Go on, son."

"I've had impure thoughts today, Father."

"Yes. Go on."

"I imagined myself beating a priest to a bloody pulp."

A sudden fear seized the priest. He tried to shake off

the trembling in his stomach. Involuntarily, he clenched his fists. He was no small man, he reasoned. And years of playing football before dedicating his life to the church had certainly taught him how to handle himself in a fight, if the situation warranted it. Still, something in the sinner's voice cut through his defenses. Something calm and terrifying in the way this other man spoke. As if ... as if he ...

"And Father? I enjoyed it."

Renault stood quickly and reached for the door.

"Don't run, Father. It will do you no good anyway."

Father Renault flew across the carpet of the sanctuary, racing toward the huge cathedral doors that led to the outside, to safety. He didn't look back.

The stranger caught him after only twenty feet or so, yanking hard on the back of his collar, releasing just in time to let Renault's head crack hard on the floor.

Renault tasted blood from the gash his teeth had cut in his tongue. He rolled quickly, instinct taking over. In a moment he was on his feet, facing the stranger and cautiously edging backward toward the sanctuary outside the doors.

"Now listen, son," he spoke soothingly, palms facing outward toward the man. "You don't want to do this."

"Yes, Father," the stranger grinned fiercely. "I really do."

Renault took his first good look at the sinner. The man was neither small nor large. Six feet tall, at best. His dark hair was long and hung carelessly down his face, where the front tickled his chin and the back straddled his shoulders. He was not large, no, but he was solid. He wore a black ribbed shirt and a charcoal-colored, thigh-length coat. Even through the clothing, Renault could make out the build of a man who had apparently spent many years in a weight room. His legs were thick and muscled, too, and judging by how fast he had caught the priest, he obviously was quick. Still, the Father figured the stranger couldn't weigh more than 175 or 180 pounds. Renault had the weight advantage. And the height advantage too. That was something, wasn't it?

The priest drew in a breath, straightened his shoulders, and closed his fingers into fists. "I'm warning you, son. I don't want to have to hurt you." His mind and his body traveled back to the football days, when it felt good to menace an opponent—and it felt better to hurt him. Confidence flooded back into his soul. Yes, this stranger had picked the wrong priest on the wrong day.

The Sinner's voice turned to ice, and his face to stone. "Don't worry, Father. You won't hurt me."

Renault never saw the blow coming, a heel to the groin that left him gasping in unexpected agony on the floor. The stranger leaned close to his ear.

"First," he said, "I'm going to break at least two of your ribs, Father."

Renault swung hard toward the voice, but his attacker was too fast and easily out of reach before the fist could land. Less than a second later the priest felt the hard toe of a boot digging viciously into his side. He yelped and tried to crawl away, but the boot landed a second time, making him curl into a soggy ball of pain. The kicks came again, harsh and relentless, until the priest felt one, then a second of his ribs crack in his side. His lungs felt like they were on fire, and he felt dizzy with pain.

"Next, I think I will break an arm. You are left-handed, correct?"

The heel of the boot stepped quickly and firmly on Renault's left forearm. It snapped with little resistance. The priest screamed; the man resumed casually kicking at the fallen priest on the ground.

"Please ..." Renault croaked finally, "please ..."

The kicking stopped, briefly, and Renault felt strong hands grab and lift him to almost a standing position.

"What did you say?"

The priest gasped, coughed, gagged on the blood in his mouth.

The stranger balled a fist and cracked a blow directly on the bridge of Renault's nose. Renault passed out then, briefly, and when he came to, he was still being held up by the attacker's hands.

"Please ..." the priest whispered over swollen tongue and through the bloody river streaming down his face. "Please ... don't hurt me ... anymore."

The savage before him leaned in close, looking deeply into the priest's eyes. The stranger's eyes were chocolate brown, calm. Controlled. But flecked behind the chocolate were tiny dots of reddish gold, as if this man had seen the fires of hell, and traces of it had been spattered into the pigment itself.

"Are you listening to yourself, Father?" the man whispered. "Haven't you heard those words before?"

Pictures flashed unbidden through Renault's memory.

He closed his eyes tightly, releasing tears of agony. "Why ... why are you doing this?" he moaned.

"Because I've seen you, Father," the Sinner said calmly, still supporting the full weight of the beaten and bloody man of God. "I know what you've done with the others. And I've seen you with Hector Gomez."

The priest shook his head in protest. "But," he grimaced at the effort of trying to breathe and speak at the same time. "But I've done nothing to Hector. Nothing."

"Right," the attacker said firmly. "And you never will."

Father Renault closed his eyes again, and finally began to pray. To plead with God for mercy.

"I'm going to blind you now, Father." The voice was still, even calm, as if it were discussing the weather or ordering coffee. "I will leave you one eye, though. One eye to remember. One eye to look for me. Because if you ever see me again, Father, I will take that one too."

Pain exploded like dynamite in the priest's left eye socket. Darkness, sweet darkness, spread through Renault's consciousness as he felt the orbital bone in his skull crack, then break beneath his skin. His body fell limp to the ground.

†

THE SINNER STOOD FOR A MOMENT, LOOKING DOWN AT THE man he had just bloodied and beaten. He absently rubbed his forehead where the brunt of his head butt had broken the priest's skull. Then with a swift movement, he removed Father Renault's personal items from a pocket in the lining of his coat and dropped them unceremoniously on the priest's unconscious body. He turned to leave the now-silent church and saw a boy standing, open-mouthed, in the doorway.

"Call the police, Hector," he said quietly as he walked toward the door. "And an ambulance." The boy didn't move. "You'd better hurry. He's going to wake up soon, and when he does, he'll be in a lot of pain."

The stranger disappeared through the door, pausing just long enough to make sure Hector had run toward the back room where a phone could be found.

†

"Nine-one-one operator. What is the nature of your emergency?"

"Um, I need an ambulance. Please hurry."

"Are you hurt?"

"No. But Father Renault is. He hurt him real bad. He needs help."

"Okay. Everything's going to be all right."

"I'm at St. Anthony's. I don't know the address. But the man hurt him bad. You've got to hurry."

"I've got the address. I've notified police and dispatched an ambulance to your location. Everything's going to be all right. Did you see who attacked the priest? Did he use a gun?"

"Yeah. I mean no. I mean, a man came in the church and beat up Father Renault. I don't think he used a gun."

"Can you see the Father? Can you tell if he's breathing?"

"No, he's in the main sanctuary. I had to come back to the church offices to find a phone."

"Can you hear the sirens yet?"

"No. Are they coming? I don't hear anything."

"Yes, they'll be there any minute. You can trust me. I promise, help is on the way. Is there anyone else there at the church with you?

"No. I don't know. I didn't see anybody."

"What's your name?"

"Hector. Hector Gomez."

"You're very brave, Hector …"   †

The dream always begins the same way. It's the eyes I see first. Large. Brown. Tired. They stare at me from behind the thin branches and brambles of the wild berry vines. A slow blink, and the eyes peek into my soul.

The smells come next. Hot, dusty, summer morning odors that mix aromas of sweat, dirt, and sticky blackberries ripe on the vine.

I move slowly, kneeling to make my eyes level with the ones I see.

"Hello there," I whisper. "What's your name?"

She doesn't answer.

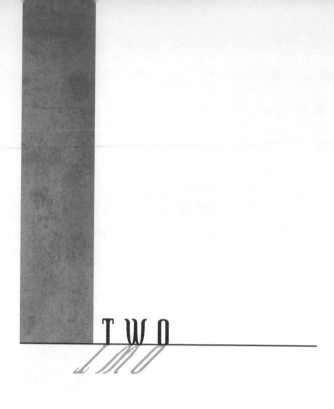

TWO

CELIA KAYE IVORS HEARD THE PHONE RINGING, SAW the blinking numbers on her caller-ID display, and turned her attention toward more important matters.

"Let's see now," she said to herself, "green can kill him. Red causes temporary, unexpected mental, emotional, or physical changes. And gold, well, gold can rob him of his powers forever."

She reached across the display case and lifted out all three of the colored Styrofoam balls from among the action figures and memorabilia that made up her collection.

"But never fear, Superman," she said grandly, "for in my hands, Kryptonite is merely a puffy ball to be juggled in childlike delight when one is avoiding whatever it is that she should really be doing."

In the background she heard the answering machine click on. "Hey, you've reached CK. I'm busy solving mysteries and winning Pulitzer prizes, so leave a message, and when I'm done I'll give you a call back." The long beep-tone indicated that at least seven previous messages had gone unanswered.

"CK!" the voice on message number eight was friendly, with an element of strained joviality. "It's John Corson. Okay, so I haven't gotten you the Pulitzer yet, but I'm working on it. Your newest book has a real shot, to be honest. And it's selling like hotcakes. Steady sales, too. Still on the nonfiction bestseller list, even though it released more than three months ago. Wow, who knew so many people would be obsessed with finding out the real story behind the '87 Cadillac murders? Well, I guess you did, right?"

The voice gave a forced chuckle, then paused briefly, as if summoning up courage. "Listen, CK, in two hours I've got that editorial meeting I told you about, and, well, I promised the team that I'd have that 'lights-out, dynamite newest' concept for your next book to show them. I've already stalled them twice, and, well, they're getting grumpy about it. So whaddya say, CK? Do your old editor a favor and give me a call back right away so I can keep my job for at least one more day. Okay? Call me, CK. Hope to talk to you soon."

The answering machine fell silent. Miss Ivors sighed and gently returned the Kryptonite to its rightful place among the Superman artifacts.

"Never shoulda signed that fifth contract," she muttered.

"What idiot signs a book contract without knowing what she's going to write about?"

The first book had been easy. It was mostly just a compilation of her newspaper columns exposing problems in the national government. Not a best seller, but it had done well enough to warrant a second book. By that time she'd become interested in what looked like a cover-up in the antiquities department of the National Museum Association. When she was done writing, her little journalistic investigation came across as "Indiana Jones meets the Bride of Frankenstein." At least that's the way *Time* magazine had described it in their review. That was the breakout book, and the one that defined her style—and her audience. Real-life mysteries, solved by the never-photographed, never-interviewed CK Ivors. Most people didn't even know whether CK was male or female, and that was just the way she liked it.

After the success of *Ancient Secrets, Modern Lies*, the publisher had quickly locked her up to write three more books, and CK quit the newspaper to do that full time. She also used her now-hefty advance money to put a down payment on a big house with some acreage in the snootier section of the city. It was there she wrote *The Real Story of John Wilkes Booth*, which came out next and soaked up rave reviews on its way to selling close to a million copies. Then was *The Mysterious Cadillac Murders*, which—if Corson was telling the truth—looked like it would pass the million-seller mark sometime in the next month or two.

Of course, CK liked the perks that came with being a successful author. It was always nice to deposit a big, fat check into her once-skinny bank account. It was also a thrill to get on a plane and see another passenger (or two) all caught up in the pages of *Ancient Secrets* or *Cadillac Murders*. But after five years of nonstop writing, investigating, writing some more, doing more research, revising, reading galleys, and so on, she felt ready for a break. A good long one, with lots of tea and side orders of chocolate and amusement parks.

"Never shoulda signed that fifth contract," she sighed again.

The sound of sirens blaring past her front door ended her self-pity, replacing it with the insatiable curiosity that was CK's most persistent trait. She hurried across the room to where her desk, computer, and other equipment sat idly waiting to be put to work. A flip of a switch and the police scanner was on.

"Ten-four, dispatch," a voice crackled over the speakers. "ETA at St. Anthony's Cathedral is three minutes. Is there a 907K?"

"Roger that," the dispatcher replied. "According to the boy, the priest was beaten up pretty good. Paramedics should be on the scene any minute."

"Ten-four." A pause. Then, "Unit F-7 to dispatch. Code 6A, out of car to investigate. We'll need backup over here. Looks like a crowd is already forming on scene."

"Roger that."

"Also code 914, requesting detectives on the scene."

"Roger."

A new voice cut in. "Unit F-2 to dispatch. We're four blocks away. ETA at St. Anthony's in two."

"Roger that. Unit G-4, what's your twenty?"

CK switched off the scanner. She'd heard enough to

understand that a priest had been attacked at St. Anthony's Cathedral less than a mile from her home, and that a boy had been the one to call for help.

"Butt out, CK," she said to herself. "Let the authorities do their jobs. You've got work to do anyway."

But why would someone barge into a church and attack a priest? The mystery beckoned familiarly to her, and she responded as she always did, mentally lining up assets and working out strategies. She picked up the phone and dialed a number from memory.

"Yeah?" The voice that answered was both guarded and warm, casual and professional.

"Junebug, it's CK."

"Ah, CK. Always nice to hear from you. Mostly because a phone call from you means I'm about to go on some wild goose chase that pays an obscene amount of money."

"Yeah, we can talk about money after I see what you can do."

"Oh, you wound me. Have I ever let you down before?"

CK snorted. "Yeah. A lot. But you're still the best, which is why I keep calling you with work."

"Well, my refrigerator is empty and my cameras are all full, so give me the details."

"Not sure yet what I'm looking for. We'll know it when we see it. Do you still have that mini-camera built into a pair of sunglasses?"

"Does a rodent wear white gloves?"

"What?"

"Never mind. Yes, I've got that one and several new beauties too."

"Great. Bring the sunglasses and whatever else you think would work, and meet me at St. Anthony's church. Don't get noticed, but do get as much information as you can."

"Undercover it is, then. Betcha a dollar I get there before you do."

CK didn't bother to respond before hanging up. After all, she never lost a bet, and she wasn't about to start losing today.

✝

JUNEBUG COLLINS WASN'T SURPRISED TO SEE THAT CK IVORS had beaten him to the cathedral. But he wasn't about to let her beat him to the information, even though he didn't yet know what it was he was looking for.

A quick survey at the scene showed a growing number of neighborhood folk migrating toward the front doors of the church. An ambulance was parked nearby, and paramedics were rushing equipment in and out of the ornate entryway. Two blue uniforms were cordoning off the area with yellow crime scene tape, and two others were urging the crowd to back away from the church. A plainclothes detective was standing next to an unmarked car, mentally measuring distances and casually looking for clues. CK headed toward that police officer. Off to the side, a female officer was comforting a young boy beside one of the cruisers. Junebug stuck a hand in his pocket and silently clicked the remote that activated the shutter on his sunglasses/camera. He zoomed in and clicked again.

CK should be able to ID the kid from those pictures, he thought with satisfaction. Now the real task was to get a glimpse of what was going on behind those big wooden doors.

"Hey, officer," Junebug tried to act his role, working both to get the attention of the blue closest to the doors and to get his camera aimed into the shadows behind the policeman.

"Sorry, sir, you can't come in here. Back away from the yellow line, please."

"Right. Listen, officer, what's going on?" Click. *Got to remember to open the aperture and apply enhancers.* "I dropped my nephew off here an hour ago for communion class, but now I can't find him." Click. Click. Click. "Have you seen ... Oh wow ..."

Four paramedics burst open wide the doors to the cathedral, wheeling out a priest who was writhing in pain. If the IV unit attached to the priest's arm had painkiller flowing through it, it obviously wasn't doing much good.

"Back away *now*, sir."

"Right, right," Junebug said, pausing long enough to snap more digital images of the wounded man before taking a step back.

"The pictures," the patient groaned as he passed by. "Burn the pictures ..."

A sudden fright seized the photographer. How did this priest know he was taking pictures? Had he seen him before?

"Mick," one of the paramedics stopped briefly to speak to the cop. "Tell Detective Stepp there's some evidence he'll want to secure on the floor inside there." He looked disgusted and nodded toward the ambulance. "Almost makes me want to leave that priest where I found him."

"Yeah, I saw 'em too," the guard responded with a sympathetic grimace. "I'll let Stepp know."

Junebug turned as if he were leaving. The police officer paused, saw the photographer ambling away and apparently figured he could spare a moment away from guarding the door. He moved quickly toward the police cruiser to inform the detective about the evidence inside the building. He had barely turned his back before Junebug slipped inside.

Click. Click Click. There were bloodstains on the floor, and at least two dozen Polaroid pictures scattered in the aisle nearby. An unmarked videotape, spattered with blood, was shoved to the side as well. Click. Junebug reached for one of the pictures on the floor.

"Hey! Don't touch those!" The police officer's voice was both authoritative and peeved. Junebug jumped in spite of himself. "Back away from there."

"Uh, sorry, uh, I'm looking for my niece. I dropped her off here an hour ago, and …"

"Well, she's not here now," the officer said firmly, "and this is an off-limits crime scene. You'll have to leave. *Now*."

"Right. Um, sorry. Thanks."

Junebug backed out the door, heart racing with excitement and revulsion. Whatever kind of beating that priest had gotten, he had apparently deserved it.

✝

"WELL, IF IT ISN'T CLARK KENT, INVESTIGATIVE REPORTER and sometime superhero."

"CK will do just fine, Detective. And I'm always a superhero, just like you."

Sean Stepp smiled and extended his hand. "I'd ask what brings you out on this fine day, but I'm guessing you already know."

"Not really, Sean. Just following a hunch. What's going on?"

Detective Stepp nodded toward the cathedral. "That your photographer?"

CK didn't bother to follow his look. "Never seen him before in my life. C'mon, Sean. What's the fuss about here? Got a fugitive locked up in there or something?"

The detective grimaced and scanned the crowd. "Nah. The perp is out here somewhere. Or long gone. Not sure which yet."

"So what can you tell me?"

Detective Stepp took an appraising look at the woman beside him. She looked younger than she should have, and gave no hint that she'd made her first million by the time she hit twenty-nine. She'd been a big help to him on cases in the past. And he'd returned the favor by helping her plod through the evidence in the Cadillac Murders. They were even, at least for the moment. But CK Ivors was a good person to have in your debt, and a little morsel here might pay off sometime down the road.

"See that boy over there with Officer Chilson? Appears he was scheduled to meet with one Father Renault today to go over altar boy duties for Sunday services. When he got here, he found a man in a gray overcoat beating the living daylights out of his priest. The stranger told him to call the police, and then he left. We showed up soon after, and that's where we are right now."

"Hmm. Any leads on the stranger? Any motives?"

"Not yet. Just got here a few minutes before you did, CK. Give me a break already. We're not all Supermen."

"Can I talk to the boy?"

Detective Stepp choked down a laugh. "You know the answer to that." He glanced back up at the cathedral doors. "Now where'd that photographer of yours disappear to?"

"Told ya, Sean. I've never seen him before in my life. Must be one of yours."

A uniformed officer approached, ignoring CK. "Detective Stepp," he said. "One of the paramedics advised that there is evidence you'll probably want to secure on the floor inside."

"Thanks, Mick. Keep everybody out of that church for now, and I'll be up there in just a minute."

"Right, sir."

Detective Stepp noted that the first of the television news crews had just arrived on the scene. Cameramen were hurriedly unloading equipment while a reporter scouted the best angle from which to deliver her report. An assistant was already flashing credentials to one of the blues and demanding to know what was going on inside. The ambulance pulled away, sirens blaring and lights flashing. Overhead a news helicopter approached, flying low. This would be a real circus soon.

"Time to go to work, CK." Just then he spotted someone backing out of the doorway and groaned. "And get your man off my crime scene before I have you both arrested for tampering."

"Remember your heart, Sean," CK grinned. "Stress is bad for your heart."

Detective Stepp grunted and headed toward the steps to

the front doors of the church, but not before he made sure CK had signaled the photographer that it was time to leave.

†

THE ROOM WAS COLD AND EMPTY, SAVE FOR ONE LARGE OAK desk, a weathered file cabinet, and an old black telephone. The door to the small office was locked, and dust and spider webs were its only decorations.

The phone rang fifteen times, then went silent. Thirty minutes later, it rang again. Fifteen rings, then silence. This process repeated itself for two hours before a gruff figure stuffed a key in the lock and threw open the light of day into the musty cubicle. The visitor tore through the spider webs and picked up the receiver on the eighth ring.

"Wrong number," he grumbled, and hung up before anyone could respond.

Ten seconds later, the phone rang again. The gruff man swore and answered before the first ring could finish.

"I told you, you've called the wrong number."

"I don't think so, sir."

"Listen, don't call this number again, or I'll have you traced and thrown in jail for harassment." He slammed down the receiver and gathered his keys to leave.

Fifteen seconds later, the telephone rang again. Before the man could let loose his rage on the caller, a voice on the other end spoke.

"Please don't hang up, sir. This is important, I think."

"What makes you so sure of that?" the man asked sarcastically.

"Well, sir, you told me it would be."

There was silence for a moment, then the gruff man spoke again. "Who is this? What's this about?"

"Well, sir, I think you know who this is. I work at the Union Colony Bank. You told me to call you, to call this number if …"

"So there's been a change?"

"Well, sir, there's been activity at least. New activity."

"After eleven years?"

"Yes, sir. After eleven years of dormancy, the account has gone live again."

"Go on."

"A transfer was made on yesterday's business. A large sum of money was taken out of this account and deposited into another at a different institution across town."

"Is that it?"

"Well, I have the account number at the other location, if you want it. And the exact amount taken."

"That's irrelevant. Did anyone see who made the transfer?"

"No, sir. It was done electronically."

A pause.

"Is this good news, sir?"

"Never call this number again. Good-bye."

"Sir, about the promised paym—"

The gruff man hung up without listening. He tapped a key on the desk for a moment, then shuffled out of the office, locking the door behind him.   †

William Hazlitt once said, "No man is truly great, who is great only in his lifetime. The test of greatness is the page of history."

What he neglected to tell was when the page of history begins—or when it ends. Is it the start of a life that marks the beginning of greatness? Or the start of death? And how is one supposed to know the difference between greatness and debasement? Between heroism and ignominy? Between judgment and grace?

The answer, I suspect, is in the dreams.

THREE

CASSIDY REYES GLANCED UP FROM HER POSITION in the teller booth to check the clock on the wall by the sliding glass doors of the Union Colony Bank, Cole Street branch. Eight minutes to quitting time. The bank had closed almost half an hour ago, and now employees were totaling up the day's business, organizing their drawers, and getting everything ready to start all over again tomorrow.

Cassidy took a second look toward the front. The lobby security guard seemed distracted by something outside. He stood frowning, arms folded across his chest, staring at something or someone. Cassidy hit the total button on her adding machine, breathed a quick "thank you, God" when it matched the cash in her drawer, and quickly slid everything into envelopes and bags. After she'd cleared out her position, she grabbed her coat and purse and approached the front.

"Whatcha looking at, Link?" she asked.

The security guard didn't let his gaze out the front door waver. "Watching a suspicious character. Not sure what to make of him." He nodded toward the glass.

"Oh, him? He came in here a little before closing. Withdrew a chunk of money from a money market account at my teller window. Wonder why he's still here?"

Lincoln Sayles shrugged and frowned more deeply. "Don't know. I saw him come in. When he left, he walked out to the curb, pulled out that little book, and sat down. Been reading that thing ever since. It's like he's waiting for someone, but he's not in any hurry."

Cassidy took a long look at the stranger. He didn't look too much out of the ordinary. Seemed to be average size, muscular. His long, dark hair was pulled back into a pony-tail. His face was obscured, turned away from the front door.

"Nice coat, though," the security guard said. "Looks comfy, too."

"Yeah," said Cassidy. "Charcoal is a nice color in a jacket. Wonder how he gets it to hang so well?"

Lincoln smiled for the first time. "Careful, Cass. It's not wise to flirt with the customers. Or criminals. Whichever this guy may be."

She nodded. She'd learned the hard way on that score. "So, you think it's safe for me to walk out to my car? I'll have to go right past him."

The security guard shrugged. "Not sure, really. He hasn't done anything but sit there. And he's already got money. If he was a burglar or a mugger, I guess he would have done something by now."

"Okay. Well, keep an eye on me anyway. You'll be my hero if I need one, right, Link?"

The guard smiled and gave a half-hearted bow. "At your service, madam. Just be careful, and don't stop between here and your car. Better safe than sorry."

Cassidy nodded, buttoned up her coat, pulled her keys from her purse, and stepped out the door.

†

"SO HOW LONG DOES IT TAKE TO DOWNLOAD THE IMAGES from that funky little camera of yours?" CK Ivors was terribly curious, and whenever she was curious, she was also impatient.

"Just give me minute to hook up the USB cable, and we'll have the images on your computer screen in a heartbeat. That is, unless you have one of those ancient, slow pieces of garbage from a year ago."

Junebug couldn't help needling his friend and current employer. After all, she kept this office like a Fortress of Solitude, stocked with the latest and greatest technology—and decorated with memorabilia from her silly Superman fixation. He ran the cable from the earpiece of his sunglasses into the back of the computer tower and waited for the software to load itself.

"That new?" he asked, nodding toward a framed, oxygen-sealed comic book on the wall.

"Hey, yeah. Cool, huh? It's the very first issue of *Superman's Pal, Jimmy Olsen.* Came out in nineteen fifty-four. Cost me more than I really wanted to pay, but it's so hard to find in this kind of condition—and it's a must for any real collector."

Junebug smiled. The quickest way to get CK off your back was to get her talking comics. He tuned out her enthusiastic details until his pictures loaded.

"… was really a landmark for its time. Nobody thought a nonsuper superhero would—"

"Okay," he interrupted. "We're up and running. Check these out. I got twenty-seven shots total. Hopefully they'll give us something worth, you know, getting paid for."

CK was all business again. "Okay, let's see. Nice shot of the boy. I'll get Elko working on identifying him. Detective Stepp said he was the only witness. That the priest?"

"Um-hm."

"Whew. Whoever this attacker was, he meant business. But why leave him like that? Looks like he could have killed him just as easily. Why let him live? Okay, what's that?"

"Sorry. Didn't get the lighting fix right on that one. Was supposed to be a shot of inside the doorway. Unfortunately, there was a mean, burly police officer threatening bodily harm on me at the time."

"Wimp."

"Hey, you better be careful, or I'll just take my pictures and go home."

"Now you're just pouting. Okay, what's … whoa. What's all this stuff on the carpet there?"

"Bunch of Polaroid pictures. And a videotape."

"Hmm."

"Got a close-up of one of the pictures. Let's see, here it is."

"Ugh. That's disgusting. That the priest in the Polaroid?"

"Yeah."

"At least now we know a motive."

"Think the attacker is related to the boy being abused in the picture?"

"Maybe. What about the other pictures? They more of the same?"

"Well, I only got a quick look at them, but yeah. They're all of the Father in, um, compromising situations with children. Boys and girls both."

"Which means we can guess what's on that videotape."

CK sat back in a chair, thinking. So that was it, then. Just an angry relative retaliating for a victim of abuse. Sad, yes. But no real mystery to be solved. No need for a superhero.

"CK, one more thing." Junebug motioned for her to look at the computer monitor. "I clicked this last picture just before I was kicked out of the sanctuary. It was on the floor, but over to the side, under the end of a pew. Didn't get a good look at it then, but snapped the picture anyway. Now I'm glad I did."

CK leaned in close. "What kind of symbol is that? Ever seen it before?"

Junebug shrugged. "Nope. I thought you were the one who knew that kind of stuff."

CK hit a button on the computer keyboard and zoomed in closer on the golden object. "It looks like ... but that's been ..." she paused. Finally she spoke. "Congratulations, Junebug, We've got ourselves a mystery."

The photographer clapped his hands together gleefully. "Excellent. Does that mean I'm getting paid?"

"Yes, Junebug. You're getting paid. And your work schedule just got booked up for the foreseeable future."

He reached for the phone. "Just let me find someone to feed my frog."

†

CASSIDY REYES BREATHED A SIGH OF RELIEF WHEN SHE passed safely by the stranger on the curb. She was just pointing her car key toward the lock when she heard his voice.

"Excuse me, miss? Ma'am? Excuse me."

She glanced back and was surprised to find the stranger standing right next to her. Her heart was suddenly in her throat. How had he moved so quickly? So quietly? How could she have let him sneak up on her like this?

"Um, yes?"

He smiled, and his features seemed to relax into someone familiar. His skin was clear, a little pale but still tinted with color. He was clean shaven and smelled faintly of flowers.

"Sorry to bother you, but do you have the time? I seem to have lost my watch."

Over his shoulder, Cassidy saw Lincoln Sayles step out the front of the bank door. He gave her a questioning look.

"Sure. It's um," she glanced at her watch. "It's 5:35." She turned to go.

"Excuse me, miss?"

"Sorry, but I really need to get home now. You understand. Thanks."

"Right, of course," he said, still smiling. "But," he
looked earnestly into her eyes, "haven't I seen you before?"

Cassidy took another step backward, and shot a look of
concern toward Lincoln. "You mean besides in the bank?
No, I'm afraid not. Sorry. Have a nice day, sir." She moved
another step closer to her car.

The stranger seemed nervous. She saw his eyes start
measuring distances, noticed his muscles tense when he recognized the security guard slowly walking toward them.

"It's just," he said quickly, "I was wondering if, well, if
you'd like to get a cup of coffee with me." He nodded across
the street in the direction of a coffee house franchise, the
smile still frozen on his face. "I'd be honored to buy you a
latte and a pastry or something. I'm sort of new in town and
don't really know anybody yet."

Cassidy visibly relaxed. So, he was just hitting on her.
Flattering, a little embarrassing, but not necessarily dangerous. She hoped. "Thanks, but no. It's not good policy to
date customers."

"I could close out my accounts." There was a pleading
look in his eyes now. Not for himself, but almost as if he was
pleading for her.

"Thank you, but no." Cassidy had finally edged her way
to her car. She slid her key in the lock. "Good night."

"Cassidy," the stranger reached out and touched her
arm, causing her to jump in alarm. Lincoln broke into a trot
in their direction. "Don't go home. Not yet."

The teller looked wildly from her car, to the stranger, to Lincoln, her hero coming to the rescue. "Listen, mister," she said in a shaky voice. "Leave me alone or I'm calling the police."

"Cassidy," he almost whispered now. Pleading again. "Cassidy, he's there. He's at your apartment. Kinsey's at your apartment."

"Okay, back off, sir. Step away from the lady before you get hurt." Lincoln positioned himself between Cassidy and the stranger, with his nightstick drawn and at the ready. "You okay, Cass?"

She felt her hands trembling, saw the stranger sizing up the security guard, saw his eyes go flat and calculating. Though they were close in size, she didn't doubt that he would make short work of her friend in a fight.

"What did you say?" she asked.

"I said, are you all right?"

"No, what did *you* say?" She nodded toward the stranger. He took a step backward, away from the security guard. He appeared to be weighing his options.

"Listen, Cassidy," Lincoln said, refusing to take his eyes off the stranger. "I want you to take my cell phone and call nine-one-one. Tell them to get out here right away." He glared at the stranger. "That means you're going to jail for stalking, buster."

"No," he replied evenly. "I'm not."

"Hold on," demanded Cassidy. "What did you say?"

Both the stranger and the security guard were startled by the intensity of Cassidy's outburst. They turned toward her and found her trembling, fearful, and angry all at the same time. A softening glaze filtered over the stranger's face. He dropped his hands to his sides.

"Cassidy," he said quietly. "Kinsey's at your apartment. Right now. I've seen him. You can't go home yet. I won't let you."

†

"I FEEL LIKE A DORK." JUNEBUG COLLINS COVERED THE mouthpiece of the telephone to whisper loudly at CK. "All I can say is you better make this worth my while."

CK nodded vigorously. "It'll show up in your final paycheck, if that's what you mean."

He held up a hand and stood at attention. "Yes, John Corson, please." He nodded into the receiver, trying to feel less dorkish and more professional. "He's in a meeting? Yes. May I leave a message for him? Thank you." He covered the receiver again, and mouthed "waiting for voicemail" to CK. She nodded expectantly. Then, "Hello, Mr. Corson. This is, uh, Olsen. James Olsen. I'm the personal assistant to CK Ivors. She asked me to return all her calls while she's away. Out of the country. Gone for at least two more weeks. I'll, uh, be sure she knows you called while she was out. Out of the country. For, you know, at least two more weeks. I'm sure she'll call you when she's back. From being, well, out of the country …"

CK hung up the phone before Junebug could ramble any further.

"I am so busted," she muttered. "Did you have to say 'out of the country' a half-dozen times? You sounded like a twelve-year-old phoning in his own excuse for ditching school."

"Hey, I'm a professional photographer, not a professional liar. Or a professional 'personal assistant.' Where's Kelly anyway? Doesn't she usually do this kind of stuff for you?"

"She's 'out of the country.'" CK grimaced. "Actually, she's lucky not to be in jail. Caught her trying to sell my Lex Luthor statuette on eBay. She thought I'd never notice it was gone."

"Big mistake."

"Yeah, big mistake." CK sighed. "Okay, James Olsen—"

"Hey, it was the first name I could think of. Didn't think he'd believe me if I said my name was Junebug."

"Nobody believes your name is Junebug."

"You wanna work, or you wanna get personal?"

"Right. You're right. Sorry. You hungry?"

"Starving."

"Good. Let's go pick up some chicken and lay down the plan. Might be a long night."

"Regular, or extra crispy?"

"Both. I have a feeling we're going to need all we can get."

✝

THE COFFEE SHOP HUMMED WITH CASUAL CONVERSATION, whirring machinery, and smooth jazz playing softly through the speakers carefully placed around the room. Lincoln Sayles and Cassidy Reyes sat uncomfortably at a table near the rear of the establishment, cautiously eyeing the stranger at the counter.

"You sure this is a good idea, Cass?"

The bank teller shook her head slowly. "No, I'm not, Lincoln," she said. "But I figure it's safer than watching that guy take you apart in the bank parking lot."

"Huh. Right. I can handle myself."

Cassidy softened immediately. "Yeah, I know you can, Link," she said, squeezing his hand. "And I want to thank you for coming to rescue me out there. That was brave, and I appreciate it."

"So why are we here? Why not just call the cops and get this creep behind bars?"

She glanced up at the counter and saw the stranger paying for two double lattes, two scones, and a cup of hot tea. "Because … because I get a feeling about this guy. How does he know my ex-husband? Or where he is? Nobody's seen Kinsey for more than a month—thank goodness. Then this guy shows up and tells me not to go home because Kinsey's there. That's enough to make me want to know more."

"Kinsey was bad news, huh?"

She sighed, and said nothing.

The stranger stood for a moment at the table, then placed a scone and a latte in front of each of the two bank employees before sitting down. He looked first at Lincoln.

"So, Mr. Sayles," he said cordially. "I don't believe I've seen you. How long have you worked at Union Colony Bank?"

"How long have you been stalking our tellers?"

The stranger suppressed a grin, nodded, and turned to Cassidy. "Thanks for coming to have coffee with me."

"Listen, Mr. … I'm sorry, I don't remember your name."

The stranger smiled a relaxed and comfortable smile. He took a sip of hot tea, then glanced up at a clock on the wall behind the coffee counter, saying nothing.

"Okay. Well." Cassidy raised her eyebrows at Lincoln. He gave a slight shrug.

"You mentioned something earlier about my ex-husband," she continued, "and I'm curious to know how you know about him—and what you know about him."

The stranger took another sip of tea and shot a quick glance back at Lincoln before continuing. "I've seen him," he said quietly. "And I've seen you. And I've seen that he intends to, intended to, hurt you."

Cassidy paled. "Well, you know, he tried to hurt me. After I found out about … well, and after the divorce, too. But he didn't hurt me, not really. And now there's a restraining order against him, so I'm sure he wouldn't do anything that would violate his probation. He wouldn't want to go back to jail." She took a trembling sip of her latte, then leveled her gaze. "You know, I'm tougher than I look."

The stranger sneaked another peek at the clock on the wall. "I know you are, Cassidy. I also know that when Kinsey is drunk there's no telling what he'll do."

"And just how do you know Kinsey Reyes? Are you one of his runners? A collector? What?"

The stranger's lips tightened. Was he going to laugh?

"No, Cassidy. I don't work for your ex-husband. I just didn't want to see you get hurt anymore."

The man stood abruptly and put a hand out toward Lincoln. "You're a good man, Mr. Sayles. It's been a pleasure."

Lincoln shook the hand warily.

"Cassidy," the stranger said, "it's after six. It should be fine for you to go home now. By this time your neighbors will have heard Kinsey's racket in the apartment, and the police should have already arrived. He's going back to jail. Where he belongs. Meanwhile, you be safe. And happy. You deserve it."

"What are—"

The stranger turned and headed for the door. He was gone before Cassidy or Lincoln could think of anything more to say.

"Well," the security guard said finally, "that was strange."

Cassidy Reyes wasn't sure what to think. "Hey Link," she said after a moment, "give me a lift home?"   †

"What's your name, sweetheart?"

She still doesn't answer; she just stares at me with those big brown eyes. She doesn't show fear, nor does she seem glad to see me. She simply looks at me with blankness in her pupils. Tired.

Only then do I notice that she's not alone. Behind her, squeezed back into the bush, a man is kneeling. He slowly wraps his arms around the girl and pulls her protectively to himself. He's a darkie, lean and muscular. Scars on his arms, dirt on his face. Barefoot. Deep stains under his eyes, as though he's been awake for a long, long time.

"Please," he says urgently, "she din mean no harm. She jes' hungry is all. H'ain't had nothin' to eat since yest'day mo'nin'. She jes wanted t' try a few o' dem berries is all. She din mean no harm. Please."

He looks pleadingly at me. I say nothing. He pulls farther back into the brambles of berries and vines.

"Why are you hiding in there?" I ask stupidly. "Why not come out here on the road? This is my family's farm. I'm sure no one cares if you pluck some wild berries for yourselves. Besides, I'm the only one here today. Everyone else has gone to visit my aunt for the weekend."

"Thank yeh," he nods ingratiatingly, grabs a few berries and presses them into the girl's hand. She raises them to her mouth with a mechanical motion, but never takes her eyes off me.

The early morning sun is beginning to grow hot in the sky. I feel warmth soaking into the clay and dirt of the road beneath my feet. A trickle of perspiration drips past my left temple.

"Why are you hiding in there?" I ask once more, though I am beginning to suspect that I already know the answer.

He closes his eyes, and a low sigh escapes his lips.

I know I am dreaming. I know I have lived this before. Please. Please, God. Don't make me live it again.

FOUR

THE NEWS ANCHOR'S POLISHED FEATURES AND PLATinum hair gleamed through the television screen. "Turning to local events," she said with professional warmth and sincerity, "more bad news for the leaders at St. Anthony's Cathedral. One week after Father Michel Renault was savagely beaten by an unknown assailant, the parish priest has now been charged with multiple counts of sexual misconduct and child pornography involving young people from his church's congregation. Police are keeping mum about details, but Detective Sean Stepp did advise Channel 7 News that evidence gathered at the scene of the beating led the district attorney to file the charges."

In the background, to the left of the anchor's head, an artist's rendering of a man with a small, dagger-shaped birthmark on his left cheek pixeled into view. "Meanwhile, police are also circulating this artist's sketch, based on eyewitness descriptions, of the priest's attacker. Anyone with information about this person is encouraged to notify the local authorities. Now, for an update on sports, here's Wayne Brody—"

CK Ivors paused the DVD burner/player and turned to the team assembled in her office. "That's the man we're looking for," she said. "And we're going to find him."

†

HECTOR GOMEZ LIKED TAKING THE SHORTCUT BEHIND THE used bookstore on his way to school. The alley there was almost always deserted, and sometimes he was lucky enough to find a box of old paperbacks that the store was tossing out with the recyclables. Once he'd rescued three worn but readable copies of *Prince Caspian*, and a coverless copy of *The Hobbit* to boot. He had spotted a box behind the store today, but a quick inspection showed it to hold only romance novels—something Hector was definitely not interested in.

He repositioned his backpack, adjusted his jacket, and turned to continue the walk to school. That was when he saw the man sitting next to the big Dumpster across the alley. The man's eyes followed his every move closely, waiting.

Hector felt an unexpected terror flash through his body.

He didn't know whether he should just casually continue walking down the alley or forget about appearances and break into a run, get out of there as fast as possible. He started breathing in shallow, nervous gulps, and looking for the best way out of the alley. Then the man spoke.

"It's okay, Hector. You don't have to be afraid of me. I think you know that already."

KEENA COLLINS TRIED TO STARE INTENTLY AT THE SKETCH on the TV screen, but she couldn't help being distracted by the person who pointed at it. So this was *the* CK Ivors. Being Junebug's cousin, Keena knew that he had worked with the famous author, but she never really expected to actually meet her—let alone get hired on as CK's personal assistant. When Junebug gave her the news a week ago that Miss Ivors was looking for a new "right-hand man," she'd been interested. When CK herself called to offer her the job—"based on Junebug's recommendation"—Keena was even more excited. She'd been out of work for two months already, and any paying job was looking mighty good. To get paid a decent salary for tagging along with her favorite cousin and his famous friend seemed a dream come true. But when she'd entered the back office at CK Ivors' home for today's strategy meeting, all that excitement had quickly transformed into nervousness.

Three things caught Keena's attention when she walked through the door into CK's office. First was the size of the room. This place, apparently added on to the back of CK's house sometime within the past few years, was huge. About the width and length of a basketball court, Keena figured, with room for a small set of bleachers packed in as well. Second was the unnerving neatness of the whole place. Sure, there were a few desks and chairs, the obligatory filing and supply cabinets, low cubicle walls, a few computers and accompanying office machinery. But every desktop was clean, every "in" tray neatly trimmed, every chair pushed under its appropriate desk. In short, it looked like an office that would make a drill sergeant proud—and that made Keena worry what kind of drill sergeant CK Ivors would turn out to be.

The third thing Keena noticed was an entire wall of display cases filled with children's books and toys. A closer inspection revealed a carefully arranged collection that included comic books, action figures, statuettes, even a metal lunchbox and matching trash can. Gaps in the display case indicated that there were special places awaiting the arrival of other, still-sought-after items.

"CK's got a kickin' Superman collection, huh?"

Keena almost jumped at the sound of the unexpected voice in her ear. It belonged to a guy who appeared to be about her age—twenty-three or twenty-four—who wore a friendly smile and carried two cups of orange juice. He offered her one, and then his hand in greeting.

"Name's Chance Elko. I'm CK's information grunt. Whenever she needs to know something that most people don't know, I'm the guy she calls."

"Nice to meet you, Chance. I'm Keena. So you must be pretty smart then?"

He had laughed then, an easy comfortable laugh, as if he'd known Keena for ages. "Oh, no," he said quickly. "I'm not all that smart, really. I just know where to look for information, so people think I'm smart. Makes me look good for the ladies."

"Hey, Elko," a voice had called out from across the room. "Stop flirting with the new girl and help me get these chairs set up. Everybody's going to be here in five, and I've still got to get the plasma screen warmed up and check the DVD-R too."

Chance nodded apologetically toward Keena. "Gotta go," he said. "When the boss says jump, I say, 'how high?'" He'd turned toward the voice that called him. "Coming CK, but I don't see why Junebug didn't do this dirty work before he left."

"He had another job to do this morning," CK answered warmly. "He'll be back soon enough." She'd hesitated for a second, then said, "Nice to have you here this morning, Keena. We'll get started in a few minutes. Meantime, make yourself at home, and, um, be careful not to spill that juice by the display wall. Could make an expensive mess."

Keena had nodded quickly and stepped over to help Chance set up two rows of chairs in front of the plasma screen. She sat with the others, trying to watch the screen, trying to pick up the details that CK was giving about the new job. But she kept stealing looks at the author and her lair and the people gathered around her. She noticed how everyone in the room hung on CK's every word. They never questioned her leadership or her goals. They were like a sports team prepping for a big game, listening to the coach tell them exactly what it would take to win. Keena pulled out a spiral notebook and a pen, ready to take down notes.

When I grow up, she thought to herself, *I want to be CK Ivors.*

✝

HECTOR FELT HIS HEARTBEAT SLOW BACK TO NORMAL AT THE sound of the stranger's voice. "So it's you, then? You're the guy who ... who hurt Father Renault?"

The stranger rose slowly to his feet and grimaced. "Yeah," he sighed. "That was me."

"You hear what they're saying about Father Renault now?"

The stranger nodded, looking grimly in Hector's direction. The boy ducked his head, avoiding eye contact, as if he were surprising himself with the boldness of what he was saying to this stranger.

"Is it true? What they say he did to those other kids?"

The stranger nodded again. Hector responded in kind, slowly.

"I thought so." He adjusted his backpack. "Was he ... was Father Renault going to hurt me, too?"

"You know the answer to that, Hector."

The boy nodded again. "Yeah, I guess I do."

The stranger produced a folded sheet of paper from his coat pocket. "I guess that's why you lied to the police sketch artist about me, huh?" He unfolded the paper to reveal the "Wanted" poster the authorities had distributed regarding the priest's attacker.

The boy just shrugged.

A wry grin cracked the stranger's chiseled face. "I see you told them I was black."

Hector shrugged again.

"And that I had a military haircut. And a goatee. But personally, I liked the knife-shaped birthmark on my left cheek. That was a nice touch."

Hector giggled. "They kept asking me if you had any 'distinguishing marks.' They asked me that probably ten times. I got tired of them bugging me about it, so I gave them one. My friend's uncle has a tattoo like that. But he's not black, so I figured it wouldn't be a big deal."

The stranger folded up the sketch and returned it to his pocket. He reached out and patted Hector on the shoulder. "C'mon," he said. "I'll walk you to school."

Hector fell in step with the stranger as they headed down the alley. "So why'd you come back? Aren't you worried someone will see you with me or something?"

It was the stranger's turn to shrug. "I figured you probably had questions, and that you deserved some answers."

"Yeah, I do have some questions still."

"Shoot. If I can answer them, I will."

"Okay. Well, for starters, what happened to your hands?"

†

CK IVORS TOOK A MOMENT FOR AN APPRAISING LOOK AT the team she'd assembled over the past week. She was pleased to see Keena Collins take out a notepad without being prompted to do so. Details were important in this kind of work, and Keena seemed to pay attention to details. Junebug had recommended her highly as well, and Junebug was rarely wrong when it came to judging people's character.

Elko was his usual friendly self. *Kid must have an IQ of 160*, CK thought to herself. *But you'd never know it to talk to him. Not the kind to show off. Much.*

The best thing about Elko was his pit bull-like tenacity when it came to getting information. The guy simply would not give up. He'd search obscure files on the Internet, dig through the basement stacks of any library, interview any-one and everyone, call the president himself if that was the only place to verify a fact. CK paid him well, sometimes even asking him to dig up facts she didn't need just to keep him busy. She didn't want his unique talents wandering too far off to the next-highest bidder.

Rebel Feine and James Dandy sat next to Elko. CK had had to convince them to come out from Oklahoma City, but they were worth it. Rebel was networked to the max, able to connect with just about any private investigator in the country. She always seemed to "know a guy" who knew somebody who could get details from someone else. She was especially good at tracking down people who wanted to stay hidden. James was supposed to be her bodyguard, but in reality was more an equal partner in their detective agency than he liked to let on. Together, they were a formidable team.

Then there was Galway. Nobody knew what his last name really was (though CK suspected that Elko might have dug it up anyway, just out of curiosity). Galway was … well,

Galway. At sixty-two, he was the old man of the bunch. As the resident conspiracy theorist, he was also the most paranoid. But CK had learned on more than one occasion that the twists and turns his inventive mind took often led somewhere important. She kept him on the team as the thinker, the person to prime the pump and get her mind working in new directions. One never knew what he might come up with, and CK was always curious to find out.

CK's reverie was interrupted by Galway's thunder. "Where's Junebug?" he shouted suddenly. "Have you murdered Junebug? Is that why we're here? You'll never pin his death on me, lady. I don't care how much you offer to pay."

"Galway, please," Elko responded. "We've got newbies here this morning." He nodded toward Keena. "And guests." He gestured toward Rebel and James. "Try to behave yourself just for once."

"No worries, Gal," CK soothed. "Junebug's out on a special assignment. He's been following the eyewitness to the priest beating. We're thinking that the guy who whupped up on Father Renault is probably a relative of the boy who called nine-one-one. I tried to arrange an interview with the boy, but his parents turned me down. They said he'd told everything to the police and were adamant that he would talk to no one else—especially not to me. They accused me of just wanting to profit from the boy's experience." CK shrugged. "So Junebug's been shadowing him as he goes to and from school every day. We're hoping that sooner or later the fighter will make contact with the boy again. But don't worry, Junebug'll be here soon enough."

Galway nodded, apparently appeased. CK took another look at her crew and smiled. "Now," she said with authority. "It's time to get to work."

✝

HECTOR WATCHED THE STRANGER STEAL A QUICK GLANCE AT his hands. Both of the man's palms were bandaged with white gauze strips, wrapped from the middle of the hands, around the thumbs, down below the wrists and into the sleeves of his charcoal gray coat.

"What happened to my hands?"

Hector nodded.

The stranger put on a disarming smile. "Nothing, really. Just old scars from a riding accident. Sometimes they get irritated, so I cover them up for protection."

Hector nodded again. "What about those other kids? The ones Father Renault hurt. Why didn't you protect them?"

The stranger's face grew serious. "I didn't see them in time."

"But you saw me?"

"Yeah."

"Where? When did you see me?"

"It's hard to explain, Hector. But I saw you with Father Renault once, and I knew I had to protect you. I knew he wanted to … to hurt you."

They walked in silence for a few minutes until they arrived at the outskirts of the school property. The man and the boy stood together, looking at the building ahead, but neither moving. Finally the stranger spoke.

"You better get going or you'll be late."

Hector turned and looked up at the big man next to him. "How do I know you're real?" he asked. "How do I know you're not just my imagination? Or an angel or something?"

The stranger snorted. "Believe me, Hector. I'm no angel. Just a sinner, like everyone else. Worse than everyone else."

Hector waited.

"Here," the stranger said. "Give me a piece of paper, or a card or something."

Hector fished an index card out of his backpack and gave it to the man. The stranger pulled a silver pen from his coat pocket and, with a practiced hand, inked a few quick strokes across the card. He passed it back to Hector.

"Whenever you see that symbol," he said, "you'll know I was here. With you. Okay?"

Hector looked at the drawing. It appeared to be a thick wooden cross, with a calligraphied *S* wrapped around the center beams. Hector nodded approvingly. "Okay," he said. "And thanks."

But when he looked up again, Hector realized the school bell was ringing, and that he was alone.   †

"Phil'de'fia?"

She speaks for the first time, and I feel myself jump at the sound of her voice. It is surprisingly rich, musical. Like laughter in water. Her eyes crease in uncertainty, locking onto mine.

"Hush, chil'." The man whispers it in her ear, but loud enough that I hear him anyway.

"What did she say?" I stand and find I am looking down on the man.

"She din' say nothin'. She jes' tired."

"Phil'de'fia?" She interrupts again. She is asking me a question. There is a moment of silence between us three.

Finally, "No. This isn't Philadelphia," I say, looking directly into the eyes of the man. "You're still in Virginia. But you're getting closer, I think. Maybe four or five more nights of steady walking, and you'll be in Philadelphia. Maybe."

The man nods, knowing that I know he is a runaway. Knowing that I won't be calling the sheriff. Trusting his life—and his daughter's life—into my white hands.

FIVE

JUNEBUG COLLINS WATCHED THE MAN SLIP AWAY with a frustration that bordered on vengefulness. He noted carefully that the boy had not seen—and apparently not heard—when his companion turned, took three broad steps, and was lost behind the corner of the schoolyard. Junebug was also well aware that the stranger had managed to walk five blocks to Hector Gomez's school without ever exposing a clear view of his face. It was almost as if he knew someone was trailing them, as if he timed every dipping tree branch or parked car to intrude on the scene just when Junebug lifted his camera to snap a quick shot of the pair. The only image the photographer managed to capture plainly on his camera's digital disk was the coat—a long, charcoal gray covering that hung unwrinkled from the man's shoulders to his thighs like the dressing for a department store mannequin. Junebug didn't recognize the material. It looked like something expensive, though, smoother than leather but tougher than wool.

For a moment, Junebug considered abandoning his surveillance of Hector and chasing after the stranger in the long coat. But doing that would also expose him to Hector, and CK had been adamant that the boy shouldn't know anyone was following him. "He's been through enough trauma with the priest and the police already," she'd said. "Let's not make our little investigation another reason to upset this poor kid."

After a moment, Junebug saw the boy look up, realize he was alone, and shake his head in mild surprise. The man had drawn something on a card—a map maybe? Or a letter?—and given it to Hector. The boy placed that card carefully in his backpack and headed up the sidewalk toward the school doors.

"Wish I could have seen what was on that card," Junebug muttered to himself.

"Why?"

Junebug nearly jumped out of his skin at the sound of the unexpected voice.

"No, don't turn around," the voice commanded calmly. "You wouldn't like what you saw if you did."

Junebug felt his adrenaline kick in, felt his muscles tremble ever so slightly. "What is it?" he asked. "A gun or something?"

The voice was silent for a moment, then it continued as if Junebug had never spoken. "Why?" it said. "Why do you wish you could have seen what was on that boy's card?"

Whoever this mugger is, he's got good hearing, Junebug thought. His mind raced with options for what to say and do next. "Um, just curious, I guess," he said finally. "Looked like it might've been important."

"Only to some," the voice said. "So why were you following us?"

Busted, Junebug thought. *Time to change the subject.* "So that was you, huh? Nice to meet you. My name is Junebug Col—"

"Why were you following us, Junebug? Have I seen you before?"

"No, I don't think so." Junebug laughed nervously. "Hey, nice coat, by the way. What is that? Leather? Hangs real good in the back. Been thinking about getting a new coat myself. Where'd you—".

"Why were you following us, Junebug? And what are you going to do with those pictures?" The voice was growing impatient.

"Hey, man," the photographer sputtered, "no need to get upset. I was just doing my job, checking up on the kid and all."

The voice hardened suddenly, becoming flat and emotionless. "Who do you work for? Johnson? Or someone else? Who?"

"No, man. Nobody like that." Junebug sensed the shift in tone, and it made him nervous. "I don't know any Johnson, at least not any that could hire me to work for them. Listen, can I just turn around and introduce myself properly? I'm sure this is all just one big misunderstanding."

The voice was silent.

"Sir? Mister? Listen, how about I turn around slowly and—" He chanced a short glance behind him, then a longer one, then he issued a disgusted snort. "Geez, that guy is so *quiet*. Must be a Navy SEAL or something, to be able to appear and disappear like that."

Junebug let himself exhale and felt the tenseness loosen itself from his upper body. Then he turned and walked briskly toward the front door of the school. A sudden urge had made it very important for him to find the nearest bathroom.

†

RUNNING ALWAYS FELT GOOD.

Something about the rhythmic pounding, the steep inhale and shallow exhale, the intensity of focus. It always seemed to clear the cobwebs from the mind. "When I run, I feel his pleasure ..." Didn't Eric Liddell say something like that? Well, he had little hope of feeling God's pleasure, but running down the pavement, across the emptied park, and into the upper downtown area still felt good. Exhilarating, almost.

The first bullet snicked past his right ear, grazing the shoulder of the jacket but doing no damage. He smiled.

In one smooth motion he flicked the hood of the coat up over his head, made a cut around a street vendor's hot-dog cart, and steamed into a parking garage. He'd already covered two miles outside. Now it was time to try an indoor setting.

Have to get the sniper away from bystanders, he thought. He saw the ramp up to the second level and didn't hesitate, putting on a burst of speed and feeling a slight burn in his throat; a good feeling. One that reminded him of childhood. He could run like this for a long time, unless one of those bullets got lucky and put a stop to it.

He heard a car screech into the garage, brakes protesting the stop-and-go treatment required to maneuver in here. He was already at the bottom of the ramp up to the third level when the car wheeled into view. A black Mercedes. Four teens inside, wearing red and gold and draped in jewelry. All except one. He held the sighted rifle capped with a silencer, and this one apparently wanted no dangling chains or thick-fingered rings to interfere with his work.

Four more steps and I'll be out of the sniper's sight, at least for a moment.

The second bullet struck him squarely in the back, just above the third vertebrae of the spine.

✝

CK IVORS LEFT THE PLASMA SCREEN ON, THE POLICE sketch of the priest beater frozen in close-up for everyone on the team to refer back to. "Elko," she said, "flip on that projector, please." The space next to the TV set illuminated with the desktop of a computer monitor. CK quickly clicked into a PowerPoint file on her laptop, and images began to appear on the wall.

First was a young boy, eleven or so. He was Hispanic, handsome in a prepubescent way, and looking very serious. A police officer knelt next to him, apparently saying something that was intended to be comforting.

"Hector Gomez," CK announced. "The only witness to the crime." She clicked again, and a different picture of Hector appeared. This time he was walking out of the police headquarters, accompanied by a police escort and two people who appeared to be his parents. A small crowd of photographers and reporters obscured part of the view in the picture, but the boy's face was still clearly seen. He had his head tilted away from the police officer, and looked very calm in spite of what must have been a noisy, slightly chaotic environment. He held a backpack tightly to his chest and hunched his shoulders away from the crowd.

Was he grinning?

CK clicked again, and this time Hector was alone, walking toward a school building, carrying books, and looking serene, as if he were just any other normal kid on his way to see his buddies.

"Go back." It was Galway.

"Gal, let her—"

"Go back. Please."

CK nodded. She trusted Galway's instincts. Tapping the mouse pad on her laptop, CK returned to the first picture of the boy. Galway stood up to study it. After a moment, he nodded, and CK clicked to the second picture outside the police station.

Rebel Feine leaned over and whispered something to James Dandy. Galway stared so long at this picture that Elko finally gave up and went to get another cup of orange juice. Dandy pulled out his own notebook now and jotted something down, showing it to Rebel, who nodded tersely.

Galway now turned his attention to the plasma screen, lingered on the image there, and then let out a soft chuckle. "Okay. Thanks, CK," he said.

CK nodded. Galway knew something, and he knew that they knew he knew it. Now he would wait for just the right moment before sharing it with the others. That, of course, was his way.

†

Generally speaking, Maria Eliza Garces didn't love her job. Oh sure, being a Maximum Maid wasn't terrible—certainly better than many other occupations. It wasn't all that difficult once you got into a routine, and it paid enough to keep the family current on their bills. Medical and dental benefits were nice too. But it wasn't what she'd expected to do with her life, and definitely not how she'd expected to fill the last eight years. Still, she'd grown comfortable with the predictability of it, and even had a sort of fondness for the homes that had become "regulars" on her assigned route.

Once a family had had Maria Eliza clean their house, they almost always requested her again. She was the kind who worked quickly, but also with a ruthless intolerance of clutter, stains, and unsanitary situations. As a result, she was soon the highest-paid worker at Maximum Maid Service—and with her rank came a few privileges. That was why, once a week, for about four hours of the day, Maria Eliza Garces genuinely loved her job and all that went with it.

It had started five years ago, when her friend Candy had quit to stay home with her young children. "Maria Eliza," she'd said. "I recommended you to take over the cleaning of one of the houses on my route."

"*Aiee*, Candy," Maria Eliza had said. "I am full to the brim with houses already. I can barely finish my route each week as it is. Let Grace take it."

Candy had just grinned and patted her shoulder. "Grace can take one of your current houses. Trust me, this one you want. It's a cottage really. A guest house behind an old manor in the suburbs. Just take it, *hermana*. You'll like it, and I can't trust it to someone who doesn't deserve it, if you know what I mean."

She looked narrowly across the room at Elise, the boss's daughter. They called her "Lazy Elise" behind her back because she always seemed to disappear when real work was to be done and reappear when a clean-up was in its finishing stages.

"Besides," Candy continued, "I already got Robert to agree. Elise gets Grace's house on Fourth Street, Grace gets your two-story on Abingdon, and you get the cottage once a week, four hours a day minimum." She smiled. "You can thank me later," she said breezily. Then she'd walked out of Maximum Maids for good.

Now, five years later, Maria Eliza said a prayer of thanks for Candy once a week, four hours a day.

✝

He felt the nub of metal press against his lower spine. If he hadn't been running at near-top speed, he might have laughed at the insult. He'd spent decades perfecting the complex weaving and layered temper and chemical treatment of this cloth, and almost a full year finally putting it all together into this thigh-length, charcoal gray coat. He couldn't even remember the last time a bullet had been able to nick its way through the layers and actually touch his skin. A knife, well, that was different. A knife, if it were sharp enough and driven with sustained force at a slower rate of speed, could probably cut through the narrow fibers of the jacket and do some damage. But not a bullet. It came in too fast and flattened out too quickly. It would barely even crease the outer shell.

He didn't wait to hear the clinking sound of the bullet sliding off the back of his coat and bouncing on the pavement. Instead he put on a burst of speed and ran up to the third level of the parking garage.

He figured he had two, maybe three seconds alone before the car with his would-be assassins would come screaming up the ramp behind him. Fortunately it had been a busy morning at the garage, and three seconds was about one and a half more than he needed. With a lithe twist, he dove to the right and rolled, flattening his body to fit— albeit snugly—under a Ford Ranger. Then he waited.

The Mercedes didn't disappoint, zooming onto the third floor with a squeal of tires and speeding halfway across the lot before the squeaking of brakes indicated a change of heart.

He could hear the teens now, their voices low and buzzing just above the idling of the car. Their words were still indistinct, though, murmurs of half-dreams one tries to remember and wishes he could forget. One door clicked open. Then a second. Then a third. The car accelerated forward slowly, finally coming to a stop at the entrance of the ramp to the fourth level of the garage. Sneakered footsteps gently slapped the floor as he heard the walkers begin to separate and spread out across the parking garage. They were apparently going to try to trap him here so they could finish their work.

Great, he thought. *Now I'm going to have to kill them all.*

†

CHANCE ELKO SWALLOWED A GOOD AMOUNT OF ORANGE juice before realizing that if this turned out to be a long briefing, his bladder would not be happy about the extra liquid. But sitting around waiting for Galway always made him feel both bored and anxious, and when he was either bored or anxious, he tended to fill his mouth with food or drink.

He sighed, willed himself away from the doughnuts that seemed to call his name, and took a seat next to Keena. She was pretty, he admitted to himself. Junebug didn't seem to know any ugly women. Still, he was Chance Elko, computer nerd extreme. Women just didn't go for his type unless they thought he'd invented Google or something.

Wish I could see what Galway is seeing right now, he thought, trying to concentrate on the pictures of Hector Gomez. *Guy's a nut, but I'd never want to go up against him in a poker game.*

Galway finally finished his goofy staring at the pictures, and CK Ivors now brought up one last photo in her PowerPoint slides.

"Whoa." It was Rebel who spoke this time. "Is that for real?"

CK nodded. "Junebug saw it himself. Snapped the picture inside St. Anthony's Cathedral just after the beating took place."

Galway stood hesitantly. "CK, I don't know that we should be messing with something like, well ... Are you sure you—we—want to pursue this?"

CK only tilted her head in response. "Right," Galway muttered. "Of course. I forgot. With CK Ivors, if it's not dangerous, it's not fun."

CK dimpled. "Oh c'mon, Gal. You know you're the one who taught me that motto."

Galway waved a hand in her direction. "Yah, I know. Still doesn't mean you have to keep dragging me into crazy stuff like this."

James Dandy politely raised a hand, something that seemed out of place for a man of his size and incongruent with the informality of the group surrounding him.

"James," Rebel groaned. "You're not in second grade anymore. You got something to say, just say it. CK's not going to give you a bad grade or anything."

Dandy ignored his partner, and waited. CK finally stopped chuckling and acknowledged his hand. "Don't listen to Rebel," she said, shooting a semiserious glare to the rest of the group. "Politeness is its own reward, James. You have a question?"

The big man nodded. "I think I'm missing something, he said. "All I see up there is a gold pocket watch with some kind of engraving on it. Might be an antique, I'll grant you that. But what's the big deal for us about an antique pocket watch?"

CK nodded approvingly. "Good question," she said. "And I can see it's the same question that Elko and Keena are asking as well." Their nodding heads confirmed CK's assessment. "Elko," she continued. "Would you describe the engraving that you see on the cover of this watch?"

Elko gave it a hard look, then said, "Looks to me like a cross with a snake wrapped around it. But I don't see a head on the snake, just the snake's body."

CK nodded. "Galway, why don't you tell him what it really is."

The old man leaned back in his chair. "That, youngster, is the sign of the Sinner."

MARIA ELIZA FELT HER MUSCLES RELAX AS SOON AS SHE SHUT the door behind her. Everything was as it should be. She hadn't realized it at first, but something about this little out-of-the-way cottage breathed peace into her soul. The main house wasn't even visible from out here, obscured by trees but evidenced by a lightly worn pathway that wound around the pond and into civilization. Other Maximum Maids would have scheduled this assignment on Friday afternoons and simply skipped away for an extended week-end. But not Maria Eliza. She came here at all times. Some weeks she'd come out on Monday, already needing a break from the hassles of the real world. Other times she'd schedule this enclave for Wednesday, a serene midpoint to a busy week. Only rarely did she let herself in here on a Friday, and even then she made sure to stay the full four hours anyway.

"Television would've been nice," she muttered for the hundredth time, knowing she didn't really mean it. Part of the attractiveness of this place was the isolation. No TV, no phone, not even a radio. But plenty of comfortable chairs, and wall after wall full of books.

As was her custom, Maria Eliza took her shoes off at the door. She told herself that it was just more comfortable that way, but deep down she also knew that something about this location almost required it. There was a somber reverence inside these walls, and one always goes barefoot on holy ground.

She took a cursory glance around the room. Same as always. Untouched. The living area with a large, late nineteenth-century couch and two matching chairs. A rocker by the fireplace. A rolltop desk—locked, always locked—and several lamps spread throughout the room. Straight ahead was a small kitchen and dining area. The refrigerator was always running, but always empty, too. The only signs of food were in the pantry, where canned goods from who knows how long ago still dotted the sparsely arranged shelves. "Ought to just toss out those dusty old cans," Maria Eliza mumbled time and again. "I'm sure they're all past their expiration dates." But she never did; something about her upbringing made it hard for her to knowingly waste food, and there was no way to tell for sure that the beans and things in those cans were bad until somebody opened them to check. That was a line Maria Eliza was unwilling to cross, opening somebody else's food.

Down the narrow hallway was a bathroom and two doors. One door, she knew, led to a fine master bedroom with a queen-size bed, a hand-carved wardrobe, and a matching dresser. It always smelled faintly of potpourri or incense or something, though Maria Eliza could never find where that smell came from.

The last doorway ... that one was the great unknown for the maid. Some days she'd stand and stare at it, barely breathing, trying to guess what could be behind it—and why it had been closed and locked and dead-bolted two times over. Depending on her mood, she dreamed that it held hidden treasure left over from pirate booty, or that a corpse sat rotting in there, or that inside revealed an elaborate tunnel to some even more secret place where great mysteries were routinely revealed. Once she thought she heard a man groaning on the other side of that door, but that had been years ago and she wasn't the kind to believe in ghosts. When only silence answered her calls through the door, she assumed it was merely the settling of the wood floor or a branch scraping a window. She never heard a peep from that room again, and after a few years, she learned to simply ignore that last door. It faded in existence like a tree that grows silently by a second-story window, unnoticed until suddenly you realize that, with a little effort, you could actually climb out your window onto a branch and scurry away into the adolescent joys the night offers while your parents slumber unknowingly.

Today Maria Eliza was ready for this plum cleaning assignment. Truth be told, the place needed only a little dusting each week. Nothing else was ever moved or disturbed. Sometimes she'd forget and leave out a book on the couch, or bring a magazine from home and leave it on the table by the door. It was always in its same spot, the very place she'd left it, the next time she came in to clean. Today was no different.

Maria Eliza breathed in the scented air and felt again like she was coming home. She reached on the shelf and found the immaculately kept first edition of *Uncle Tom's Cabin* that she'd been admiring for weeks. A woman of lesser moral fortitude would have stolen it a long time ago, along with several of the other rare and valuable tomes sprinkled on the shelves. But she was content simply to enjoy it here in the company of the cottage. She sat in her favorite chair and checked her watch. Plenty of time for a little reading, a little nap, and then a quick twenty minutes of dusting before heading back to the Maximum Maids office.

She opened the book carefully, wary of creasing the spine or tearing a page. She'd read only half a page when something triggered a warning inside her mind. She cocked her head, listening, but heard nothing. She tried to return to reading, but a vague uneasiness settled in the air and made it difficult for her to pay attention to—and translate—the old ways of phrasing things. She set the book in her lap and placed her hand gently across the page.

A glint of light flashed across her vision.

"Who's there?"

She said it involuntarily, standing to her feet and immediately feeling foolish. This cottage was empty. It was always empty. She sat again, feeling nervous and cross. This time she caught the reflection of the light on the face of her watch as it glanced across the room. She looked at the front windows, saw that the curtains were pulled, and found herself more curious than afraid. She spotted a gleam of light narrowly displayed on the wood floor beneath her feet, but it seemed to come from behind her, where it didn't belong. Slowly, she allowed her gaze to follow the light back to its source, and then her breath caught in her throat.

At the end of the hallway, standing only slightly ajar, the door to the last bedroom was open.   †

She looks at me, and even in the morning heat I feel a shiver. Her eyes open themselves like a butterfly's wings, and I am mesmerized. They blink, and more than sadness spills forth.

Tired, so tired. Those eyes are used to being tired. But still they hope. For rest. For peace. For sleep.

I can't give those eyes everything they desire, though I would give them everything I have. Rest comes only to the free, and we are, none of us, free at this time. Peace comes only to the strong, and we three are struck dumb by the power of our weakness. But sleep …

Sleep requires only a bed. A place to lay the head, a safe moment in which to drape the spirit with the blackened curtains of dreaming.

And this, this is something I can give.

I steal a glance behind me. The barn doors are closed, left that way from when I milked the cows earlier this day, then sent them out to pasture. The cool of night still sticks within the tattered brown walls, I know, and its shadows will protect what's inside from the growing heat of the summer sun. Only my horse is stabled in there. The others were taken when my family left yesterday, taking the two-day journey to visit my father's sister downstate. She might be well by the time they get there.

And while they are gone, the eyes before me just might sleep.

I hear a shuffling. The man, the father, seems unsure of what to do in the awkward silence we share. The eyes say nothing; they just wait.

"C'mon," I finally say to the child standing before me in the berry brambles. "I'll take you someplace safe."

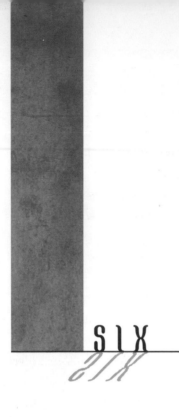

SIX

LOFTIS JOHNSON DESPISED THE PASTY-WHITE SYCO-phant sitting in the stiff metal chair beside his desk, waiting. He despised them all, really. The toadies who called him "sir," who smiled ingratiatingly and jumped to fulfill his slightest whim. Money did that to people, took away their self-respect and replaced it with power or influence or simply arrogance and a deep satisfaction that anything and anyone could be bought if the price was right.

So he hated them all.

Used them, yes. Paid them, empowered them, and even bailed them out of occasional misfortunes. But he never liked them, never pretended to respect them. They were all simply porous sponges filling their souls with the oily slime of greed and the disgusting motives of arrogance.

They were, in fact, people just like Loftis Johnson.

Which is, of course, the real reason he hated them. Particularly this one, who sat silently, subserviently, money-lust so easily written on his face. *I wonder how long I can ignore him before he gets fed up and says something*, Loftis thought. But he knew the answer. This man was a high-ranking bank official, and he'd been promised a fat payday today. He would wait with that pathetic plastic smile on his face until hell froze over, as long as he knew he could wrap his bony fingers around that money afterward. And if there was one thing you could count on about Loftis Johnson, it was that he always paid what he promised.

The once-forgotten office had been swept and cleaned, oak desk polished, and telephone replaced with a high-tech, "electronic receptionist" phone system. But it was still a cold and empty place. No pictures on the walls, no personal items decorating the desk. This was a place for business and nothing more. The fact that it was buried deep inside a large home in one of the finest neighborhoods meant nothing. It still resembled mostly a closet in a basement, cleaned, starched, bleached, and ready to be used for blank, passionless purposes.

But when it came to dealing with the Sinner, this stale little office was anything but a passionless workspace. It was something of a ruse in that sense, for the intensity of Loftis Johnson's hatred permeated the very walls. Loftis Johnson hated no one with more passion than he hated the Sinner. Not even himself.

The electronic receptionist on the desk lit up, flashing a caller-ID scan and news that line three was about to start ringing. A second later the trill of electronic chimes fulfilled the receptionist's prophecy. Loftis ignored it.

The bank official shifted uncomfortably in his seat. For some, the ringing of a telephone is akin to an itch that must be scratched. To put it off only makes it worse. To let it stop ringing, unanswered, is nearly unbearable. This man was obviously of this sort.

On the eighth ring, the banker dared to speak. "Excuse me, Mr. Johnson, sir. Would you like me to get that for you?"

"Only if you enjoy broken fingers."

The banker nodded and sat back in his chair—on his hands—and clenched his teeth while trying to ignore the impenetrable itching that apparently crawled up his neck and into his temples.

The phone grew silent after the fifteenth ring. Loftis simply stared at it. The banker cleared his throat. "Sir, about that promised payment?"

Loftis switched his stare from the phone to the man. Silence reigned again. Finally the gruff man pulled a calculator from the top drawer in the desk.

"Eleven years, is that right?" he said

"More or less," the banker removed his hands from under his seat, genuinely enthusiastic about the new direction this meeting was taking.

"Which is it?" Loftis said coldly. "More? Or less?"

"Right, sir. Sorry." The man pulled a calendar out of his briefcase and checked a few dates. "It was exactly eleven years, two months, and four days. But I believe the bonus kicked it after the tenth year, so—"

"Stop talking." Loftis's fingers were already flying over the calculator. After a moment, he flipped the display toward the banker. "Does that look appropriate to you?"

The banker involuntarily took in a breath. "Mr. Johnson, sir, you are very generous."

"And you are still employed."

The banker smiled, slightly faded teeth showing behind the curve of his lips. "Of course, sir. I will keep watching those two accounts religiously. Any activity, and I will know about it. Anything significant, and you will know about it."

"And?"

"And when the Sinner makes a mistake, when he—or his servants—withdraw money in person or via an ATM, we will of course capture it on our bank surveillance cameras and immediately forward those images to your e-mail account. Immediately, sir. You have my word."

Loftis Johnson hated this worm of a man. But he definitely wanted to use him. The gruff one slid open the middle drawer on the left side of his desk, passed over the revolver, and pulled out six bundles of cash instead.

The banker went home a very happy man. This time.

†

By the time Junebug entered the back door of CK Ivors' office building, he was surprised to find the place empty. The plasma screen was on, though, with a police sketch of the perp from the St. Anthony's beating in the middle of its focus.

Next to it, the projection unit was shining a PowerPoint slide of one of his photos—the one of the gold watch he'd spotted under the pew at the church right after the priest was taken away. There were a few half-filled juice cups, a few doughnut scraps, and other signs of recent occupancy in the room, but no people anywhere.

"Hello?" Junebug called out. "CK? Keena? Elko?"

He walked over to a computer and absent-mindedly began downloading the latest surveillance photos he'd taken of Hector Gomez and that mystery guy who'd accompanied the boy to school. He paused to examine the police sketch of the priest beater still frozen on the plasma screen. Could it be the same guy he'd talked to at the school? He shook his head quickly. Nah, the guy at the school had been white; the guy in the police sketch was black. A witness could mix up things like height or facial features, but it'd be pretty hard to confuse a person's skin color.

Two cold hands suddenly reached out from nowhere and grasped Junebug's face. One palm covered his eyes, the other his mouth, yanking him away from the computer. Without a sound, he tumbled backward and down toward the floor.

†

TUCKED NEATLY UNDER THE FORD RANGER, THE TARGET willed his muscles to relax. In the next few moments he was going to need fluid movement and speed, something that can hurt if one's muscles are tight and tense. He took a deep slow breath and started counting.

Ten.

"Sucker's got to be somewhere in here," one of the teens said aloud.

"Runs fast, though, don't he?" another snorted.

"Shut up," said a third—the sniper? "Check behind those two pillars over there."

Nine.

Eight.

The target slowly flexed his palms. He considered, briefly, trying to unwrap the bandages on his wrists, then decided against it. He would just have to be extra careful not to let the gauzy padding interfere with the work ahead of him.

Seven.

"You hear something?" It was the second voice, now closer than was comfortable.

Six.

In the distance, the wail became more clear.

The Mercedes suddenly honked, three quick taps. A yell from the direction of the car. "Cops!" the driver shouted. "Headed this way. Just heard it on the police scanner."

Five?

"Go! Go!"

There was a clattering of footsteps, then a successive slamming of metal doors. The tires squealed in a circle and the engine gunned toward the exit, slowing just before it reached there.

"Hey, Sinner man!" the adolescent voice crowed. "This ain't over yet, brother. There's a price on your head, a big one. And we aim to collect."

The engine revved and silence returned to the parking structure.

The target took in a shallow breath and waited. Just when he was ready to roll out from under the truck, he heard another sound. New footsteps, walking slowly and carefully toward the middle of the lot, apparently from the direction of the elevators on the east end.

He listened. This was unexpected.

"You can come out now." A new voice. Familiar ... but why? "You're safe for the moment. But the police will be here shortly, and I'm guessing you don't want to be under that truck when they arrive."

So he'd been seen after all. That was interesting.

†

MANIACAL LAUGHTER FILLED JUNEBUG'S EARS, MAKING HIM wish his mouth were open just enough to bite the lower hand that covered his face. Instead he simply tumbled backward until the hands finally released their grip and left him lying face-up on the floor.

Keena was still giggling when he opened his eyes. She gazed down at him with a mixture of sympathy and hilarity in her expression. "You okay, Cuz? You should know by now never to turn your back on me, right?"

Junebug sighed, letting the coolness of the carpet gently seep through his shirt, willing his muscles to relax. "Keena, you have no idea what I've been through today."

The girl snickered again. "Oh c'mon, wimp. Like you've never scared the living daylights out of me before."

"That was different." Junebug started to protest, then remembered one particularly satisfying Halloween night that involved his cousin, her car, and several gallons of partially soured milk. "Okay," he grinned, reaching a hand up for help, "so I deserved it. But still, after what I endured this morning, you could at least have waited a few hours before springing your revenge."

She laughed even harder, reaching down to peel her cousin off the floor. "Revenge? That? Please. That was just goofing around. When it's time for revenge, well … all I can say is, 'when you least expect it, expect it.'"

Junebug smoothed down his shirt and looked around. "Right. Okay, psychopathic need for revenge aside, where is everybody? I thought CK was having the first meeting with the team today."

"She is. Was. Will be. I mean, we started the meeting, and partway into it, she got a call from some detective who wanted to talk to her. She and Galway went over to the police station, and she told the rest of us to keep ourselves busy for an hour. That girl from Oklahoma and her bodyguard went off somewhere to make a few phone calls. Chance invited me to try out some new video game he wrote for Nintendo. I think he's in a game room somewhere. I was going to join him, but this house is so big I couldn't find the right room, so I came back here."

Junebug nodded thoughtfully. "Game room's on the second floor. You have to go up the main staircase by the front hall, then turn left. You can't miss it. Chance's game is a kick, too. You'll enjoy it."

Keena nodded, then squinted over his shoulder. "What're those?" she asked, waving toward the photos that now appeared on the computer screen.

"Surveillance pictures of Hector Gomez."

"Who's the stud with the kid?"

Junebug gave Keena a quizzical look. She shrugged, "Hey, guy's got a nice build. A girl can't notice these things or what?"

"Yeah, well, that 'stud' threatened physical violence on your favorite cousin," he said. "So you'll excuse me if I'm not thrilled with your choice in men."

Junebug leaned over the computer and started clicking through the pictures. Keena peeked over his shoulder and kept quiet while he worked.

"Never got his face, not even once," Junebug muttered. "Explain that."

Keena opened her mouth, then closed it again.

"Nothing usable," Junebug pushed the computer mouse aside. "But I am pretty curious about who that guy is. And how he managed to avoid getting his face captured on film. And how he was able to sneak up on me so easily when I was supposed to be hidden from both him and the kid."

Keena leaned in closer to the computer screen. "Nice looking coat he's got, though. Don't recognize that material. Looks tailor-made … which means the guy isn't just good-looking; he could be also be rich."

Junebug just groaned.

†

REBEL FEINE SPOKE WITH AN AUTHORITY THAT CAME FROM rarely being denied anything as a child. She expected certain things in life, and because she expected them, she often got them. James Dandy, having grown up on the other side of the tracks, typically found her attitude annoying. But he had to admit there were times when it was nice to be associated with Rebel Feine's name and family influence. Right now was one of those times.

"I understand your concerns," Rebel said curtly into the telephone. "You must also understand that my time is short, my purpose is clear, and I need to see that information within the next hour. Now, what can we do to make that happen, hmm?"

She motioned for James to hand her a pad and pen.

"Fine, I'll hold."

James looked around the little library where he and Rebel had commandeered a phone, guessed that he'd find writing instruments in the ornate, polished antique desk, and began digging through the drawers. His search was rewarded in the second compartment, where he found several ballpoints and a small yellow pad of paper. Rebel palmed the mouthpiece on the receiver when he handed her the materials.

"Thanks," she said. "Need a phone book too."

James returned to his reconnaissance of the desk while she continued talking. "The research library doesn't open until eleven," she said, "but they've got a strong collection of Civil War archives, so I'm trying to get us in right now. I have a pretty good idea of what we're looking for—think I saw it in a textbook during college. With any luck, we'll be in, get what we need, and get back here before CK even knows we—"

She held up a finger and returned her attention to the

telephone. "Dr. Gramercy, how kind of you to take my call." She mouthed her thanks when James placed the phone book in front of her. Then she grimaced slightly and rolled her eyes a bit. "Of course I'll tell Daddy you said hello. He always speaks so highly of you. I just knew you'd be the right person to call."

She tucked the receiver between her ear and shoulder and started scribbling words on the yellow pad with one hand, and flipping through the phone book with the other, barely seeming to pay attention as words spilled out of her mouth. She'd played this little influence game so many times, she had it memorized. And whenever she was bored, multitasking was her natural response.

James couldn't help but check the windows and door once more. Some instincts never die out. His eyes ran over the cracks along the edge of the window sills, looking for signs of any recent, forced entries. There were none. He checked the latches; they were locked and dusty, indicating no one had opened them for some time. He started plotting escape routes in his mind, just in case a mad bomber crashed through the doorway and he had to take drastic action to protect Rebel from harm. *Once a bodyguard, always a body-guard,* he chuckled to himself. But CK's house seemed safe enough. At least for now.

"Why, you are a dear, aren't you?" She cooed into the telephone, thickening the Southern hints in her accent just enough to sound both grateful and flirtatious. She tore off the top sheet of the yellow pad, folded it in half, and wrote "CK" across it. "Well, my partner and I can be there in about fifteen minutes, if you could ... yes ... right ... very good.

Thank you so much, Philip. I certainly owe you one." She grimaced again. "Of course I'll tell him. We'll be right over."

She replaced the receiver with practiced precision and turned toward her bodyguard, partner, and friend. "Put this somewhere CK will find it, James," she said, handing over the note, "and let's get out of here. Time waits for no man."

She caught herself, and then gave the big man a wry look.

"Well," she added, "except maybe the Sinner."

MARIA ELIZA'S LOWER JAW MUSCLES RELAXED INVOLUNTARILY while the rest of the maid's sturdy frame stiffened with a tenseness she felt mostly in her neck. How long had that door been open?

In the silence of the moment Maria Eliza could hear the air rushing through her lungs as she breathed in and out through her slightly opened mouth. She found herself still fascinated by the sliver of sunlight that now flickered across her stockinged foot. Yet something prevented her from doing anything more than standing, staring, and breathing in the direction of the forbidden room.

LINCOLN SAYLES SNEAKED A GLANCE AT THE MAN WALKING beside him. For a guy who had just narrowly escaped death, the man was remarkably calm. And barely sweating at all.

When Link had parked his car this morning, he expected just another average day in the lobby of the downtown headquarters of Union Colony Bank. This week the security guard was scheduled for three days at the expansive downtown building, and only two at the Cole Street branch. He considered himself lucky when he'd spotted a parking space near the elevator on the first level of the garage attached to the bank building. He'd barely gathered his things and gotten out of his car before a man in a long gray coat swept in from the outside, running—no, sprinting, at top speed—toward the ramp to the upper levels. Before Lincoln could satisfy the nagging thought that he'd seen that guy before, a glittering Mercedes screeched into the garage as well. When he caught sight of a gun barrel poking lazily out the front window, his instincts kicked in. After all, six years in the army and a scar on his left calf had taught him the dangers of a gun in the wrong hands.

Flipping a switch on his radio, Lincoln called in the situation to the security team dispatcher. She'd call the police, and also send a few guards toward the parking garage for backup. Lincoln then made his way, cautiously, up the ramp toward the upper levels of the garage.

By the time he reached the third level, a dozen scenarios had played themselves out in his mind. And he was never the hero in any of them. But that didn't stop him from peering around the pillared corner to see the car idling across the bay, and subsequently counting one, two, three young men with guns carefully searching the garage for something or someone.

Lincoln breathed a short curse and quickly muted the volume on his radio. No sense taking a chance at being mistaken for the man in the gray coat … gray coat? With a hood? Now why would a runner be wearing a coat like that on a morning as warm as this one?

Slowly the images began to fall into place inside Lincoln's head. He closed his eyes to replay a second look at that thigh-length coat fluttering past as the man ran by. It was a match.

"Him." The security guard said it like a curse. *Just who is this guy,* he thought with frustration, *and why does he keep turning up in all the wrong places?*

Still, he had been right about Cassidy's ex-husband. And by delaying her from going home, he had probably rescued her from a nasty confrontation with a drunken ex-con out to make his ex-wife pay for testifying against him in the pre-liminary hearing.

Lincoln Sayles could have easily slinked away and waited for the police to arrive, but loyalty learned in combat forced him instead to crouch behind a red Camry and begin crab-walking toward the concrete wall to his left. After several silent shuffles, he worked his way around the edge of the lot to within twenty feet of the elevator shaft. He peered over the hood of a sleek brown Buick LeSabre and formulated a plan.

Now, twenty minutes or so later, in what Lincoln considered one of the most surreal moments of his life, the two men were walking casually down the halls of the bank building complex, headed toward the lobby area where couches and coffee awaited. When silence finally became louder than Lincoln could bear, he spoke.

"So," he said. "Been in town long?"

†

IT TOOK SIXTY-SEVEN HEARTBEATS BEFORE MARIA ELIZA Garces realized she had been counting the thumping in her chest. "*Aiee, chica,*" she whispered to herself. "You are a superstitious, silly girl." She inhaled a deep breath and took a step forward, feeling her pulse rate calm itself to almost normal. "And besides, that room hasn't been cleaned in years. Looks like you've got work to do today after all."

The Maximum Maid carefully returned *Uncle Tom's Cabin* to its proper place on the bookshelf, then smoothed her skirt and headed toward the threshold to the now-unlocked room. She paused a moment in the doorway to take in the surroundings of the room. Like the rest of this cottage, the furniture was spare, functional, almost antique, but in very well-kept condition. A sleigh bed dominated the space of the room, with an upright dresser nearby, a small table and chair, a rocker, and an open closet that appeared empty except for two gray overcoats, one floor-length, the other hip-length. Maria Eliza glanced to the right and saw, without surprise, another wall full of bookshelves, also two-thirds full of what appeared to be hardcover and leather-bound antique books. Tucked away in the back corner of the room was a narrow door, half-open, that apparently led to a small bathroom that barely had room for a toilet, tub, and sink.

After a moment of silence, Maria Eliza realized that she'd been holding her breath, let out a soft sigh, and caught the faint scent of potpourri or wildflowers. "Whoever uses this room," she said softly, "must like flowers."

She stepped into the room and walked around the bed toward the bathroom, scanning the room out of habit. She noticed someone had stripped off all the bedclothes and wondered where she might find clean sheets to remedy that situation, when she saw the linens piled in a tumble on the floor at the foot of the bed. She knelt to pick up the dirty laundry and noticed rusty stains dried onto the fabric. She examined the stains more closely, ready to unleash her arsenal of cleaning skills to make the sheets shine bright white again, when the realization of what she was looking at suddenly hit her.

Who has been bleeding in this bed?   †

Time, it seems, is an indifferent ally—firing minutes like loaded weapons, passing hours as a soothing salve, counting moments blindly into eternity.

Too late I see that time is merely a created toy, wound up and left spinning in the wounded hands of One for whom it holds no meaning. Eons and ages aren't enough time for that which finds its fullness in a day. An hour. A moment.

Celia.

I would kill it if I could. Wrap my fingers round its steely neck and squeeze forever to still the pregnant pauses, to grind to silence the ticking beast. But I am weak. Helpless. Also a created thing.

Left spinning.

Time, my enemy, my friend, you heal all wounds, yet leave open the festering sores of memories burned indelibly on the soul.

Celia.

Please forgive.

I didn't know that time, which was my friend, would betray you as my enemy. I didn't know his blessing would be my life-saving curse.

Would that I, like you, could escape forever the indifferent hands of time.

SEVEN

CK IVORS ALWAYS FELT LIKE SMILING WHEN SHE SAW Detective Sean Stepp—probably because that always seemed to make him feel like she was hiding something, and he hated being left out of a secret. But she knew that beneath his police detective professionalism there also lay a man of deep faith and loyalty, a devoted husband, and someone CK would—and did—trust with her life. So when CK and Galway entered Detective Stepp's cluttered office, Galway, as usual, started checking for listening devices, but CK gave the detective a warm smile—and meant it.

"Thanks for coming in, CK," he said, rising from behind his desk. He was polite enough to pretend not to notice

Galway and the way the old man was peering under lamp-shades and indiscriminately shuffling papers on his desk.

"Anything for you, Sean," CK replied. "We superheroes have to stick together, right?"

"Ah, are we superheroes today? I thought we'd given up that calling."

"Well, maybe we're not super. But we're pretty close, don't you think?" She took a seat in front of the detective's desk and kicked Galway in the foot to indicate that he should sit down too.

"Detective," Galway finally nodded toward Sean, before glaring at CK and sitting down.

"Nice to see you again too, Galway," Detective Stepp said, though it was obvious he only half meant it. "Although, I don't remember asking you to come down with CK. Perhaps you'd like to wait down in the lobby? We won't be long, and I believe the doughnuts down there are only a few days old."

"Actually, he's got something to tell you, Sean. That's why he came along."

Detective Stepp raised his eyebrows toward CK and settled back into his own chair behind the desk. "All right. What is it, Galway?"

The old man just smirked a moment, then said, "Nah. You don't deserve to know it. After all, you just tried to kick me out of your office. Me, a fine, upstanding citizen—"

"With thirteen arrests in the last twenty-four months."

"Trifles, all, and you know it, since you're probably the one who drummed up those bogus charges against me, Detective—"

"Galway, you tried to steal the fire hydrant from in front of the police station."

"As you'll remember, the court didn't see it that way, *Detective* Stepp. And I'll thank you not to slander me so in front of genteel company like CK Ivors—"

CK snorted and held back a laugh. "Gal, please. We're *guests* here."

"Fine. But I'm not talking to this pawn of the corporate conspiracy until he apologizes."

"Galway! You were the one who insisted on coming along with me to see Sean. You said you had valuable information for both him *and* me and that you'd wait to tell it to us together. Now, what? You're backing out? Or you didn't really have anything to begin with?"

"No, CK, don't pressure him," Detective Stepp protested. "A promise that Galway won't speak is worth its weight in gold around this department. Now if I could just get my mother-in-law to make the same vow."

Galway started to respond and then remembered that he was punishing the detective with his silence. He then turned to say something to CK, saw her palm placed defiantly in front of his face, and finally just "humphed" and sat back in his chair, waiting.

CK finally shook her head and then turned back to the detective. "Okay, Sean, let's see, do I owe you a favor, or do you owe me this time?"

The detective reached into the top drawer of his desk. "Well," he said, "I think we're even at present, so this one will have to be something for both of us."

CK leaned forward, always eager to get in on secrets

Sean Stepp may have been hiding. Galway sat up in his chair despite himself.

"Look, CK," the detective continued, "I know you and your photographer were nosing around at St. Anthony's last week. I don't know why, but I'm guessing it had something to do with this."

He placed the gold watch with the sign of the Sinner on the desk, deliberately putting it closer to Galway than to CK. The old man's eyes glowed with the light of a thousand conspiracies, but to his credit, he restrained himself from picking up the watch and beginning an immediate examination of it.

"Okay, I'll give you that much, Sean," CK grinned. "But how did you know we'd even seen it?"

The detective waved a hand, dismissing the question. "I also know this watch is at least one hundred years old, that the symbol on here has been around for even longer than that, and that it's associated with some kind of urban myth."

CK and Galway both nodded, waiting.

"What I don't know," the detective said, "is why that symbol is also on this."

He now pulled a sheet of folded notebook paper from the top desk drawer and placed it in front of his guests. The Sinner's symbol had been inked at the bottom of the page. The top of the page was simply a jumble of numbers.

"Or why the man who gave me this paper keeps telling us that it's a death threat and that he needs immediate protection by a half-dozen officers in my department."

CK pulled the paper closer to her. The handwritten numbers at the top of the page were confusing:

55
34-1-28657-8
6765-8-8-610
121393-987-17711

CK's mind instinctively started ciphering through what she knew of codes and numbers while she talked. "Who gave this to you, Sean?"

"I can't reveal that person's name to you, CK, for his own safety. But I can tell you that this person is a respected member of the community and a professor of applied mathematics at the university."

CK grinned. He had just given her enough information to track down the identity of the bearer of the note, without actually revealing that person's identity. Detective Stepp was tricky that way. It made CK wonder what kind of tricks he was playing on her at the moment. But apparently that was enough information for Galway to get over his recent grudge against the police officer.

"Detective," he said seriously, "this is a death threat. Give the guy the protection he's asking for." He paused and moved his lips while looking at the sheet in CK's hands, a process she recognized. Galway always moved his lips when he was committing something to memory. Then he stood quickly.

"Let's go, CK. We need to get the team into action— before we're too late." His forehead furrowed into deep thought; he was present physically, but long gone from the room inside his head.

"Wait a minute," Detective Stepp started.

But CK knew Galway, and she knew that when he took a break from being smug and superior, when he was lost to the working out of some problem in his head, that was the time to act first and ask questions later.

"Sorry, Sean," CK said quickly, "gotta go. But I'll call you later with more info. I promise."

"You'd better!" Detective Stepp shouted as he followed them toward the door. He stopped abruptly as CK dodged backward out of the doorway when Galway leaned briefly back into the room.

"Oh, and by the way, Detective. You've got the wrong guy on your wanted poster for the priest beating. You'll probably want to let the public know that before you arrest an innocent man."

CK shot a quick look at Galway, then looked back at Detective Stepp and shrugged. "Hey, I didn't know it either, Sean," she said on her way out. "But now that I think about it, it does make sense. I'd say take it down too."

"How can you be so sure?"

CK didn't have time to answer. She didn't want to lose sight of Galway as he marched down the hallway toward the exit.

†

CHANCE ELKO FELT LIKE STARTING A CLUB FOR MORONS who invite pretty women to play video games and only realize later that pretty women don't play video games—at least not with morons. He checked the hallway once again before finally resigning himself to the fact that Keena Collins not only wasn't coming, but that she wasn't even the slightest bit interested in coming. "Probably downstairs with that bodyguard somewhere," he muttered. "Probably already married to him or something."

Chance wandered back into the game room and flicked off his prototype for *Council of War*. Nintendo was telling him they expected it to be a moderate hit during the Christmas season, and that if the current trends continued, he should begin thinking about *Council of War 2: Retribution* pretty soon. But right now Lucinda Elko's youngest son just didn't care.

He walked over to the row of gaming computers and logged on to the Internet. Maybe if he solved this Sinner mystery, that would make the chicks dig him. He glanced down at his T-shirt and had to smile. It was a plain blue shirt with the words "My mommy says I'm special" on it. Lucinda had given it to him for his birthday last October. It was cheesy, yeah, but in a funny way. And it was nice to feel special to somebody.

Chance skipped over to Google.com and started half-heartedly entering search strings. He didn't really have to do this yet—CK still hadn't given him any clear search criteria to use. But Chance always felt more comfortable in front of a computer, so he started tapping letters into the Web browser. After thinking a bit about the priest beating at St. Anthony's Cathedral, he had a fit of inspiration and entered "Sinner Legend God." He stopped when he came to an obscure entry on the third page of his results list. The page was titled "Legends I Have Met" and appeared to be a personal page of someone somewhere in California. It had last been updated about thirteen months prior.

The page had mostly just photo scans of a rather plain blonde woman—apparently her name was Samantha—standing next to famous people. Judging from the progression of the pictures, she appeared to be in her midthirties. Each photo had a caption from Samantha (or "Sammy" as she sometimes called herself) describing the scene.

"This is me next to Charles Grodin on the set of *Beethoven's Fifth*. (Don't ask how I got in there!) Super nice guy, but the dog slobbered all over my leg."

"Here I am with Paul Newman! Can you believe it? He was at this restaurant and stopped to let us take his picture on his way out."

"This is me with Sonny Bono. Saw him at a taco stand in DC (note the stains on my shirt!). He didn't know my friend Kimmy was taking the picture, so that's why he's turned a little to the side."

Near the end of the page, however, was one last entry—without a photo. Instead it framed a sketch of a man in a long coat. He had dark shoulder-length hair and a muscular torso. On his chest Sammy had drawn a careful replica of the symbol Chance had seen on the watch. Next to him, she had drawn a young girl holding his hand and looking up at a halo over his head.

"This is, well, I don't know who he is. He just said he was a 'sinner' like everyone else. But he's the reason I started believing in God again. I think he might have been an angel because he saved me from a really bad man (can't talk about it, but trust me, he was bad). I haven't seen him since I was six, but he was there when I needed him, and I know he'd be there if I ever needed him again. As far as I'm concerned, he's legendary … and I hope you never have to meet him. But I'm sure glad I did."

Chance stared at the drawing. Sammy certainly had some artistic ability, but even so, the face of the "sinner" was obscured in shadows. *Maybe she couldn't remember his face,* he thought to himself.

And maybe it's time I got serious about discovering the history of this guy they call the Sinner.

He reflected on what Galway had told them, and realized again that Galway had only given them a sketchy summary of the legend surrounding the Sinner. He had first appeared just before the Civil War. Then disappeared. Then appeared again at odd intervals, usually going on some vigilante crusade before disappearing for some time again. Some said he was a hero, others said he was as bad as Hitler. Then there were those who claimed he could fly, that he could magically transport himself through time, that he was an alien from Mars, and all kinds of other weird things. Chance knew there had to be a lot more information out there somewhere, and if someone were diligent, he could probably piece together what was true and what wasn't. But whether it was all truth or fiction didn't make a difference at this point. What mattered was putting together the full picture of the man behind that snake-and-cross symbol.

He looked at Sammy's sketch again and clicked on the print button, sending it to a printer downstairs in the main office. He had a feeling he was going to need the deep paper supplies that CK always kept in those machines down there.

†

LOFTIS JOHNSON GOT THE CALL AFTER THE FACT AND, AS usual, felt his blood pressure rising just a bit higher.

"We saw him," the adolescent growled, "actually had him cornered in the parking garage at the Union Colony Bank, downtown."

"But you let him walk away?"

"Hey, the cops showed up. What were we supposed to do? But we'll get him. We know what he looks like now, and we got scanners all over the downtown area. They'll spot him. And when they do, we'll get him."

"Fine. Call me when your work is finished. Don't waste my time with any more stories about failure."

"But you wanted us to verify—"

Loftis Johnson tapped his fingers on the desk after hanging up on the gunman. He was a patient man, when patience was called for. After all, he had waited more than eleven years this time around, hadn't he?

He leaned back in his chair and waited for the phone to ring. He knew he wouldn't be waiting long.

†

REBEL FEINE BREATHED A SIGH OF RELIEF WHEN THE GOOD Dr. Gramercy finally excused himself and left her and James to work through the Civil War archives in the university library. He promised to check back in fifteen minutes, and Rebel vowed to herself to be done by then. Otherwise James would have too much information (from the free-talking

Dr. Gramercy) to make into stories for CK and the others when they gathered for lunch later. After all, Rebecca Feine had a reputation to maintain if she expected people to keep calling her Rebel … and she did.

James had followed Dr. Gramercy to the door, and now stood sentinel in front of it. Rebel shook her head.

"James, how many times have I told you that I don't always need a bodyguard? Can't you just stop with the little protection thing every once in a while? I mean, look around you. There's nothing but books and papers down here. It's not like one of those maps on the wall is going to try to strangle me or something."

Mr. Dandy simply smiled and stayed exactly where he was.

Rebel looked disgusted. It was hard to fire a bodyguard when Daddy was the one signing his paycheck.

"Fine," she said. "At least help me look for the letter."

The big man hesitated, peered out the door and down the hallway, then finally came over to stand by Rebel. "So you think it was 1862?"

"Yeah," she said, "1861 or '62. Not sure which. But it was a part of the Englander collection that they discovered in 1929. A personal letter from one Judge John Northcutt Simmons to a slave owner in Georgia. Interestingly, nobody knows the name of that slave owner, but rumor has it that he and his family fled to Florida after receiving the judge's letter."

"But that's just a rumor?"

"Yes. What we know for sure is that Judge Simmons wrote the letter, that somehow it ended up in Pennsylvania, where somebody in the Englander family rolled it up with a bunch of newspapers and used it as insulation for the wall of a small house. When builders came to remodel the house in 1929, they found the letter along with several other artifacts that dated back to the Civil War. One thing led to another, and before long the whole set was in the Smithsonian."

"And now, years later, that obscure piece of information seems worth plundering the archives at a respected university. Right?"

"Shut up," she grinned. "Can I help it if I like history? Besides, they are supposed to have duplicates of the entire Englander set right here in this room, and if you expect to get back before CK knows we're gone, you'd better get busy."

The bodyguard grinned back. He knew a race had begun. The first one to find the letter in question would win bragging rights for at least an hour. And James Dandy did like to brag.

THERE ARE TIMES WHEN SIMPLE CURIOSITY IS ENOUGH TO make a grown woman forget her senses and her place, to make her take chances she might not otherwise take. To make her forget for a moment that she is simply a maid, lost in a forgotten cottage, hidden behind a sprawling manor, secreted away from a busy city where traffic runs unconcerned, where crimes are committed and love is made. For Maria Eliza Garces, the world had gone away, at least for the moment, and only curiosity remained.

She stared hard at the sheet in her hands and thought she noticed a pattern in the blood stains. She peered down at the empty bed and was not surprised to see faintly matching rust stains in the appropriate places on the dark blue mattress. She carefully spread the sheet back into its original place on the bed, pulling the corners tight out of habit.

"It must have been a man," she said to herself, noting that the distance from the top stain appeared to be around six feet or so from the ones at the bottom. "Or a very tall *chica.*"

She breathed in the scented air of this forbidden room, and felt a little thrill at her current task. She tried to take in the story of the sheet as a whole, trusting that she was sensing something more than deducing it. She started at the top, where pinpricks of brown spots indicated rows of tiny wounds that dripped then quickly congealed against the sheet. Tracing a medium-sized figure down from there, she could connect the invisible sufferer to a once-sticky palm print on the right, and a small pool of blood toward the left side of what must have been a torso, and what could have been a clenched, bloody fist on the far left. From there to the bottom, the sheet was relatively clean until it came to one large, smeared rust spot that might have signaled that two ankles had writhed within its mess.

"*Madre de Dios,*" the maid whispered when the picture finally sank in.

She quickly stripped the sheet off the bed and threw it in a heap with the rest of the bedclothes. She scanned the rest of the room and was surprised to discover no blood stains on the floor or even in the bathroom. She traced what would have been a normal path from the bed to the bathroom, to the door, or even to a window, thinking there must have been some sign of the way the sufferer had been taken from the bed and out of the room. She saw years' worth of dust, but no cobwebs or other signs of decay. She made out what she thought might have been a set of footprints headed from the bed to the bathroom and inspected them as closely as she could. Still, no sign of the bleeding that had been so profuse on the sheets.

She stood, confused and worried. The rest of the world began to slowly seep back into her consciousness. Did Candy know about this? Or Robert? Should she call the police?

She felt herself backing toward the door, wondering where she would find the nearest phone. At the main house, perhaps? She turned for one last look into the room, and then her foot kicked against something solid.

Maria Eliza felt her heart rate quicken.

LINCOLN SAYLES SHRUGGED TO HIMSELF WHEN THE MAN next to him didn't respond. He motioned to a chair on the edge of the lobby. "Can I get you some coffee or something?" He was trying to be polite, but this guy was beginning to get him agitated anyway.

The man in the gray coat paused then, and took a long hard look at Lincoln's face. Lincoln willed himself not to look away. He had never backed down from anything in his life, and he wasn't about to back down now. After a strained moment of silence, the mystery man's face relaxed just a bit.

"No, thank you. Sayles isn't it?" The stranger's eyes were still locked onto Lincoln's face, but they were unguarded, at least just a bit. Just enough that Link felt his shoulders relax and realized his hand was still hovering comfortably close to his gun.

"Yeah. Lincoln Sayles. Met you a few days ago at the Union Colony Bank on Cole."

The stranger nodded, thoughtful. "I remember," he said. Then he turned abruptly and began to survey the scene in the lobby. The workers and customers in there seemed blissfully unaware that anything dangerous had transpired just a few floors above them only minutes ago.

Lincoln watched the stranger. Judging from the way his eyes flicked about the room, he appeared to be counting exits, monitoring possible threats, and marking the positions of innocent bystanders. The whole process took less than ten seconds. Lincoln felt his shoulder muscles tense up again.

"Listen, you want to tell me what that was all about up in the garage?"

The stranger didn't respond, instead turning his attention to the surveillance cameras scattered around the room.

Lincoln shook his head and snorted. "Let me guess," he said. "You're finally going to get around to telling me your name?"

The stranger turned back to the security guard. "What's interesting, Mr. Sayles," he said, "is that I've never seen you."

Lincoln began to wonder about the man's mental competence. "What are you talking about? We met just a few days ago when you nearly scared one of our bank tellers out of her wits. Now it turns out that you did Cassidy a favor, and that's the only reason I didn't let the police come and get you out from under that truck. But I gotta tell you, you're not doing yourself any favors with this big mystery game you're playing."

The stranger grinned, the first genuine expression Lincoln had seen in his face. "I suppose you must have questions," he said comfortably.

"As a matter of fact, I do. For starters, who are you? And why were those kids with guns trying to shorten your life span? And how did you know that stuff about Cassidy's ex-husband? And, well, just who are you?"

"Unfortunately, Mr. Sayles, I don't have any answers for you today."

Lincoln felt his face flush red with anger, but tried to keep his voice calm and under control. "Listen," he said, "I saved your life up there. I'm the one who called the police to scare away the gun boys. I'm the one who was ready to put my life on the line to help you face down those gang punks. And I'm the one who helped you get safely down here instead leaving you to police custody—and to *their* much more invasive questions."

He paused.

"Look, I think you owe me something," Lincoln said when a moment had passed in silence. "After all, I'm going to have a lot of explaining to do—like why I called the police and then let you leave the garage before the police got to you. They're not going to be happy, you know. They just rushed to an empty parking lot, and now they probably already think I just called in a false alarm. So the least you could do is tell me who you really are."

Lincoln waited, and the two men stared at each other in silence for a moment. *Interesting that we must be about the same height,* Link thought after a moment, *because he's looking at me level, right in my eyes.*

The stranger looked thoughtful, then delivered a slight nod. "Thank you for your help in the garage," he said in a tone that indicated their time together was about done. "I would have been fine without your help, but I appreciate the intention anyway."

Moving more swiftly than Lincoln had expected, the stranger slid to a counter where pens and deposit slips awaited. He quickly scratched out something on the back of a slip of paper and then handed it to the security guard. Lincoln glanced at it and saw a cross with a snakelike *S* wrapped around its center.

"Mr. Sayles," the stranger said formally, "I am in your debt. If you ever have need of me, tack this on the public announcements board at the local library. I'll find you soon after."

The stranger held out his hand. Lincoln shook it warily, not sure he was ready to let this man leave the bank yet. But before he could say anything to stop him, the stranger turned toward the row of bank tellers across the lobby.

"Now," he said, "if you'll excuse me please. I have business to attend to."

†

THE ONLY WAY CK IVORS HAD GOTTEN GALWAY TO SLOW
down and eventually stop was to loan him a cell phone.
Now he stood by CK's car, mumbling in low tones to the
third or fourth person he'd called in the last few minutes.
CK gave him credit, though. Always aware that CK (or
some hidden adversary) might be trying to read his lips, he
cupped a hand over his mouth the whole time and period-
ically made eye contact with his companion to draw her
gaze away from his mouth. Finally he flipped the phone
closed and tossed it toward his friend.

"Finished with the secrets and lies?" CK said tersely.
"Thought you were working for me on this Sinner thing."

Galway smiled, the kind of smile that CK thought he
must have used back in his flirtatious days—if he ever had
any. CK had never heard of a Mrs. Galway, nor had she ever
seen any trace of an interested woman around Galway
either. Once he had mentioned a name, Roseanne or something, in passing while they were following up a lead, and
CK got a hint that there was more to that name than her
old friend let on. But he was much too paranoid to let anyone know he cared about anything too much, so CK was
left to guessing.

"Actually, CK," Galway said warmly, "I never work *for*
anybody. You know that."

"Then why do I keep giving you cash-filled envelopes to
keep you on retainer each month?"

Galway patted her on the shoulder. "You give me those
payments to work *with* you. And I'm glad to do so. But
never *for* you. That would be unethical."

CK threw up her hands. "Fine. Whatever. Now tell me what you know because we're supposed to be back at my office finishing up our briefing right about now, and if I have to be late I should at least know what's going on."

Galway leaned back against the hood of CK's car. "Okay, well, for one thing the person in that police sketch of the priest beater doesn't exist."

"The boy was lying? How can you be so sure?"

Galway tilted his head to the left and gave a small frown. "Look at Junebug's picture, CK. The one of the boy leaving the police station with his parents."

"Listen, Gal, something you should know. Not everybody has a photographic memory like you do, okay?"

Galway now tilted his head to the right. "No, I suppose they don't," he said. "But I do know that your memory is still quite good, even if it's not photographic. In fact, I'm betting you memorized that code in Stepp's office before I did."

CK nodded curtly. "Makes no sense to me, though," she said. "And right now I want to know about that boy."

"Look at the picture."

"Galway!"

The old man stood up, and now he really frowned. "Listen, girl. I didn't take you under my wing so you could be lazy and stupid. If you're going to play a detective, you'd better do the work of a detective."

CK wanted to be angry at her old friend, wanted to tell him off and let him know that she'd done fine for many years before they met, and would have (well, might have) done just fine if he hadn't joined her team during the antiquities investigation. But she looked at his face, so serious, so proud, and realized that what made him proud was the fact that she was his prize pupil. And she hated knowing that he knew something she hadn't figured out.

"Okay," she closed her eyes. "I'm looking at the picture." *My mind is a camera lens,* she thought to herself. *The black behind my eyes is a canvas. My brain will paint the picture …*

"Good," she heard Galway's voice. "What do you see?"

She mentally blocked out the crowd. They were there, but they were a faceless, formless blob in the background. The parents were dropped in place, one on each side of the boy. But again, they were just forms, faceless, but standing in protective postures.

"The boy," she said. "Hector Gomez."

"And?"

CK let her brain fill in the space she'd reserved for Hector. What did she remember about that picture? What made her take a second look?

"Is he grinning?"

She could hear the smile in Galway's voice when he responded. "Yes, he is. Good for you. That was the first 'tell' I noticed too. Go on."

Tells? Of course. CK mentally kicked herself. It had never occurred to her that she might be playing poker with Hector Gomez. He was a kid, right? Witness to a horrible crime. What did he have to hide?

"I see what you're talking about, Gal," she said, keeping her eyes closed to hold on to the image in her mind as much as possible. "Kid's hunched over, leaning away from the police officer. He's trying to avoid letting the police officer in on a secret, but his body posture is revealing that anyway. Instead of walking between his parents, he's over to one side, keeping both mom and dad between him and the cop. Unconsciously using them as a protective barrier between him and the police officer. Backpack is carried in front, serving as another barrier, instead of carrying it on his back where it would normally go."

"And?"

"And he's just starting to grin. All the way to his eyes. He knows he's just about to get away with a big, fat lie, and the relief is showing itself involuntarily in his face."

CK opened her eyes to find Galway nodding with approval. "The boy is lying to the people around him, and appears most concerned about the police officer's reaction to his lie. What have the police been asking him about?"

"A detailed description of the attacker."

"So we must assume that's what his lie is about."

"Which means he faked the details in the description of the suspect. But why would he do that, Gal? What's he got to gain?"

"Don't know," Galway shrugged. "At this point that's irrelevant. What matters is that we don't know what our attacker looks like after all."

"And that means he could be anybody, we could have seen him a dozen times by now, or not at all."

"It also means we need to redirect our investigation. The boy is an unreliable source. So what's left?"

CK let things fall into place in her mind. "The symbol on the watch. The legends about the Sinner. The priest who was beaten."

"Sounds like we've got some work to do."

CK's cell phone rang unexpectedly. She flipped the cover and held it up to her ear. "CK," she said.

"CK," the voice belonged to Junebug. "Listen, Chance and I just put something together, and we're thinking you should see this. When are you coming back?"

"We're on our way," she said, motioning for Galway to get in the car.   †

She steps toward me without hesitation. What have I done to deserve this child's trust? Nothing but given a promise. Someplace safe. A cool spot to rest. This is my promise to her, and she believes my promise as though it were truth.

I am determined to make it so.

I begin to stand and she raises her arms to me, eyes expectantly fluttering, looking into mine. I don't think; I merely respond, stretching my own hands back toward her. She melts into them, and I feel her head lie heavy on my neck. A soft sigh escapes her lips, and I feel her thigh muscles twitch with weariness as I stand up.

"You a strong one," the man says to me admiringly. "But she heavy, I know. You wan' me to cawrry her fo' yeh?"

"No," I say. "It's not far." And I am thinking that I would never give up this precious package in my arms, even if the barn were miles from here. I made her a promise. And I will make it so.

I brush the thick, matted hair away from the child's ear and whisper. "What's your name?"

She doesn't answer.

She has already fallen asleep.

EIGHT

RANCE ACKERS SHOULD HAVE BEEN IN COLLEGE. IN fact, his parents still thought he was there, still sent the occasional letter (and sometimes cash) to the dormitory address he'd given them last year. But Rance Ackers had never been to college, never broken out a notebook or sat through a lecture on Middle English literature or anything even close to that. Letters to that dormitory address were automatically forwarded to a friend who was happy to hold on to Rance's mail in return for a few illegal favors now and then. Rance lived wherever he found a bed, and his only pursuit was to find a way to recapture the thrill and the peace of days spent away in his mind.

He knew in high school that he had to get away, to get to a place where he could feed his habit without having to cover it up from his parents or his teachers. He knew he had to get to a place where he could simply take what he needed instead of asking for it. A place where his strength was other people's weaknesses.

So this morning, after watching the green house on Minkin Avenue for four days, he knew he was ready.

First he lifted his spirits with a needle in his arm. That would last him a bit, but not long enough to his liking. If he were to get more, he'd have to pay old man Dunn for it. And he had to get more.

Then he climbed the fence to the backyard, and went to the window over by the kitchen sink. They always left that one open. Or at least unlocked.

Once inside, he found the master bedroom and barricaded himself inside the closet. He had to let the spirits fly in his brain. They were angry today. Angry like the time they made him stab that old man for his wallet. Like the time they made him cut that girl's face 'cause she was just too pretty to look at.

Rance doubled over and retched for a moment … but it was only dry heaves. He tore some clothes off the bar hanging in the closet and made himself a comfortable niche in a corner. He toyed with the idea of simply robbing the place. There were plenty of things he could trade for money or favors in here.

But he'd been watching this house for four days now. He knew the first person to get home would be the girl. She was maybe sixteen, maybe seventeen. Came home from school in a bright red car and stayed here alone for at least an hour before anybody else got here.

And the spirits screaming inside his head now were so, so angry.

She was, they shouted over and over, just too pretty to look at.

†

JUNEBUG COULD SEE THAT CK WAS NOT HAPPY.

"So where are they? Didn't I tell everyone to stay here until I got back?" She glared at Chance. "Couldn't talk them into playing your war game or something?"

Junebug was surprised to see Chance blush and glance furtively at Keena.

"Hey, CK, c'mon." Junebug figured somebody had to say something. "It's not his fault that Rebel and James took off. They're grown-ups, you know. They get to do what they want to do, when they want to do it."

CK fumed silently, staring hard at Junebug.

"And besides, *Council of War* rocks."

That finally broke her. CK let a half smile play on her face. "Yeah, it does," she said. "And next time I'm going to kick your armies all the way to Athens."

Junebug watched both Chance and Keena exhale with relief.

"Well, what do you think, Gal?" CK said. "Should we wait for them or go ahead?"

Galway busied himself with a pitcher of orange juice and just shrugged.

"Oh." It was Keena. "I almost forgot. James left this note for you, from Rebel." She passed the paper over. CK gave it a quick glance and then nodded to herself.

"Gather the chairs at that round discussion table, guys. It's time we made up a game plan."

†

REBEL FEINE SOMETIMES FELT SO IMPATIENT THAT SHE wanted to pull her ears out of her head just to see if she could use them as wings to go flying through the atmosphere.

"James," she said in frustration, "let's *go*. We found the letter ..."

The bodyguard paused and gave her a questioning look.

Rebel grimaced. "Okay, *you* found the letter."

James Dandy relaxed his face, nodded, and returned to his work.

"We made the copy. We even took a digital scan of the letter to bring back to CK's office. So why are we wandering around the stacks looking for old Edgar Allan Poe stories?"

James Dandy was sometimes so patient, it made Rebel want to pull *his* ears out and go flying. Surely those oversized lobes of his were big enough for something like that.

"Just a minute, Reb," he said, apparently unaware that she was losing her temper. "It's got to be in one of these books." He flipped open a thick tome and quickly scanned the table of contents. Not finding what he wanted, he flipped open the next one and did the same. At the third book, he looked up and smiled. "Got it," he said. "Think they'll let me take this without a library card?"

"No."

"Me neither." He smiled and looked up at the ceiling. Rebel instinctively followed his gaze. When she looked back at him, the book was gone.

"Learned a new magic trick, did we?" she said.

"I have no idea what you're talking about. Now come on, we can't goof off around here forever."

Rebel started marching toward the door, all the while devising exactly how to shape a large man's earlobes into fancy, aerodynamically efficient wings.

†

IT WAS A BOOK. LEATHER BOUND. WORN.

Maria Eliza Garces let her breath out in relief. The book was upside down, with a pen stuffed inside it, all the way to the spine. She picked it up and opened it. The pages toward the front had been filled by handwritten entries, all in a meticulous cursive that suggested the author took his or her time and made each letter in a careful, practiced flow. Before the middle of the book, however, the writing entries stopped. The rest of the book was blank.

Without thinking, Maria Eliza slowly sat on the edge of the stained mattress. She looked for dates on the entries but found none. She noticed a page near the end of the written part that had apparently been torn out, crumpled, then flattened, and then folded in half and inserted back into the book again. She gently unfolded it and read:

let me be forgotten by posterity. an old worn
black-and-white photo showing a group of
unnamed people that family members look at
during reunions though they can't ever remember
just exactly who was who. let my words be
overlooked and dismissed like doggerel scribbled on
napkins then quickly abandoned and later used
for kindling to tempt the flames in a fireplace on
a cold winter's night. let my voice be erased like
an overused tape leaving only sustained blank
hissing to remind that thoughts were once spoken
here. let my life's work crumble into ruin carelessly
eroded by the ceaseless tides of time that spill over
and then through the countless sandcastles of
individual existence. let the very memory of me
become only a memory in the fading imagination
of a slumbering universe where sleep turns quickly
into death leaving me simply as one who is no
more. and when i am finally unremembered
maybe then i too can forget that this world is
what it seems to be: a hurtful, hateful place where
people carve apart the souls from bodies of men
and women and children. and themselves. until in
ultimate hypocrisy they scapegoat God judging
him as guilty for the wicked, wounded world their
very hands have made.

Maria Eliza wondered at the words she read, curious to
know more about the person who had written this entry—
but unsure that she wanted to actually meet that man or

woman. She flipped the book closed and saw that the leather had been stamped … or maybe tooled by hand. The image now carved there was not one she'd seen before. It was a cross and a snake, held inside a circle. There was no title on the book, only the symbol.

The maid became lost in thought for a moment, letting her eyes wander around the room toward the bookshelf built into the wall. She was surprised to see two whole rows of leather-bound books similar to the one she held, stored low, on the bottom of the bookcase. She stepped carefully to the wall, then knelt down to look at the long rows of leathers. Each book bore the same symbol on the front, and no other outer markings. The ones to the far right were obviously newer; the far left were so old as to be antiques. She peeked inside a few and discovered what she expected: that same, careful handwriting filling up line after line on each page, front and back.

She gently removed the first book in the line, taking great care not to crack the old leather or tear the brittle pages. She sat down on the floor and opened the first page. She felt like a little girl with a secret glimpse at a magic book. But before she could read very far, she thought she heard a thump somewhere nearby. She held her breath and waited, heard the soft thump again, this time followed by a light scratching. She turned her head toward the sound and was relieved to see a tree branch swaying outside the window. It blew gently against the window, delivering a rhythmic soft thump followed by a light scratch as its leaves brushed across the pane.

Her eyes went back to the original book she'd picked

up, and the page that was torn out of it. Holding the antique book in her left hand, she returned to inspect that crumpled page with her right. It was then that she finally thought to turn it over. On the back she saw these numbers:

55

34-1-28657-8

6765-8-8-610

121393-987-17711

She had no idea what they might mean. Then she noticed a small entry on the inside left corner, near the bottom of the page, rising horizontally up the page. It looked like a calendar notation.

And it had been dated this very morning.

†

After everyone huddled themselves around the table, CK showed the group Rebel's note. It said:

> *CK—*
> *Kid's lying about something. Took me awhile*
> *to figure that out— sorry. My guess is the police*
> *sketch is a fake. So when you can't track a face,*
> *you've got to track a wardrobe. Back soon.*
> *Reb*

"She's right," CK said. "Galway figured that out right away." She paused to glare at him. "Only wish he'd told us sooner."

Galway, of course, just smiled.

"What's she mean about tracking a wardrobe?" Keena asked.

Chance looked at Junebug and could barely contain himself. "Well, when you don't know a target's face, you can sometimes track that target by style instead."

Keena looked puzzled. "Is this what you and Junebug were talking about earlier?"

"Yeah." It was Junebug. "Everybody has an individual style, something they don't think about. Some guys always wear caps. Some girls always wear a certain brand of makeup."

Keena sat up straight and flattened both her palms on the table. "Oh," she said. "And the Sinner always wears a coat, doesn't he?"

Chance and Junebug both nodded. "Gray jacket. Straight."

CK knew enough to know she didn't know enough. "Show me what you got, guys."

Junebug laid out a stack of freshly printed pictures. "Okay," he said, "here's a few photos I snapped of Hector Gomez this morning. See that guy walking with Hector? I could never get a frame on his face—but I did get several clean shots of his coat."

CK had to admire Junebug's talent with a camera. These shots had to have been taken from awkward distances and with a handheld camera, yet each image was clear and bright, almost like it had come from a portrait studio.

"Nice jacket," CK said. "Gray. Hip length. Hangs very well. You make out what the material is?"

"No," Chance replied. "It has the texture of wool, but

also a polish like satin. I'd have to look at it in person to make it out."

"Okay," CK continued. "So we have a guy with a nice jacket. Think that's our perp?"

"Well, after the morning I had, I'd have to say I'd be suspicious anyway," Junebug started to retell the story of his encounter with the man in the coat, then opted to save it for another time. "Anyway, I was looking for clues to this guy's identity when suddenly this popped out of the printer."

He placed the sketch from Samantha's Web site next to the top photo in CK's stack.

"I was upstairs, uh, doing some Internet searches and found this," Chance said. "Thought it was interesting, so I printed it out down here, along with a few other tidbits from some obscure Web pages around the world. When I got down here to pick up the pages from the printer, Junebug had everything spread out on a table and was comparing it all."

The hair in the sketch was different from the photo. Also the guy in the sketch was definitely more muscular, and probably taller than the guy in the photo. But the coat was almost exactly the same.

"How old is this?" CK asked.

Chance shrugged. "My best guess? Maybe twenty, twenty-five years. The lady who put this sketch on her Web site said she hadn't seen the guy since she was six, and she was definitely a grown woman, judging by the other pictures on the site."

"Then it's not the same guy."

Galway snorted.

"How can it be?" CK continued. "Look at the guy in this sketch. He's maybe midtwenties, right? And look at the guy in Junebug's surveillance shot. It's hard to tell without seeing his face, but judging by his body, he can't be more than early thirties, and might be as young as twenty-five. If twenty years have passed, we'd see some signs of aging, right?"

"Maybe he got the jacket from his uncle or something?" Keena suggested. "A family of vigilantes?"

Galway snorted again.

"A possibility," said Junebug. "But look at this." He placed another printout on the table, this time from a newspaper archive of the *Philadelphia Inquirer*. The headline read "Mysterious Hero Rescues Local Teen from Car Trunk."

"Let me summarize this for you," Chance said. "Local teen goes to a night hangout. Gets into an argument with another guy over a girl. Seems he was black, and the girl was white, and the partygoers didn't like them talking to each other. The white guy disappears, returns with a few friends. They grab the first teen and lock him in a trunk and go for a joyride. About an hour or so later, the car stops. The kid in the trunk hears a commotion and even a gunshot. Next thing he knows, some mystery man pops open the trunk and tells him to call the police. On the ground around him are four of the guys who stuffed him in there, beaten, bloodied, and groaning. Then the hero is gone."

"Sounds like an after-school special. But what does that have to do with our guy?"

Junebug put the next printout on the table. "Two days later, the police ran a description of the hero, trying to track him down to make a statement."

CK read aloud. "Caucasian male in his midtwenties. Short, cropped black hair. Medium build and around five ten to six feet tall. Last seen wearing a long gray coat with a hood attached to the neck."

"Okay, sounds like our guy," she continued.

"Can't be, according to you," Galway smirked.

"What do you mean?"

Galway pointed to the corner of the article. "Date says this took place in 1966. That guy would be ready for retirement by now, don't you think?"

Junebug sat down. "CK, Chance came up with more than a dozen sightings of this coat in the last fifty years. In every one of them, the guy wearing the coat is midtwenties, medium to larger in size. So many similarities that it has to be the same guy. But the sightings are all over the decades. So either this guy keeps himself in really good shape, or there's more than one Sinner out there."

CK nodded thoughtfully. "So, Galway, what do you think?"

"Well, the legend says he's been around a long time."

"How long?"

"CK," Galway said, "there are a couple of things you should know about the legend of the Sinner."

Chance broke in. "Well, for starters, the crackpots on the Web," he nodded toward Galway, "no offense intended …"

"None taken."

"Well, they back up what Galway told us earlier. They say this guy's been around since the 1800s. They claim that his first known appearance was in 1860. At least that was the first time anybody saw the sign of the Sinner—that cross and snake thing."

"That's impossible."

"Which means," Junebug said, "what we're probably dealing with here is a whole underground society of vigilantes. Like the Knights Templar or something."

"CK," Galway continued now, "the other thing you should know. The Sinner apparently doesn't take kindly to people who try to track him down. And we've all seen what he can do to people he doesn't like."

CK nodded, undeterred. The back door to the office building opened just then, and Rebel Feine called out, "What? You started without us? See if I ever invite you to my slumber parties again, CK."

"Your parties are boring as Junebug here anyway," CK called back. "Where have you been?"

Rebel and James pulled up two new chairs and joined the circle around the table.

Junebug pouted, "What do you mean I'm boring, CK? You didn't like that time we went butterfly spotting or something?"

Rebel pulled a photocopy from her bag. "Went to the university library to track down a copy of this."

Galway leaned over to get a good look at the paper. "From the Englander collection?" he quizzed.

Rebel nodded. "Supposed to be the first written reference to the Sinner, back in 1861 or '62."

"Does it say anything about a long gray coat?" asked Keena.

"No," Rebel said, "but it does include a sketch of this." She pointed to the corner of the photocopy where, hand drawn in the text, was a small cross with an elongated *S* around it, wrapped in a circle. "I thought I'd seen that symbol on the watch before, and I was right. I saw it in a college textbook, in a graphic image of this letter."

"Good work," CK said. "Gives us a place to start."

"The author of the letter says this was the sign left behind by a 'man full of vengeance,'" Rebel continued. "The letter doesn't name the Sinner, but that symbol is the same one that has come to be associated with him over the years."

"Wait a minute," Junebug said. "This letter is, like, a hundred and fifty years old, right? There's no way the guy in this letter is the same one we're tracking."

Galway snorted again.

"Gal," CK said without turning her head, "tissues are over on my desk. Use them."

"Fine," the old man responded. "But your mundane assumptions are coloring your judgment. Remember, there are such things as miracles."

Junebug rolled his eyes. "Look, Galway, I've got no problem with miracles. I've read the New Testament, and I'm pretty convinced that Jesus did some amazing stuff. But that was thousands of years ago, and there haven't been any authentic Son of God sightings since then."

CK chimed in, "And besides, Galway, we need to pursue serious leads in this case. We can't get distracted by the myths surrounding this guy. We need to stick to the facts."

But then Rebel spoke. "I think Galway's right. We've got to keep an open mind here. If we are going to 'stick to the facts,' we need to accept that we may not understand them at first sight. Is it likely that this Sinner guy has actually hung around for a hundred and fifty years? Of course not."

"The more likely explanation is a secret society of Sinners who keep the legend going down through time," CK mused.

"Still," Rebel continued, "is it *possible* that all these stories could be referring to the same person?"

"That's absurd," Junebug said.

"Well," CK said, "I did read an article in a science magazine a few weeks ago that suggested our current sciences are nearing the creation of technology to extend human life spans past one hundred years."

Junebug started to snort, but caught himself when CK glared his direction.

"Look," CK said. "Anything's possible. But we've got to assume our guy is flesh-and-blood reality today, not some Civil War ghost come back to haunt us."

"So how do we track down the guy to find out for sure?" Chance asked.

James Dandy produced a book and tossed it on the table. "*The Murders in the Rue Morgue*," he said.

CK felt herself racing with Rebel to make the connection that James Dandy had obviously made. Then it hit her. "Oh, that's good," she said, noting with pleasure the annoyed look that passed briefly across Rebel's face. *Score one for the home team*, she thought.

Aloud CK said, "Good thinking, James. If we can't get to the Sinner, we'll make him come to us."

†

SEAN STEPP KNOCKED ON THE OFFICE DOOR AND WAITED. When no one responded, he contemplated leaving, going back to his office and simply trying to call the professor later. But if that nutcase, Galway, was correct, and if that string of numbers really was a death threat, then he figured he'd better do his job and project the innocent.

Assuming, of course, that Professor Cyril Strand was indeed innocent.

Detective Stepp muttered a little prayer, wondering to God about the good professor. Something inside Sean didn't trust that man.

He was still standing and whispering when Professor Strand rounded the corner of the hallway. "Detective Stepp," Strand said, quickly adjusting his suit coat. "Thank God. Have you finally decided to send me some protection?"

Sean looked the man over carefully, quickly taking in his slightly nervous air, the flabby folds under his chin, and the starched white shirt and tie under the man's basic blue suit coat.

"Yes, Professor. We have. I wanted to talk to you about the arrangements. One of my men is expected to be here in about half an hour."

"One man? That's all? Detective, you've seen what this monster can do. Do you want me to end up like that priest over at that Catholic church?"

Sean gave a questioning look. "What makes you think it's the same guy?"

The professor gave an exaggerated harrumph, then absently rubbed his nose and brushed lint off his shoulder. "Oh come on, Detective. The Sinner has come back, and he's the one who nearly killed that poor priest. You know it and I know it. The symbol on my terror note was the same as the one Michel Renault received. Only he couldn't decipher the code, and I could."

Red flags went up inside Sean Stepp's head.

"Those horrible, faked pictures of that priest doing God-awful things. Who knows what kinds of faked evidence this monster will plant on me?"

A siren sounded inside the detective's head now too.

"And I'm this killer's next target—I've shown you the proof. Every minute we waste could have terrible consequences. And you can bet that if he gets me, my lawyer will be coming after you." The professor crossed his arms, uncrossed them, then shoved them into his pockets.

Sean motioned to the door beside them. "Professor, perhaps we could talk in your office?"

Strand took a step toward the door, then hesitated. "Actually, I've got all my papers strewn about in there. Would you care to go to the lounge instead?"

Sean made a calculated decision. "That won't be necessary. I think we're about done here anyway." He pulled out a pair of handcuffs.

"What are you doing? Have you gone mad?"

"Professor Strand, you're right. One man isn't enough to protect you from this Sinner character. I think you'll need the protection of a dozen men or more. And the only place I've got that many men ready to serve you is in jail."

"What?"

"So, I'm going to arrest you—for your own safekeeping, of course. Protective custody, you know. And don't worry, I'll put you in your own private cell. And shoot, I'll come by to visit you as well. I want to learn a few things anyway. Like how you know about the note that Father Renault received before the beating. How you know about the pictures from the crime scene. And what connection you happen to have with Father Michel Renault and this Sinner character."

"This is absurd! I won't stand for it!"

Detective Stepp clicked the first cuff into place. "Professor Cyril Strand," he said firmly, "you have the right to remain silent."

†

MARIA ELIZA COULDN'T STAY, BUT SHE JUST COULDN'T LEAVE either. Whoever owned this journal would be coming back. Whoever owned everything in the supposedly empty cottage would want to know why their Maximum Maid had pilfered the previously locked bedroom.

She glanced out the doorway into the hall of the cottage. Everything was, as usual, as she had left it.

She turned and surveyed the forbidden room once more. Then she made a decision, one she regretted immediately but refused to go back on. First, she carefully returned the newer journal back to the floor where she had originally kicked it. Next, she straightened the leather books on the bookshelf, careful to cover the fact that she had removed the very first one. Then she folded up the torn, crumpled journal entry and stuffed it in her pocket for a closer look later. Finally, she tucked that antique first journal under her arm and walked into the hallway and out the front door. She would call in sick for the rest of the day.

What Maria Eliza didn't notice, though, was that when

she walked out of the forbidden room, the door automatically locked behind her.

†

RANCE ACKERS FINALLY HAD TO SCREAM. THE SPIRITS IN HIS head were begging him to do it anyway. He took a switchblade out of his boot and started cutting and tearing at the fabric of the clothing that surrounded him. He heard another scream, and then laughed when he realized it was his own. His eyes burned with the heat of unexpected passion, and he started singing a song about screaming. He made it up, and he liked it, so it was good. The spirits said it was good, and that made him feel invincible. He smelled blood somewhere, and he liked that, too. Then with a sudden force, all the noises in his head went silent. He heard himself breathing heavily, felt his own sweat— or maybe blood?—dripping off his skin. He wondered if he were dreaming, or if he had been dreaming and was now awake. He felt his body cramped and twisted inside the closet, but he felt no pain.

He stopped singing.

He saw an image walk into the room. A ghost? The girl?

The ghostlike person seemed to fade in and out of existence, and Rance felt like singing again, but without the spirits in his mind he had no screams to harmonize with. The image finally solidified in front of him. Definitely not the girl.

"Get out."

Rance started laughing and stabbing at the torn pile of

clothes in which he was sitting. He spat in the direction of the ghost.

"Get out, Rance. Or I will come in there after you."

Must be one of the spirits, Rance thought, *since he knows my name.*

Rance breathed in deeply and smelled a faint flowery smell. Something like potpourri, but harder and yet more elusive.

The ghost crouched down now, and whispered through clenched teeth. "I've seen you, Rance Ackers. And I never want to have to see you again."

"Go 'way," Rance finally muttered. "I'm waiting for someone."

The ghost stood up, but didn't go away. Rance bared the blade again, forced his eyes to focus on the ghost. "Go 'way," he screamed, letting the spray fly from his mouth and all over the ghost. Then the spirits began singing in his head again. "Now you've done it," he glimmered. "Now you've done it."

Rance struck out with the knife, slicing without warning, cutting hard across the sleeve of the ghost's gray coat. The knife hit solid, but didn't break the weave of the fabric. Rance was happy now. He liked it when the spirits told him to hurt something. It made him feel powerful, invulnerable.

"Now you've done it," he said again, standing and readying himself for attack. "You see, man, I'm the Devil. The honest-to-God Devil who's gonna cut you into a thousand pieces."

The ghost seemed unconcerned, and Rance hesitated at that reaction. Then in a fluid movement, the ghost slapped his waist and slid a belt from the loops on his pants.

"Your daddy ever whip you, Rance?"

The cacophony in his head changed to the sound of a thousand whimpers.

"That's one thing belts are good for." The ghost leaned in conspiratorially. "But I've discovered something else they're good for too."

Moving faster than Rance could follow, the ghost darted into the cramped closet space. Rance felt the belt wrap around both his wrists, cracking them together, forcing him to drop the switchblade. He felt a hard tug, then understood that the ghost had just broken at least one of his wrists. The blinding pain from that break reached his consciousness a split second after, and Rance screamed again, feeling the pain clear his muddled senses.

He felt the belt slide off his mutilated hands, and as he tried to sink to his knees, felt the belt wrap twice around his throat. He tried to kick, then felt his left leg pinned to the floor at the ankle. A hard shove, and he knew that ankle was broken too. The tightening belt muffled his cry and a sudden, startling clarity came over the young man.

He's going to kill me, Rance thought. *Or worse, he might let me live.*

The ghost now slid his end of the belt over the hanger rod in the closet, and Rance felt his head being raised by the neck, bruising his vocal chords and depriving him of oxygen. He felt the ghost tilting up his chin, felt his wild eyes staring into the calm, red-flecked eyes of his abuser.

Then the voice finally spoke. Controlled. Cold. Businesslike.

"You do resemble him a bit, Rance. The Devil, that is.

But I've seen old Scratch close-up, and even he doesn't scare me anymore. Know what I mean?"

Rance Ackers felt his eyes bulging, craved a clean breath of air, welcomed the swirling blackness that clouded his vision. While he was out, he dreamed of drowning, first in the liquid of a thousand giant syringes, then in blood that spurted from a thousand broken needles. He awoke gasping, unable to move, lying sprawled among a pile of shredded laundry. He couldn't feel the effects of his blessed needle anymore. He could feel only pain, deep and constant. His moaning filled the closet until ...

Until that voice broke through his sobs.

"You have a decision now, Rance."

The would-be college student could only whimper.

"Death. Or agony. What'll it be?"

The boy moaned and tried to crawl farther back into the closet.

"Cheer up, Rance," the colorless voice said. "At least you get two choices. I got only one."

Rance Ackers suddenly, in the very worst way, wanted his mommy. Longed for the times when his dad used to carry him to bed and whisper good night in his ear. But this time the whisper came from the Devil himself.

"Agony it is, then," the voice said.

In a moment, the screaming inside Rance's head had resumed. But this time there were no spirits. Only Rance. Screaming.

Jessica Kenyon caught her breath when the stranger came out the front door of her house. "Is he still in there?" she asked.

The man in the gray coat nodded. "He won't hurt you—or anyone—anymore."

She bit her lip. "You killed him?"

The stranger shook his head. "No. But almost. I already called an ambulance. They'll be here soon."

"He would have hurt me." She shivered in spite of herself. "I heard him singing about it when I went in there." She couldn't stop herself from crying now. "He was singing about doing terrible things to me. Terrible things."

"I know. He won't do those things. Not ever."

She shook with sobs until the stranger finally wrapped her in strong arms. After a moment she regained control, but lingered in the comfort of his embrace. "How did you know he'd be in there?" she asked.

"I had seen him," the stranger replied. "And I knew what he would do if I didn't stop him."

Jessica stepped away from the man and nodded. "I guess I'll have a story to tell when the police arrive."

"Just tell the truth. About how I met you just after you left for school. About how I brought you back here and how we watched him break into your house. About how we went in and heard him, and all that happened next. Do that, and everything will be fine for you."

She nodded again. In the distance the sound of sirens began to cry. She looked down the road toward the sound. "Will I ever see you again?"

There was no answer.   †

We stand in the shadow of the doorway to the barn.

My mare, Destine, snorts softly, and her long lazy head swoops over the wall of her stable, regarding us with her large horse-brown eyes. She is comfortable in here, but she doesn't recognize the man next to me, and this makes her just a little nervous.

I walk to the last compartment in the back of the barn, the one that usually holds my father's horse. I cleaned it out for him soon after he and the rest of my family left for their trip. It is still fresh and swept.

"Please," I say, nodding toward the hay stored nearby. The man says nothing, but springs into action and in a moment a makeshift bed of hay has filled the stall. I move to lay down my precious package, and her eyes open sleepily when her head leaves my shoulder.

"What's your name, sweetheart?" I whisper.

"Celia," she mumbles, eyelids resting heavy again.

"Sleep well, Celia. You still have a long journey ahead of you tonight."

It strikes me as almost a nativity when I pause to glance back at the child in the hay. Like a manger scene, with a dark new miracle alive in its midst.

I turn to find the man standing near me, also gazing tenderly into the stall. "Thank yeh," he says quietly. "She real tired. She need to rest."

I remember that, of course, he must be exhausted too. "You want to make a bed for yourself in that stall over there?" I ask.

"Nah, thank yeh," he says pleasantly. "I kin sleep jus' fine right up agin this stable doorway. I don' wan her to be 'fraid, wundrin' where I is when she wake up." He waits expectantly. After a moment I realize he is waiting for me to leave before allowing himself to sleep.

I point to a spot near the front of the barn. "When you wake up," I say, "look there for some sandwiches to take on your journey tonight." He nods. I start to leave, then turn back.

"And when you wake up, if it's dark outside, just leave. Don't stop to tell me when you go. It's better if I don't know." He nods again.

I glance back at the child in the manger. "Tell her my name was Beverly. Tell her I will never forget her, and I hope that she will remember me too."

He nods, more solemnly this time. "Thank yeh," he says, "for yo kindness. God will bless yeh, Ahm sure."

Now it's my turn to nod in solemnity. "You'll be safe here," I say as I open the gate to Destine's stall, preparing to lead my mare out of the barn and into the harsh sunlight outside.

It is the last time I will see these people.

Except, of course, in the dreams.

NINE

TEN DAYS REALLY ISN'T THAT LONG A TIME. TEN DAYS
on vacation can seem to speed past like a motorboat. Ten
days of a first-time romance seems to flash by like sunlight
across a pond. But ten days in a jail cell can feel like forever.
Especially if you are used to a more comfortable lifestyle
where people don't watch while you're using the toilet,
where food tastes like food, and where there's something
more to do than lay on a bare cot and stare at the ceiling for
hours on end.

And that's one of the many things that was puzzling
Sean Stepp about his "guest" in transitional holding at the
block cells adjacent to the police building. Professor Cyril

Strand simply was not the type to adapt well to life in solitary confinement. Yet there he was, placid, peaceful, and sealed up like a tomb on the other side of Stepp's surveillance video feed.

Detective Stepp pulled a cell phone from his pocket and called number four on his speed-dial list. It was time to get help from an outside source.

✝

CK Ivors scanned the listings on eBay and wanted to get really excited. After all, there, with only nineteen minutes left at auction, was a collectible edition of Superman #7—the 1940 issue where Clark Kent's boss, Perry White, first appeared. It had been graded at 5.5 (out of 10 possible) by the Comics Guaranty, which was pretty darn good for a book that old. The bidding had been active, but the price was still within a range that CK would consider, although she knew the last-minute snipers like herself could change that in a hurry. She wanted to feel excited about the find, but something in her just wouldn't let her feel the joy that comes with snagging another rare collectible purchase.

It had been ten more days since they'd started their investigation in earnest. In that time, at least one more beating—which may or may not have been associated with the Sinner—had occurred. Galway had gone practically underground to try to ferret out more history on the Sinner, and the rest of her team was following leads as well. Still, they were no closer to unraveling the riddle of the priest beater than when they had started the investigation. CK was not generally a patient person, and to go ten days without any appreciable progress was grating on her. It was like an insult to her intelligence—and the insult came from within.

"Superman's got a Fortress of Solitude," CK muttered to herself for the fifteenth time, "and Batman's got that secret cave. Everybody has to sleep somewhere. So where does the Sinner sleep nowadays? Find the hideout and you find the man, CK." Of course, she'd been repeating this line of reasoning for more than an hour already, and she was finally ready to admit she was stuck.

She heard Keena walk into the private office. "Find anything great on eBay?" the assistant asked cheerily.

CK closed the Internet window and turned toward the girl. "Nah. Can't seem to enjoy it today. I've got Sinner on the brain."

Keena nodded sympathetically. "Got messages for you. Rebel's in California. Said she's working one more lead and then will be back as soon as she can get a flight."

"That's good," CK said. "Maybe she's got something that will get us all back on track. Is Galway done with his scenarios?"

Keena shrugged. "Actually, he only came in for a short time earlier this morning. Every time I got near him, he started shouting about spies and moles and shooed me away."

CK laughed in spite of herself. "Don't take it personally," she said. "He does that to everybody."

"That's what Junebug said too," Keena dimpled. "Thanks. One more here. Detective Stepp called from the police headquarters. Wondered if you were available for 'consultation.' That's what he called it."

"Means he wants my advice about an interrogation." CK said. "Might as well go, since I've got nothing better to do here. Want to come along, Assistant?"

"Sounds good to me. Shall I call the detective back and tell him we'll be there in fifteen minutes or so?"

CK felt her spirits improving at the prospect of having something to do again. She felt her fingers get itchy at the computer mouse button as well.

"Let's go with nineteen minutes instead."

✝

MARIA ELIZA GARCES HAD SEEN THE ADVERTISEMENT IN the paper at least a week ago. Normally the lost-and-found notices simply gave a description of a particular item, but this ad included a photograph along with its description. The ad read:

> Found: One antique pocket watch. Gold, with wind-up action and no chain. Engraved with a cross and a large *S* on the front. If not claimed within 10 days, watch will be donated to charity. Contact Junebug Collins to verify your claim on the watch.

The ad then listed only an address, no phone number, where a person was to go to claim the watch.

Maria Eliza had wanted to call this Junebug Collins person, just to ask a few questions. Where had he found this watch? And how old was it? And did he know anything about that engraving on the front?

But there was no phone number. Anyone with questions about that watch would have to go meet Mr. Collins face-to-face, and Maria Eliza just wasn't ready for that. Not yet.

She thought again about the leather-bound book she'd stolen from the forgotten cottage. It worried her. The nightmares written inside it scared her too. But she'd read each page, feeling trapped by the person who wrote them but unwilling to try to break free. This person needed her, even though by now the author would be long dead. But maybe someone knew more, maybe whoever owned that watch could tell Maria Eliza more.

She had gone back to the cottage the next week, secretly hoping to return this first volume of the leather-bound books and steal away the second. But when she arrived, it was empty as usual, and the door to the forbidden room had been locked up tightly once more. So she kept the book, and the torn page she'd stolen as well. They burdened her, but she couldn't release them, couldn't even tell anyone about them.

She held the image of the cross and its *S* shape in her mind's eye again. The engraving on the watch was identical to the symbol on her book. Whoever had the watch had to know something more about the author of the book ... and maybe even knew what caused that tortured soul to bleed the wounds of Christ in that bed in the forbidden room of the cottage.

Somebody out there needed Maria Eliza's help. And it worried her that she just didn't know who.

†

A KNOCK AT THE DOOR ANNOUNCED THE EXPECTED VISITOR. Sean Stepp called out, "Come in," and was pleased to see CK Ivors enter with another young woman.

"How's it going, Sean?" she said. "Have you met Keena Collins? She's working as my assistant now."

Sean stood and shook the young woman's hand. "Any relation to Junebug?" he asked.

"Cousin," Keena said pleasantly.

"Sorry to hear that," Sean said just as pleasantly.

"Making any headway in your case?" CK asked.

The detective gave a tight-lipped shake of his head. "Still at a dead end," he said. "They finally brought Father Renault out of his medically induced coma, but he's not talking. Claims he's got nothing to say about the incident at the church, and that he doesn't even remember it anyway."

"Hmm. I guess being exposed as a child abuser and sexual predator can really shut a guy up." CK looked at the video monitor in front of her friend. "Professor Strand," she said. "I heard that you got to him before I did. Didn't know you'd locked him up, though. What's the charge?"

"No charges yet. We're holding him in protective custody. Right now he's only a 'person of interest' in relation to the charges against Father Renault. But I'm going to have to let him go before too long. Two weeks is the legal limit for protective custody in this state. Same for the 'person of interest' designation unless I file charges against him. But I don't have enough evidence to accuse him of a real crime yet. Still, he's lying to me, CK, and I can't figure out exactly why or what he's trying to cover up."

"Been questioning him every day?"

"At first I did. Then I skipped a day, just to see how he'd react. Rattled him some, but not enough. Then he had a visitor two days ago—somebody named Lee Jeffries. Banker in town. Far as my team can tell me, the two had never met before then. But ever since that visit, Professor Strand down there has been calm, collected, even optimistic. And even more closed-mouthed than before."

"What about his lawyer?"

"After meeting with that Jeffries guy for five minutes, the professor fired his lawyer. Said he didn't need one anymore."

CK considered the oddity of this situation, but wasn't sure what to do next. "So why am I here, Sean? I've got my own investigation going on, and I should be working on that."

"I'm going down there to interview Professor Strand again. I want you to observe the interview from here and see if there's something I'm missing. Maybe something in his body language or expressions. Something."

CK nodded. "Okay, let's get the party going. Got places to go and people to see, you know."

†

JUNEBUG COLLINS HEARD THE DOORBELL RING AT CK's sprawling estate, knew it was probably for him, and kicked a cushion on the floor in front of the Nintendo box. "You're a lucky man, Chance," he said. "I was finally about to beat you at your own game."

Chance just laughed from across the room. "Get over it, Junebug. There's a reason why I'm here skimming the

Internet while you're over there still trying to figure a way out of my *Council of War* battle trap."

Junebug made a show of pretending to catch his foot on the electric cable to the game box. "Oops! Accidentally unplugged the game. Guess we'll never know who would have won after all."

"We already knew who won, buddy," Chance said. "The only question was how long it was going to take you to admit defeat."

The doorbell rang again, and Junebug heard James Dandy calling his name. "Gotta run," he said quickly. "Can't keep the big man waiting, if you know what I mean."

Junebug took the steps down three at a time, bracing his leaps by leaning hard on the arm rails. He raced into the main entryway and saw that James was already in position behind the door. He mouthed a quick "sorry!" and then moved to open the front entrance.

Standing on the covered porch were two men, both in suits, both looking uncomfortable in those suits. One was likely in his midthirties. The other, barely past twenty-one.

"Yes?" Junebug knew at first look that these guys were imposters. Unless … maybe they were here as representatives?

The older suit spoke first. "I, uh, understand you've found my watch."

Junebug shot a glance at James behind the door. The bodyguard rolled his eyes.

"Thank you for stopping by," Junebug said. "But I'm afraid I don't have any watch after all. That ad in the paper was just a prank. A practical joke a friend of mine pulled on me. Sorry."

He started to close the door, but the older suit prevented him. "Listen, son," the man said. "I did a little checking. That watch is a pretty valuable piece, and the only way you—well, your friend—could have pictured it in the paper was to see it firsthand."

Junebug noticed the younger man starting to fidget. He tapped his middle finger on the back of the door, signaling the bodyguard.

The older suit continued. "So why don't you just tell me where that watch is, so I can go ahead and get it."

"Sorry, friend. Can't help ya."

"Maybe this will motivate you." The younger suit reached under his coat and produced a small revolver.

The older suit spoke again. "My friend here has an itchy trigger finger. And he wants that watch. Word is that it's worth close to two hundred thousand dollars to some antiques collectors. So I'll ask again. Where's the watch?"

James Dandy stepped from behind the door, looking just like a butler heading to hang up a coat. Both the suits' eyes widened at the size of the bodyguard, and each involuntarily took a step back on the porch.

"Is there a problem, Mr. Collins?" James said formally.

Junebug swallowed, stepped back a few paces himself, and nodded in the direction of the gun.

James glanced at the gun, then turned back toward Junebug. Before anyone could say anything else, the big man spun into a turning back-kick that hit the younger suit's wrist, just behind the barrel of the gun. The revolver went flying in the air, and the younger man cursed and fell to one knee, cradling his bruised hand against his body.

"Anything else, sir?" The bodyguard stared menacingly at the older suit.

The older thief grabbed his companion by the shoulder and started dragging him backward off the porch.

"You seem to have lost a gun, sir," James called after them. He reached inside his own jacket and pulled out a long-barreled .45 pistol. "Perhaps you'd like this one instead?" He fired a warning shot over the intruders' heads, then watched casually as they started running, profanities spewing, back toward their car.

When they were gone, Junebug looked over at the big man. "You really get into that whole butler-who-kicks-butt role, don't you?"

James just chuckled. "You're welcome," he said. "Again."

"Hey, this was the first time you got to pull a gun, wasn't it? Good for you, big guy."

James sighed. "Well, maybe *The Murders in the Rue Morgue* idea wasn't such a great one after all."

Junebug went out on the porch to retrieve the abandoned handgun left by their previous visitors. "No," he shouted back over his shoulder. "CK and Rebel both said we just have to be patient." He returned back to the main entryway and closed the front door, hearing it lock behind him as it closed.

"Seemed like the right idea," James said. "I mean, in that mystery story, when they want to bring the villain out of hiding, they run an ad in the paper that they know will be irresistible to the bad guy. Next thing you know, the guy shows up right at their front door and, bang, mystery solved."

Junebug slapped James on the shoulder. "It's still a good idea," he said. "We just have to be patient. Now come on, I'll take you on at *Council of War*."

"Again?" the bodyguard said as they walked toward the stairs. "Aren't you tired of getting beat at that game yet?"

†

LOFTIS JOHNSON SAT AT HIS DESK, NEVER TAKING HIS EYES off the city map spread out before him. To one side sat the folder that insipid banker had given him more than a week ago. Just past that folder, the insipid banker sat in his own chair, waiting.

Loftis had kept the folder on his desk ever since he had received it. He knew it had to be true, of course, but simply seeing it—seeing him—again made the rage inside turn icy hot. He had tried to file the folder away in a drawer more than once, but every time, he fished it out again for another look in just a few minutes time. Finally he gave in to it, and left the folder on his desk, reviewing the contents a dozen times a day. Remembering and hating all over again.

He took a pencil from the desktop and started plotting a route through the upper downtown area. He circled a spot on the map.

"Here," he said. "Take him here. There's a restaurant with an outdoor seating service. Put him in plain sight, next to the gated entry."

"What if someone is already seated there?" the banker asked.

"Then you'll have to make them move, won't you?"

"But, well, how ..."

Loftis Johnson flung a one hundred dollar bill into the banker's face. "That should do it, shouldn't it Jeffries?"

"Of course. Right. Yes, I see now." After a moment, the banker spoke again. "Today, then? You want me to get him out today?"

The gruff man shook his head. "No, let him stew a little while longer."

"Well, he's been in jail ten days already, sir. It seems—"

"I'm not talking about that insignificant professor, Jeffries. I'm talking about *him*. Every day that professor is out of his reach he suffers another day of dreaming. Another round of nightmares. And he deserves to suffer."

There was an uncomfortable silence, and in the silence Loftis felt the need to look in the folder yet again. He no longer even tried to resist that urge. Instead, he reached carefully over and flipped open the file. On top was a still image, taken from the video surveillance camera at the downtown, home office branch of the Union Colony Bank. Beneath it was a photocopy of a cashier's check made out to "Cash" for a very large amount. Enough money to keep a family of four comfortable for decades. But Loftis was uninterested in that check, only in the picture.

"You were right, sir," Lee Jeffries said happily. "Eventually he had to come after the money. Unfortunately, he closed out the account completely, so I can't follow that trail anymore. At least not until he cashes the check. But we caught his face on the video camera at the teller's booth. Now we know what he looks like."

Loftis Johnson growled. "I already knew what he looked

like." *I could never forget that man's face.* "I just wanted to make sure it was really him, that he really was still alive."

The banker shook his head in admiration. "Eleven years," he said. "You were very patient to wait eleven years just for this."

The gruff man slapped shut the folder. "I killed him once, eleven years ago," Loftis Johnson said. "And this time, I plan to kill him off for good."

REBEL FEINE WHEELED HER RENTAL CAR INTO THE PARKING lot at Jade's Dixieland Diner and wondered what a place like this was doing four miles off the I-10 freeway outside Indio, California. Inside she expected to find chicken-fried steak, fried dill pickles, and, if she'd done her homework, one Samantha Lancaster, who was supposed to be part-owner and manager of this particular franchise.

Although she had been the one to insist that James stay behind on this trip—after all, Junebug was likely going to need protection—she had to admit she missed the big lug after all. It was surprising how easily you got used to having a bodyguard around, even if you didn't want one in the first place.

Rebel cut the engine of her Ford Focus and quickly checked the scene outside before exiting her car. In the past week she'd already interviewed four people who, supposedly, had come into contact with this Sinner character over the past few decades. Chance had given her a list of eleven people who, based on his research, had given a legitimate reference to meeting the Sinner at some place and time. Of those eleven, three had already passed away and three more had been untraceable in a timely way. So Rebel took the final five names and started looking them up all over the country. So far she'd been to Detroit, Philadelphia, Augusta, and Portland. Now in California, this Samantha Lancaster was her last stop, and she was ready to get back and report to CK and the others.

Surprisingly, her previous interviews had yielded only a few new clues to the identity of the Sinner. In Augusta, the man she met with was in a wheelchair, paralyzed from the waist down. When she'd mentioned the name Sinner, the poor old guy had turned ghost-white and refused to talk. Just as he was wheeling himself away, he'd given Rebel a warning. "If you don't want to end up like me, paralyzed for life, then stay as far away from the Sinner as you can. Because that guy never dies. And he never forgets either."

She thought it odd that yet another person, a contemporary, could so easily buy into the idea of a single immortal vigilante. Every scenario she ran in her head had to have a group of Sinners working through the decades. But the other three interviews yielded similar sentiments, though that old woman in Philadelphia had said she thought the man who rescued her back in 1949 was probably dead by now.

At any rate, she had something of a profile on the guy by now, and hoped to learn more by talking with Ms. Lancaster. She took a moment to look at a photo of Samantha that Chance had dug up from somewhere, hoped it was at least a recent picture, and then stepped out of her car toward the front of the diner. She braced herself for the worst, but it still came too soon. She heard the twangy Dixieland tunes floating her way before she ever reached the door.

†

HE FELT THE SHARPNESS IN HIS WRISTS FIRST AND WONDERED whether the rest would follow this time or if he might be spared the full treatment, as sometimes happened. He knew the light was trying valiantly to penetrate the cracks surrounding the window, but he'd kept the curtains closed tightly anyway. And the door to the room locked and bolted. He'd even placed the lightweight pillow over his face, breathing the hot musty darkness that surrounded his face.

A man like him deserved only darkness.

He lay in the bed and waited, feeling the blood trickle across his palms then slowly begin to dry and clot where the scar stayed fresh. Only the hands today, it appeared. One had to be grateful for small favors.

Then he felt the sudden agony of a piercing in his side, felt the skin rip apart beneath his left, bottommost rib and his insides tear at the force of … of nothing. Some years ago he might have cried out in response to this pain, but now he knew better. Now he knew that the terrible splitting in his side would soon heal over and allow him to breathe again.

But next would come the dreams.

He groaned softly to himself. Lately the same dream had

started his every sleeping time. The same man, doing those same vile things, and no one there to stop him. Not ever.

And then would come the others. Or maybe just one this time. He hoped for just one. But no matter. A man like him deserved to dream these dreams. Only a man like him could suffer these dreams without dying. And only a man like him could stop these dreams from coming true.

The darkness left the room and closed in beneath his eyes. Before the darkness took its full control, a thought flicked briefly through his mind.

I wonder if anyone has finally dreamed of me.

†

"SEE IF YOU CAN FIGURE OUT HOW TO TURN OFF THE sound, Keena." CK Ivors motioned to the control knobs on the video monitor.

"You don't want to hear what they say?" the new assistant asked.

"Not now," CK said. "I can always listen to the recording later. Right now I want to watch."

Professor Cyril Strand had sat up straight when Detective Stepp had entered the cell. Now the two men were sitting and facing one another over a folding table a prison guard had set down in the middle of the small floor space.

"Don't they usually do this kind of thing in an interrogation room or something?" Keena asked while she flicked the volume knob on the monitor.

"Yeah, but Sean likes to change things up sometimes, just to see if he can break the rhythm of a suspect."

The detective started by placing the Sinner's death threat on the table. Strand immediately leaned over the paper, pointing to the numbered sequence and speaking animatedly.

"So those numbers are all a Fibonacci sequence, huh?" Keena said. "That's kind of cool. In a weird, whacked-out, death-threat kind of way."

CK nodded, watching the mathematics professor apparently explain the concept again to Detective Stepp. "Yeah," she said. "According to Galway, Leonardo Fibonacci discovered the sequence in the early 1200s as the solution to a math problem about rabbit reproduction."

"Right. So in the sequence, every time two numbers are next to each other, they always add up to whatever follows them in the line."

"What made Fibonacci's name stick around for so long is that mathematicians started discovering this unique sequence all over nature. In the thorn pattern on roses. In the nodules of a pine cone. In the proportions of growth in a snail's shell. They have even discovered Fibonacci patterns in the asymmetries of atomic fission."

"So when you apply the Fibonacci sequence to that code on the professor's death threat, it spells a message."

"Yeah. If you assume that A=1, it spells out the phrase, 'I have seen you.'"

"Seems like an odd thing to say for a death threat."

"Well, again, according to Galway, the person who sent this note intended for it to be decoded pretty quickly. If he hadn't, he would have made it much more difficult, for instance, by assigning Fibonacci numbers randomly to letters of the alphabet instead of in an ordered fashion."

"But why the phrase, 'I have seen you'? And how did Galway know that was a death threat?"

CK shrugged. "He wasn't sure about the phrase itself, but it was sent to a mathematician who would easily figure out the code, and a similar note was sent to a priest who was beaten senseless shortly after. Same guy sends the same note, in this situation you have to assume the threat level is the same—or worse. Galway made a logical assumption that the intent was harmful."

Keena nodded. "Makes sense."

They watched the two men in the cell in silence for a moment. Then Keena said, "Boy, that guy sure gets happy about math."

CK nodded. "Good catch, Keena," she said. "Look at his posture and his arm movements. All externally focused. At this moment, he's unconcerned about his image or appearance. He is confident in what he's talking about and not even thinking about the rest of his body."

"Thanks," Keena said. After a beat she added, "Um, I guess that means something important?"

CK chuckled. "It means he's probably telling the truth right now. He's not trying to project anything because he doesn't have to. He's just talking math, his specialty."

"So how does that mean he's telling the truth?"

"Think of it this way," CK said. "When you go out on a first date with a guy, what's going through your head?"

"Well, I'm really self-conscious. I worry about whether my hair is straight, or if I have food in my teeth or toilet paper stuck to the bottom of my shoe."

"Right. Your concern about how you appear to your

date makes you internally focused. You want to make a good impression, so you think about it and that makes you seem more stiff and nervous. Now let's assume you're grabbing lunch with Junebug, or somebody else you know well. Do you worry about any of those things you just mentioned?"

"Of course not. I mean, Junebug is just Junebug. He doesn't care what I look like."

"Exactly. In that situation, you are free to be externally focused. You're comfortable, relaxed, and confident around Junebug, so you don't worry about what kind of impression you're making on him. All that other stuff becomes a secondary concern. The same principle applies to lying and telling the truth. When a person tells the truth, he's comfortable, relaxed. Externally focused, like Professor Strand talking about mathematics. He's free with his movements, confident with what he's saying, and his body responds accordingly."

Keena nodded thoughtfully, staring at the monitor. "So when he's lying, he must look something like that."

Detective Stepp had now placed a second note on the table, one that looked almost identical to the first. This time the professor's spine stiffened just a bit, and he leaned back in his chair instead of forward toward the note. His hands had dropped into his lap, and he occasionally smoothed an imaginary wrinkle on his pants while he talked.

"Yep. He knows something he's not saying."

"Where did the detective get that second note? Is it a copy?"

"Nope. It's one the priest had in his pocket the day he

was beaten. Apparently he got a warning just like our professor down there, only he didn't come running to the police with it."

Detective Stepp now placed a row of three Polaroid pictures on the table. CK couldn't see what was on them, but she knew what they were and flinched just the same.

"Those the pictures I think they are?" Keena said grimly.

"Yeah. Makes me almost glad that priest got the beating he did. But look at the professor."

"What? He looks mostly calm."

"Right. Sean told me he hadn't shown these pictures to this guy yet, that he was going to try them today to see what kind of reaction they might get from the professor."

"And?"

"The guy didn't even flinch. The only thing he did was rub his nose for a second, then look away."

"So what does that mean?"

"It means, Keena dear, that Professor Cyril Strand has seen these photos before."

"What? How?"

CK didn't answer. Instead she flicked open her cell phone and quickly dialed a number. On the video monitor, Sean Stepp interrupted his questioning and pulled another cell out of his pocket.

"Stepp here," the voice crackled in CK's ear.

"Hey, Sean," she said to him. "Ask him who took the pictures."   †

The sun sits high overhead, daring anyone or anything to stir under the intensity of its gaze. Destine is unhappy, tied to the live oak tree about 30 paces from the barn. She stands in the shade, but the buzzing horseflies keep her tail busy with flicking, and the water trough is still too far away for her to reach. She whinnies loudly when she sees me exit the house, but my hands are full at the moment. A burlap sack with meat sandwiches and a few apples in one hand. A glass pitcher of lemonade in the other. After all, they will be thirsty when they wake up, I reason.

"I'm coming to you next, Destine," I holler to my mare. "Be patient. I'm coming."

Destine whinnies again, but with a different tenor, in a different voice. I stop in spite of myself, and look in her direction, but she is looking away from me. I follow her gaze, staring down the dirt road that leads out of our family farm and into the community of farmers beyond.

In the distance, a dust cloud is rising.

TEN

Galway eyed the pretty brunette serving drinks to the businessmen at table number four. He recognized the fake laugh she used when someone made a joke she felt wasn't funny but she wanted to be polite anyway. After all, a girl had to work to get good tips, even in a nice place like this. He lifted a cup of hot chocolate off the table and let the sweet, liquid smell flavor his senses for a moment, then he set it back down without drinking.

The waitress shot a quick glance his way before she disappeared into the kitchen. Galway counted. If she didn't come out of that kitchen before he reached seventy-nine, he was leaving. No sense in wasting time on what was probably a setup anyway. Those CIA spooks could reach anybody, anytime, but Gal wasn't going to make it easy for them.

He had just whispered "seventy-one" when he caught sight of the brunette's ponytail flicking past the serving window. At "seventy-four" she'd breezed through the entryway and back into the dining room. She paused to refill a few coffee cups at table six, then handed off the pitcher to another server and made her way toward Galway's table. In another moment, she slid herself into the booth across from him and smiled.

"Okay," she said, "I've got ten minutes before I have to get back on the floor—unless those guys at four finish early. Can't miss that tip. I've worked too hard for it."

"Another dumb blonde joke?" Galway asked.

The pretty brunette wrinkled her nose. "Yeah. Guess they think that since I've got dark hair, I don't care how they insult women."

Galway felt himself start glowing inside. He loved it when she squinched her nose that way.

"Can I have a sip of your hot chocolate?" she asked.

Galway smiled, then drained the now-cooled cup himself. "Not necessary this time," he said. "But I appreciate the offer. Never can be too careful, you know."

"Galway!" she said in mock anger. "This time I was serious. I really wanted a sip!"

"What? Oh, well. Sorry. Thought you were just offering to test it for poison or something."

"Never mind," she pouted. "I'm glad at least you enjoyed it."

Galway smiled again. She was adorable when she pouted.

"You get the information I needed from Ranger 5?" he asked.

The pretty girl rolled her eyes. "Yes, and *Henri* said to pass on his greetings to you and to let you know he and Kaylynn want you to come for dinner sometime."

Galway stiffened in his seat, and quickly checked the surroundings of the dining room. "Watch what you say!" he hissed. "We're in public!"

She just giggled. "You deserved it for hogging the hot chocolate. Which I got you for free, if you remember."

"Fine. Just give me the envelope."

She reached into her apron and pulled out a fat letter envelope and started to pass it across the table until Galway hissed again.

"Do we have to do that *every* time?" she asked. Galway only hissed in response.

The pretty girl shook her head in resignation, then carefully slid the envelope under the table toward the old man. He coughed, covering his mouth with his right hand while reaching under the table to grab the envelope with his left. When the transaction was complete, he winked at the girl across from him.

"Listen," she said. "I read that report about this Sin—" Galway hissed, so loudly that the women at table one glanced over and tittered at the old man.

The waitress lowered her voice. "I read that report. Seems wacky—as usual. But this one could also be dangerous. They're saying this is the same guy that nearly murdered a priest a few weeks ago."

"No need to worry about me, sweetheart," Galway said winsomely. "I know kah-rah-tay."

The waitress stood up, leaned over the table and kissed the old man on the cheek. "I know, Daddy," she said. "But he might know a few bigger words than that. So be careful, okay? Don't let CK talk you into anything that might cost you a few years of your life."

Galway felt himself glowing again. "You kidding?" he said. "CK is more protective than you. I'll be fine. I always am, right?"

He patted her cheek, and felt treated by her smile. "Time to get back to work, baby," he said. "You to yours here, and I off to mine."

†

SEAN STEPP WALKED TOWARD THE SURVEILLANCE ROOM feeling optimistic, in a disgusted sort of way. Professor Strand had barely known what to do when he had asked him who took the photos.

"What? Who? Well, I'm sure that I don't know," he'd blustered at first. When Sean didn't say anything, the pompous fool just kept talking. "What are you insinuating, Detective? Are you saying I took those pictures?" Sean had kept silent, watching the mathematician flounder. "How dare you accuse of me that! This charade is over. I've been here ten days. I've answered your every question. I even explained the Sinner's code to you because your people here were too simpleminded to learn math in high school. But to accuse me of somehow being complicit in the sexual abuse of a child—that's just too much! And pretty soon, I won't have to stand for it anymore. Once Mr.—" The professor stopped himself.

Sean had seized the moment. "Mr. who? Jeffries? He seems to have disappeared at the moment. Didn't report to work yesterday or today. Maybe he's on vacation? Or maybe he's sold you out and left you to take the rap for his crimes?"

The professor had simply looked smug.

"Who took the pictures, Strand? Was it you? Was it Jeffries? Are you all involved in this priest's dirty little secret?"

The professor had leaned over the table and stared at the detective with pure disdain. "I feel sorry for you, Detective," he said. "Because Loftis Johnson is now aware of my situation here. And soon he will walk through that cell door, and I will walk out."

That had been the end of the interview today, and now Sean was headed back to debrief with CK and her assistant. But he felt good, for once. Like he was finally getting somewhere, or that he at least had a place to start.

Loftis Johnson himself, he thought. *Now things are starting to get interesting.*

REBEL FEINE FELT UNCOMFORTABLE IN THE BACK OFFICE OF Jade's Dixieland Diner, but she had to admit it was nice to have that god-awful music muffled by the hall and doorway that led back to here. Samantha—or Sammy, as she insisted on being called—Lancaster was a woman in her midthirties with a hardworking air about her. She had a pleasant, though unremarkable, face, and hips that looked like she'd eaten a few too many of her "world famous" Dixieland dessert specials. When Rebel had shown her a printout of the sketch she'd done of the Sinner, Samantha had smiled and invited her to come back to the office where they could "talk in private."

Now Sammy placed a cup of coffee on Rebel's side of the desk and instead of taking the place behind the desk, sat down in a chair next to Rebel.

"So," Sammy said kindly, reaching out to touch Rebel lightly on the knee. "What did he rescue you from?"

"What do you mean?" Rebel asked, genuinely surprised by the question.

"That's what he does. Rescues young women from evil people. So what did he do for you?"

Rebel thought about her next approach. An honest person would have explained right then that Sammy had mistaken her visitor's intentions. But James Dandy was the honest one. And there was a reason they called her Rebel instead of Rebecca.

"Well," she dragged out her response, pretending it was hard to talk about while formulating her story. "Actually," she said after a moment, "he beat up a priest. Nearly killed the man with his bare hands. For me."

Sammy nodded knowingly, and her lips grew tight. "What had the priest done to you?"

Rebel covered her eyes with her hands. "I ... I don't really like to talk about it," she said with faked emotion.

Sammy gave Rebel's knee an affirming squeeze and gently pulled her visitor's hands away from her eyes. "You don't have to worry anymore, honey," she said, speaking as if she were counseling a small child. "Once he takes care of a problem, it stays taken care of."

Rebel nodded.

"They call this guy the Sinner," Sammy continued, leaning back and getting comfortable in her chair, "and a devil. But if he's a devil, at least he's one that's working for God. In fact, I think he's an angel, 'cause he saved me from a real devil when I was only six years old."

Rebel couldn't believe her luck. This kind lady was in a chatty mood and ready to open a whole new window on CK's investigation. If only Rebel could just keep her talking.

"Tell me more about him," she said with sincere interest, remembering almost too late to reach out for Sammy's hand as a sign of feminine friendship. "I want to know all there is know about … about the guy who set me free."

Sammy just smiled.

†

THE MAN IN THE LONG GRAY COAT WIPED BLOOD FROM behind his ears and wondered how it had managed to spray all the way up there. He checked the mirror and admired again how liquids just spilled off his coat, never leaving permanent stains. When he'd perfected the bulletproof weave, he hadn't expected it to be waterproof as well. But it was a convenient side effect.

He had not slept long, and when he awoke he knew he would have to hurry. He'd been late a few times in the past and always regretted it deeply. Sometimes he couldn't help it. Sometimes he was prevented from arriving in time, and the agony was always worse when the dream returned, reminding him of his failure. He'd had too many failures over the years. Too many.

But not today, at least. Today he'd made it in time after all.

He turned on the faucet of the sink below the mirror and washed the mess off his hands. The scars had healed up nicely while he slept. No need for bandages today at all.

He found himself casually admiring the linoleum floor in the public restroom. Whoever had designed this place had made a good choice. It would be easy to clean up the spattered blood off a floor like that.

He glanced back up into the mirror and caught a reflection of the dead body in the stall behind him. He hadn't really wanted to kill this one. But sometimes he got carried away. And the guy had certainly been trying to kill him. Thought he was somebody named "Jonesy" at first, and even fired off two shots before he'd realized that (a) this guy wasn't Jonesy, and (b) this guy was wearing a bulletproof coat. Kind of ruined the effect of capping his gun with a silencer and hiding in the stall before making the attempt to murder his ex-girlfriend's new love interest. But the would-be killer had paid for his mistake.

The man in the gray coat heard the bathroom door open and turned to face the guy who entered.

"Oh, excuse me," the new guy said, starting to make his way past the gray coat to the stall on the left. Then he stopped, eyes going wide and fear glistening across his face.

"It's okay, Lance," the gray-coated stranger said quietly. "He'll never hurt you or Melissa ever again."

Lance just stood, openmouthed and staring.

"Call the police, Lance," the stranger said. Then he dried his hands and walked out the door.

Now, he thought, *maybe I can get some sleep.*

†

CK PACED IMPATIENTLY, WAITING FOR SEAN STEPP TO RE-enter the surveillance room. When he finally did, she wasted no time. "Did you get anything?"

"Maybe," the detective answered. "He finally dropped a name."

"Well, he's lying about most everything he said, Sean. So you should be careful when you follow the lead on that name."

"Right. Will do."

There was a pause, and CK could tell the detective was enjoying making her wait. "He took the pictures, Sean," she said after a tight moment. "That vile man is a pedophile just like your priest. Get a search warrant for his house or his office or someplace like that and I bet you'll find the camera."

Sean shook his head. "He's had too much time to get rid of evidence. He would have done that before coming to us with the note from the Sinner." CK frowned. "But, of course, we'll search his office, his home, even his bathroom cabinet to see if we can find something he overlooked that ties him to the priest and to those children in the pictures."

CK nodded, waiting.

Detective Stepp opened the door, "Thanks, CK. You've been very helpful." He nodded toward Keena. "Nice to meet you, Ms. Collins. I'm sure we'll see each other again in the future."

CK simply smirked and sat down in a chair. Keena followed suit, although she didn't quite feel comfortable smirking in the detective's general direction.

"Fine," Sean said with a smile. He took a third seat nearby. "What do you want to know?"

"The name."

"It's private police business and classified information that could taint a future jury pool, but, hey, what's that between friends?"

"C'mon, Sean. Without me you'd still be sitting in there wondering if Fibonacci was a French chef down the street."

The detective nodded approvingly. "You're right. I wouldn't have connected him to the camera, at least not yet." He glanced at Keena.

"I'll vouch for her," CK said.

"And?"

CK sighed and quoted from memory. "And I'll make sure that any pertinent information I get in my investigation will be duly transmitted in a timely way to the police department of this fair city, specifically addressed to one Detective Sean Stepp."

"Thank you," Sean said, "although we really need to define that term 'timely way' because in the past that—"

"Sean!"

"Right. We can discuss that later. Well, the good professor down there seems to have made a powerful acquaintance. He could be bluffing, but he said that Loftis Johnson is coming here to get him out of jail."

"Loftis Johnson, the investment banker?"

"Is there any other?"

Keena scratched her head. "Isn't that guy like a billionaire or something? Never leaves his mansion in Northern Connecticut, except to meet with world leaders and stuff?"

CK nodded thoughtfully. "Think the professor was bluffing?"

"No way to tell," Sean replied, "except wait to see what happens."

CK nodded again. After a moment she said, "Let him go now, Sean."

"What?"

"Release the professor, then put a tail on him."

"He's a flight risk."

"Maybe. But if Loftis Johnson really is interested in this guy, he's not going to be here long anyway. If you release him now, you leave him to his own devices, at least for the time being. And I'm betting our professor isn't as smart as Loftis Johnson. Let him go now and he leaves tracks— tracks that might lead you to the evidence you need. Let Loftis Johnson take him and he disappears into the night, never to be seen again."

"What if he's bluffing? What if he's not really connected to the Johnson family?"

"Then your guys follow him around for a few days, eat a few doughnuts at taxpayer expense, and pick him up again when you think you've got all he can give you. Then you file formal charges and hope you can make them stick. You can't keep him here much longer anyway, not without some kind of evidence to hold him. Let him go now. Maybe you'll get lucky."

"I don't believe in luck," Sean Stepp grumbled. But CK could tell he didn't believe in Professor Cyril Strand either. Finally he said, "That means more paperwork. And I hate paperwork."

†

Maria Eliza Garces finished the house on Magnolia Avenue early and realized with surprise that she had the rest of her day free. That had sneaked up on her. She had forgotten that the two-story on Carmelita was canceled for today while its occupants were on vacation.

She thought about taking a bus back to the Maximum Maids office to see if anybody needed help on another house this afternoon. She considered simply going home, since all her work was done for the day. She even toyed with the idea of calling her sister to join her for coffee somewhere nearby.

Instead, she found herself walking casually under the spring sun, not lost, but not really going anywhere either. She stopped when she saw the familiar outline of St. Anthony's Cathedral looming down the block. This had been her church for a few years, until she and her family had moved farther west in the town, closer to better schools and into a house with an honest-to-goodness backyard for the kids. She had liked the church, though. Even enjoyed Father Renault and his rambling sermons on forgiveness and faith. It had never occurred to her that this pleasant, gentle man might have been capable of the things for which he was now accused. She felt sorry for him, and for the people who had trusted him. *It must be heartbreaking to know you are living a lie*, she thought. *To preach of the Christ, yet live like the Devil.*

Maria Eliza checked her watch and wondered why she still didn't feel like going home. She stuffed her hand in her pocket and felt a familiar ruffle of paper, felt her hand tingle at the memory, and caught her breath slightly. She clutched her handbag to herself, knowing the hardness she felt within it was the outline of the leather-bound book she'd stolen. She felt a pang of guilt at her crime and, almost out of habit, lifted her face toward the sky.

Then, unexpectedly, Maria Eliza Garces felt her soul opening and knew where she wanted to be. She moved quickly in the direction of the church. In there, she felt certain, she would find peace.

REBEL FEINE WASN'T SURE WHAT TO BELIEVE IN THE STORY this woman was telling her. Her cognitive logic told her the woman was a liar, that maybe as a frightened little girl she had made up an imaginary friend and imbued him with all kinds of wonderful characteristics. Common sense told her that Samantha Lancaster, though certainly a nice person, was actually just a bit nutty in the head.

But her heart told her that Sammy was simply telling the truth, that perhaps something extraordinary had happened in this woman's life, and that she would never be the same because of it.

"So," Sammy finished, "he left then. I've never seen him again since, though I've sometimes read about a mystery man in the newspaper and wondered if it was him. And I've never forgotten him, though, isn't it funny, I can't remember his face. I can close my eyes and picture his hands, his arms, even the gait of his walk. But I can't remember his face. I wonder sometimes if I dreamed him, but whenever I think that, I feel the scar on my arm. If he wasn't there to pull the knife away, then how am I still here today?"

Rebel Feine breathed out a sigh and realized she'd been holding her breath. "Wow," she said finally. "You were only six years old at the time?" Sammy nodded. "And trying to commit suicide? That seems, that sounds …"

Sammy laughed lightly. "Hard to believe, right? It's okay. You don't have to believe me." She patted Rebel's hands. "But, well, you know he doesn't come unless the situation is serious. And I really thought, even as a six-year-old, that I was going to die anyway if that old man touched me one more time. I wanted to die. But he saved me. I think he was an angel sent by God. I've never been the same since."

Rebel shook her head, decided it was time to line up the facts so she could jot them down correctly when she got in her car. "Okay, so, you're in the bathroom—in the bathtub—trying to cut yourself with a dulled kitchen knife, and suddenly this man in a gray coat is standing over you."

Sammy nodded. "Even then I was a clean freak," she said. "Was worried I'd get blood on the bathroom rug and get my mom in trouble."

"And you don't know where this guy came from, how he got in your bathroom without making a sound?"

She shrugged. "Like I say. I think he was an angel."

Rebel nodded. "Right. Beginning to wonder about that myself. So he takes the knife out of your hands, wraps a towel around your arm, then just sits down on the floor, without saying a word?"

"And when I started shivering, from fear, or relief, or cold or whatever, he took his own coat off and wrapped it around me like a blanket."

"This was that charcoal gray coat, right? Was it heavy? Did it have pockets inside?"

"It was, well, all I really remember about it was that it was warm and that it smelled a little bit like rose petals."

"After awhile …"

"I think maybe an hour, but it could have been only five minutes. I wasn't real good at telling time back then." She laughed lightly again.

"So, after an undetermined amount of time, he patted you on the head, then stood up and faced the door. When your stepfather came limping in, drunk and with his prosthetic leg unattached, he saw the, um, angel and went berserk."

"It was like he knew the angel, like he'd seen him before. And I think he had because the angel just said, 'I warned you,' then just attacked the old man."

"And you covered up inside the Sinner's coat, still curled up in the bathtub."

"Yeah. The old man kept screaming that he was going to kill me right in front of the angel's eyes, just so he could see it. Well, he said, 'Just so you'll have to see it again,' but obviously that didn't make any sense. Then after just a minute or two, everything was quiet."

"And when you looked out from under the coat, your stepfather was lying dead on the floor, and the Sinner was leaning against the sink bleeding from the abdomen."

"Right. Apparently the old man got hold of my knife and stuck him through. When I think about it now, I realize he must have punctured the guy's liver, but that seems impossible. Still, a lot of things seem impossible about the Sinner. The stranger pressed a towel against his wound to try to stop the bleeding and keep from making more of a mess on the floor."

"Then he says to you, 'I need a place to sleep. A hidden place.' And you take him to the abandoned storage room in the basement of your apartment complex?"

"Mm-hm. He tells me to call the police, but not to tell anyone he was there. And that I don't have to worry because the old man will never hurt me again. Ever. Then he curls up in a ball in the back corner and, well, he falls asleep. I tried to clean up some of the blood in the bathroom, but mostly I ended up just smearing everything together and ruining a few of my mom's favorite towels."

"The police come, and they figure your stepfather slipped on the wet floor and hit his head against the sink?"

Sammy nodded. "I never told them any different, and they never checked the blood. I figure if they had, they would have seen right away that I was lying because they probably would have found two different blood types in the mess. But they knew my stepfather—he'd had a scrape or two with the law before. Honestly, nobody mourned too much over his death."

Sammy let out a soft sigh and paused for a moment.

Then she continued. "I didn't tell my mom about the angel until I was twenty-five. But she didn't believe me, and just said she was 'right glad the old man had had the decency to die before we both got really hurt by him.'" Sammy shrugged. "But I saw the angel every day for the next five weeks after my stepfather died. Just sleeping in that dirty, old abandoned room. Spiders crawled all over him. I'm pretty sure mice lived around him too. But he never moved a muscle. Just slept, breathing in shallow breaths. I kept thinking he was dead, but he was always breathing."

"For five weeks straight? You're sure about that?"

"Marked each day on a calendar in my room," Sammy said. "Then one day I went in and he wasn't there anymore. I looked all over and never saw a trace of him. About two weeks after that, there was a note on my bed. It said, 'Thank you. Grow up happy. And strong. If you ever need me, I'll be there.' And it had that cross symbol with an *S* snaked around it."

"Have you ever seen him again?"

Sammy smiled, genuine and warm, as she looked Rebel deeply in the eyes. "You know, honey, I've never needed him again."

MARIA ELIZA STEPPED INSIDE THE FRONT DOORS OF THE cathedral and admired again the ornate furnishings that draped the sanctuary in regal religiosity. She contemplated entering the confessional to her left, but decided instead to move toward the altar near the front. Several candles burned behind the altar, a silent testimony that others had been here today as well.

Maria Eliza took a seat on the front pew of the sanctuary and enjoyed the quietness that filled her in that moment. She bowed her head slightly and let her heart pray words she couldn't formalize in her mind. She was unaware of the minutes as they passed by, though she did, briefly, wonder how anyone could go through an entire life without recognizing the fact of God's existence. True, one might not see his face in this life. But one could certainly feel his hands of comfort—and yes, sometimes discipline—gently touching the soul.

Before long a parish priest—a new one, she thought, and mighty young at that—knelt in front of her.

"Is there anything I can help you with, mother?" he asked.

She patted his shoulder and smiled at his kindness. "Not today, thank you, Father. I just wanted a quiet place to pray today."

The priest nodded knowingly and stood again. "The Lord be with you," he said by way of an exit blessing.

"And also with you," Maria dutifully replied.

When she was alone again, she felt the memory of the leather-bound book pushing its way to the fore of her prayers. She tried to fight the interruption, but finally could no longer. She reached into her bag and pulled out the book, turning to the last page to reread what might have been a poem or perhaps a letter. It had no title, just steady lines of words that read:

I want to breathe beauty like a fire,
To run naked into everbeing
Where stooping lower takes me higher.

It stinks here in this place
with all the blind men seeing;
I want to breathe ... Beauty like a fire

sears my lungs with its hot grace,
consumes my ashes until I am leaning
where stooping lower takes me higher.

Sacred perfume and smoky choir
are fetid stand-ins for the meaning
I want. To breathe beauty—like a fire—

devastates me; yet it is my soul's desire,
it swills me into powder in a place foreseeing
where stooping lower takes me higher.

It's terrifying to long for undoing
by One never undone, but still
I want to breathe beauty. Like the Fire
Who once stooped low to take us higher.

Maria Eliza understood that longing, that deep, deep hunger for the blessed undoing that comes with meeting God face-to-face. She yearned to read more in the second journal, to know if the writer had reached that heaven he had apparently so desperately desired. It frightened her to think that maybe, just maybe, the writer had not.

"*Santo Padre,*" she whispered, "*ayudanos, por favor.*"

Maria Eliza tried to pray longer, to recapture the peace she'd experienced just moments before. Finally she crossed herself and stood, turning to face the large cathedral doors that opened to the outside world.

It was time to go see this Junebug Collins.   †

They are riding fast, kicking up dry road behind them like a thresher spitting grain. Three of them. All men. All rough at the edges, browned and leathered by their travels. Hard men, I think. My mind races with uncomfortable thoughts.

They are here before I know what to do, reeling in their lathered horses, prancing to a stop in the courtyard before me. They don't say anything at first; they just turn in circles and survey the land and buildings around us.

I stand there, sandwiches in one hand, pitcher in the other. I don't know what else to do. I wait.

Finally, one leans over his saddle and tips his hat my direction. "Afternoon," he says amiably. "We hear tell they's a coupla runaway slaves somewhere round here."

He says it like it happens every day, like there's nothing unusual about it at all. But the air around me feels electrified. My throat dries within me, and I am suddenly, painfully aware that I have never been a good liar.

I swallow. They wait. Finally I say, "Haven't seen any today. Have you tried over at the Turner place, 'bout two miles south of here?"

The first man smiles comfortably, nods. He takes a kerchief from his shirt pocket and wipes his already-dry forehead with it. The two men beside him dismount, but the leader still holds my gaze from up high on his horse. He nods at the pitcher in my hand.

"That for us? 'Cause that sure is kind of you, what with a hot, dry day like today. Haveta tell you, that lemonade looks sweeter than mama's milk to me right now." He plays to the crowd now. "What do you think, boys? That lemonade look good to you?"

"Yessir, Mr. Jennison," says the fat one. "Reckon I could drink it all up myself." The narrow one just grins. He's played this game before.

A beat passes between us before I force myself to say, "Of course. Saw you coming and thought you might be thirsty. Here." I hand the pitcher to the narrow man, who hands it up to the leader, to Jennison.

He nods approvingly, takes a long deep breath above the top of the pitcher. Then he throws the pitcher hard against the ground between us, shattering the glass and scattering lemonade like dynamite in a wide, wet circle that somehow touches all of us with the spray of its sticky explosion.

"What's your name?" he asks me quietly.

"Beverly," I say, just as quietly. "Beverly Thomas."

"Well, Bev, here's the thing. Much as I want that drink of cool lemonade, I want them two niggers even more. And I'm vowing not to drink anything until you tell me where they are. Understand?"

It is an involuntary reaction. I will myself to look directly in this Jennison's face. But I feel my eyes betray me. I feel them flick, for the briefest of instants, toward the wide, closed doors of the barn.

Celia. Please forgive.

"I don't know where they are, mister," I say, trying to convince myself as much as anybody.

"Bev."

He says my name like we are old friends. Like he hasn't seen me in weeks and is delighted to become reacquainted. Like my father and his father play poker together every Thursday night. Like he's about to ask how my lovely mother is doing with her vegetable garden this year.

"See, the thing is, Bev. I think you're lyin' to me."

ELEVEN

CK FELT THE CLUTCH RELEASE UNDER HER FOOT AND eased her Honda into traffic several car lengths behind the bright yellow cab. "You're sure that was him, right?"

"You know it was him, CK," Keena said. "He walked right past our car to catch the cab. Are you sure he didn't recognize you?"

CK changed lanes so she was no longer directly behind the cab, and at the same time wished that she had some magical control over the thickening traffic patterns that quickly enveloped her. One poorly placed vehicle, and she could easily lose the good professor.

"I'm sure. Nobody—well almost nobody—knows what

CK Ivors looks like, or even that she lives in this city. My face is something I work kinda hard to keep a secret."

"Shame," Keena responded. "'Cause it's such a pretty one, with those emerald eyes giving such a contrast against your skin."

CK rolled her emeralds. "Flattery will get you nowhere, Assistant." But she smiled inside anyway.

"Why do you think it took so long for the detective to release the professor?" Keena asked. "I mean, it's nearly dinnertime now."

"The wheels of justice move slowly," CK intoned, "if they move at all. But regardless, I don't want to lose that cab, so help me keep an eye on open spaces in traffic."

"Did you spot the police tail yet?"

"Think so. My guess is that they're in that blue Toyota back there. Sometimes they can get a decent car from impound. Did you call Junebug?"

"Yeah. He said he'd get a camera and call us when he was closer to downtown."

"Good. We may need his photo skills if Professor Strand stops anywhere interesting."

As if on cue, the cab ahead flashed its blinker and then turned right into the parking lot of an Italian restaurant with a bright green awning that covered a festively decorated outdoor seating area.

"Whoa," CK said. "What's the point of that? Why take a cab to go less than one mile to a restaurant?"

CK and Keena rolled slowly by as the cab disgorged its customer. "Well," Keena sniffed, "judging by his belt size, our professor is not much of a walker."

"Mm-hm. But obviously something of an eater."

CK drove up to the next light, then circled around the block to take another pass by the restaurant. She noticed the blue Toyota, now situated in a parking lot across the street, but saw no sign of the professor.

"Come on," she said to Keena as she wheeled into the lot beside the restaurant. "We're going inside."

✝

CHANCE ELKO DIDN'T MIND BEING ALONE IN CK IVORS' SPAcious house—in fact he kind of liked it. Made him feel like he was the one with the big bank account and fancy toys. He was too embarrassed to study CK's Superman collectibles when others were around, but when he was alone, one of his favorite activities was to see what new items his boss had acquired.

"Wow," he said aloud to nobody, "that is one *nice* copy of *Jimmy Olsen* #1. Wonder how she found one in such good condition? Must have cost her a mint." He chuckled at his own wordplay, even though he knew it wasn't really funny. He was tempted to take it out of the hard plastic case that kept the comic in pristine condition, just to page through the inside and look at the advertisements. It was always fun to see the wacky things companies tried to sell to kids back then. But he resisted the urge. A comic that old, and in that kind of shape, might show a crease on the cover where he had opened it up.

It had not been long since Junebug and James Dandy had left. Chance thought that Junebug actually might have been relieved when Keena had called and asked them to come out and meet her and CK. The bodyguard had maneuvered his *Council of War* forces so adeptly that Junebug had been losing the game pretty convincingly for some time. The only thing that had kept it from ending was James' pitying pullbacks and second chances. It struck Chance as funny that James referred to his general as "The Quarterback" and to his foot soldiers as "The Heroes on the Line of Scrimmage," but he had to admit the guy knew what he was doing. Might even be able to give Chance a run for his money.

Next time maybe I'll give Junebug one of the cheat codes for extra armies or a genius general or something, just to make it more competitive.

Chance was moving down the display case with casual confidence, now admiring a 1950s vintage, unrestored Lex Luthor action figure when he realized the one thing he didn't like about being alone in CK Ivors' house.

There was no one to back him up when the doorbell rang.

✝

LOFTIS JOHNSON SAT WITH HIS EYES CLOSED, FEET ON HIS desk, visualizing what he intended to do to the man whose rebirth maddened him so. He would wait two more days, then bail the professor out of jail and use him as bait in his trap. He'd already called the leader of the Crux and informed him to prepare his gang for an ambush at an Italian restaurant about a mile from the police station. He had trained this young man himself in the art of war, under the guise of a charitable work-training program for the underprivileged that was run by his company. He had no doubt the gang was scouting the territory even now, getting ready for a quick hit followed by a quick, and untraceable, exit.

Loftis still remembered the day his life had changed forever. He had gone to work a boy—a weak, immature, spoiled little boy—and come home a man. A man with a deep, angry need for vengeance. It took him eight years, but he had finally tracked down that Sinner who had scared his father so. And he had made him pay.

The phone rang on Loftis's desk, but he ignored it. He was reliving his arrival at manhood, rekindling his hatred. His hand reached involuntarily for the folder on his desk that held the photos of the Sinner. He had memorized that face nineteen years ago.

Loftis had been twenty-three at the time. Recently graduated from Princeton. Ready to learn the ropes of his family's financial empire, he had stepped into a position as a junior investment banker, focusing on start-ups and bond buyouts. For a man with Loftis's upbringing and education the job was easy, and he was already bored by it. He was actually driving home early that day, meandering down the long, winding driveway to the mansion when he'd seen a man running awkwardly away from the big house where they lived.

Was that his father?

Loftis had stopped his car, and the man had run to his door.

"Junior!" Loftis's father had gasped. "Thank God! Quick, we've got to get away. He's here, Junior. Just like he said he would be. And he's going to kill us all."

Suddenly another man had appeared, almost out of nowhere, before Loftis Senior had even opened the door to the car. He stood in front of Loftis's automobile, in the middle of the wide driveway, practically daring Loftis to do something. So he did. He gunned the engine and tried to run down the intruder, to crush him beneath the wheels of his fancy new car.

But the stranger was fast. Too fast. In what seemed like a heartbeat, he had jumped to the side, rolled, and come up standing only a dozen feet from the father. Loftis slammed on the brakes and rushed back to intervene. When he got there, he was dumbfounded to find his powerful, strong, world-moving father kneeling on the pavement, weeping and begging for mercy.

The stranger had ignored the father's pawing and spoken to Loftis instead. "Go inside," he said. "Call the police. And an ambulance. Your father is going to need them."

The old man had wailed then, begging forgiveness, promising restitution, promising riches and more. It was pathetic and disgusting. Loftis had vowed at that moment that he would never beg for anything, ever. If he wanted something, he would take it. He would make others beg.

"Who are you?" Loftis had asked.

"Just a sinner," was the stranger's calm reply.

"What do you want?"

Loftis's father grew quiet.

"I want to stop seeing your father in my dreams. I want

to stop watching him rape and rape and rape the women who serve on your household staff. I want to stop seeing him force himself on their daughters. I want to stop watching him bury their husbands so they won't interfere. I want to stop seeing him imprison entire families on the grounds of this cursed estate, threatening them with deportation or prison, just so he can use them up to fulfill his own wicked desires."

Loftis's father moaned, and the younger Johnson felt as though someone had swung a baseball bat against his stomach. "Father?" he said.

"Please," the older man begged, "I'll make it right. I'll give them all money. I'll adopt the ones that are mine. Please, just don't hurt me again. Not again."

Loftis felt anger burning inside him. He cursed and spit and leaped on the stranger's back, intent on tearing the man's head off with his bare hands. The stranger eluded his grasp with ease, and Loftis felt a sharp blow to his skull. The concussive after-effects left him reeling. He was vaguely aware of a scuffle, then his senses cleared and all was silent.

He was sprawled on the ground, looking up at the cottony blue of the evening sky, wondering if everything he'd just witnessed had really happened. He sat up and saw a bloody, mangled mess on the pavement. His father was unconscious, blood draining from a fractured skull, his hip twisted at a macabre angle. Loftis knew his father needed medical attention in the worst way. But he was now horrified by the man before him and now wished him dead after all.

Loftis stood and returned to his car. He drove carefully

into the garage and went inside, sequestering himself in his suite within the big house. It had actually been one of the maids who finally called an ambulance and the police. Loftis always wondered if she was one of the ones his father had abused. But it made no difference. Not anymore.

The old man had recovered in time, though he was blinded in one eye and crippled in one leg ever after. He never left the house again, either. Too afraid. He died five years later. Alone, and a shell of the powerful magnate he once was.

Loftis despised his father for that. So he took over his company and turned it into a lithe mercenary organization that grew fat on the misfortunes of others.

And Loftis despised—with a loathing that could make him choke on his own breathing—the Sinner. He had spent eight years planning and tracking that man. And then he had thought it was over. But it wasn't. Now, eleven years after his revenge, Loftis Johnson's loathing came back to the surface, and he had to admit he liked it. It gave him purpose, meaning. It gave him the cold hatred he needed to succeed at anything. If only it didn't leave him so hollow as well.

Loftis heard the phone ringing again, and finally opened his eyes. He had indulged his hatred long enough. Now it was time for action. He picked up the receiver and waited.

"Mr. Johnson," a cocky young voice said hurriedly, "there's been a change of plans."

✝

CK and Keena got out of the car and headed toward the entrance to the Italian place. CK scanned the area quickly, looking for any unusual reason why Professor Strand had chosen to stop at this particular restaurant. She couldn't see anything. *Maybe he just likes pasta and red sauce,* she sighed to herself.

"Not the best neighborhood in town," Keena said under her breath, nodding toward a group of unsavory characters smoking cigarettes on the sidewalk.

"Crux Crue," CK said. "Members of that gang always wear a gold braid, like that long one on the skinny guy. Just ignore them. They usually keep to themselves unless you challenge them."

"You never grew up in my neighborhood."

CK nodded. Her assistant had a point.

They were halfway across the parking lot when a voice called out. *"¡Hola, chicas!"* he laughed. "Mm, you both so fine. How 'bout you come over here and talk with me 'n' Renzio awhile?"

They just kept walking toward the restaurant.

"Aw, don't be like that, baby." More laughter. "We be real nice to you both."

A beeper sounded. A brief pause, then, "Maybe later, *chicas!* Me 'n' Renzio got to go to work now. *Vaya con Dios!*"

And then CK and Keena were inside the doors. Keena shook her head, "Whatever."

CK just nodded, then quickly surveyed the darkened interior of the restaurant. It was already half full and bustling with the sounds and smells of an imitation Italy within the walls.

"There," Keena whispered, nodding to the right. CK followed the nod and saw Cyril Strand seated at a table near the exit to the patio. He was already looking hungrily at a menu and sipping on a glass of ice water.

"Will there be more in your party?" a friendly hostess asked.

CK shook her head. "Just the two of us tonight," she said. "And may we have a table on the patio? It's lovely weather outside."

†

SEAN STEPP CLICKED THE SEND BUTTON ON HIS RADIO. "Myers, what's your status?"

"We're just sitting here looking pretty, boss," a voice drawled back.

"Amazing what makeup can do for a monkey these days, isn't it Myers?"

"Oh, Detective," the radio said, "you wound me. I think I'm about to cry."

Sean smiled in spite of himself. "Update, please."

The voice on the other end grew serious. "Suspect took a cab out of the station, then stopped at Little Italia just about a mile down the road. Entered there about ten minutes ago. We're now staking out the location from across the street."

"What about CK Ivors?"

"Yeah, she's here too, boss. Just like you said she would be."

Sean tapped a thumb on his radio. "Okay," he said

finally. "Don't interfere with her. But, you know, don't let her get hurt either."

"On it, boss. Over."

"Out."

Detective Stepp actually picked up his keys for a second, ready to drive down to the restaurant and pull CK off the scene. Then he returned them to his pocket and sighed. There was no way to show his face near Professor Strand, not without giving away the fact that Strand was under police surveillance.

He picked up a phone instead and dialed her number from memory.

"CK Ivors," the voice answered on the second ring.

"What do you think you're doing?"

Even over the phone line, Sean could hear CK's voice smiling. "Why, Sean, how very nice to hear from you. It's been so long, hasn't it? At least half an hour or so."

"CK, I've got two men on Professor Strand right now. You tailing him too could blow the whole operation."

"Are you ordering me to leave this nice Italian restaurant, Sean? 'Cause me and my assistant are just about to order some delicious entrees."

Detective Stepp felt his blood pressure rising. "Yes, CK, I am ordering you to exit the premises and stop interfering with an ongoing police operation."

CK laughed lightly. "Nicely said, Sean," she said. "But I don't work for you. And I'm in a public place, about to enjoy a public meal, so you can't order me to do anything here."

"Okay then," Sean said, "I'm *asking*. CK, would you please leave?"

CK's voice grew immediately warm. "Thanks, Sean. But I can't leave. Not yet. And besides, Strand doesn't know me. I can get closer to him than you or your officers can, keep a closer eye on what he says and does."

Sean sighed. "Where are you, exactly? And where is he?"

"Oh, yes, I'd love a tall glass of strawberry lemonade," CK cooed away from the phone. "Thank you. Okay, Sean. Let's see. Keena and I are sitting out in the patio area of the restaurant. We're right next to the railing by the sidewalk. Bad idea, really, as exhaust from rush-hour traffic blows by here every few minutes. But it does give us a clear view of both your blue Toyota across the street and Professor Strand inside the restaurant."

"Where's he exactly?"

"He's at a table just inside the door to the patio. There's a big plate-glass window between us, and his chair is facing about a quarter turn away from us. But still a clear view. In fact, I think he just ordered the chicken Parmesan."

"CK—"

"I know, Sean. I'll be careful. And if anything starts to go down, I'll alert your boys in the blue Toyota. Okay?"

"Fine."

"Love you, too, Sean. Say hi to Terri for me when you get home tonight."

Detective Stepp hung up the phone. CK Ivors was often a big pain in the neck. But she was also very good at what she did. Sean was prepared to trust her. Again.

✝

THE KID WHO ANSWERED THE DOOR SEEMED TOO YOUNG TO own a place like this and too old to be a freeloading college dropout living off mom and dad's income. He also seemed just a little unsure about opening his door to find a security guard standing on his porch.

Lincoln Sayles made a point of keeping his hands away from the gun strapped to his waist. *Should've taken that thing off before I got out of the car*, he thought. *Don't want to scare this kid before I get some answers.*

"Um, can I help you, officer?" the kid said meekly.

Lincoln tried to put on a comforting smile. "Thanks, but I'm not a police officer. Just got off work—I'm a security guard at Union Colony Bank—and haven't had time to go home and change yet."

"Oh," the kid nodded, but didn't relax. There was an awkward silence between the two of them before the kid finally spoke again. "Um, can I help you, Mr. Security Guard?"

Now Lincoln was feeling uncomfortable and nervous. "No, listen, my name's Lincoln Sayles. No need for all the formality."

"Oh," the kid nodded again. Lincoln felt like an idiot.

"I'm looking for a Junebug Collins?" Lincoln said it as a question.

Now the kid relaxed. Go figure. "Oh," he said. "He's not here right now. Is it about that watch?" Lincoln could see the kid giving him an appraising look.

"Yeah. Sort of."

"Sure. Well, thanks for coming by and all, but Junebug's already taken care of that, so, you know, it's all taken care of."

Expecting someone specific to come for that watch, then, Lincoln mused. *And I don't fit the description.*

"So, you know, thanks for coming by."

"The owner came by and claimed the watch already?" Lincoln asked before the kid could close the door.

"Yeah. Sure did. Thanks. Guy came by earlier today. Boy, was he happy to get his watch back. So, you know, thanks for coming by."

"Actually," Lincoln took a chance, "he didn't come by at all. Because he's not the kind to be drawn into a trap like the one you've set, now is he?"

The kid froze up, eyes flicking around the room for help from no one who was there.

"It's okay, kid," Lincoln said. "I've met the owner of that watch myself. At least I think he's the owner. And that's why I came here to see this Junebug person."

The kid nodded, mute.

"If you really want to catch the Sinner, you're going to need more than an advertisement in the lost and found pages."

"The Sinner? Who's that?" feigned the kid.

Lincoln shrugged. "I had reason to do a little Internet research on the symbol engraved in your watch. Couldn't find a whole lot, but what I did find always mentioned a 'Sinner.' So I'm betting that he was the guy you're looking for."

The kid nodded, glanced around the room again, apparently weighing a decision. Finally he opened the door wide. "Maybe you'd better come in, Mr. Sayles."

†

REBEL FEINE HATED WAITING FOR PLANES TO TAKE OFF. She hated the claustrophobic, cramped, stale-smelling experience of sitting in an airplane seat before it taxied away from the gate. For that reason, she always waited until the very last minute before boarding a plane. Some idiots liked to jump up and get in line to be first on a plane, where they'd then sit for half an hour in their tray-tables-in-the-upright-position mini-coffins disguised as seats (which could be used as a flotation device). But Rebel Feine was no idiot.

She heard the announcement for the last call for boarding her flight. She checked her watch, checked the activity of the flight attendants at the gate, and figured she had at least four more minutes before committing herself to several hours in a flying cargo hold. She flipped open her cell and spoke into it.

"Name dial. CK Ivors."

A moment later, she heard the ringing of a telephone on the other end. Then, "Hello? I mean, CK Ivors' place. Hello?"

"Chance," Rebel said, "Let me talk to CK. I've only got a couple of minutes before I get on my flight back, and I wanted to give her a quick update."

"Um, hey, Rebel. This is Chance."

"Right. Got that already, buddy. You okay?"

"Well, there's someone here."

"Okay, fine. Just let me talk to CK real quick and I'll let you go."

"Actually, Rebel, CK's not here. She went on some kind of stakeout with Keena."

"Okay, Let me talk to James then."

"Actually, James and Junebug went out to meet up with Keena and CK."

"Fine," Rebel said, watching the gate attendant gather her things to board the plane. "So who's there with you?"

"Just the security guard," Chance said.

CK hired a security guard? Rebel thought to herself. *Weird.* Aloud, she said, "Okay, well, tell CK and James that I should be back sometime after midnight. I'll come straight to CK's place from the airport and will give everybody a full report in the morning."

"Okay."

"Meanwhile, tell CK to be careful. This Sinner guy we're chasing may be the real thing, not just a copycat. And if he is the real thing, he's a killer. A vicious one. Glad CK was smart enough to hire a security guard. Tell her to stick close to James as well. He's pretty good in a tight scrape."

"Okay, but—"

"Gotta go, Chance. Change the world, buddy." Rebel saw the gate attendant move to close the door to the passenger walkway.

"Okay, but—"

Rebel flipped her phone closed and sprang toward the entrance to the Jetway. "Hey, wait for me!" she shouted.

CK hired a security guard, she thought again. *Wonder why she hired only one?*

✝

HE'S IN THERE, THE GRAY-COATED MAN THOUGHT. *EATING his dinner. Evil thoughts swirling in his mind.*

The Sinner leaned back into the shadows of the alley-way just down the block from the Little Italia restaurant. He could wait. In the next half hour or so, Professor Strand would finish his meal, leave a 20 percent tip, then walk toward a taxi headed uptown to where he lived. And that was where he would finally meet the Sinner face-to-face, on his way to the taxi. And after that, he would never frighten her again. Never degrade her. Never make her lie and cry.

And the Sinner would never have to see his stippled, greedy, cruel face.

It had been hard, knowing what was to come yet being prevented from stopping it. To see the professor so clearly each time he slept, and to be powerless with impotent rage, unable to touch the professor while he sat comfortably in a jail cell. But he had learned patience over time. He'd had to. And he knew that if he waited it out, if he endured these dreams for now, he could make them stop forever in the future. He never dreamed about the successes again. Only the failures. They were the ones that kept coming back, the failures. But tonight he was determined to make Professor Cyril Strand a success, so he could forget about him forever.

He wanted to check his watch, to calculate the minutes just right, but he still hadn't replaced the one he'd lost at Saint Anthony's a few weeks back. He had to rely on his senses. At least the sun was still shining this time of year. He closed his eyes and centered his thoughts on the minutes passing. He could feel them now, when he wanted to. He understood better how created things can speak to each other. And he, like time, was a created thing. Shortly, his senses had fixed on the moment. Still plenty of time. The fat man would keep eating for at least another ten minutes. Nonetheless, maybe it would be good to change position, to move down past the restaurant and toward the spot where the cab would be waiting.

He scanned the street. Nothing unusual. Not yet. He saw two men in a blue Toyota in a parking lot across from the restaurant. They'd been there for a bit now, never leaving their car. Waiting for a friend? Or watching for someone or something? He decided to risk their attention. If necessary, he would handle them before or after he'd handled the professor. There were only a few people in the tables on the restaurant's patio. Two women near the gate. A man and a woman in the corner. Another woman, eating alone, beside the doorway into the main dining area. They'd never notice one more pedestrian walking briskly past them on the sidewalk.

He closed his eyes for another moment and pictured her face. He had never seen her smile, and that was tragic because he imagined that she had a beautiful smile. But every time he had seen her, Cyril Strand had been there. Or Michel Renault. And in their presence the best she could muster was a brave resignation mingled with fear and a trembling lower lip. The men smiled, leering and prompting with unholy hunger in their voices. But never her. Not ever.

"I will save you, little one," the gray-coated man whispered aloud. "I will save you because I can't save myself."

He opened his eyes and felt the glare of the evening sun. He had an unexpected urge to raise his hood, though he was unsure why. Something made him feel uneasy at this moment. He scanned the street again, found nothing different, felt the minutes ticking by inside him. He wouldn't wait any longer.

The stranger flipped the hood of his coat over his head and stuffed his hands in his pockets, ignoring the fact that it was really too warm for this kind of bundling. He stepped out of the shadows and into the light. He chose a spot about one hundred feet past the restaurant, a place next to a lamp-post, and began walking toward that place.

Inside the pockets of his coat, the Sinner flexed his fingers, then tightened them into the familiar form of fists.   †

FROM THE JOURNAL OF BEVERLY SCOTT THOMAS:

There is no purgatory.
Only hell.
And I am in it.
I deserve to be here. I earned it. It is my just reward. My
righteous judgment.
So why do I still dream of heaven?

TWELVE

CYRIL STRAND WAS IMPRESSED. FOR STARTERS, this chicken Parmesan he was eating was exquisite. After so many days eating prison food, it was sheer pleasure to taste something actually made with the palate in mind. He took a long draught from a glass of wine and dabbed his mouth with the cloth handkerchief. *Heaven*.

What really impressed Cyril, though, was Loftis Johnson. Two days ago Johnson's man, Jeffries, had appeared out of nowhere and insisted on a visit with him. They'd met for the first time looking through the smeared, bulletproof plastic of the visiting area down the hall from his cell.

"Mr. Strand—" Jeffries had begun.

"Doctor, actually," Strand interrupted. "PhD in applied mathematics."

"Dr. Strand, then," Jeffries said. "I won't waste time for either of us."

Actually, I appear to have plenty of time on my hands, Strand had thought. But he kept quiet.

"I have a message for you from Loftis Johnson."

"*The* Loftis Johnson?"

Jeffries nodded. "He wished me to inform you that he is aware of your situation, and that he has an interest in the party who sent you that threatening note."

Cyril perked up then. Maybe this little visit was going to be worth something after all. "Yes? And?"

"Mr. Johnson has suggested that you fire your lawyer and wait for him to act instead."

"He'll get me out of here?"

Jeffries nodded.

"And the Sinner?"

"Mr. Johnson has plans for him as well. You'll be safe under Mr. Johnson's protection."

"And what does Loftis Johnson want from me?"

"Only your cooperation—when it is required."

Professor Strand felt new hope surging inside him. This could be just the break he needed. "Of course. Anything Mr. Johnson wants."

Jeffries stood then and nodded curtly toward the professor. "We'll be in touch."

Now, only forty-eight hours later, that arrogant Detective Stepp himself had been the one to escort him to freedom. "We can't hold you any longer, Strand," Stepp had said. "Not without charging you. And so far we haven't found the evidence we need to charge you. So I'm letting you go. But count on this, Professor, as soon as I round up the evidence that I know is out there, I'll be bringing you back in myself. Got it?"

Inside, Strand had smiled. He'd taken care of most of the evidence within twenty-four hours after poor old Renault had been sent to the hospital. All that was left was a small lockbox of photos he'd stored in a hidden compartment of his desk at the university. He would wait until late tonight, sneak back there, and destroy those pictures. Then he would disappear into Mexico or Eastern Europe or someplace else where no one would come looking for him. He didn't even need Loftis Johnson to do that much. He had money and friends all over the world.

He considered trying to contact Jeffries to advise Mr. Johnson of his plans, but then opted against it. A man like Johnson would find him if he was needed. And, of course, Cyril Strand would be most cooperative.

Cyril pushed his plate away and contemplated what kind of dessert he would be ordering tonight. Something with chocolate drizzles would be good. He loved chocolate drizzles, and had been denied anything remotely sweet during his last ten days in a holding cell.

Suddenly the thought of chocolate drizzles reminded him of something important. Chocolate was that one girl's favorite treat. What was her name?

Professor Strand frowned. That was a loose end. He'd

have to take care of that tonight also, before he left. Then he smiled.

Yes, he'd take care of that tonight.

†

CK WATCHED WITH CAREFUL DISTASTE AS THE GOOD PRO-fessor chewed his food. They'd been here for nearly forty-five minutes and nothing unusual had happened ... yet. The other patrons eating on the patio had left a good ten or fifteen minutes earlier. A busboy had come out and cleaned the dishes off the other tables, and then CK and Keena were alone on the patio. There appeared to be a lull in the restaurant traffic, because no one else joined them in eating outside near the sidewalk. But that was okay. CK preferred a little solitude when stalking a subject. She glanced over at Keena and noticed her assistant fidgeting in her chair.

"Problem?" she asked. The sun was finally starting to show a few gray streaks in the sky. The evening would still be light for another hour at least, but the heat that had been building up all day was lessening.

"CK," Keena said, "I know I should have thought of this earlier, but, well, I was kind of caught up in the moment. I mean, I've never been on a stakeout and tailing a suspect and all that." She let her fork twist a few strands of pasta together, then let them fall apart and back onto her plate.

CK felt a moment of awkwardness and realized she'd forgotten that not everyone could afford to pop into a nice restaurant on a moment's notice. "Not a problem, Keena," she said quickly. "This is a business dinner. It's on CK Ivors Enterprises, LLC." She reached in her purse and flashed a credit card. "So be sure to order the expensive dessert," she whispered conspiratorially. "I promise not to tell the boss."

Keena laughed and pursed her lips. "Thank you," she said. "That's very generous of you, and I appreciate it. But—"

"No, really, Keena. Ask Junebug. When we're on the job, it's an all-expenses-paid kind of deal. I think that's what he likes best about working for me, to be honest. Well, that and the fact it allows him to raid my refrigerator at home."

"No, really, CK, I—"

"Fine," CK cut her off. "If it's that big of a problem for you, keep track of what you spend, and then let me know a total when we're all done. I can deduct it from your end-of-project bonus. Does that sound fair?"

"CK," Keena's eyes widened unexpectedly. "I love getting free food, so I'm happy to have you pay for my dinner. And I thank you. But I think you should know something else."

CK tilted her head, curious now.

"I noticed a guy about half a block down awhile ago. Didn't think much about it. He was just standing in the shadow of that doorway over there—don't look! He's been there this whole time, and I just started thinking it was kind of weird that someone would stay in that one place doing nothing for that long. I know I should have thought to say something earlier, but I was kind of caught up in the whole keep-an-eye-on-Professor-Strand thing, and it didn't really register with me until now."

"What didn't register?"

"Well, that guy in the doorway? He's wearing a long, charcoal gray coat."

"What?"

"And CK? He's heading this direction."

GALWAY HEARD LAUGHTER COMING FROM THE DIRECTION of the game room on the second floor. He started to ignore it and just continue down to the work area where he could put together a visual of all the facts running around in his head. Most of what Ranger 5 had given him was information that Galway already knew. But there were a few things that might be helpful. That part about the Angel of Antietam, for one. And the stint inside Nieswiez, though it was hard to believe that he might have gone all the way to Poland. Still, Galway wasn't about to dismiss anything that might be remotely credible at this point. But he needed to see the facts, not just read them. He needed to start making notes on little yellow stickies and pasting them on the large white board in CK's war room. Then he could rearrange and organize them as much as he wanted, sorting the individual bits of information into a larger whole that would make sense. At least to him.

So at first he walked past the stairway that led to the second floor, ready to continue working on this mystery of the Sinner. Then he heard a voice, a rumbling man's voice that he didn't recognize.

Was there a spy among them?

He retreated back to the bottom of the stairs and strained his ears to listen. "No good," he muttered. "Can't make out the words. Sounds like two of them, though."

Galway looked around for something to use as a weapon, saw an umbrella in a stand by the door and figured that had possibilities. Not that he really intended to use it. His mind had always been his best weapon anyway. But sometimes it was helpful to have something threatening to wave around.

†

MARIA ELIZA GARCES NEVER FELT SILLY PRAYING. BUT SHE did feel a little silly marching around this beautiful big house while she was praying. It had not taken her long to walk the mile or so from Saint Anthony's Cathedral to the address in Junebug Collins' lost and found advertisement. She'd gotten turned around once and made a wrong choice partway here, but she'd figured out her mistake and righted her path within about twenty minutes or so. But once she arrived she just couldn't bring herself to ring the doorbell on that ornate front door.

She was curious. And not afraid. So she began praying and letting her feet lead her. They led her around the right corner of the house, through the garden fence, and into the back area behind the house. She called it a "back area" instead of a "backyard" because it obviously stretched out a few acres, both behind and to the side of the house. She noticed a large addition in the back that had likely been added on to the main house at some point in the recent past. She kept walking. She liked this place. It had a comfortable spirit about it.

By the time she'd walked all the way around the house, she was almost ready to go ring that bell. But then an old man had pulled up in an old car and parked along the wide driveway out front. He was obviously distracted by his thoughts, and he entered the front door with a key, so that meant he probably lived in this big house as well. Could this be the "Junebug" from the advertisement?

The old man had not seen Maria Eliza when he went into the house, and now she thought maybe she should wait another few minutes before ringing the bell at the front. It would be nice to give that man a chance to get settled in at his home before he had visitors.

Maria Eliza remembered a wooden bench back by the garden area. That, she figured, would be as good a place as any to let some time pass by.

†

APPROPRIATELY ARMED WITH HIS UMBRELLA WEAPON, Galway walked stealthily up the stairs toward the game room. He paused outside the door, heard the crack of a cue ball hitting another ball, and then the soft gloving sound of that second ball sinking into the pocket of a billiard table.

So, the spy was obviously making himself at home.

He heard Chance's voice now, clear enough to recognize who it belonged to, but still too mumbly to make out the words.

Galway dared a peek through the open doorway.

A cop. A cop?

Wasn't CK supposed to be with the cops right now? And if so, then why had they called her away, only to send another cop here in her absence?

"Sneaky bluecoats," he muttered. It was the oldest trick in the book. First, you trick your enemy into leaving his headquarters. Then, when you know they are gone, you send in mercenaries to litter the place with bugs and all sorts of listening devices. Poor CK. She was such a trusting soul. Detective Sean Stepp calls and she goes a-running, all the while leaving her house defenseless to the sugarcoated poison of spies in their midst.

He was a little confused about Chance's involvement, though. The kid was kind of, well, geeky, but very smart. And seemed to be dangerously loyal to his boss. Galway wondered how the spy had managed to gain Chance's confidence. Or if Chance was actually the spy and this cop merely his accomplice.

Galway retraced his way back down the steps to the main entryway of the house. He snapped his fingers lightly, a nervous habit when he felt stressed. Should he confront the spies? Call CK?

Finally he decided simply to get out of the house. He would go back to the public library, bury himself in the stacks, and think through the situation while he organized facts about the Sinner. He opened the front door and was very much surprised to find a woman standing there, smiling and holding a leather book.

"Oh," she said kindly, "I was just about to ring the bell."

Galway shot a furtive glance behind him toward the

stairs to the second floor. "Yes, of course," he said. "May I help you?"

The woman nodded gratefully. "Yes," she said, "are you Junebug Collins?"

Galway's eyes narrowed. "Is this about the watch?"

"Only a little bit," she said. "It's mostly about this." She held up the leather-bound book, and Galway immediately recognized two things: (1) it was an extremely old piece, possibly from the late 1800s or early 1900s, and (2) it bore an etching of the sign of the Sinner.

"Where did you get that?" he asked.

"I can show you, Mr. Collins," the woman said boldly. "And then maybe we can help each other find the person who owns this book and your watch."

Galway nodded, and realized he was still holding his umbrella weapon. He set it down hurriedly. "I am free at present. Can you take me there now?"

The woman smiled warmly. "I didn't bring a car."

Galway returned the smile. "Not a problem. I can drive—unless you object to riding in a 1981 Ford Escort?"

"That will be just fine, Mr. Collins."

Galway proffered an arm, like any gentleman would. "This way, Ms. ... I'm sorry, I don't believe I caught your name."

"Maria Eliza Garces," the maid said. Together they walked toward the driveway and over to Galway's car.

†

CK Ivors fumbled for her cell phone and tried not to make it look obvious that she was angling for a glimpse of the man in the gray coat. "When he gets almost to our table," CK whispered to Keena, "cough. That'll be my cue to look up and check him out."

"Right," the assistant responded. "Do you think it's really him? Do you think he's here to make good on that threat to Professor Strand?"

"We'll find out soon enough, won't we?"

"What do we do if it is him?"

"We'll deal with that in a minute. Right now, just stay alert."

CK set her eyes on Keena, and kept her thumb hovering over the dial button on her cell phone. If things got out of hand, she wanted Sean to get his stakeout buddies over here as fast as possible.

Keena's eyes suddenly went slightly wider, and the assistant gave a hearty cough which she then buried in a glass of tea. CK let her eyes dart out and upward as she caught sight of the coat in her peripheral vision. For a lightninglike instant, she felt her eyes connect with the eyes of the gray-coated man as he looked down at her, apparently drawn by the sound of Keena's cough and the quick motion of CK's head.

His eyes were dark and flat, splayed with flecks of red deep within the pigment. He glanced at her in passing, and at the same time seemed to peer deeply into her mind. Just before he turned his head and continued walking by, CK saw a glint of recognition in his gaze. But his face remained a stone, and just as quickly as their eyes had met he was past her and walking purposefully down the rutted sidewalk.

"It's him," she whispered to Keena. "It's him. It's the Sinner."

Keena sucked in a breath and then blew it out in a strangled sigh. "Should we call Detective Stepp?"

CK didn't answer. She was trying to remember the number to Junebug's cell phone, but something in her memory wasn't working correctly and she couldn't remember the fourth digit. Junebug had been offended when CK refused to add his name to her speed-dial list, but CK had reasoned that his was one of the few numbers she actually knew by heart. She would never need to speed dial. Except, of course, until now when her mind had betrayed her like a rookie quarterback who forgets the play he called in the huddle.

"We need Junebug first," CK said in a low breath. "We can't let this guy out of our sight. We need to have Junebug follow him, photograph his hideout, his hangouts, everything." She glanced across the street at the blue Toyota and briefly registered that someone was leaning in the driver's window, talking to the two cops. But she didn't have time for that right now.

The Sinner was about twenty paces away now and slowing down just a bit. CK still held her cell phone in her hand, cursing herself for forgetting one little, but important, digit of a phone number. She reached into her purse and pulled out the credit card.

"Take this," she said to Keena.

"What? Why?"

"So you can pay for our dinner. Give a good tip. I'm going to follow the Sinner. You can take my car afterward and catch up to us."

CK bent down to dig her keys out of her purse. Keena whipped her head around to follow the progress of the gray-coated man and then let out a little gasp.

"CK," she said. "You might not have to follow him after all."

"Why not?"

"He's coming back."

†

RENZIO MORALES FINGERED THE SMALL, SILVER-HANDLED pistol. It felt good in his hand. Warm, comfortable. Small enough to fit in his palm. Powerful enough to kill a man with one shot. He rubbed the gun across the stubble of the cop's unshaven neck and then let it rest, barrel down, against the man's chest.

"So you see, officers," he continued quietly. "We need you to take a short break, okay? Not long, maybe ten, fifteen minutes or so. Imagine yourself eating a doughnut or something nice like that."

Detective Myers didn't respond. He simply kept his gaze on the gun pressed against his sternum.

"Oh, and your other officer over there? Do us a favor and roll down your window for my brother Marcel. I think he wants to have a word with us too."

The second detective, Gates, slowly reached over and rolled down the passenger window.

"Thank you very much, officer," Marcel said. Then he leaned inside the window and quickly removed Gates's handgun from its holster. Renzio did the same with Myers's gun. Next, Marcel reached over Gates and yanked the speaker off the police radio. "Can't have anyone catching you on an unscheduled break, now can we, officer?"

"You know we can identify you," said Myers. "Our people will have you in a jail cell within forty-five minutes of the time you leave here."

Renzio looked thoughtful. "You know, you're right, officer. Maybe I should just go ahead and pull the trigger now and get it over with, huh?"

Myers said nothing, so Renzio continued.

"No, I don't think you'll identify us back at the station, officer. You see, my brothers back there," he motioned to seven other young men surrounding the blue Toyota. All wore gold braids somewhere in their hair. "They can identify you and your partner here. And if anything happens to Marcel and me, well, our brothers come looking for you. Know what I mean?" He smiled and finally pulled his gun out of the detective's chest. Immediately, another gun from one of the other gang members slipped into the window and positioned itself against the back of Myers's head. Another gang member filled the same function for Gates, effectively rendering both the police officers helpless.

"Now," Marcel said as he backed away from the Toyota. "Is everybody in place?"

Renzio glanced quickly toward the rooftops, noting three black shapes against the setting sun. He nodded.

"Good," Marcel said. "Then let's get busy."

†

CK IVORS LOOKED UP TO SEE HIM STANDING IN THE MIDDLE of the sidewalk, staring at her.

"Keena," she said quietly. "Get up and go inside. Find a phone and call Sean Stepp at the police station. Then hide in the restroom until his men get over here."

Keena didn't move.

"Keena!"

"Shut up, CK," she said patiently. "I mean, boss, I'm not leaving you to face this guy all by yourself. Junebug would never forgive me."

CK didn't know whether to be angry or flattered by her assistant's loyalty. But she decided now was not the time to argue.

The Sinner was still staring. Even from this distance, CK could see his eyes blazing with meaning. He took a slow step forward, then another, never taking his gaze off CK.

It was a surreal moment for the unshakable Miss Ivors. When the Sinner reached the table, CK stood to face him, and Keena quickly followed suit.

"Can we help you?" Keena asked, and CK admired the girl's courage. She sounded both casual and disinterested, perfectly covering what CK knew had to be a rapid heartbeat.

The Sinner looked at CK and finally whispered, in a raspy, dry-throated voice, "I have seen you."

CK felt herself flinch inside, and heard Keena's breathing get a little ragged.

Wasn't that the phrase the Sinner used for his death threat notes?

"No," he said after a moment, almost in wonder. "Not

you. Your eyes are green, not brown. But your face, the shape of your eyes, the flatness of your cheek and the strength of your jaw. I have seen you."

Now the man was spouting gibberish. CK wasn't sure what she'd expected upon meeting the legendary Sinner, but something had made her think he'd make more sense when he spoke.

"Celia."

She flinched again, outwardly this time.

"How do you know my name?" she said angrily. An instinctual reaction.

His face softened, as if things were finally falling into place in his head. He almost smiled. CK heard a ringing in her ears. She followed the Sinner's gaze as it traveled from her face down her arm to her hand.

Her cell phone was flashing.

†

CYRIL STRAND NEARLY SWALLOWED HIS FORK WHEN HE happened to glance out the plate-glass window next to his table. He saw two women standing and talking to someone on the sidewalk. Then he saw the coat, that horrible, charcoal gray coat, and he knew the Sinner had found him.

No! he thought. *Too soon. Has Loftis Johnson betrayed me into the Sinner's hands?*

His breathing became frantic, and he tasted the soured flavor of partially digested cheesecake. He had to run, to find a place to hide. He thought about bolting for the door, then faced the grim realization that there was no way he could outrun the thickly muscled man who was stalking him.

He froze in his chair, panic clouding his thoughts. He would start screaming, he decided. He would scream like a little girl on a roller coaster if that's what it would take. This was a nice dining establishment. They'd come running to find out his problem. They'd surround him with helpful waitresses and restaurant managers. They'd protect him, simply by being near him and being innocent. The Sinner would never attack him in such a crowded place. He would wait to catch him alone, but Cyril Strand would never let himself be alone. He would stay holed up in this Italian sanctuary until … until what?

Until he could call Lee Jeffries. Until Lee Jeffries could call Loftis Johnson. Until Loftis Johnson could get here and kill that wicked man standing just outside.

Professor Strand reached for his wine and downed it all in one gulp. He would scream. At just the right moment, he would scream.

CK IVORS STARED AT HER CELL PHONE AS IF IT WERE A FOR-eign object, then looked up at the Sinner standing before her. He only smiled, crossed his arms, and waited. *Looks almost normal when he's like that*, she thought to herself.

"CK?" It was Keena. "Want me to answer that?"

Of course Keena's right, CK thought. *It's probably Junebug. Or maybe Sean. I need to answer this phone.* She shook her head quickly and flipped open the phone.

"CK Ivors," she said brusquely.

"CK Ivors? In the flesh? My goodness, I can't believe my good fortune!"

CK groaned inside.

"CK," the voice continued happily, "It's John Corson. How's my favorite author today? When did you get back from being out of the country? Were you in Europe? Or South America? Or some other magical place doing research for that new dynamite lights-out fantastic book you're working on?"

Keena snorted and covered her mouth, and CK realized with embarrassment that her editor's enthusiastic voice was leaking out the back of her cell phone and into the ears of anyone nearby. The Sinner stood impassively, as though waiting were an art form that he had perfected.

"John," CK said finally, "hey, listen, can I call you back? Now's not a great time, and—"

"Oh no you don't," Corson insisted. "You are *impossible* to get in touch with. If I let you go now, it'll be weeks before I catch you again. If I hadn't promised a bribe to that kid back at your house, I might not even have caught you now either."

"You mean Chance gave you this number?"

"Yep. Nice kid. You should give him a raise."

Or a swift kick in the butt.

"Listen, John, I really can't talk right now. Really."

"Okay, okay, just tell me a little something about our new book. Will I like it? Will it be on time? What's the title so far? You know, our marketing department is planning to—"

"John!" CK saw the Sinner suddenly tense and look toward the rooftops.

"C'mon, CK. Don't be one of those ego authors. Think of all we've been through together. Think of where we're going with your career in the future. Now, give me some dirt, honey. What's cooking in that creative brain of yours?"

Two men were approaching from across the street. She heard Keena groan. "It's the dorks who tried to pick up on us when we came in."

The Sinner's eyes suddenly went flat and his face taut. CK saw his hands form fists and noticed him lean slightly forward, balancing his weight on his toes as he turned to face the approaching gold braids.

CK felt suddenly worried—not for herself but for this Sinner. She pressed the cell phone into Keena's hand and leaned forward, touching the Sinner on his left shoulder.

"Listen," she said fiercely. "I think you and I should talk. But not here, not now. Those guys are part of the Crux Crue gang, and they mean business. You need to get out of here. Just tell me where I can find you again. Please."

The Sinner didn't turn around. "Just sit down," he said. "I won't let anything happen to you."

"Hi, uh, Mr. Corson?" Keena spoke into the cell phone. "CK can't come to the phone right now. She's, uh—" Keena shrugged. "Well, she's suffering from a bout of irritable bowel syndrome. And she may be awhile, if you know what I mean. I'll have her call you back as soon as possible. Thank you. Good-bye!" Keena flipped the cell phone closed before the editor could respond, then pressed the "off" button so it wouldn't ring again.

The Crux members were now standing warily before the Sinner.

"Hey Sinner man," the leader said. "Told you we'd see you again." The gray-coated man said nothing. "Me and Renzio, we been looking for you for a while now. Got to say you're pretty good at staying hidden when you want to."

"You can't hurt me," the Sinner said evenly. "Not even your snipers up there. But I can hurt you. And I will, if you're not gone in the next sixty seconds."

CK looked frantically for help from the blue Toyota across the street. Her heart sank when she saw a cluster of gold-braided teens draped around the car.

Marcel looked over the Sinner's shoulder at Keena. "Mm," he said to her. "Baby, is this man bothering you? 'Cause me and Renzio got a nice little crib where you can come over and have a good time. You can bring your friend, too," he said, nodding toward CK.

"Forty-five seconds," the Sinner said, letting his frame settle into an attack posture.

"See, what you're missing, Sinner man, is that we don't aim to hurt you with our snipers," he pulled a pistol from his pocket, "or even with this gun here."

CK started measuring the distance between her table and the doorway into the restaurant. The restaurant workers and other customers seemed blissfully unaware of the drama unfolding out on the patio. CK wasn't sure if she should be grateful that no one else was out there—which meant fewer people were in danger—or annoyed because then there would be others to call for help. Still, she was used to handling things herself. She turned her attention back to the men on the sidewalk.

"We intend to hurt those two pretty ladies standing behind you," Renzio said. "And that, Mister Sinner, is something we *can* do."

The Sinner froze for a breath, then relaxed his posture and stood up straight, arms at his side.

"What do you want?"

Renzio leaned in close and studied the gray-coated man's eyes. "Tell me," he said. "Have you seen me, man? Have you *seen* old Renzio in your dreams?"

The Sinner shook his head tightly.

"Well that's interesting," Renzio continued. "'Cause Mr. Johnson has seen you. And he wants to see you up-close again. Right now."

"Loftis Johnson?" Keena asked boldly. "What's Loftis Johnson want with this guy?" CK admired that even now Keena seemed unafraid. The two gang members and the Sinner ignored her.

"Fine," the Sinner growled. "Let's go."

"Uh-uh," Marcel said. "First things first. The coat."

The Sinner unwrapped the charcoal gray from his body, then carefully handed it over the gate to CK. "Put this on," he said. "Over both of you." CK and Keena obeyed.

Now Renzio produced handcuffs. "I believe you know what to do with these?"

The Sinner placed both hands on his head. Renzio grabbed one hand and pulled it behind the Sinner's back, snapped a cuff on it, then grabbed the other and repeated the process.

"One last thing," Marcel said. "Mr. Johnson's suggestion. I thought it was a good one." He unwrapped a length of what looked like guitar string or thick wire from around his waist and formed one end into a noose, which he quickly slipped over the Sinner's head. The other end he wrapped around a glove on his hand, then he jerked, causing the Sinner to step forward involuntarily.

"Okay, Sinner-man. We're ready. And if you try anything that looks even a little bit threatening, I will garrote you around your neck until your head pops right off. How well you think you'll be able to rise from the dead without a head attached?"

CK looked at the captured vigilante before her. He did not move his head, but he spoke directly to CK. "Raven," he said urgently.

CK had no idea what he was talking about.

"Raven," he said again. "Raven Ann Rinehart. Say it."

"Raven Ann Rinehart," she repeated.

The Sinner nodded, and then Marcel yanked the wire again. The three men started walking down the sidewalk.

"Ladies," Renzio said. "It's been a real pleasure. I'm real hopeful we will all see each other again under much more, um, *friendly* circumstances." The gang member winked at Keena, and then he strutted merrily away.

CK Ivors watched the odd little procession disappear around a corner. She heard a commotion in the restaurant. It sounded like a little girl screaming for help, but it was quickly overwhelmed by the thoughts running through her head. And one thought quickly rose above all the others.

How did he know my name?

†

CHANCE ELKO HAD TO ADMIT THERE WAS SOMETHING HE liked about this security guard. He had a casual confidence that immediately put others at ease. He talked to everyone as an equal and didn't appear to be afraid of anything. Plus, he'd paid off the bet right away—without complaining—when Chance had beat him with a lucky shot in their game of pool. Something about that experience had tipped the scales in Chance's mind. He'd decided he was going to trust this guy and see what happened.

Of course, he'd have felt more comfortable trusting Lincoln Sayles with James Dandy—or even Junebug—at his side. But they were still frantically searching for CK and Keena somewhere downtown. Junebug had called earlier, frustrated and concerned because he and James were driving around the downtown area and hadn't been able to find the boss or her assistant as planned.

"Why don't you just call her cell phone?" Chance had asked. "She carries that thing everywhere."

"Tried that already," Junebug said curtly. "Keep getting dumped into her voice mail after the first ring."

"Oh," said Chance. "That means she's turned it off."

"Knew that, Chance. Not a moron, okay?"

"Sorry, Junebug. But why would CK turn off her cell phone? She doesn't even do that when she's at the movies."

"You took CK to the movies? When was that?"

"Whenever. We all go to movies, Junebug."

"Well, where do you think she could be?"

Chance ran the possibilities in his head and came up

with nothing. Almost nothing. "She was going to meet with that detective at the police station. Sean something."

"Sean Stepp?"

"Yeah, sounds right. Did you check with him?"

"No, not yet. That's a good idea. We're pretty close to the station right now, so we'll just go over there and see if we can catch him."

"Okay."

"Meanwhile, if CK calls in, tell her we're scouring the streets looking for her."

"Gotcha. Will do."

There was a pause. "So what movie did you take CK to see?"

"Gotta go, Junebug. Chasing a Sinner and all that."

"Right. Okay. Thanks."

Chance had hung up then and found the security guard standing near the pool table, trying to pretend he hadn't been listening to the whole conversation.

"Well, Mr. Sayles," Chance had sighed.

"Lincoln," the security guard said for the fifth time. "Some people just call me Link."

"Right," said Chance. "Well, Lincoln. Link." Didn't sound as goofy out loud as it had sounded in his head. "Looks like it may be awhile before anybody important gets back."

The security guard stroked his chin thoughtfully. "Well, tell you what, Chance. I'm going to show you what I came to show that Junebug person, and you can tell me what you think we should do next, okay?"

Chance had nodded. Lincoln had reached in his shirt pocket and pulled out what looked like a bank deposit slip.

He turned it over and revealed, hand-drawn in black ink, the symbol of the Sinner.

"Where did you get that?"

Lincoln had handed the paper to Chance for inspection, and said, "The guy who gave me that wouldn't tell me his name. But he did say that if I ever needed him, I could use this to contact him."

Chance had nearly done jumping jacks in excitement. "Wow, we gotta call CK—no wait, can't do that. We could call Junebug—no, he's not going to want to stop looking for CK just yet."

Lincoln waited patiently.

"Let's see," Chance had continued. "Rebel's still flying in. Galway ... Where's Galway?" He'd started toward the door, then stopped and turned back to look at the security guard.

"Well," Lincoln said carefully. "We could just go try to contact this guy ourselves."

Chance remembered what kind of beating this Sinner had given that priest back at Saint Anthony's, and the thought of meeting him without the team around was a little unsettling.

"You think that's safe, Link?"

The guard shrugged. "Here's the thing, kid. I've pretty much decided to do it anyway. I'm just inviting you to come along. If you want."

Chance had hesitated, but in the end he'd decided to go along with the security guard, figuring that's what CK would have done if she'd been there. Now Chance's belly was grumbling nervously, and he was standing just inside the doors of the public library. Behind him, on the other side of the doors, the sun had just completed a spectacular sunset. In front of him, Lincoln was carefully studying the public announcements bulletin board in the lobby.

"Well," Lincoln was saying, "should we put our little symbol next to the flyers to help prevent bed-wetting or the advertisement for 'expert drum lessons—rock 'n' roll style' from Kelly Moore?"

Chance shrugged. "If I were the Sinner," he said, "I'd want to be next to that girl in the workout suit advertising twice-a-week aerobics sessions."

Lincoln grinned. "Makes sense," he said. Then he stole a look over his shoulder back at Chance. "When this is over," he said, "remind me to introduce you to my niece." He grinned.

Chance blushed in spite of himself. "Yeah, sure. Whatever." There was an awkward moment before Lincoln just chuckled and turned to pin up the Sinner's symbol on the board. He stepped back to look at it, then he glanced at Chance.

"So what are we supposed to do now?" Chance asked.

"Just wondering that myself," Lincoln said. "I guess I should have gotten more instructions."

"What did he tell you exactly?"

"Well, he said that if I ever needed a favor, I should put this up on the announcements board at the library. That was it."

Chance looked around the lobby, then checked the door for the closing time of the library. "So do you think we should just wait here, or what?"

"Well, seems kind of silly to wait here," Lincoln said

thoughtfully. "I mean, it could be days before he sees this board again, right?"

"Yeah. I guess that's right."

They stood in silence a moment longer. Just when Chance was about to suggest that he and Lincoln swap cell phone numbers and call it a night, a voice spoke behind them.

"He's not coming this time."

Chance and Lincoln turned to see a boy, maybe ten, eleven years old. The boy had a serious look about him and was staring up at the symbol Lincoln had just tacked to the announcements board.

"What do you mean?" Lincoln asked, kneeling down to be eye level with the boy.

The boy cocked his head to the side, questioning. "Are you trying to arrest him?"

Lincoln smiled, a genuine smile that Chance wished he could fake. "No," Lincoln said. "I'm not a cop. Just a security guard for a bank. Didn't have chance to change after work."

The boy nodded. "Well, it doesn't matter because he's not coming. He can't."

"Who's not coming?" the security guard asked.

The boy pointed to the symbol on the board. "Him. I don't know his name. But the guy who gave you that drawing. He's not coming."

The tumblers finally fell into place in Chance's head. "Wait a minute," he said. "I know you. You're Hector Gomez."

The boy took a step back in alarm.

"No, it's okay," Chance continued. "I recognize you from the pictures in the paper. After that priest beating thing a few weeks ago."

Hector nodded, but said nothing.

"What are you doing here tonight, Hector?" Chance asked.

The boy nodded toward a table where a woman sat reading a book. "My mom brought me so I could get some books for a homework assignment."

Lincoln nodded. "How do you know the guy we're looking for? Is he a friend of yours?"

Hector looked thoughtful. "No, I guess not. Not really. But also, yeah, maybe he is. If that makes sense."

Chance shook his head and started to say something, but Lincoln cut him off. "Yeah, I know what you mean," he said. "I've met him only twice, but I can't help feeling like he's both dangerous and someone I could trust."

"Yeah," Hector looked carefully at the security guard. "But he's not coming. So if you put that note up there to signal him, you probably should take it down before too many people see it. Before the wrong people see it and come after you too."

Chance was now thoroughly confused. What was this boy talking about? Were they in danger? Well, more danger than expected?

Lincoln put a hand on the boy's shoulder. "Why don't you tell me what you know, Hector? Maybe we can help."

Hector studied the security guard's face for a long moment, then nodded. "Okay," he said. "Well, they got him. The Crux got him. My friend Jorge's big brother was bragging about it on the phone earlier when I was at their house. They said they're going to keep him in a secret place. An old haunted mansion that's been empty for, like, twenty years or something."

"Why did the Crux Crue want this guy? Is he from a rival gang or something?"

Hector shrugged. "Dunno. But Jorge's brother was calling in other gang members to go to the house and guard him."

"Do you know where the house is?" Lincoln asked.

Hector shook his head. "But I did hear the address."

"That's great, Hector," Lincoln said kindly. "What's the address?"

"You gonna help him?" Hector asked.

"Well, I guess we're going to try," Lincoln responded.

"You gonna call the cops? 'Cause the cops will just put him in jail, and then he's no better off than being caught by the Crux."

Lincoln tilted his head to the side, realization dawning. "This guy rescued you from that priest, didn't he, Hector?" he said quietly.

Hector studied the floor, then looked up again into the security guard's face. "You gonna call the police?"

Lincoln finally stood up and traded glances with Chance. There was a pause while the security guard thought through the implications of withholding important information from the police.

Finally he said, "No, Hector. I won't call the police. Not unless it's absolutely necessary. Okay?"

Hector nodded. "Then," he said, "I'll tell you the address."

†

LOFTIS JOHNSON MADE ONLY ONE PHONE CALL. WHEN THE receiver on the other end picked up, he said, "Your services are no longer needed."

"Mr. Johnson? Wait, what are you talking about?"

"Your services are no longer needed, Jeffries. Our agreement is terminated."

"But—"

"You would be wise to take your earnings and disappear as planned."

A pause. Then, "Right." Another pause. "Okay then. Well, thank you, sir. If you ever need—"

Loftis Johnson hung up. After all, he had a plane to catch.   †

I feel the blood drain from my face. I don't know what to say, so I simply stand there, stupidly holding a bagful of sandwiches. The absurd thought runs through my mind that if I leave these meat sandwiches in the sun much longer, they are going to spoil.

"Nice mare you got there, Beverly," the leader says. "Fine horse. Looks healthy. Well-cared for."

I nod, following Jennison's gaze to where Destine is tied to the tree.

"Know something, Bev?" he continues. "If I had a pretty little horse like that, there's no way I'd tie her up outside during the heat of the day like this."

He nods to one of his men, the narrow one. "That horse looks thirsty," he says to him, "but she can't reach the water trough." Jennison scratches his head and turns back to me. "That make sense to you, Bev?"

"I think it's time you left my property," I say finally. "I've got chores to do and all."

Jennison grins. "Can't leave yet, Bev. Got chores of my own today."

It happens again; I think afterward that I could have prevented it. But I don't. My eyes flick back toward the big barn doors. I hastily avert them and stare at the ground. But it is too late.

Jennison makes eye contact with the narrow henchman.

The fat one ambles closer to me. "Beverly Thomas," Jennison yawns. "Odd name for a strapping young man like yourself. Family name?"

I nod. "Grandfather."

Jennison scratches his left ear. "No substitute for family," he says. "I'm guessing you're what, twenty years old? Twenty-one?"

"Nineteen," I say.

"A man's age," Jennison nods approvingly. "Not a boy any longer, are you, Bev?"

I summon my courage. "Mr. Jennison," I say firmly, "I need to ask you to leave. Now. And if you don't, I will have to call on the sheriff."

Jennison ignores my request. "See, the thing about family," he says, "is that the family bond ought to be unbreakable, right, Bev? I mean, your father feeds you, raises you, puts clothes on your back. You ought to be grateful for that, right, Bev?"

I say nothing, noticing only that the fat man is now uncomfortably close to me.

"And when somebody ungrateful breaks that bond," Jennison continues, "when, oh let's say, a slave disrespects that family bond. When he steals away a daughter and leaves his pregnant wife behind, alone. When he shows utter disdain for everything his kind and fatherly master has done for him and his family, well, that just ain't right, is it, Bev?"

So the runaway's wife is pregnant. Now I understand why he runs with the daughter alone. With Celia. And then another thought strikes me.

"Who is the father of the child about to be born?" I ask. I am surprised by my boldness. But I suspect that I already know the answer.

Jennison laughs. "Well, now, there is a question," he says, winking at the fat man behind me. Then he shrugs. "Seeing as the master made plans to sell the first little girl to a good family down in Florida, the master felt it would be only proper to give that nigger mama a new baby to keep her happy. Ain't that nice o' him?"

The fat man chuckles derisively in my ear. The narrow man just grins and shakes his head. He stands over by the barn door now, waiting.

"What are you going to do?" I ask through clenched teeth, feeling the fear I've been fighting finally begin to seep into my sweaty palms and drying throat.

"Gonna set things right again, Bev. That's all. Just gonna set things right."

THIRTEEN

"OK, I'M WORRIED."

"I know. We all are. But we've taken every precaution. We just need to stick to the plan."

"No, I mean I'm worried about Galway."

"I know."

"Nobody's heard from him since this morning."

"We can't do anything about that right now."

"But isn't there some way to contact him? Signal fires or something?"

"No. He refuses to carry a cell phone. Says they're concealed tracking devices for the government."

"Maybe we should send Keena or somebody to check

out where he lives. What if he had a stroke or something?"

"Nobody knows where he lives."

"Guess I should have expected that."

"Galway will have to take care of himself. He's always managed to do that up to this point."

"Right. You're right."

"We have to stay focused. Got a job to do tonight."

"I understand. If I'm going to be here, I need to be all here."

"Good."

"Good."

"Hey, it's okay, though. Galway is special, and I'm worried too."

†

HECTOR GOMEZ WOKE UP CRYING. IT TOOK SEVERAL MINutes for Hector to regain his orientation, to recognize that he was home, he was safe, he was in his own bed. Even then, choking sobs involuntarily eked their way up his diaphragm and out his mouth. Hector was a big boy now, and he disliked crying. But this time, in spite of his best efforts, the tears would not stop, at least not yet.

He was finally beginning to quiet himself down when his mother entered the room. The muted glare from the nightlight revealed a face that was tired—exhausted, really—but also pained with concern for her son.

"What's wrong, baby?" she said, coming to sit on the side of his bed. She reached out a tender hand, wiping tears and stroking his face. "Shh, it's okay. Mama's here."

Hector felt silly, but just the touch of his mother's hand brought a fresh round of weeping. He sat up and leaned into her comforting warmth.

"What is it, baby?" she asked again softly. "What's wrong? Did you have a bad dream?"

Hector nodded, now gaining some control over his emotions. "A nightmare," he said.

"It's okay," she said, rocking him gently in her arms. "It was just a dream. Nobody's going to hurt you."

Hector shook his head forcefully. "Not me. It wasn't about me."

His mother reached across the nightstand and retrieved a tissue, using it to expertly clean Hector's increasingly messy face. "What do you mean, baby?"

"The dream wasn't about me. It was about a man. A man on a cross."

Hector's mother waited, curious and concerned.

"And they were hurting him. People were there, hurting him."

"Where were you?"

"I don't know. Just watching. I couldn't do anything. Nobody did anything to stop them. And he just kept getting hurt by them. Why didn't anybody stop them?"

"It was just a dream, honey. It's okay now. Everything is okay." She gently laid her son back into the folds of the covers, arranging him for a return to sleep.

"But I have seen them, Mama," he said as he submitted to his mother's nighttime ministrations. "And they were hurting him."

"Who was on that cross, baby? Was it Jesus?"

Hector shook his head, trying to make sense of the vision in his head. "No," he said finally. "It was a sinner. Just a sinner on the cross."

✝

MEDICAL AND PSYCHOLOGICAL EXPERTS CALL IT "LUCID dreaming"—that is, a dream state in which the dreamer is aware that he or she is actually dreaming. So it was no surprise that he considered his current situation a lucid dream.

Except that, technically speaking, he wasn't dreaming.

Instead, he was enveloped in the healing blackness of sleep, hearing himself breathe, feeling the gentle thumping of the heart within his chest, but unaware of anything going on outside his subconscious state.

It was as close to heaven as he had ever been, and a reminder that there is indeed a God who is active in the lives of his created. Of course, that revelation was always dampened by the cold fact that God hated, in particular, him.

But for now at least, he could push that knowledge to the dim recesses of his mind, to the waking man instead of the sleeping one. In the darkness there was no pain, no sorrow, no memory of loss and regret. No face, no body, no soul. Only healing. And rest.

Peace.

At some point, though, as in every lucid dream, the whisper of reality began to jog the mind, to remind it that it is not normal to be awake while you are sleeping. The mind, against its own will, talks itself out of peace.

He felt the bruise under his right eye first. Then the cut

that fat diamond ring had left stretching from under his cheekbone all the way back to his ear. Something about lefties, they always seemed to peg his right ear sooner or later.

His insides, below the lowest portion of his rib cage, felt scrambled and damaged. He was pretty sure his collarbone was cracked. And was his shoulder dislocated too? Possibly. Probably.

He heard somebody groan, not loud or wailing. But softly, nearby, as though within the dream.

Then he felt the familiar tingling, the drug to which he was addicted but which he longed would stop infecting his body. He felt like laughing and crying at the same time. In the darkness he knew the pain—the physical pain at least— would soon be over. But the other pain, the one marked by scars on the soul rather than on the body, that pain would persist in silence and shadow. As it always did.

The blackness swirled. The mind had to make a choice. Release lucidity and give in to dreaming? Or embrace the discomfort of wakefulness? His mind chose the waking nightmare, and for a moment the mind was triumphant. But only for a moment. Then the body asserted its will— God's will?—and trumped the awareness that beckoned from the outside.

He felt his lucidity fading, and could nearly taste the bitterness of his disappointment.

Please, he prayed, knowing his prayer would go unanswered. *Rescue me from dreaming ...*

†

GALWAY KNEW IT HAD TO BE WELL AFTER MIDNIGHT, BUT HE
didn't care enough to check the watch on his arm. Janine,
good daughter that she was, wouldn't start worrying until
he'd been gone three days at least. And even then, she'd call
CK before calling the police. So he had plenty of time.
Plenty of time.

That nice maid had taken the bus home hours ago. Said
she needed to go fix supper for her family, and would "Mr.
Collins" mind locking up the cottage when he left?

When they had left CK's house earlier, Maria Eliza had
assumed that Galway had placed the ad regarding the gold
watch, and thus also assumed that his name was Junebug
Collins. Galway saw no reason to disabuse her of this
notion, at least not yet.

They had chatted comfortably for the first few minutes
of the drive, and then Galway had moved to the issue at
hand.

"So tell me," he said, "what a woman like you is doing
with a book like that?" He motioned toward the leather-
bound tome in her lap.

"It's kind of a confusing story, actually," she responded
with a nervous laugh. "And one that could get me in trouble at work."

"My lips are sealed, madam," Galway said gallantly.

"Well, you see, there's this old abandoned house.
Actually, it's a mansion, over in the old Highlands Hills part
of the city."

"I know the area," Galway said. "Out where most of the
old money lives, by the really big country club, right?"

"Right."

"Is that where you found the book?"

"No. Well, sort of."

Galway waited patiently.

"You see, behind the big house are servants' quarters. Three small family cottages, down a path and hidden behind a grove of trees. The cottages are empty too—at least they have been as long as I've known about them.

"Well, not completely empty," she continued. "Like the big house, they still have furnishings inside them. You know, tables, chairs." She paused, collecting her thoughts. "Beds. In the big house everything is covered for storage, you know, large sheets and things over the furniture. But in the cottages the furniture is still uncovered."

"If the estate is uninhabited, then why—and how—did you go in there?" Galway's eyes narrowed. He wanted to ask if the woman with him was homeless, a squatter perhaps? But her appearance and manner seemed inconsistent with that possibility, so he kept that thought to himself.

"Well," Maria Eliza said, "I work as a maid for Maximum Maids. Several years ago—maybe ten or fifteen years from what I can gather—somebody hired our company to service one cottage on the estate. The middle one, a two-bedroom cottage. Apparently they paid in advance for some ludicrous number of years—twenty, or fifty, or something. Robert, my boss, never told me exactly."

Galway made a mental note to try to get Chance following the money trail on that later. *Follow the money and you'll find the man*, he said to himself.

"Anyway, I've been cleaning this cottage for five years now, and it's always the same."

"Empty?"

"Um-hm. Not just empty, though. Untouched. Nothing moved or changed at all."

"So every week you go to clean an empty house? Seems unusual, doesn't it?"

Maria Eliza shrugged. "I'm just telling you how I found the book."

"Right. Sorry. Please continue."

"Well, the one thing about this cottage—other than the fact that somebody paid to have it cleaned every week—is the second bedroom in the back. It's been locked for as long as I've been cleaning that place. No access to the back bedroom at all. Most days I even forgot it was there. Then—"

"Ah," Galway's mind had started racing by this point. "Somebody opened it?"

"Well, I guess so. I still have never seen anyone in the cottage. But one day I was there, and the bedroom door was open. When I went in to clean it, I saw a bookshelf that had dozens of these kinds of leather-bound books on it. And all of them had that same cross-and-snake symbol."

"It's actually an *S* you know." Galway couldn't help correcting the maid on this point. "It stands for Sinner—the name of the guy who owns the books."

Maria Eliza nodded slowly. "That makes sense. Oh, turn here," she said. "We're getting closer."

Galway rolled his car into an obviously richer area of town, full of flowing gardens, gated manors, and large houses surrounded by green expanses of property.

"Well," she stopped, reordered her thoughts, then continued. "Tell me, Mr. Collins, do you believe in miracles?"

Galway snorted in spite of himself. "Actually, my dear," he said, "I believe it takes more faith to disbelieve miracles than it does to believe them."

"Well, Mr. Collins—and this is the part that could cause me problems at my work—I took this book from that second bedroom. And I read it. And it makes me believe in miracles all over again. So much so that I feel strongly that I need to find this man, this Sinner."

"Why is that, Maria Eliza?"

"Because," she'd said quietly, "I believe he needs a miracle."

They had traveled the rest of the distance to the cottage in silence. When they arrived, Maria Eliza directed Galway to a secluded parking area behind the three cottages. Once they entered the middle home, Galway had had to nearly choke himself to keep from examining the rare books in the living area, and from trying to figure out the ages of some of the more obviously antique furniture in there.

They walked down the short hallway to the second bedroom, which was now closed and locked.

"I wanted to return this book," Maria Eliza said. "But now I can't get in there."

Galway grinned. "No worries, Maria Eliza," he said. "I've never been one to let a locked door keep me from important business. Just ask the file keepers at the IRS."

Maria Eliza stood by, apparently impressed, while Galway removed a shoe, removed a hollow heel on the shoe, and then removed a tiny set of lock-picking tools from the heel. Galway timed his efforts on the door and was proud to discover that he could still pick a lock in under sixty seconds.

And then he saw the books.

Now, hours later and into the wee hours of the morning, he was still looking at the books. He carefully turned another page in the sixth leather-bound book and paused briefly to reconsider the maid's reaction when she'd been here earlier.

Maria Eliza had seemed almost transfixed by the sight of the books when they'd entered this bedroom. She'd gently handed Galway the first book, then quickly walked to the shelf to remove the second book. She didn't even bother speaking to Galway at the point. She simply sank into a corner of the room and began reading, turning pages carefully and quickly.

Galway had decided not to interrupt her, and instead took his first close look at the leather-bound tome Maria Eliza had been carrying. He'd opened the cover and confirmed his suspicions that it was indeed somebody's journal, apparently the first in many volumes of journals. He'd turned to the first page, seen the clean, careful handwriting and noted with some concern the yellowed, brittle signs of aging on the pages. Then an unusual sense of, of *something* washed over him. He thought he smelled flowers or potpourri or perfume, but he wasn't sure.

Almost involuntarily, he too took a seat on the floor, leaning his back against the wooden bed frame. He had let his eyes focus on the page before him and read these first words:

The dream always begins the same way ...

†

CYRIL STRAND FOUND THE KEY UNDER THE BRICK BY THE side of the house, just where he'd expected to find it. His hands felt dirty after fumbling for it in the dark, though, and the professor hated to feel things crawling beneath his fingernails.

"Should have remembered to bring a flashlight," he muttered to himself.

Cyril paused to wipe the dirt from his shoes on the grass beside the driveway. "No need to leave any sign that I've been here," he whispered softly to no one in particular. While there, just on a whim, he peeked through the small window and into the darkened garage. Then, in his excitement, he moved to another window that benefited from the slight illumination of a neighbor's porch light.

Cyril Strand couldn't believe his luck. He knew the child's mother sometimes worked the night shift at the bakery, but he'd thought that was only on weekends. Still, the garage was empty, so the mother must have had to go to work tonight. Leaving, as she often did, her delectable little girl home to sleep through the night alone.

The professor did a little calculation in his head. He knew that when the mother worked a night shift, she was usually off by 5:00 a.m. She had always been so tired in his 8:00 a.m. calculus class after working through a long night, barely able to stay awake, let alone comprehend the principles he was teaching his students. Cyril had been happy to tutor her a few evenings at her home. He was known as a professor who cared. The bakery where the mother worked was not far—maybe ten minutes from here, given that there would be virtually no traffic this time of the morning. Cyril illuminated the dial on his watch and checked the time: 3:31 a.m. More than an hour and a half.

The professor smiled inside. He'd already taken care of that lockbox at the university, and this was his last stop before leaving the States for good. *Plenty of time*, he thought. Time enough to get what he needed to recover. And perhaps to, well, indulge himself before leaving town.

"You are an evil man," the professor snickered to himself. "They ought to call *you* Sinner."

Cyril Strand slithered up to the front of the house and was grateful this porch light was not on tonight. He slipped the key into the lock, felt the satisfying clink of tumblers moving out of his way, and quietly let himself in the door.

"Now, if I remember correctly," he whispered to himself, "Raven's room is the first one on the right."

†

WHEN THE DARKNESS FINALLY GAVE WAY TO LUCIDITY, THE Sinner found himself in the same place as when he left.

In an unfinished room, apparently in the basement of a house he didn't recognize.

Stripped to the waist.

Stretched out on what appeared to be a man-sized, wooden cross. The base of the cross was tipped into a hole in the cement floor. The top of the cross leaned precariously against a concrete wall.

His torso was wrapped in a thick, braided wire that swirled from behind the wooden axis, over his shoulder, across his chest, down around his waist, and behind the lower portion of the center beam. This thick wire bore the brunt of the Sinner's weight, though not enough to prevent an uncomfortable gravitational pull on his arms and feet. It appeared as though that wire was supposed to represent an *S* like the one in his sign.

His left hand was pulled awkwardly toward the end of the crossbeam and handcuffed to a hook embedded in the wood. His right hand was secured the same way on the other side.

His feet were bare and tied with another braided wire that wrapped his ankles together and pressed painfully against the wood about twenty-four inches above the cement hole at the base.

And his neck was wrapped in a noose made of rope, which also used a hook embedded in the top of the cross to securely attach it to the wood. There was play in the rope, however, and he could move his head freely. Apparently that part of the game would come into play later.

He kept his eyes closed at first, listening.

There was no movement in the room, though a light was apparently on. He heard breathing. Three people? Four? A mixed smell wafted by, a combination of sweat, aftershave, and fresh laundry.

He waited, and finally a voice spoke, one that he remembered with disgust.

"Amazing," the voice said. "Almost worth eleven years just to see that."

The Sinner kept his eyes closed, centered his attention toward the sound of the voice, and spat hard in that direction.

†

CHANCE ELKO KNEW WHY LINCOLN SAYLES WAS HERE. After all, he was the one who had gotten them this far. And besides, the security guard was still in his uniform, gun still faithfully at his side.

He had a pretty good idea why James Dandy was here too. The guy was huge, after all. And could obviously handle himself in a scrape.

It was also obvious why Rebel was here. For starters, trying to keep her from coming would have been like trying to jump into a swimming pool without getting wet. Rebel was used to doing what she wanted, and she wanted to be involved in this. And besides, Reb was pretty tough herself and unafraid of anything—even James Dandy. If it came to blows, Chance would probably bet on James, but Rebel was a dirty fighter, and he wouldn't count her out too fast either.

What Chance didn't know was why *he* was here. He hadn't been in a fight since Patsy Freeman had kicked him all over the schoolyard for dumping her best friend in eighth grade. He didn't have leadership skills like Rebel, or even cloak-and-dagger skills like Lincoln. Put Chance in front of a computer and he'd wipe the floor with his companions. But out here, in the real world, in the real dark of night, with what appeared to be danger lurking at every corner, and Chance had to admit he was the weak link in this team.

He tugged briefly on Rebel's sleeve. "Hey, Reb," he whispered, "tell me again why I'm here?"

Rebel just put a finger to her lips and motioned up the driveway. Chance nodded and shut up immediately. There were three cars parked by the front entrance of the mansion—a Mercedes, a Toyota pickup, and a Jaguar. Lounging around the cars and smoking cigarettes were two young men who appeared to be carrying two very large semiautomatic weapons.

Chance turned behind him to point out the guns to James, and was chagrined to discover the big man was already gone. He turned back to the front and nearly slugged himself in frustration. Lincoln Sayles was gone too.

"Reb," he rasped again, and this time she responded by clapping her hand over his face. She pulled him by the head until they were nestled in a row of bushes that lined the long driveway. Then she released his mouth and nodded in the direction of the guns.

Chance followed her gaze and made out a dark figure—James?—now crouching beside the Toyota truck, out of view of the two guards. He still didn't see Lincoln. Was he on the other side?

James twisted his body into an almost-sitting position, putting his weight on the balls of his feet and pressing his back against the driver door of the truck. He looked back in the direction where Rebel and Chance were hiding, then tapped the back of his head with his palm.

Rebel pushed Chance deeper into the bush as she stood up. "That's my cue," she said. "Stay here and don't move."

†

"WHERE'S JUNEBUG?"

"He's here. With me."

"Are his cameras all in place?"

"Yep. Three of them."

"Are they working?"

"Yep. Got a good, clean feed on all three."

"Good. Are you two in position?"

"Yep. Unless you want us somewhere else?"

"No. Just stay there."

"So what's next?"

"Now we hurry up and wait."

GALWAY FINALLY PUT DOWN THE NINTH VOLUME OF THE journals. These books definitely answered a few questions. Poland, for instance, was a myth. Antietam was not.

He felt a weariness and wished he had a steaming cup of highly caffeinated coffee. He'd brought a comfortable chair from the living room into the bedroom earlier, and that helped—better than sitting on the floor at least. But he realized that sooner or later he was going to have to get some sleep. A man his age couldn't just pull all-nighters anymore.

He looked around the bedroom, taking his first real assessment of what was in there. That was when he finally noticed the bloodied sheet and the stains on the mattress. Curious, he spread the sheet out on the bed and gave it an appraising look. Little dots of dried blood up where the head would be. Larger blood stains at the feet and torso areas. More stains where the hands would be if they were stretched out on the bed a bit.

So, he thought, *this is what the stigmata does to laundry.* He sighed, yawned, and stretched. He looked again at the bed.

Maybe I'll sleep on the couch.

†

MARIA ELIZA GARCES FELT THE MEASURED BREATHING OF her husband beside her as it gently rustled the quiet of the night. She glanced again at the digital display on the clock by their bed and wondered if she should continue to hold out hope for that elusive sleep or give up and go read or eat and wait for that last hour or two to pass before she would have to get up for work anyway.

She listened to the world around her and was struck by the way silence so often speaks to the soul.

She turned her gaze on her husband and smiled. He was a good man. Loyal, caring, hardworking. He took special pride in being a carpenter, a trade he learned as a teenager. It was only years later that he realized he'd chosen the same career path as Christ, and now whenever his clothes shed sawdust onto Maria Eliza's carpet, he would laugh and quiet her fussing. "*Amante*," he would say, "remember that Jesus was a carpenter like me, so walking on sawdust is like walking on holy ground."

"Well, that 'holy ground' is about to get sucked into my sacred vacuum cleaner," she would say, and he would laugh again, kiss her, and go change into clean clothes.

"*Gracias a Dios*," Maria Eliza whispered, thinking about the blessing of being married so long to a man she not only loved, but also really liked. And then her mind wandered back to the cottage behind the big house, and the rows of journals in that last bedroom that held so many secrets. She wondered what time that nice Mr. Collins had finally left, or if he even had. She wondered if she would find him still there the next time she opened the front door and went in to clean that little place once more. She hoped he would be there. She had more questions she wanted to ask him.

Then she thought about the one who owned those journals, the one Mr. Collins had called the Sinner.

Where is the Sinner right now? She wondered. And what kind of miracle was he seeking?

She felt a troubling within her and stole another glance at the slowly ticking clock by the bed. Sleep was such a fickle thing. But she knew something that was not so fickle.

She carefully rolled out of bed so as not to wake her husband. Then she reached into the darkness beside her mattress, retrieved a worn Bible, and made her way into the kitchen where she started a pot of coffee. While waiting for it to percolate, Maria opened her book and saw a vision.

A man, bloodied and beaten.

His face set in defiance and resignation, but not set in anger.

A cross, bearing the load of the weight of the world.

A sinner in need of a miracle.

The vision faded so quickly that Maria Eliza couldn't be sure she'd seen it at all. She breathed rapidly, wondering. She wasn't used to this kind of experience.

Her eyes focused on the open Bible before her, and she saw that some years ago she'd highlighted the reference: Luke 23:39–43. She read the words there and felt their power tingling in her mind.

"Of course," she whispered. "Of course."   †

I am a foolish, naïve little man. I am the worst of sinners, the betrayer of innocent blood. I am, and always will be, damned by my sins, by the moments that encompass eternity. By the weak-willed glance, by the eyes that are unfaithful.

By my eyes. They widen at Jennison's words and the realization that something ungodly is about to happen. I turn my head to the barn and stare. They are in there, I think to myself. They are supposed to be safe. I promised them this. I promised Celia this.

My world feels like molasses. Time slows its pace. A roaring sound begins in my ears.

Jennison looks at me carefully now, then nods once. Just once.

The fat man reacts more quickly than I would expect for a man his size. Before I can blink, he has twisted my arms painfully behind my back, forcing me to drop the sandwiches and immobilizing my body.

The narrow man slips expertly into the barn, barely making a sound.

Shout, I think to myself. Warn them. Tell them to run. Maybe there's still time.

But my open mouth refuses to respond. It is paralyzed by the fear that sinks deep within my heart.

Jennison sits like a king upon his stallion. He wipes a trickle of sweat off his brow. I see his tongue lick his chapped and dry lips. He is eager for this. He is entertained by it. And still I do nothing.

It feels like hours, but I know only minutes have passed. Five? Ten? It doesn't matter. There is no noise from the barn.

The silence speaks. It condemns me. It condemns me to hell.

Then the barn door slips open and the narrow man slides out. He is grinning. Like the Devil when he first saw Eve. He makes eye contact with Jennison and nods. Then he looks at me and gives me a tip of his hat. He is thanking me. And I feel like retching.

I finally begin to struggle, to fight against the fat man's grip. But he is strong, stronger than I am. He has a man's strength, and I am still a boy despite my age and size.

"Settle down, youngster," he hisses in my ear. I wonder if his is the voice that man and woman first heard in the Garden and which they have never been able to un-hear since. "Stop fussin', boy," he says again, wrenching my shoulder nearly out of its socket. "The smoke'll get 'em first anyway. They'll never feel a thing."

Smoke?

I look back at the barn and realize the other men are also staring expectantly at it. Hungrily.

Destine begins to pull on her bindings. She, like me, feels uncomfortably close to danger.

It begins with a wisp that puffs out under the bottom of the big barn doors. A charcoal gray fabric of ash and air. In seconds that wisp becomes a billow of smoke streaming steadily through the cracks in the barn.

The roaring sound in my head becomes audible on the outside. My barn is filled with hay, and hay burns so very, very quickly. I hear the fire inside eating, devouring the hay scattered throughout the barn's belly. I hear it gnawing on the wood within. It growls at me and reminds me who I am. And what I am.

There is no sound of human voices. No screams or cries for help. No great crashing as a man breaks through a wall with his precious daughter in his hands. No coughing or sputtering or frenzied pursuit of breath and air.

Just the fire, eating, always eating, always hungry for more.

We all stand transfixed, watching as the first flames crack through the roof of the barn, and then lick their way down the walls and around the building.

Would it have been so hard to shout a warning? I think to myself. You promised her a safe place. A resting place. You promised.

The barn is engulfed in fire now. I feel the sparks fly around me, feel the terrible heat of the day dwarfed and consumed by the blazing flames in my barn. My eyes burn, as though they are being sprinkled with red-hot cinders.

The barn, my family's barn, it burns so fast, like the fabric of my soul.

The fat plume of smoke rises high into the sky. Maybe my neighbors will see it. Maybe they will come. But for now I stand mute with my tormentors, watching in awe and sacred sadness as the consuming fire sucks the life and breath out of anything it touches.

And finally it is over. The fire seeks more to burn, but simply cannot find enough to fuel its voracious appetite. The roaring subsides. The walls and roof and those great big doors have long since collapsed. There is more to burn, and the fire will still lick greedily for some hours to come. But the worst has past. It will burn itself out before nightfall.

Just a few hours ago, in the promise of morning, I held in my arms a miracle. I held on my chest a beauty of creation. The majesty of God placed its little head on my shoulder and trusted me enough to sleep there.

And I failed her. No, I betrayed her, like Judas and his kiss.

Jennison finally turns back to me and nods. The fat man releases his grip, and I feel the pain of blood rushing back into my arms. I drop to a knee, still staring at what used to be my barn.

The narrow man is returning to his horse. Jennison looks grim. He reaches into his pocket and pulls out three gold coins.

"For the trouble," he says, tossing them at me. They fall dead at my feet, like thirty pieces of silver strewn in a temple. The fat man hesitates, then picks them up and stuffs them into the pocket of my vest.

"Well, gentlemen," Jennison says with finality. "I believe our work here is done." The fat man and the narrow man respond immediately, mounting their horses and turning them toward the road that leads off my family's farm.

Jennison nods cordially to me. "Thank you much, Mr. Beverly Thomas. We could never have got those slaves without you." He turns his back on me, and all three men ride casually away. I am left with only my sorrow, and with my unforgivable guilt.

I am a foolish, naïve little man.

I am the worst of sinners, the betrayer of innocent blood.

I am, and always will be, damned by my transgressions, by the moments that encompass eternity.

I am, now and forevermore, worthy of only one name:

Sinner.

FOURTEEN

CYRIL STRAND STOOD IN SILENCE FOR A MOMENT, holding his position in the doorway until his eyes adapted to the shadows reflected by the princess night-light. He waited until he could distinguish the child from the mound of plush animals and blankets on the little pink bed in the corner of the room.

He felt hungry.

"Raven," he spoke softly, so as not to scare the child, but loud enough to interrupt whatever pleasant dream she might be having. She didn't stir, so he said it again. "Raven. It's time to wake up."

The child fluttered a bit, almost like a butterfly spreading its wings as it tried to decide whether to fly away. Then she became still again.

Cyril frowned. "Raven," he spoke more loudly this time, firmly. "Wake up."

The child sat up suddenly, obviously scared by the voice she'd heard in her sleep. She stared toward Cyril with uncomprehending eyes. Cyril finally smiled.

"Raven, it's me. Professor Strand."

The child's lower lip quivered. "Where's my mom?"

"Still at work, honey. She'll be home soon."

"Are you watching me?"

Professor Strand chuckled at the thought. "No, honey, I'm not your babysitter tonight."

Raven nodded, silent.

Cyril took a step closer to the bed. "Raven, you remember those pictures we took before? The ones of us with Father Renault?"

Raven swallowed hard. She was apparently trying to fight back tears. Cyril watched her clutch for one particular plush animal—an elephant with pink ears—and noticed her hands were already trembling. He relaxed. He had her now. She was too afraid to do anything but what he told her to do.

Cyril continued, "You know which ones I'm talking about, don't you, Raven? Remember how we laughed and called them our 'naughty pictures'?"

The child was crying now, softly. "Yes," she said.

"Remember how we hid some of those here in your room, Raven? So we could look at them together sometimes as our fun little secret from your mom?"

Raven simply nodded, still crying without making a sound.

"Well, I need to get those pictures now, okay, Raven? I need to take them away so some bad men don't find them and think that you're a bad little girl for taking your clothes off with two older men. You understand, Raven?"

The child nodded again. "I don't like you, Professor Strand." She choked out the words. "I don't like those pictures or when you come over here to take more. I want my mom."

Cyril frowned again. "Well, you are a rude little girl tonight, aren't you, Raven?" Then he softened. "But that's okay. I forgive you, sweetheart. I know you are just tired."

"I want my mom."

"Well, she's not here right now, is she?" Cyril snapped. "Now, get me those pictures before I get angry."

The child slid obediently out of bed and went to her closet where she dug around among the toys and clothes that covered the floor. In a moment she emerged with an envelope. She handed it to the professor, then quickly ran back to her bed where she pulled the covers over her head.

Cyril Strand walked toward the night-light and pulled the contents of the envelope out for a quick inspection. Yes, they were there. All of them. He smiled. Those had been good times. Before, of course, the Sinner had shown up and nearly killed Renault.

He shuddered. He had to leave soon. Get away before the Sinner could find him as well. He licked his lips, and paused.

"Raven?"

There was no answer from underneath the covers.

"Raven, your mom won't be back for at least another hour or two," he cooed. "Would you like me to stay with you for a while, to make sure you're safe until she gets back?"

The child still didn't answer.

"Raven, I'm speaking to you."

"No," she said finally. "I want my mom. Call my mom."

"You know I can't do that, honey," the professor sighed. "But I can stay with you, for an hour at least. I can comfort you."

He licked his lips and wondered if Raven was still crying.

"Move over, honey," he said hungrily. "Make room so I can lie next to you for a while."

Professor Strand removed his belt. He was pretty sure Raven was still crying.

✝

REBEL MUSSED HER HAIR A BIT AS SHE WALKED DOWN THE long driveway. She consciously relaxed her limbs and gave a little wobble to the heels of her feet. She figured music was appropriate for a night like tonight, so she started humming "The Eyes of Texas" in a slightly off-key voice.

The two gang members picked her up almost right away. She saw them raise their guns instinctively, and watched as the one on her right took a step forward.

"Hey, lady," he called out. "You're on private property. You better leave. Now."

Rebel kept wobbling toward the front of the house, now breaking into a big smile. "Oh, excellent! There is somebody here. Woo-ahh! That's a relief."

Rebel watched as the second gang member paused to check out her figure and then whisper something into the ear of his partner. They both grinned for a moment before the first one became all business again.

"Not messing with you, lady. You can't be here."

"Lissen, fellas," she said carelessly, "my car just hit a tree about a half mile down the road, and now the stupid metal can won't drive 'cause the wheel well is all bent in, and—" She pretended to finally notice the two guns waving in her direction. "Woo-ahh, you guys don't mess around, do ya? Whatcha got those guns for?"

"To keep drunks like you out on the road where you belong," the second one said.

Rebel put a hand to her mouth in mock surprise as she carefully positioned herself on the opposite side of the cars, standing between the Toyota truck and the Mercedes. She could see James out of the corner of her eye, still crouching with his back against the truck. She had not yet spotted the security guard, and she worried briefly that maybe he wasn't as reliable as James. She forged ahead anyway.

"He is a little spicy, isn't he?" she said conspiratorially to the first gun. "But that's okay," she winked, "'cause I'm a little spicy myself sometimes." She laughed at her own joke.

The first gang member seemed to relax a bit, obviously not sensing any real danger from a woman too drunk to drive a car home safely. The second one was not so comfortable.

He cursed her angrily, then started toward her with his gun waving.

"Such language," Rebel mocked as she took a step or two backward to give James a little more room. "Lissen, honey, I just want to use a phone to call somebody, and then I'll be outta your hair in nothing flat."

The first gang member just stood there grinning, enjoying the drama unfolding before him. But the second gun stepped between the truck and the Mercedes and ordered, "No, 'honey,' you gonna be outta my hair right now or else you won't—"

James sprang from behind the truck with the speed and ferocity of a linebacker. He knocked the gunman at least eight feet down the pavement before collapsing on top of him. The gun went clattering under the Mercedes, forgotten in the collision. Rebel looked up and was pleased to see Lincoln standing with his firearm behind the other gang member's left ear, effectively disarming and immobilizing him in seconds.

James stood to his full height, hauling his gang member up until his feet dangled a few inches off the ground. Rebel saw that her bodyguard had wrapped his burly biceps under the young man's armpit and clamped his wrists together on the side of the gang member's neck.

"Sleeper hold," she murmured. "Guatemalan security officer taught him that one. James is a little unorthodox in the way he executes it, but also extremely effective. That kid'll be out pretty soon."

Lincoln now held the first gang member's automatic weapon and was forcing him to lie facedown on the concrete.

James continued to squeeze the other one's neck. Most people crushed the victim onto the ground during a sleeper hold, but James liked to keep his subjects dangling just off the ground. He said it helped the "emotional, instinctual fear response" because the victim felt more helpless when he couldn't touch the ground, like a rat dangling from the mouth of a cat. Rebel took a step closer so she could better hear what was going on between those two.

"—mama ever teach you how to treat a lady?" James was saying. "Then you wouldn't need me to teach you that kind of stuff, now would you?" He gave an extra squeeze, and Rebel could see the young man pale. His eyelids fluttered as his brain was being denied oxygen.

"You will have a headache when you wake up," James whispered. "If I let you wake up."

The gang member tried to thrash a bit then, but it was a feeble attempt. His knees sagged, and suddenly James let go. The boy wilted to the pavement, gasping, but still conscious.

James leaned over and said, "How many?"

The gang member coughed.

"How many?" James asked again. "Five?"

The gang member raised his fist in a rude hand gesture. The bodyguard picked him back up and reapplied the sleeper hold until the boy passed out. He dragged the gang member to the back of the Toyota where he produced a pair of handcuffs and attached the boy's wrists to the bumper of the truck. Then he turned to Rebel.

"I'm going to need your cuffs too, please," he said. She tossed them over without hesitation.

The gang member on the ground had watched all the

action without saying a word. Now he began to get agitated. "Dude, what'd you do to Zee over there? Is he dead? You ain't choking me to death, no way."

Lincoln kicked him in the side, causing the young man to catch his breath. "Don't speak unless you are spoken to. Dude."

James walked over to the boy on the pavement and knelt down beside him. "How many?" he asked again.

The boy said nothing. Lincoln aimed another kick toward his rib cage, but James motioned for him to halt the kick. "Not necessary, Link," he said. "As I feel the need to rob yet another of the Crux Crue of the breath of life." He reached out with big hands and began to draw the gang member into another sleeper hold.

"Fourteen!" the boy shouted in alarm. "There's fourteen of us guarding the house tonight." He tried to roll away from the bodyguard, only to find Lincoln's boot shoving him back.

James continued. "How many outside and how many inside?"

"There's just me and Zee on the outside. The rest are stationed on the inside of this creepy house. The boss man figures the real threat isn't out here."

"Where is the real threat?"

"Down there in the basement."

†

THE SINNER LET HIS EYES OPEN NOW, AND WAS PLEASED TO see he had been on target. This basement cubicle was all concrete and studs, waiting for a visionary construction worker to turn it into a game room or a bedroom or even a bathroom and spa. The ceiling was surprisingly high for a basement, at least twelve feet up. Plenty of room to hang him later, if they wanted to do that. But right now they seemed to be enjoying the torture more.

There were two young gang members in the room with him—the same two who had abducted him from outside the restaurant. But as far as he was concerned, they were irrelevant. The real danger was the middle-aged, balding man who was now wiping spittle off his designer suit with a very expensive cloth handkerchief.

The Sinner couldn't resist. "Nice to see you again, Johnson," he said conversationally. "How's your daddy doing these days?"

An icy hatred glazed over the eyes of the middle-aged man. The left-handed gang member—Marcel?—stepped forward to respond, but Loftis Johnson stopped him with a gesture.

The Sinner began listening to the creaking and humming of the floorboard above him, trying to determine how many people were in this house, trying to guess where the exits would be, seeking clues that would benefit him when it was time to escape.

Johnson had finished wiping off his coat now and was walking toward the man bound on the cross.

"You really are an amazing specimen," he said. "I always wondered how you seemed to last forever. You look no older than the day I first saw you. And yet here I am, squarely in middle age, even though we were both about the same age when—" he paused, then said, "well, before."

"Flattery will get you nowhere, old man," the Sinner said.

Johnson pulled a pen from inside his coat pocket. He used it to point to an area along the Sinner's collarbone. "My friends here broke that bone at least once during the previous beating," he said. "I heard it crack myself." He pointed to his captive's jaw and eye. "Cuts up here, contusions in this area. Look, you can still see the blood from those wounds staining our fine cross here."

He stepped back again. "I'll give you credit. You can take pain. But you, my friend, were one pulpy mess when you finally passed out." Marcel grinned proudly and exchanged glances with Renzio.

"And that's when it got interesting," Johnson continued. "Oh, not at first, of course. But not long after."

He leaned in close to the Sinner's face, so close that the captive briefly considered biting his enemy's nose before dismissing the action as futile. "Strange things happen when you sleep," Johnson said with an air of dramatic mystery.

"Got that right," Renzio muttered from near the doorway. "Guy freaks me out just to look at him."

Johnson ignored the comment. "First, the hands," he continued. "Is it like that with all stigmatics? The wounds from the hands appear first?"

"I don't control it," the Sinner said evenly. "It controls me."

"I see. So sometimes the other wounds appear first. Interesting. Well, tonight at least, it was the hands first. Gashed open so fast I felt like I was in a horror movie. Then the feet and head, almost simultaneously. Last was the side. That one looked like it hurt."

The Sinner calculated the distance between the cross and the door. "Where am I?" he asked abruptly, ignoring Loftis Johnson's story. He'd heard something like it before.

Johnson merely smiled, a smug satisfied smile that told the Sinner this man had been planning his revenge for years. "That's right," he said, "you've never actually been inside this house, have you? You did all your dirty work out there on the driveway leading in from the front gate."

The Sinner nodded. So it was the elder Johnson's old estate. How ironic.

"Place feels old and empty."

"It is," Johnson said. "After your last visit, I could barely stand to be here. So when my father finally died, I fired the entire servant staff, moved Mother to Connecticut, and closed this house up for good." He gave a rueful look. "But I never sold this estate. I always knew that someday you'd come back. And when you did, I knew I'd need this empty old house just one more time."

"So thoughtful of you to keep this estate just for my visits."

The hatred flared in Johnson's eyes again. "I killed you once, but it was sloppy, unfinished. I really am going to kill you this time. But first I'm going to make you suffer, the way you made my father suffer. And it will be for years. Years before I finally let you die."

"You don't know the meaning of suffering."

"Well, then," Johnson growled. "Perhaps I'll learn something about it from watching you." He studied the Sinner's face for a moment before continuing. "It's the dreams, isn't it? It all happens in the dreams."

"You don't know what you're talking about."

"Of course I do. And you know it too. Tell me, have you seen all this in your dreams?"

The Sinner's nostrils flared. "Yes."

"Oh, convenient," Johnson smirked. "And how did it end?"

"Badly."

"Of course."

"For you."

†

"IF ANY PART OF YOUR POISONOUS BODY TOUCHES THAT child, I will personally break it off."

Cyril Strand jumped at the sound of the voice coming from the closet. "Who's there? What do you want?"

A woman stepped out from the darkness of the closet. Angry. Fit. Ready for battle.

"First I want you to put your fat, pasty-white hindquarters back into those ample pants of yours. Next, I want you to back away from that child's bed before I have to hurt you."

Cyril contemplated the situation. He weighed at least twice as much as this woman. Perhaps he could overpower her?

She settled into a fighting pose. Apparently she knew some kind of martial arts or something. And she definitely showed no fear.

Cyril hastily trousered himself. "Now just take it easy, young lady. You wouldn't want anybody to get hurt, would you?"

She gave a grim chuckle. "Actually, there is one person I'd like to see get hurt quite a bit."

Cyril started to say something, but the look she gave him made him think better of it.

She stared hard at him, as if she were deciding what to do next. Cyril considered simply turning and walking out of the room, out of the house, and out of the country. But now there was a witness to his misdeeds, and he knew he would need to do something about that. So he waited.

The woman finally spoke, but not to him, though she never took her eyes off him. "Raven, you okay, sweetie?"

"Uh-huh," the child said, now peeking out from beneath the covers. "Did I do it right, CK?"

"You were perfect, sweetheart. Just perfect."

Now the woman spoke into thin air. "Junebug? You get it all?" She nodded, apparently hearing a positive response from somewhere. Was she wearing an earpiece?

Cyril began to get really nervous. "So, miss," he said in what he hoped was a dignified, threatening tone. "What do we do now?"

The woman relaxed her posture a bit. "Well, Professor," she said, "I'd really like to just beat the crap out of you. But I think I'm going to have to get in line." She nodded toward the door behind him.

Cyril turned quickly and felt his heart sink. Standing in the doorway was Raven's mother. And behind her was that detestable police officer, Sean Stepp. The detective reached around the mother and switched on the bedroom light, suddenly revealing two surveillance cameras and a third still photography camera ensconced in corners of the ceiling.

"I trusted you," the mother spoke with disbelief in her voice. "I took your classes because I thought you were one professor who really cared about his students. How could you do this to her? To me?"

Cyril Strand only said, "I want my lawyer."

The mother pushed past him and went to her daughter in the bed. "Oh, Raven," she wept, "I'm so sorry. Mommy is so, so sorry. I will never let this man hurt you again. Not ever."

"My thoughts exactly," the detective said now, holding up a pair of handcuffs.

The fighting woman spoke into the air again. "Nice work, Junebug," she said. "As usual. Get those tapes and photos ready for Sean and then let's get out of here."

Cyril Strand watched with mounting fear as Detective Stepp was joined by two blue-uniformed officers. He winced when the detective tightened the handcuffs past what he had to know would be a comfortable fit. He watched the fighting woman kneel beside the child's bed.

"You're going to be fine from now on, Raven."

"Thanks to you, CK," the mother said. "I don't know what we would have done if you hadn't come to warn us last night."

The fighting woman shrugged. "All I had was a name, given to me by, well, by a friend I guess." She motioned back to the detective. "Sean here is the one who put it all together."

The child spoke. "Is he going to jail?" she asked.

"Yes. For a long time," the detective answered.

The child favored the group with a hesitant smile.

"Thank you, CK. Thank you, Mr. Stepp." Then she looked
at the ceiling and shouted, "Thanks, Mr. Junebug!"

From somewhere in the house—the kitchen maybe?—a
muffled voice responded. "You're welcome, Raven!"

The fighting woman stood again, gave a disgusted look
to Cyril, and then spoke to the air again. "Okay, Junebug,
let's go. It's time to start looking for Galway."

Detective Stepp spoke next, "I believe you're familiar
with this next part," he said genially, "but I still like to say
it every time anyway. Let's see now. You have the right to
remain silent …"

For some reason that he couldn't quite figure out,
Professor Cyril Strand had an irresistible urge to scream just
then. And so he did.

Like a little girl.

†

JOHNSON BACKHANDED THE PRISONER, AND THE SINNER
felt the thread of a diamond ring cut the skin across the
bridge of his nose, felt the warm blood begin to drizzle
down toward his mouth. Johnson snorted derisively.

"I know that won't last," he said with a nod toward the
blood, "but it felt good to do it anyway."

The Sinner leaned his head back against the wood and
spoke cruelly. "Is now when I'm supposed to weep and beg
for my life, Junior? 'Please,'" he mocked, "'I'll make it right.
I'll give them all money. Just don't hurt me again.'"

He could see the rage covering his adversary's entire body.
That was good. Angry men make irrational mistakes, and the

irrational mistakes of others always worked in his favor. But Johnson quickly recognized the weakness. His eyes became a mask, his hands spread open beside him. There was a moment of silence, then he continued.

"Well, shortly after the wounds of the stigmata had opened, they closed again, leaving only the scars we now see." He pointed to the Sinner's hands, feet, and side. "Then the real miracle."

"Freaky stuff if you ask me," Renzio muttered, "I'm gonna have nightmares for weeks."

"I watched your wounds stitch themselves together. I put my hand on your collarbone and felt the bone mend itself. I saw your shoulder relocate itself, saw your skin become fresh and new all by itself, in a matter of hours. All while you slept like a baby."

Johnson shook his head. "I am not easily impressed, but you impressed me with that little trick. So how do you do it? Heal yourself like that?"

"I don't control it," the Sinner repeated. "It controls me."

Johnson nodded thoughtfully. "What were you dreaming when the bone fixed itself?"

"Nothing."

"Nothing?"

"I never dream during the healing times."

"Ah. Interesting." He held out a hand toward Renzio. The gang member promptly placed a switchblade in his hand. "I am curious," Johnson said, "how long does it take to heal something like this?"

He cut a quick swath across the Sinner's forearm,

looking satisfied when blood welled to the surface. The Sinner didn't flinch.

"Or this, perhaps?" Johnson now sliced hard at the Sinner's face, cutting deeply, almost all the way to the cheekbone. The Sinner felt blinded by the immediate pain. Johnson just waited.

Finally, through gritted teeth, the Sinner mumbled, "I don't control it. Sometimes it heals overnight. Other times the same type of wound will take weeks of sleep."

Johnson nodded. "Or possibly even years?"

The Sinner nodded once, fighting to compartmentalize the pain in his face, struggling for lucidity, feeling the need to fight against the darkness that was beginning to cloud his brain.

Johnson stuck out a hand in Marcel's direction. It was quickly filled with a fist-sized handgun.

"Here's what I know," Johnson said calmly. "When you wake up next—could be tomorrow, could be a year from now—the wounds I have just given you will be mercifully gone."

The Sinner felt his hearing fading. He fought to concentrate.

"In fact, it appears that the only way I can scar you permanently is to follow God's lead and hurt you in the way that he has already done so."

Please, the Sinner prayed, *just spare me the dreams this time*. He felt the blackness making him dizzy and light-headed.

"Which means I must leave my mark right here." Loftis Johnson pressed the barrel of his gun against the lower left palm of his captive. The clap of thunder that followed buried a bullet into the wood behind the hand, and easily tore open the scar of the stigmata. A second clap of thunder followed on the other side.

The Sinner could no longer see, and could only hear sounds as though they were wrapped in cotton before being delivered to his ears. His skin cried out in agony, but his mouth never opened, never groaned. He felt the gun barrel now pressed against the top of his layered feet.

"Now we'll see who begs for mercy."

He did not hear the final claps of thunder, three rapid-fire, successive shots that passed through the flesh and bones in his feet and tore at the wooden beam beneath them. Instead he was cocooned in the healing blackness of a lucid dream. But there was something different this time.

Loftis Johnson was in there with him.

✝

HECTOR GOMEZ WOKE UP CRYING AGAIN, BUT THIS TIME HE buried his face in his pillow so as not to wake up his parents. After a moment he raised his face out of the bedclothes and gulped the clean air that surrounded him.

It was the man on the cross again. They were hurting him more and more. They kept hurting him, taking turns, even after the man had passed out from the pain. And no one ever tried to stop them. Why did no one ever try to stop them?

Hector collected his breathing and stared quietly at the ceiling. Finally he knew he had to do something. He slipped quietly from under his sheets and then knelt comfortably beside his bed.

"Jesus," he whispered. "I have seen them. Someone needs to stop them, but I'm just a kid. I can't fight. But I can pray, and Mama says you answer the prayers of little boys. So that's how I will stop them. By praying for you to do something. Soon."

Hector stayed there for a while, longer than he was used to, but not so long that he was uncomfortable. When he finally stood and crawled back in bed, he felt as though he hadn't done much, but that what he had done was enough. He drifted quickly off to sleep, and while he slept, he dreamed of happy places.

He dreamed this time of heaven.

GALWAY HAD BARELY LAIN DOWN ON THE LIVING ROOM couch before he heard the muffled sound of thunder. He wondered why there had been no lightning. He heard a second faint thunderclap, but again, no lightning. Curious, he got up and walked to the window to look at the sky. It was, as was to be expected at this time of night, dark like ink and quiet like the sea. He could see the outline of a crescent moon above the tree line, but because these cottages were nestled into the seclusion of the wooded path, he couldn't see much beyond the place where he had parked his car.

He felt the sagging of his bones and knew his body needed sleep, just a few hours of sleep. He stared a moment longer out the window and heard three more faint claps of thunder, one hammering right after the next. They seemed to come from the direction of the main house up the path. Galway tensed. Was someone up there?

He waited, but now the night was silent. He wanted to wait a bit longer, or even to sneak up to the big house and check things out. But the body can take only so much deprivation. He felt his eyelids sagging even as he stood at the window.

All was still and quiet out there.

Finally he turned. "Can't solve every mystery that comes in the middle of the night," he muttered. "I am only one man."

He stretched his creaky frame back on the couch and laid his head against a throw pillow. He was asleep before he could count to ten.

†

CHANCE ELKO SAT IN THE BUSHES, QUIETLY THANKFUL THAT Rebel had ordered him to stay here until she said to move. He was also thankful that Reb had apparently forgotten him, so that he could stay out of the fray in front of the big house.

James and Lincoln had taken out the two gang members with surprising speed. Chance had watched James turn that mean one into Silly Putty, and reminded himself again that he was happy to be on good terms with the big fella. The second gang member had been no problem either and apparently had given James all the information he had asked for. After a brief interrogation, James had handcuffed the second gang member to the front bumper of the Mercedes. It was only then that Rebel seemed to have remembered her little computer geek in the bushes. She'd turned and waved for him to join them. When he reached their little circle, he heard James speaking earnestly to Rebel.

"Fourteen guards is too many, Rebel. We can't stay here. We've got to get the police and come back in force."

"Forget it, James," Rebel said. "We leave now and the two moron twins you attached to the bumpers will start screaming their heads off to get the attention of the gang boys inside. By the time we get back, they are long gone."

"Rebel, fourteen is just too many."

Rebel threw up her hands in disgust. "First of all," she said, "it's only twelve, big guy. Remember, you took out the first two already."

"Still, we have no idea where the others are positioned inside the house. We have no idea how well armed they are."

"We should assume they have guns," Lincoln said.

"Right," James said. "We need backup and, no offense, Chance, our computer hero here just isn't enough."

"None taken."

"I think your man is right," Lincoln said. "We can't take the risk when the odds are this high and with all the unknowns. We have to get the police and come back."

"Don't you get it? If we try to get the police, they'll have to get a search warrant. They'll have to get teams organized and fill out paperwork. They'll want to question why we came here from Oklahoma City, and what we were doing surveilling this private residence in the first place. With all the red tape and bureaucracy, I'm betting it'll be twelve hours minimum before we can get anybody back here willing to storm this place."

"It's a risk we have to take, Rebel," James said. "Maybe CK can get her detective buddy to speed things up with a judge or something to get that search warrant faster."

"James," Rebel was almost pleading now. "He's in there, I know it. The Sinner himself. The legend, the myth, whatever. We may never have this chance again."

James sighed, then glanced back at the house. "I'm sorry, Rebel, but as your bodyguard I can't let you go in there. Not without backup. Your father would never forgive me."

Rebel's eyes flashed at the mention of her father. She spat through clenched teeth. "Come on, Chance," she said. "We're going in and we'll leave these big sissies to stand out here and do needlework or whatever it is that cowards do in the night."

"Uh, hey, Rebel, I don't think—"

"*Et tu*, Chance?" Rebel shook her head with scorn. "Fine." She pushed past Lincoln and started walking toward the house.

"Hey, lady," the Crux from the Mercedes was calling. "Your big friend is right. You really don't want to go in there alone. Trust me."

Rebel made a hand gesture that some would consider unladylike and kept walking. Suddenly the sound of gunfire erupted from somewhere inside the house. Chance nearly jumped out of his skin, and for a moment almost dove under the Toyota truck, but when he saw that no one else was taking cover he stopped himself and edged toward the truck instead. Rebel paused on the sidewalk, cocked her head, and waited.

"Reb, please," James was angling toward her from behind. "Think this through."

A second gunshot echoed in the hollow house. A moment passed in silence, and then three successive shots fired in rapidity like a jackhammer. Then, finally, there was quiet.

"Somebody musta got uppity in there," the gang member said. "Can't have an uppity prisoner, if you know what I mean."

There was a moment of indecision on the part of the lady detective. Then she took a cautious step forward.

"Rebel—"

"No, James," she called over her shoulder, "I'm done thinking. Now is the time for action."

"Rebel, I can't let you do this."

"Try and stop me."

The bodyguard didn't hesitate. He was on her before her boots could touch the first step, applying a sleeper hold like a pit bull biting on a snake.

"You're right, Rebel," James said gravely. "Now is the time for action."

Rebel was both shocked and furious. She beat against his face and arms, flapping and gasping. She finally started to wilt, but managed to slap at James' face once or twice more.

"I won't forget this, James," she choked out as her eyes fluttered.

"I know, Reb," James whispered kindly. "But at least

you'll be alive to make me regret doing this. If you were dead, I'd regret not doing it even more."

Her body went limp, and James swept her up in his arms like a rag doll. He turned toward Lincoln and Chance and started walking down the long driveway to the gated entrance.

"Come on," he said. "Let's go get backup."   †

I do not know how long I have kneeled in the yard, staring at the smoking embers of what once was my family's barn. Minutes? Hours? Days? It doesn't matter. Nothing matters now except my guilt and shame.

Destine whinnies from her tree. She has nearly lost her mind with the panic of fire so near. She deserves better, she is better. But all she has is me, and I understand now that all I have left in the world is her.

My family is gone away. I will be gone before they get back. I will never see them again. My future is gone. I have only my past. And it is now nothing more than a nightmare.

I find myself walking, as if undead, toward Destine. She looks at me through glazed eyes, flecks of spittle still on her cheeks, harsh red marks where her bridle has rubbed her face raw while she tried to escape the nearness to the flames. She recognizes me and calms, straining now to reach me. I unhook the bridle from her head and let it drop to the ground. She is unsaddled, but that is nothing to me. I have been a country boy my entire life, and riding a horse bareback is almost like walking.

In a moment, I am astride her, and she is trotting toward the road that leads away from my family's farm. I press my face deep into her neck and feel the bitter tears mingle with her mane. I feel as though I should take one last look at the life I am leaving behind. But I cannot. I am a sinner, and sinners deserve nothing more than a memory of heaven.

I wrap my hands around the thickness of Destine's mane and kick. I do not yet know where I will go. Destine will take me and I will trust her like Celia trusted me. We run down roads and through meadows and across streams. We run, then trot, then walk until Destine finds water to fill her thirst. And then we run again.

It is two days before I finally regain my senses, at least somewhat. We have been riding, Destine and I, through night and sun. I have slept on her back while she walked, challenged her sides to run while I am awake. She is ragged and stumbling. I cannot tell if she has slept or not, though I know she must have sometimes while I was asleep.

It is late in the day now. I see the sun beginning to set on the horizon. I cannot remember my name. I do not know where I am. Destine has stopped to eat grass from a lush green meadow. I hear cicadas beating, feel a breeze blowing, see clouds forming in the sky. My tongue feels like leather, my skin rough and beaten by the ride and the sun.

I finally cry out to God.

I am alone. I am a sinner.

God forgive me.

In the meadow I hear birds chirping. I hear a small animal racing through the grass. I hear the soft whoosh *of wind working its way through leaves. But I do not hear God.*

God forgive me! Give me a sign that you will forgive me.

I shout my prayer now. I shout it over and over and over, screaming for mercy from the Creator.

But night soon falls, and there is no answer from heaven.

I am alone. I am a sinner.

I am, and always will be, the unforgiven.

FIFTEEN

KEENA COLLINS WALKED OUT OF THE KITCHEN AT CK Ivors' house and made her way quietly toward the large workroom in the back. She'd had a late lunch, but she was still the only one awake in this big house so far.

CK and Junebug had gotten back around five in the morning, just as Keena was getting up to make coffee. They had huddled for a bit to talk strategy, and then when Junebug actually fell asleep in his chair, CK had given up and gone to bed. When Junebug woke up a few minutes later, he had moved to one of the couches in the game room where he still slept even now.

James Dandy, Rebel Feine, and Chance Elko had arrived

not long after that. Rebel looked groggy and angry, with swollen eyes and an unsteady walk. She hadn't spoken to anyone, just marched upstairs to the guest room CK had prepared for her earlier. James had shrugged, stopped in the kitchen to make a phone call, and then made his way down to a room in the basement. Chance was nervous and jittery and not sleepy at all—until he went into the game room, and then he had commandeered the second couch as his sleeping pallet for what was left of the night.

And Galway? Well, nobody knew where Galway was. According to CK, that was the number-one order of business when everyone woke up.

Keena checked her watch. It was almost 1:30 p.m. already. She worried about how long to wait before waking a few people up. Finally she decided she'd wait until 2:00 p.m. If nobody was awake by then, she'd jiggle Junebug to ask how long she should let the boss lady sleep.

Meanwhile, she decided to find out what was so great about all those Superman toys CK had on her shelves.

SEAN STEPP COULD NOT BELIEVE WHAT HE WAS HEARING.

"Now just wait a minute, Judge Marks," he said angrily. "First you pressured our police chief to order a delay on my team's raid of the home, even though we had probable cause, witnesses, and full authority to go into that house right away."

"Detective, you know who owns that house, and you know what kind of negative press he could cause for your whole police department if you'd gone barging in there and found nothing. You should be thanking me for safeguarding your image with the public. Your chief of police certainly agreed with that course of action, didn't he?"

"Then you delay for *hours* making a decision on granting a search warrant that would supposedly 'safeguard' our authority to enter that house. And now you're telling me that you are going to deny the warrant request outright? You've got to be kidding."

"Watch your tone, Detective. I am a judge, and I have responsibilities just like you do. What, am I supposed to tell the fine citizens of this district who showed up for court today—that I can't hear their cases because Sean Stepp wants my attention?"

"Yes!" Sean fairly shouted into the phone receiver. "Of course you are, Judge, and you know that. When a warrant request for an ongoing investigation comes to you with a high priority label, yes, you are supposed to recess your court and address the warrant first. By now our suspects—and their evidence—may be long gone."

"Well, then you obviously don't need that search warrant anyway. And you are now wasting my time. Good-bye, Detective."

"Just a minute," Sean was seething inside. "I've got four witnesses at the scene last night who are willing to testify that the Crux Crue have broken into and taken over that mansion. That those gang members are armed and dangerous. That they heard five gunshots between 4:00 a.m. and 5:00 a.m. And that they have a strong suspicion, based on conversations with Crux members outside the house, that

someone is being held captive inside that mansion's walls.
And now you're going to deny my men the authority to
search the premises in a timely way? How can you do this,
man? What possible reason can you have for this inane kind
of decision making?"

The judge's voice was clipped and frosty. "For your
information, Detective, I have spoken with the owner of
that home, just today, in between court appointments."

"Johnson." Sean said the name like a curse.

"Why, yes. Mr. Loftis Johnson himself phoned me."

"How much is he paying you, Marks?"

"Mr. Johnson informed me that he is personally at the
premises in question, that he invited a few 'troubled youths'
to a retreat at his house in a philanthropic effort to help
these kids turn from a life on the streets."

Sean snorted.

"Mr. Johnson said that a few drunken revelers breached
his security gate last night, but they were turned away peace-
ably, and that all was quiet and in good order at his mansion."

"What about the gunshots? What were those? Loud
kisses among friends?"

"Your attitude is disrespectful and pathetic. I would expect
better from an officer of the law with your reputation."

"Listen, Judge Marks. Whatever Johnson is paying you,
or threatening you with, it's not enough. This guy is dirty,
and if you let me into that house I can prove it."

"Can you? Mr. Johnson has survived assaults on his
character in the past."

"Judge, just give me the search warrant." A pause.
"Emerson, please."

There was a brief silence on the other end of the line. Then, "No, Detective Stepp. Your request for a search warrant to the property in question is denied. Now, if you'll excuse me, I've got work to do."

Sean Stepp held the phone receiver in his hand until the recorded voice chanted, "If you'd like to make a call, please hang up and try again. If you need help, hang up and then dial your operator."

Finally he clicked the receiver until he got a new dial tone. *Well,* he thought determinedly, *there's more than one judge in this happy little burg.*

†

THE SINNER FELT HIS CONSCIOUSNESS RETURN ABRUPTLY and resisted the urge to open his eyes. He listened carefully, trying to assess the situation before letting those around him recognize that he was awake. He knew without looking that the holes in his hands and feet had healed completely. There was not even a tingle in his face where Johnson's knife had cut him to the bone.

He wondered how long he had been sleeping. In the past, wounds with that kind of severity had taken weeks of sleeping to heal. But there were a few times when wounds of a mortal nature had healed in just a few hours of sleep.

I really don't control it, he mused to himself. *If I did, I would turn it off and just sleep forever. But I haven't been given that choice.*

He tried to get a sense of time, but there was none. He couldn't tell if it was day or night, whether he'd been sleeping an hour or a decade. He centered on the low voices rumbling around the room and listened.

"Trip kings, baby," one voice crowed. The Sinner recognized it almost immediately as Marcel. "I win again."

The second voice was dull and flat. "Fine, take my money. You know I'll get it back within five hands anyway."

He heard a chair scrape across the cement floor. "How long before we can get outta here?" Renzio said. "I gotta get me some sleep, man."

Marcel laughed. "You shoulda taken that little pill I offered you earlier. Look at me. I been awake as long as you and I feel great. And I'm winning all your money."

"Whatever, drug-bug. You know how I feel 'bout that kind of stuff."

There was a brief silence, then Marcel said, "Yeah, I know, bro. Kinda respect you for it too." He laughed again. "But me, I'm not so principled as you, so I take what I can get."

"Like all my money."

"Yeah, bro!" Marcel crowed again. "You're gonna have to go rob another liquor store when I'm done with you."

"Whatever."

The Sinner heard the chair slide again.

"Where you going?" Marcel asked. "You can't leave me alone with the freak over there. Johnson said that was the number-one rule."

Renzio sighed. "C'mon, bro," he said. "I gotta empty out my insides from all that Mountain Dew. You don't want me to do that in here, do you?"

The Sinner heard footsteps drawing closer, actually

smelled the mild body odor that comes with a man who's been up and active all night long.

"Dude, Johnson said not to leave until our replacements come at five."

"Yeah, and where is old moneybags himself right now?" Renzio snapped. "Sleeping away his troubles upstairs in that fancy red bed." The Sinner filed that information away in his head. He hoped to use it later. "Loftis Johnson's not going to ever know I took two minutes to go take a leak, is he?"

"I'm just saying—"

"Besides, ol' Freaky here is still out cold."

"Yeah, but look at his hands and face. Those wounds are all healed up already. That means he could wake up anytime."

"Yeah, and look at his hands and feet and head and the rest of his body. This guy ain't moving, even when he does wake up."

"Renzio, just hold it for a while longer, man. Follow orders for once."

"Ain't no rich white man gonna tell me when I can or can't go to the bathroom. I ain't on some plantation in the South, 'massa.'"

The Sinner heard the footsteps walking away, and heard Marcel sputtering to himself.

"Whatever. Stay in there 'til you fall in for all I care, bro."

He heard a match, then smelled the stale aroma of cigarette smoke floating past his face.

So he had two minutes with only one guard. That could be a good thing. Except, of course, for the fact that he was still bound securely to this big wooden cross.

†

GALWAY ALWAYS WOKE UP WITH A FEELING OF DISORIENTA-
tion, but this time it took him even longer to piece together
where he was and why he was there. A full sixty seconds
passed in confusion before he finally remembered the maid,
which then triggered the memories of the cottage and the
long row of antique journals in the back bedroom.

He checked his watch and was disgusted to discover that
he'd actually slept over ten hours. Then he shrugged. Those
antique couches could sometimes be really comfortable.

He felt his stomach grumbling about the long interval
between his last meal and the present. But it was already late
afternoon, and Galway still had a list of things to do. He
started counting them off in his head.

Find out what that strange thunder was last night.

Eat something.

Call Janine.

Go home and change clothes.

Brush teeth. Definitely brush teeth.

Call CK.

The seventh thing on his list quickly jumped to number
one in his mind. All those other chores could wait. But then
he turned toward the back bedroom and found himself sur-
veying the lines of leather-bound books again. He reached
out and pulled the tenth volume off the shelf, then settled
into his chair and resumed where he'd left off reading last
night.

Good thing books don't mind halitosis, he thought as he
turned the first page.

†

IT WAS WELL AFTER 3:00 P.M. BEFORE KEENA HAD BEEN ABLE to rouse all the people in CK's house. Whatever had gone on last night, it had left them all exhausted.

CK felt good that her assistant had taken the initiative to get things going today. The more time she spent with her, the more CK thought Keena was going to work out just fine. She made a mental note to include a finder's-fee bonus on Junebug's end-of-project paycheck.

Keena had awakened Junebug first. Once he was functioning (after drinking a full can of cold Coca-Cola), he had advised Keena to go ahead and wake up CK. That was about when Rebel came down from upstairs as well, showered and fresh for the day.

When James came up from his room in the basement, Rebel walked calmly over to him, looked him in the eyes, and then kicked him, hard, in the shin. The big man buckled, then hopped on one leg, both yelping and laughing.

"That's for the bruise on my neck," Rebel said when he'd quieted down a bit.

"And what should I expect for your wounded pride?"

"That," Rebel said comfortably, "is something that should be a surprise."

The big man smiled. "At least you're talking to me. That's a good thing."

Rebel glared at him. "And for your information, *Jim*,"—the bodyguard winced visibly—"I spent a little time on the Internet before I came down here. I learned a few defenses against big-lug sleeper holds, so consider yourself forewarned."

James held up his hands in mock surrender. "I hear and obey."

CK had watched the exchange with curious disinterest and decided she definitely wanted to sit down with Rebel later to get more details—especially about that antisleeper-hold defense. But now she had more important things to focus on.

She held up her hands, "I don't even want to know right now what's going on between you two," she said to Rebel and James. "But I do need to know if you can still work together as a team."

"Of course, CK," Rebel said immediately. "Sometimes I can't stand this big bully, but there's nobody in the world I trust more ... most of the time, anyway."

"That's very kind," James said softly. He leaned forward, "And for what it's worth, I am sorry about last night."

"Yeah, well," Rebel tried to stay mad, "you oughtta be. But right now, let's work."

"Good," CK said. "Everybody grab something to eat from the refrigerator and meet me in the lounge area near the front entrance."

✝

THE SINNER ALLOWED HIS EYES TO OPEN TO NARROW SLITS and verified what his ears had told him. There was only one guard in the room, Marcel. He was seated at a small table that held a drawer in the center. Poker chips and two decks of cards were spread on the table. Several soda cans were strewn on the floor. Two chairs sat next to the table. And except for the oversized cross and the prisoner upon it, the rest of the room was empty.

Marcel was staring warily at him, so the prisoner went ahead and opened his eyes. There was a moment of recognition as both men locked eyes.

"Mornin'," Marcel said finally. "Though it's late afternoon now, so I guess I should say 'Afternoon.'"

The Sinner added that to his collection of facts. "What day is it?"

Marcel snorted. "You slept a long time," he said, "but not that long."

The Sinner nodded. He noted that his captor was wearing—sans jewelry—the same clothes he'd had on when they kidnapped him. So, he'd healed quickly this time—in the same twenty-four-hour period.

Marcel stretched and yawned. Then he ground out his cigarette on the cement floor and stood up.

"So," he said. "Feel like a little exercise?"

The Sinner adjusted his weight on the cross, pushing on his bound feet for support. He felt something creak within the wood beneath his soles. *Interesting*, he thought. "What did you have in mind?" he said aloud.

Marcel opened the drawer in the table and moved its contents a bit. The Sinner heard metal slide in there, and the jingling of jewelry.

"Got to look pretty for this kind of exercise," the gang leader said. The Sinner watched as Marcel placed several fat, diamond encrusted rings on his hands. Three on his left hand, two on his right. He noticed again how they all sported at least one diamond protrusion that stuck out like a nubby little spike.

"I see you got your rings cleaned."

Marcel gave a mock bow. "Only the best for freaks like you."

The Sinner returned the bow. "Where's your boss?"

Marcel stiffened. "Johnson?"

The Sinner laughed in derision. "No, he's just a crazy man with a lot of money and a penchant for pain."

"*I'm* the boss of the Crux Crue, Sinner man."

The Sinner laughed again. "Whatever makes you feel better about yourself, kid."

"What are you talking about, man?"

"You're not the boss of the Crux Crue. You're not even the boss of yourself. Renzio's the real boss. That's obvious."

"You don't know nothing, Freak. Renzio works for me. He's my second in command. He'll do whatever I say."

The Sinner nodded toward the door. "You order him to go to the bathroom so we could be alone?"

Marcel frowned. "Guy's gotta leak, man."

The Sinner now pulled outward on the braided wire around his feet. He worked cautiously, trying not to give away his actions. He felt the wire cut into the top layer of skin, but it wasn't deep and barely hurt after what he'd been through. He felt the wood give a satisfying groan behind his ankles.

"How long has he been gone?"

Marcel checked his jewel-bedecked watch, glanced at the doorway, and frowned harder.

"He'll be here, man."

"Sure, now that he's got your execution all planned out with your 'brothers' out there."

"You don't know what you're talking about, man."

"Sure I do," the Sinner said. "Renzio and me worked it all out earlier."

"What?" There was real alarm in the gang leader's voice now.

"You haven't figured it out yet? Why Renzio's not here? Why he left you all alone with me in a deserted basement room?"

Marcel flew to the cross and landed a body blow deep into the Sinner's right side. He swung with his right and came down across the prisoner's chest, leaving two bright red scars where the tips of his rings touched.

"Yeah," Marcel said as he threw another punch into the Sinner's jaw. "So I can beat the daylights out of you again."

"Wrong," the prisoner said through a newly bloodied lip. "It's so I can kill you."

The beating started in earnest then, with Marcel hitting the defenseless prisoner again and again, blinded by his anger and immaturity.

The Sinner took each blow with a practiced endurance, and every time the Crux leader hit him, the Sinner over-reacted to put more pressure on the wood beneath his feet. Sometimes he pulled on the wire, sometimes he pushed on the beam itself. When Marcel was finally starting to tire out, the Sinner smiled within himself.

This just might work. †

I am standing alone in the meadow. Dark surrounds me. It is something to which I will grow accustomed.

I feel a new emotion beginning to well up inside me. It is a familiar sensation, yet I do not recognize it at first. It begins to wash over me in cold waves. It clarifies my thinking and lays out a plan.

I will kill them. I will kill them all. I will make them suffer, and then they will die. I will be their judge, jury, and executioner. Not a single one will escape me. I am a sinner after all. A devil. And murder is what devils do.

I cluck for Destine to come to me. I see her massive shadow ambling slowly near. We will not ride hard tonight. But we will ride south, to the place where murder awaits me.

I will be a devil, then. A devil who works for God, when God refuses to work.

SIXTEEN

CX SURVEYED HER TEAM AS THEY LOUNGED ON THE furniture. They had come tantalizingly close in the past twenty-four hours, yet still had a long way to go before solving the riddle of the Sinner.

She listened attentively while Chance, James, and Rebel described the events of their previous night. She noticed that everyone glossed over the ending of their experience and that no one explained why Rebel had a large, fist-sized bruise on her neck.

"So where's your security-guard friend now, Chance?" she asked when they had finished.

Chance shrugged. "He went home. Said he had to go to

work today and he hoped to get at least one hour of sleep before reporting to the bank."

"I got a number for him," James said. "I told him we'd get in touch if anything changed."

CK nodded. When this was over, she was going to look up this security guard. CK Ivors Enterprises always had an opening for a guy who could think—and act—on his feet.

"Have you heard anything yet from Sean?"

"Talked to him about half an hour ago," James said. "He ran into a roadblock on that search warrant—"

"Big surprise," Rebel muttered. James ignored her.

"—but he's working another avenue and hopes to have everything moving in the near future."

"How'd it go with you and the detective on your stake-out?" Rebel asked CK. "Any luck?"

CK nodded again. "We got him," she said with satisfaction. "The perp broke into the house early in the morning. We nabbed him with his pants down."

"Literally," Junebug said with disgust. "I thought CK was going to make the pervert eat his own pants, she was so angry."

CK smiled. "Captured the guy on both video and in still photographs. Got him confessing to previous crimes as well as threatening the little girl with a new crime. He'll be in jail for a long time. At least that's what Sean says."

CK turned to Keena. "How about you, Assistant? Anything to report from last night?"

Keena looked a little embarrassed. "Well, compared to you, what I did just sounds silly."

"Gotta spill anyway, Kee," Junebug said. "That's the rules on this team."

Keena shrugged. "Well, after CK told me to stay here and act as 'home base,' I stayed here. I watched a little TV. Tried to read a book. Finally it was so quiet and boring around here that I went to bed."

Junebug laughed. "In bed by ten on a school night, huh, Keena?"

The assistant flushed. "Actually, by nine thirty, June." She shrugged again. "Hey, I was *sleepy!*"

CK let the team chuckle a bit, then raised her hand to redirect the focus. "Okay," she said, "that accounts for each one of us. What we don't have is an accounting for Galway. Anybody seen or heard from him?"

"Last I heard," said Chance, "he was going to a meeting to pick up some information from one of his weirdo contacts."

"Keena?"

"Haven't seen him, CK. He never came back last night, and he never called in either."

"Anybody check e-mail? Or his secret Web site?"

"Yeah," said Junebug. "Nothing in e-mail. Chance and I looked this morning ... well, this afternoon when we got up. And his site's changed its Web address again, so there's no telling where it is until he gives us the new domain."

CK looked thoughtful. "Rebel?"

"Well," she said, "I don't know Galway the same way you do."

"But he's the one who introduced us to each other back when you and James were just starting your agency."

Rebel stiffened. "Okay, for starters, CK, it's *my* agency. Feine Detection Services. James works *for* me."

Junebug snickered.

"And what's so funny?" Rebel said.

"Nothing, Reb, really," he grinned. "I was just thinking that if you guys did start an agency together, it'd be called Feine and Dandy." He chuckled, and Chance joined in.

"Hey," Rebel said in mock surprise. "Never heard that one before, have we, James? And you know what makes it really funny? That joke was made by a guy named after an insect. And an obnoxious insect at that."

"I got it," Junebug said contritely. "Sorry. No comments about names. Sheesh, it was just a joke." He looked miserably at James. "Wow, she's mean after being knocked out by her bodyguard."

"Tell me about it," James said, rubbing his shin.

"CK," Rebel sighed in exasperation, "why do you hire children to do grown-up work?"

"Because," she responded, "you kids"—she included Rebel in the sweep of her hand—"are all the very best at what you do. Now, tell me your thoughts about Galway."

"All right," Rebel said. "Well, like I said, the only time I work in person with Galway is when I'm here. Otherwise it's always long distance. But he's never been one to keep a schedule with me. Usually I just tell him what I need, then wait for a response. Sometimes I get an answer within an hour, other times it takes a few days."

"What's the longest you've ever had to wait before hearing from him?"

Rebel looked at James. "Three days," he said. "Never more than three days."

CK nodded. "Okay, so we're at about a day and a half

with him now. But he *is* working on something that he knows is time-sensitive. And whenever he's working for me, he usually stays in touch."

"What's your contact protocol with Galway?" Rebel asked.

"Same as yours," CK answered.

"Listen," Junebug interrupted. "Galway may be different, but he's really smart and pretty street savvy too. If he's disappeared, he's probably got a good reason. And he can probably take care of himself. I say we wait a little longer before we assume the worst with him. We've got lots of other things to do anyway."

CK chewed on her lip for a moment. "You're right, Junebug," she said. "We have to trust that Galway can take care of Galway, at least for now." She nodded to Chance. "Hit the Internet. I want to know everything there is to know about that abandoned mansion where the Crux Crue went last night. Find the property tax records, building blueprints, the works."

"On it," Chance said, rising from his seat, ready to head upstairs once the group broke up.

"Rebel, you and James coordinate with Detective Stepp. See if he'll let you go in with his team when they finally search the house. Even if he won't, stick around close by him and see what you can pick up." She looked thoughtful. "You really think that's where they took the Sinner?" Rebel nodded. "And the gunshots?"

"Could have been warning shots," James said.

"Or they could have killed him," Rebel said. Then after a moment she added, "but I doubt it."

"What do you mean?"

"Well, I've been thinking more about that meeting I had with Samantha Lancaster."

"You already debriefed us on that one before we left last night."

"I know," Rebel continued. "But look, that lady really believed this Sinner guy was an angel."

"And you?"

"Obviously he's not an angel. But based on what Chance found in his research, and things like that letter from the Englander collection ..." her voice trailed off.

"Not you, Rebel," Junebug said. "You are the voice of reason in this group of nutcases."

"Look," Rebel said, "I've never been a religious person, but I've never denied that God exists, either. I'm just saying if God does exist, wouldn't it be within his power to create an immortal from time to time?"

CK's jaw tightened. "So you think our guy today is the same one who first hung that slaver back in 1861? That's a stretch even for Galway, don't you think?"

Rebel's lips went thin. "I like facts, CK, you know that. But when the facts say there might be a miracle, I can't let my feelings stop me from at least considering the possibility."

There was a moment of silence, then CK said, "All right then. We don't assume anything. Maybe this guy is some kind of long-lifer. Maybe he really is invulnerable like Superman. Maybe he is over a hundred and fifty years old. There's only one way to find out."

James stood now. "Right. We ask him."

CK joined James and Chance in standing. "Keena," she said, "you and Junebug are with me. Let's go back through the documents we have on the Sinner. I want to know how he knew my name when he saw me at the Italian place last night."

Rebel stood too. "James," she said, "let's go down to the police station. Maybe if we see him in person, our friendly Detective Stepp will be more responsive to our requests."

"On it," James said.

They all moved to the front hallway and prepared to split off into their assigned directions, but then they stopped when James opened the front door. Standing there, framed by the opening to the porch, was a woman no one had ever seen before.

†

RENZIO REENTERED THE PRISON ROOM JUST AS MARCEL had decided to take a break and admire his work.

"Break any new bones this time?" Renzio asked casually.

Marcel shook his head. "Nah," he responded. "Working more on internal organs and things this time around."

Renzio gave an appraising look. "Looks like you were practicing cuts, too. That's a nice one down across the chest."

"Thanks, bro," Marcel said approvingly. "Tried to hit that spot a few times, make it deeper than the others."

The Sinner sucked in a cleansing breath and tried to block out the stinging in his flesh, wishing the blood would stop dripping from his nose long enough for him to breathe in dry air instead of moist. But that was really just a distraction. He could work around it.

Marcel looked over at Renzio. "Hey, bro," he said. "Go get me a soda, okay?"

Renzio looked surprised. "What about your whole 'Johnson said nobody should leave' garbage?"

Marcel frowned. "Who runs this gang? Loftis Johnson? You?"

Renzio responded to the other's tone of voice. "No way, bro," he said carefully. "Everybody knows only one guy runs the Crux. That's you, Marcel. Nobody but you."

Marcel's face relaxed. "Straight," he said. "And right now I'm thirsty. So I'm telling you to go get me a soda 'cause we're all out in here."

Renzio nodded. "What about the freak?"

Marcel waved in dismissal. "Look at him," he said. "He didn't move when you went upstairs, and that was when he was all healed up." He sniffed. "I figure I can handle the big bad Sinner long enough for you to get me a soda. What's he gonna do anyway? Bleed on me?"

Renzio nodded. "I hear you, bro. Back in a few." He disappeared out the doorway.

"Just you and me again, is it?" The Sinner's voice was gravelly and dry. He breathed in another long, slow breath, through his nose, encouraging the blood to clot and dry. Another minute or so would be enough.

"Shut up, Freak," Marcel said as he walked back over to the table. He opened the drawer in it and began dropping his rings, one by one, inside there. The Sinner heard a ring hit metal and suddenly placed the sound.

"What are you smiling about anyway, Sinner man? You like getting beat up or something? You weird like that?"

The Sinner pulled discreetly on the wire wrapped around his ankles. Still wasn't as loose as he would have liked it. Would probably scrape a layer of skin off his top foot, but that was a price he'd have to pay.

"No," he said calmly. "I was just imagining how I will kill you."

The Sinner now pressed again on the wood beneath his feet. *Poor Johnson*, he thought. *He had no idea that he was helping me when he hurt me.*

Johnson had never realized what the Sinner had noticed almost by accident. When the businessman had shot three angry bullets through the prisoner's feet, those bullets had also torn through the wooden beam beneath his feet. Since those bullets had been fired in close proximity to each other, they had weakened the wood near the base of the cross. Add to that the pressure on that spot from holding up the weight of the rest of the cross, and the wood had begun to splinter there. With the Sinner's steady pressure on that spot, he'd managed to do two things: First, he'd bent the braided wire just enough to allow a little slack around his ankles. Second, he furthered the weakening of the timber beneath his feet. Now he was almost ready.

Marcel just snorted. "Yeah, you do that, Sinner man," he said sarcastically. "You kill me first chance you get, okay?" He sat down at the table. "But meanwhile I'll just keep torturing you."

"Torture? You don't know the meaning of the word,"

the Sinner said. He took in another deep breath through his nose and felt the blood clots starting to take hold inside.

Any time now, he figured. *Any time.*

†

"EXCUSE ME," THE LITTLE WOMAN SAID TO THE BIG MAN standing in the doorway. "I was just about to ring the bell when you opened the door."

CK stepped out from behind the bodyguard and smiled. Why was there a maid at her door? "Yes," she said to the woman, "can I help you with something?"

The woman looked grateful, "Yes, thank you," she said. "My name is Maria Eliza Garces, and I am looking for Mr. Junebug Collins. Is he home?"

Junebug stepped forward, "I'm Junebug," he said.

The maid looked genuinely surprised for a moment, then she laughed uncomfortably. "Oh, no," she said. "I'm sorry. I mean the other Junebug Collins."

Chance looked dumbfounded. "You mean there's more than one person in this world named Junebug?"

Now it was Junebug's turn to look surprised. "The other Junebug Collins?" he said. "What other Junebug Collins?"

Maria Eliza gave him a quick look. She was obviously feeling more and more out of place in this little gathering around CK's front door.

"Well," she said, "your father?"

Keena stifled a laugh. "Junebug's too ornery to have a father," she said warmly.

"I'm sorry," Maria Eliza said. "Perhaps I'm a little confused. But I came here yesterday about a gold watch that was advertised as 'found' in the paper. I met an older gentleman who said his name was Junebug Collins—"

"Galway," CK and Rebel said it at the same time.

"Excuse me?" said the maid.

"This 'Junebug' that you met yesterday," CK said. "Was he a little chubby? Kind of Irish-looking, with light skin and a few tufts of red hair ringing around his mostly bald head?"

The maid nodded. "Yes, that was him."

CK shook her head in disgust. "Maria Eliza," she said kindly, "perhaps you should come in."

†

"HEY, MARCEL," THE SINNER CALLED FROM THE CROSS. "I've got an itch under my foot. Be a good boy and come scratch it for Daddy, would you?"

Marcel cursed under his breath and turned to shuffling the cards on the table.

"Suit yourself," the Sinner said. He took in one last deep breath—still through his nose—and then moved with a speed that was unexpected in any circumstance, let alone this one.

While Marcel shuffled his deck of cards, the Sinner slipped his top foot out of the braided wire. It did scrape off a layer of skin, but not as deeply as the Sinner had guessed it would. He was pleased.

With his top foot loose, there was plenty of room to

wiggle out the bottom foot. He tapped the braided wire and it slid quietly to the ground. He legs were free.

He raised his thighs almost up to his chest before Marcel noticed anything was happening.

"Hey!" the gang leader yelped, "what do you think you're doing?"

The Sinner didn't answer. Instead he brought his heels down with explosive force against the weakened spot of wood at the bottom of the cross. The beam splintered, cracked, and gave partly away. He quickly repeated the kick a second time and the center beam split apart near the bottom. The cross tilted and started to fall. The Sinner planted his bare feet on the cold cement floor and caught both himself and the cross. He stretched his legs and stood up straight, now free to move as long as he didn't mind a cross hanging on his back, hands and neck still attached to the upper portion of the wood, and braided wire still wrapped around his torso in a disfigured *S* shape.

He glared at Marcel. Stunned by the speed of the Sinner's movements, the Crux leader jammed a hand into the drawer to dig out the gun.

The Sinner didn't hesitate. He slid across the cement floor, covering the distance to the table in a heartbeat. He swung out with his left shoulder and brought the crossbeam cracking hard against Marcel's jaw. The gang leader was already sagging to the ground when the right side of the crossbeam crashed into his left ear.

The Sinner breathed in deeply, through his nose, and then placed a bare foot firmly against his adversary's throat.

"Come in, Renzio," he said calmly. "And drop that gun or I'll break his neck."

†

BACK IN THE LOUNGE AREA OF CK'S SPACIOUS HOME, THE team tried not to seem overeager to hear what the maid had to say.

"Keena," CK said, "would you get our guest a glass of tea or something?"

"Thank you," Maria Eliza said. "I just got off work, and the bus stop closest to here was still a little bit of a walk."

CK measured the situation before her, then made a calculated decision. "Junebug's father," she nodded in Junebug's direction, "sometimes gets confused. His real name is Galway. And unfortunately no one has seen him since early in the day yesterday. We're all concerned for his safety. Especially Junebug here."

The photographer looked grim. But when Maria Eliza turned to him, he just said, "Yes, ma'am. We're all worried about ... about Dad. Did he look well when you saw him yesterday?"

"Oh yes," Maria Eliza said, accepting the glass of tea from Keena and immediately taking a long sip. "He looked fine."

Ever the detective, Rebel asked, "Maria Eliza, why were you meeting with, uh, Mr. Collins yesterday? Are you the owner of the gold watch?"

"Oh no," the maid said quickly. "I just came to ask

Mr. Collins about the Sinner. At least that's the name Mr. Collins used for him. Is that correct?"

CK took over. "The Sinner is the correct name for the owner of the watch. Do you know the Sinner?"

"No," she said. "And yes."

"Why does everybody have to speak cryptically when they come into this house?" Chance muttered to James.

"You'll have to explain that to us, Maria Eliza," CK said.

The maid set down her tea glass. "I don't know the Sinner. I just know where he lives."   †

We ride in the darkness, Destine and me. Somehow she has managed to find a road. I do not know where it leads, only that it runs south, and that is good enough for me. I begin laying out a plan to find the bounty hunters who burned my barn. I will go to Richmond first. There are people there who will know men like Jennison and his cronies. Then I will find Jennison. Then I will find the others. And when they are all dead ... I don't have any thoughts beyond then. I will deal with that time when it comes.

I remember my foolishness in the meadow, begging for God to forgive me. Weeping for a sign from heaven. I am disgusted with myself. God certainly exists. But he has no time for one like me. Just as he had no time for Celia. Only I am not a helpless little girl. And I am no longer willing to stand by and watch evil men destroy the beautiful things of this world.

There are too few beautiful things.

I ride in silence, awaiting the sunrise that threatens to break over the horizon to my left.

I feel the slicing pain in my hands first. I have never felt this kind of agony. It is so sudden, so unexpected. Destine responds to the tightening of my muscles on her back and breaks into a trot. I wrap my arms around her neck and use my wrists to rein her to a stop.

My hands are bleeding. Deep, cavernous wounds that drip a dark red flow down my arms and smear upon Destine's *mane. I suddenly realize that the wounds in my hands are holes that drive all the way through. I pass out then. I do not even feel it when I hit the ground beside Destine's hooves.*

When I awake moments later, the wounds on my hands are already healing on both sides. I am confounded with disbelief. What has happened to me?

In response, I feel the agony in my feet. My right one explodes with pain from the top of the foot to deep inside and through the heel. My left foot quivers from the gaping hole that now runs through the front of my ankle and out through my Achilles.

I want to scream, but the pain has left me breathless.

A thousand needles prick holes in my scalp. Blood drizzles down my forehead and burns in my eyes. I can only writhe on the ground, mixing dirt and sweat and blood in the open, bleeding wounds.

And then, just as suddenly as it started, the pain recedes, then disappears. I am gasping, dirty, on the ground. Destine has cantered away just a few feet, apparently unsettled by the writhings of my madness.

I look at my hands and see the scars, marks that are both new and old. I am certain my feet bear the same, and I am frightened, truly frightened by this newfound anguish.

I begin to stand, and that's when my side erupts with blood. Someone has rammed a red-hot poker underneath my rib cage, scrambled my insides with it, and left me moaning to die. But death does not come. Only pain. Only suffering.

I crumple again to the ground unable to move, only able to whimper against the rising sun.

After what seems like days, the piercing in my side also closes, healing as miraculously as it appeared.

I lay gasping, gulping for air. I have learned something. God certainly exists, that I already knew. But now he has taken time for me and his punishment shows no mercy.

The darkness swirls in my mind even as the sun breaks over the horizon.

And I dream.

Horrible dreams. Terrifying, devil dreams. And within them it becomes clear.

God hates me.

I am that which he cannot stand. The thing for which he created hell and the grave.

I am the Sinner.

SEVENTEEN

SEAN STEPP SLAMMED DOWN THE RECEIVER OF the telephone and habitually patted the gun strapped under his coat.

"Knew I could count on you, Judge Santos," he muttered to himself. "Would have called you first, Tomas, but I had to follow jurisdictional protocol." He wasn't sure what Judge Santos had done to override Judge Marks's earlier decision to deny the search warrant, but whatever it was had been effective. Now it was time to get to work.

He was just reaching for the receiver to start calling his team off standby when the phone rang. "Detective Sean Stepp," he said into the mouthpiece.

"Detective, there's someone here to see you," the receptionist's voice cooed into the phone.

"Who is it?" he asked.

"A Mr. Lincoln Sayles."

Sean shoved the telephone between his shoulder and neck. "Take a message," he said. "Tell him I'm going out of the office for the next several hours. Suggest he call to make an appointment with me for tomorrow."

"He says it's urgent, Detective."

"Everything is urgent nowadays. Fine. Get his number and tell him I'll call him later tonight when I get back."

"Hold, please."

Sean was tempted to hang up, but something of the church boy in him figured that would be impolite. So he waited, slowly beginning to fume. After a minute or so the receptionist came back on the line.

"Detective? He says to tell you it's about a haunted mansion. Does that mean anything to you?"

Sean sighed. "Yeah, it does," he said. "Send him up."

THE SINNER DIDN'T TURN TO LOOK AT RENZIO MORALES at first. He didn't have to. If the boy had pulled his gun already, he would have fired. That meant he was still holding several cans of soda in his hands and hadn't yet figured out how to drop them so he could retrieve his firearm.

The Sinner instead focused on Marcel's battered form below him. He could feel the boy's neck cooling underneath his bare foot. He adjusted his stance and slid his big toe behind the boy's bloodied ear.

No pulse, he thought. *So I killed him after all. But that other kid doesn't know that yet.*

He slowly turned his gaze back to Renzio. The second in command stood frozen with indecision. He held three cans of Mountain Dew in his left hand and three of Coca-Cola in his right. The Sinner could see the outline of a gun in the boy's pocket.

The Sinner's eyes narrowed. "Renzio," he said evenly. "First, put down those sodas in your hands." The boy obeyed. "Now reach into your pocket with two fingers only. Pull out that gun and toss it on the floor between us."

The gang member hesitated. "You'll never get out anyway," he said. "There are a dozen more of us spread out all over this house. You'll never get out."

The Sinner exaggerated the pressure his foot was making on Marcel's lifeless neck. "Do as I say or I will kill him, boy. And then I will kill you and all your friends in this house."

Renzio nodded. After what he had just seen, the boy obviously believed the threat. He slowly reached two fingers into his pocket, removed the gun, then threw it against a wall.

"Now go get the keys to the handcuffs out of that drawer in the table."

The youth seemed in a daze, but he walked slowly past Marcel and the Sinner and retrieved a set of keys from the drawer.

"He don't look so good, man."

"That's because I'm killing him while you dawdle around with those keys."

The youth moved quickly to the Sinner's right hand and inserted a key into the lock. The prisoner flexed his forearm and the handcuffs popped open. The heavy cross-beam dropped toward the floor until the wire around the Sinner's chest halted the fall.

The Sinner reached up with his right hand and loosened the noose around his neck. Still holding his foot at Marcel's throat, he held out his hand. Renzio placed the keys in his palm. It took only another minute or so for the Sinner to extract himself from the second pair of handcuffs and the thick braided wire. He let the cross fall carelessly to the cement floor, and only then realized the scarring the beam and wires had left on his torso during his little exercise session.

"What now?" Renzio asked. He looked worriedly at Marcel.

In response, the Sinner hit him, cleanly under the jaw, right at a pressure point. The boy instantly collapsed unconscious at his feet. He considered binding and gagging him, then decided against it. If he couldn't finish his business here before the boy woke up, then he deserved to be recaptured by the roaming Crux Crue in the halls upstairs.

But what he had to do wouldn't take long.

CK SAT BACK IN DISBELIEF. WAS THIS MAID TELLING THE truth? "How did you find out where the Sinner lives?" she said.

Maria Eliza shrugged. "I explained it all to Mr. Galway yesterday."

Junebug leaned forward. "How did Gal—I mean, Dad, respond when you told him this?"

"He wanted to go over there. So we went last night."

"He went there alone? Without telling anybody?" CK felt her anger rising again. "Chance," she turned on the young man. "You were here yesterday. You were the home base. Why didn't you stop him? Why didn't you at least call somebody and tell them where Galway was going?"

"Hey, wait a minute, CK," Chance said. "I was here all afternoon, and—no offense, Maria Eliza—but nobody came back before you did yesterday. Well, besides that security guard. We played pool upstairs for a couple of hours, just waiting for someone to show up."

"You were here yesterday, too?" Maria Eliza asked. "I saw only Mr. Galway."

CK turned to the maid. "Did you ring the bell?

She shook her head. "Mr. Galway opened the door for me before I could ring." She motioned toward James. "Like what he did today."

"Did you come into the house?"

"No. We talked in the doorway. And then he asked me to show him where the Sinner lived. And so I did."

"No," Junebug said. "It doesn't make sense. Not even Galway would chase down the Sinner all alone. Are you telling us everything, Maria Eliza?"

The maid looked uncomfortable. Finally she reached into her bag and pulled out a leather-bound book with the symbol of a cross and snake imprinted on it.

"Now I'm beginning to understand," CK groaned.

"This is the third book," the maid said. "There are dozens of others at the Sinner's cottage."

"And you showed Galway this?"

Maria Eliza shook her head. "Not this one. I showed him the first book."

"Figures," said Rebel.

"What?" said James.

"Showing Galway a mysterious, antique book is like, well, like showing Junebug a new camera."

"Oh," said Junebug. "I get it now."

"That kind of stuff is like a drug for him. He would have crawled through barbed wire for miles just to get a glimpse at the rest of those books."

Maria Eliza returned the journal to her purse.

"Please," she said. "I need to speak with Mr. Galway."

"Well, at least now we know where he probably is," said Rebel. "At this Sinner's house. Alone."

"Still?" Maria Eliza asked. CK gave her a narrow look. "Oh," she said. "Of course." She stood to leave.

"Wait," CK said. "You can't leave until you tell us where that Sinner's cottage is."

Maria Eliza looked indecisive. "I think," she said haltingly. "Please don't be offended, but I'm not sure about that."

"You mean you're unwilling to divulge that information," said James.

The maid nodded. "You don't understand," she said. "I may have already made a mistake by bringing Mr. Galway to the cottage. But to think he might still be there! What if the Sinner returns and discovers him there? He might no longer feel safe there, and leave for good, and I will lose my chance to help him." She stood to her feet. "No, I'm sorry, but I will not tell you where the cottage is. I will go there myself and see that Mr. Galway is all right and that he does not overstay his welcome."

The maid hesitated, then locked eyes with CK. "This Sinner needs something from me," she said. "Something important."

For once, CK was speechless.

"We understand," James Dandy said unexpectedly. "But will you do us at least one favor?"

Maria Eliza waited.

"Will you at least tell Galway to call us?"

The maid nodded and moved toward the door. "James," Rebel started, but he silenced her with a wave. "Maria Eliza," he said formally as he opened the front door. "I would be honored to accompany you back to the bus stop—if you'll allow it."

The maid looked up at the big man's eyes, saw something she liked, and gave a brief smile and nod.

CK watched them leave and then shot a questioning glance at Rebel. She shrugged. Only Junebug was smiling.

"That guy is smooth," he said approvingly. "Now all we have to do is wait for him to call us from the Sinner's cottage."

†

Loftis Johnson knew the sun was shining outside, knew the day was in its latter half, but he still tossed upon his large red four-poster bed, refusing to give in to the impulse to get up. He wanted to wait until nighttime to visit the Sinner again, to see if he was healing once more from the wounds he'd last inflicted. These were more serious than the beating Marcel had first given the man on the cross, and Johnson reasoned they would take longer to heal than the last time. But Loftis was a patient man. He would wait and watch, even if it took weeks or even months for the sleep to heal his enemy.

Loftis actually hoped the Sinner would sleep longer this time. He wanted to try a few experiments, to see what would happen if the man were wounded while he slept. Would that prolong the healing time? Or shorten it? Would the Sinner feel the pain while he slept? All questions Loftis wanted answers to, and all answers he intended to get.

He let his eyes open and look toward the ceiling. He heard the shuffling feet of the guards outside his door, heard their low voices vibrating through the walls. He began wondering if he should move the Sinner to a different location, at least for a while. He'd bought off that judge easily enough, though. It's amazing what money can do to a man, even a man of supposedly high principles. Still, the question was how long that judge would stay bought. And whether those unexpected strangers from last night would return.

He would have liked to know more about those three people who had so easily disarmed the guards in front of the house. Or was it four? The gang guards couldn't be sure. One of them saw only two; the other one thought there were four. At any rate, they had been embarrassingly overpowered and neutralized—left handcuffed to car bumpers. Loftis worried about things like that—not about the fact that his guards had been caught napping, but that someone out there (or two someones or four someones) was nosing around in his business. Still, this house was the place that had been prepared for the Sinner, and this house still held the best accommodations for the long, drawn-out plans Loftis had made for his enemy. Finally he decided. When he next saw Marcel or Renzio, he would order them to bring more guards—eight or ten more should be enough. And he would put at least two on the roof with sniper rifles, just in case.

Loftis felt the silk sheets rub against his back and wondered how they compared to the harsh wood that now chafed against the skin of his enemy. He couldn't help but smile at the thought that every time the Sinner healed, he would be subjected again to the same chafing as before, feeling it all over again each and every time.

He felt a soft shudder rumble through the floor and up the posts of the bed and noticed all of a sudden that his house was unusually quiet. He sat up, listening hard. He heard the door open softly, slowly. Even in the forced darkness of his heavily curtained room, he could make out the shadow behind the door. The figure stepped slowly inside, and for the first time Loftis felt a twinge of fear.

The voice was hard, even. Businesslike. He could hear the sneer as it spoke into the void between the two men.

"You look like hell."

†

CK FACED A MOMENT OF INDECISION. SHE WAS READY TO move ahead in her fact gathering, ready for the team to dig deeply into their assignments so they could return and piece together more of the mystery of the Sinner. Yet, if Junebug was right, if James Dandy was gaining the confidence of that maid so that she would lead them to the Sinner's cottage, then simply waiting for the bodyguard to call could make all their current assignments obsolete.

The team stood in the lounge, uncertain, waiting for CK to give the word.

"Rebel?" she questioned finally.

The private detective shook her head. "I don't know, CK," she said. "James is enough of a Goody Two-Shoes that he could just be walking her to the bus stop."

"Junebug?"

"I say we wait for James. At least for an hour or so."

"Why?"

Junebug looked a little embarrassed.

"Just tell her," Keena said. "It's not like your techniques are a secret, Cuz."

Chance Elko suddenly became very interested in the conversation.

Junebug sighed. "Well," he said, "sometimes when you are, um, meeting a girl, she's reluctant to give you her phone number at first."

CK rolled her eyes. "You're giving us pickup advice?"

"Just listen," he said. "This stuff works."

Chance appeared to be looking for a pen and a piece of paper. CK frowned at him.

"When you're talking to a girl—excuse me, a lady—and

she seems to like you but she won't give you her number, the best way to play it is to go with the superpolite plan."

"Junebug, please be serious."

"I *am* serious. You convince her that you respect her distrust. You make it seem like the last thing in the world you want is to get her phone number. You offer to get her coat, you talk about your mother, you do anything that (a) keeps you near her, and (b) makes her feel like you've given up on getting her number."

"And that transparent scam really works?"

Junebug leaned back and put his hands behind his head. "Don't you remember how we first met, CK?" he said with a grin.

CK felt herself flush. "Okay. Fine. Whatever," she said, trying to recover by changing the subject. "So you're saying that James is just flirting with Maria Eliza until he can get the information he wants from her?"

"Yes," Junebug said. "That's what I'm saying."

"It does make sense," said Keena. "It could work."

Chance nodded, a look of increasing respect in his gaze toward Junebug.

CK looked at her watch. "All right," she said. "We'll give James one hour. We'll wait just one hour and then we go back to our assignments. Got it?"

Everyone nodded except Rebel. She looked thoughtful for a moment, then finally gave her assent as well.

"You all are forgetting one thing, though," she said. "Knowing James, he could be just being nice."

✝

SEAN STEPP GAVE HIS VISITOR AN APPRAISING LOOK. THE man was medium size, looked to be in decent shape for a guy approaching his thirties. He carried a mailing tube and, most interesting, appeared completely comfortable inside the confines of a police station.

"Mr. Sayles?" Sean said cordially.

Lincoln reached out and shook the detective's hand. "Thanks for taking time to see me," he said. "I think it'll be worth your while."

"Let me guess," Sean said. "You are the fourth person from CK Ivors' little reconnaissance team at the Johnson mansion last night."

Lincoln gave a mock bow. "At your service."

"Well," Sean said, "I am kind of busy today, Mr. Sayles. What have you got for me?"

Lincoln opened the mailing tube and pulled out a few sheets of rolled paper. Sean was impressed.

"Satellite photos?" he said, looking at the first sheet. "And heat signature comparisons?"

Lincoln nodded. "I figured you and your team might want these before you went into that Johnson mansion."

Sean counted the heat signatures. "Sixteen inside," he said. "How many hostiles?"

"My guess is fifteen of the sixteen. Although that sixteenth one could be the most hostile of all. Hard to tell."

Sean nodded. "Where did you get these images?" he asked.

Lincoln grinned. "When you serve in special forces for two tours in Afghanistan and one in another place that I can't reveal, you make a few friends in intelligence circles."

Sean cocked his head questioningly.

"Army Rangers," Lincoln said proudly, and he gave a short salute.

"Hmm," Sean hesitated. "Using government satellites to spy on a private domestic residence seems something of an unlawful search."

Lincoln grinned conspiratorially. "You'd think that," he said. "But actually 'looking down' on a house is not any more illegal than parking your car out front and staring at it from the road. It's just a matter of getting access to the satellite that's looking, and fortunately I knew a guy who was willing to let me take a peek."

Sean nodded thoughtfully. "So, Mr. Sayles," he said after a moment. "You busy right now?"

†

HE STEPPED OUT THE BACK DOOR OF THE MANSION AND flexed his fingers and hands. There was some bruising on his knuckles, but given the sorry state of the rest of his body he didn't even notice.

The cuts across his chest and abdomen had mostly clotted over, but a few of the wider tears had reopened during his most recent "exercise." He felt the familiar weariness that preceded the need for sleep and knew he needed to find a secluded place nearby to let the healing process take over. He also knew he didn't have far to go to find that place.

He almost pitied Loftis Johnson. In the end, this man had begged too. Maybe not as pitifully as his father, but he had still begged for mercy. Unfortunately for Johnson, mercy was a dead concept for the Sinner.

He sucked in a breath of fresh air, felt the evening sun glowing on his chest. He knew that if he looked in a mirror he would see a wreck of humanity. So he hadn't looked in a mirror when he had made his way out of the house. But he could tell by the way the two teens before him gaped that he must look awful.

They stood at a stalemate for a few minutes. The Sinner said nothing. One of the gold braids before him held a handgun; the other held a semiautomatic rifle. They were too close to the door, though. The Sinner figured he could get to the semiautomatic without any trouble. The handgun might get off one shot before he too was extinguished, but the Sinner felt confident he could use the first gang member's body as a shield. Or he could just take the bullet, finish the job, and then go lie down for a while. It was unlikely that his body would hurt worse than it did right now anyway.

Finally the handgun spoke. "I'm guessing you left a mess in there." He motioned to the big house behind them.

The Sinner nodded.

The semiautomatic looked frantically from the Sinner to his fellow guard and back to the Sinner again.

"All of them?" the handgun said.

The Sinner shook his head. "Just enough to get the job done."

Handgun nodded and adjusted his grip on the weapon. "So if I were to call out my signal, how many of my brothers would come running?"

The Sinner hesitated, then said, "Six. Maybe seven."

Handgun nodded again.

"What do you wanna do, Kex?" the semiautomatic said nervously.

"Shut up," the handgun responded. "Let me think."

The Sinner glanced up toward the sky. "Running out of time, friend," he said quietly.

Handgun frowned. "Loftis Johnson?" he said.

The Sinner shrugged. "It's unlikely that Mr. Johnson will ever walk again."

The gang member looked thoughtful for a moment, then dropped the gun to his side.

"Kex?" the other youth said, his voice rising in pitch.

The handgun motioned for his companion to lower his rifle as well. Then he spoke to the Sinner. "We don't see you, man," he said. "If you can get out of that," he motioned toward the house, "even looking like you do, you deserve to get out all the way."

He walked past the Sinner and into the house. The semiautomatic quickly followed.

The Sinner sighed. "Thanks, boys," he muttered. "Saves me the trouble of having to kill you both."

He took a step toward the path that led to the cottages behind the garden.

†

"Now these sat images are two hours old—I couldn't get real time," Lincoln was saying as he rode shotgun in Sean Stepp's unmarked sedan. "So we have to assume there's a possibility that things have changed some out there."

"We'll be ready," the detective responded. "My team has already studied the blueprints of the place and created an entrance plan that should minimize direct confrontation. Then we'll take it room by room until we're secure. Once we've collared all the hostiles, we can begin collecting the necessary evidence to keep these animals in prison."

Lincoln nodded. "Thanks for letting me come along."

Sean glanced over at his passenger. "Well, it's a big mistake, really. But I figure you deserve to see how it all goes down. Just do me a favor and stay in the car until you hear my 'all clear' on the radio, okay?"

"Wouldn't have it any other way, Detective," Lincoln grinned.

Sean grinned back. "For some reason, Mr. Sayles, I don't especially believe you."   †

I awake to find the face of a woman looking down at me. She is young. My age or so. But with lines around her eyes that say she has lived longer in her years than I have in mine. She is dabbing my neck with a cool, moist rag. She is so intent on her job that at first she doesn't notice my eyes have opened. Then she sees the flutter of blinking in her peripheral vision, sees my open eyes staring at her.

"Oh," she says softly. She immediately draws back. I catch her hand.

"Where am I?" I ask.

She looks wistfully at the door behind her, tugs gently on her arm. I release my hold and she pulls back completely, now standing over me.

"Where am I?"

"You've been sleeping a long time," she says. "You were hurt."

I nod. I feel no pain now. Nothing. But I still have memories of what I have dreamed.

"I have to go," I say.

"You were hurt," she repeats. "Ansel found you in the road, moaning."

"When?"

She hesitates, looks at the ground and back at the door.

"How long have I been here?" I ask, rephrasing my question. "How long did I sleep?"

"A fortnight," she says finally. "A fortnight plus two."

Sixteen days? How have I slept for sixteen days?

My body feels good, healthy. Fresh.

"Are you hungry?" she asks. "Do you want something to eat or drink?"

I shake my head. I have been sixteen days in the darkness, yet I feel full, as though I were just fed.

She takes a step backward, but still cannot leave the room.

"There's more, isn't there?" I say.

She nods. "You were hurt. Even while you slept."

I notice now that bandages cover my wrists, wrapping halfway up my palms. Another set of bandages warm my feet. She steps closer and tentatively pulls the sheet down to my waist. A large scar devastates my left side, just below my rib cage.

"I couldn't keep that one covered," she says apologetically. "And it didn't appear every time, so Ansel said just to leave it and to wash the sheets well afterward." She touches my forehead lightly. "Same with those," she says. "They were the most rare ones."

I sit up on the side of the bed and begin unwrapping the bandage on my left hand.

"You should rest," she says timidly.

"I'm fine," I say. And I am. Except for the memories. Except for the dreams. "Never better." I pause. "Thank you. For your kindness to me."

She flushes lightly and gives me a shy smile.

"Father Kensington said to call him the moment you awoke. I'll go tell Ansel, and he will fetch the Father for you."

I shake my head. "I know no Father Kensington. And I have no need of religion. It's time for me to go."

She looks worried. "But Father Kensington is a good man, a godly man. He tended to you himself for three days, even before we knew … before we knew of your gift."

I am lost. "Gift?" I say. "What gift?"

She reaches nervously toward my now-unwrapped palm, gently traces the arc of the scar that is painted in my skin.

"You bear the marks of Christ," she says. "You hold in your body the stigmata of God. Father Kensington says this is a great miracle. A sign that God has chosen you for himself, that he has bestowed his love on you with the most intimate of gifts."

"Father Kensington is a fool."

She covers her mouth in shock at my words. "But the wounds of Christ inhabited your body. They appeared before my very eyes, then healed of themselves and left only these scars. It is the same as what happened to Saint Francis. It is a miracle."

"It is the vengeance of God."

She begins to tremble. "How can you speak such blasphemy?" she whispers hoarsely to me.

I do not answer. I do not tell her who I am or what I have done. I stand and rip the remaining bandages off my hands and feet. She backs from the room in fear, hand still frozen over her mouth. I retrieve my shirt and shoes and vest. In my pocket I find three gold pieces.

Blood money.

I leave one gold token on the table that holds the basin of water. And then, before Ansel or Father Kensington or anyone else can come, I slip out the door. I am grateful to find that it is nighttime, and to see Destine tied to a water trough not far from the door. She whinnies in recognition and in only a moment I have mounted and turned my horse toward the road.

I have a man to kill, and I intend to fulfill my murderous intent sooner rather than later.

Maybe then the dreams will stop.

EIGHTEEN

GALWAY HAD FINALLY DISCOVERED THE PANTRY. Sure, there wasn't much in there, but a can of black beans and a glass of cold water can go a long way if you're hungry enough. It helped to wash away the sour taste of morning breath as well, and for that the old man was grateful.

He had settled back into the bedroom, reading and forgetfully spooning beans into his mouth from time to time. The way he figured it, he should be done with the final volume—either number forty-three or forty-four, he couldn't remember—by morning. Then he probably should go find a telephone and call CK. He especially wanted to talk to CK now, wanted to clarify something that might be very important.

He was feeling quite at home, reading, reclining, eating, and drinking. He was wondering what it might cost to get himself a little private cottage like this one someday when he heard the front door open and then quickly shut.

Galway froze and felt just a bit like the intruder that he was. "Maria Eliza?" he called out tentatively.

There was no answer. Instead a bloody, disfigured man stepped into the doorway of the back bedroom.

Galway said nothing, though he did almost spill the half-eaten can of beans on the opened book in his lap.

The bloodied man stared at the old man, quietly taking in the situation. Galway waited, not sure what he should do. After a moment, the bloodied one turned away from the intruder and toward the bed.

"Lock up on your way out," he said. Then he stretched out on his back and closed his eyes.

Galway sat still like a statue for several minutes. When it became apparent that the man was sound asleep, Galway quietly stood, gathered his beans and glass of water, and tiptoed out of the room. He tiptoed back in a moment later and carefully removed the first journal from the shelf. The wounded man didn't stir.

Galway quietly exited the little cottage with the book under his arm. He made sure to lock the door on his way out.

†

IT WAS FORTY-FIVE MINUTES BEFORE JAMES DANDY OPENED CK's front door. He seemed to find it unexpected that everyone was standing nearby, apparently waiting for him.

CK caught him first, before he even had a chance to close the door. "Well," she said, "what did you find out?"

"Did you get the Sinner's address?" Rebel quickly followed.

James looked genuinely surprised. "No," he said. "She said she wouldn't give it to us, remember?"

"Well, did you find out anything?" Junebug asked. "Like what part of town it's in, or how long the Sinner has been using it as a hideout, or whether or not Galway might still be there?"

"No," the big man said.

"For goodness' sake, James," Rebel said. "Then what were you doing all this time?"

James shrugged. "What? I was walking Maria Eliza to the bus stop. Then I waited with her until the bus arrived to pick her up. She's a very nice person, and I figured it was the right thing to do since she was our guest and all."

Rebel smacked him on the arm. "You big lug!" she exclaimed. "You were supposed to schmooze her into telling you where the cottage is."

CK shook her head ruefully. "No, it's okay James," she said after a moment. "Politeness is its own reward." She gathered herself up and then clapped her hands. "Okay, people," she said. "We've got work to do. We need to locate Galway and find out what he knows about this cottage."

They all nodded. "Keena," CK added, "better order a few pizzas. Could be a long night around here."

"I'm on it," Keena said.

"Did I hear someone say something about pizza?" Galway bounded up the porch with an eager smile.

"Pepperoni for me," he said happily. "And get me a large one all to myself, okay, Keena?"

"Galway!" CK and Junebug called out in unison.

"Fine! Fine!" he said quickly. "I'll share with the rest of you. But believe me, I really could eat one whole pizza by myself right now."

Galway surveyed the team standing in the entryway until his eyes fell on the young computer geek. "Oh, CK," he said casually, "I think Chance Elko might be a spy. You'll probably want to check that out sometime."

"What?" Chance's voice was shrill, and he was immediately embarrassed that Keena had heard it.

"Is there any coffee in the kitchen?" Galway asked as he started to move in that direction.

"Galway—" CK started, but the ringing of her cell phone interrupted her. She grabbed the old man by the collar with her left hand and pointed him toward the lounge while she slipped her cell phone out of its case with her right hand.

"Um, don't forget to check the caller ID," Keena said.

CK nodded curtly and waved for everyone to follow Galway into the lounge. She glanced quickly at the caller-ID number, then flipped open her cell. "Sean? What's happening?"

"Just wanted to let you know we finally got the search warrant on the Johnson mansion."

"Excellent. When are you going in?"

"My team is here and getting into position right now."

"What? Sean, why didn't you call me earlier?"

"Because," the detective said calmly, "I want you as far

away as possible from here for at least the next hour. Got it?"

"Now you're not making any sense. First you *don't* call me because you want me to stay away, and now you *do* call me because you want me to stay away?"

"One of my men on stakeout here saw a car roll out from behind the mansion about half an hour ago. We matched the license plate to one Francis Mickey Galway—"

Francis? Mickey? No wonder he just goes by Galway.

"—and that means you are involved."

"Sean, listen—"

"No, you listen CK. This could get really messed up if you interfere at this point. This could be the break we need to pull the lid off Loftis Johnson's little enterprises—and a key to cracking down on the Crux Crue. So I'm asking you, for me, your old buddy Sean. Just stay away from here for at least an hour. Okay?"

CK sighed. "Promise me you'll call as soon as you've got an all clear?"

Now Sean sighed. "Yes, CK," he said. "I promise."

"Fine." She hung up her cell and checked the digital clock in the display window. She'd keep her promise. But only for sixty minutes and not a minute more.

✝

MARIA ELIZA WAS SURPRISED TO SEE A SMALL ARMY OF police cars surrounding the front entrance to the main house on the estate where the cottages were kept. She wasn't sure what to do. If she tried to walk past the gate toward the garden cottages, the police officers were sure to stop her. But if she didn't walk down there, she wouldn't know whether Mr. Galway was still there, or if, as she feared, his presence in the cottage might have scared the Sinner away for good.

She looked back over her shoulder and contemplated going back to Junebug Collins' house, or even going home to wait until everything settled down out here. Then she saw the blue-uniformed man by the gate lean into his car and say something into his radio. He listened for a moment, said something else, then straightened up and trotted away from the gate and toward another group of officers down the sidewalk, motioning for them to follow him inside the gate and down the long driveway. A half-dozen policemen jogged inside the estate walls, apparently headed toward the front entrance to the mansion. In a moment, Maria was surprised to find that she was now, at least briefly, alone.

Maria Eliza never considered herself a lawbreaker. She always supported the police's efforts and reputation in the community in general, and in her family specifically. But she couldn't help feeling that this was an opportunity—perhaps given to her by God—and that if she didn't take this opportunity she might regret it for a long time.

Maria Eliza took a quick breath and began walking. Her heart beat uncontrollably when she slipped off the sidewalk, onto the grass, and through the gate. She saw more activity down the driveway, near the front of the house, but that was okay because she didn't need the driveway to get where she was going. Once inside the gate, she quickly turned to the right and slipped behind the gazebo that was covered with vines. The whole thing had taken only seconds, and had apparently been unobserved by the police officers who were intent upon the house itself and not paying attention to the grounds behind them.

She found the pathway behind the gazebo with ease. This would lead around the hedges and down the secluded walk all the way back to the cottages. With any luck, she'd be inside before anyone even knew she was there.

†

WHEN CK WALKED INTO THE LOUNGE AREA GALWAY WAS already showing off the antique book in his possession. He placed the leather-bound tome on the table and carefully turned to the first page. CK stared down at it and saw smooth, careful handwriting. It said:

The Journal of Beverly Scott Thomas

"Find something in your travels, did you?" CK said. "Mind telling us where you've been for the last two days, Galway?"

Galway looked up at her mysteriously. "Tell me the story, CK," he said.

CK was dumbfounded. "What are you talking about, Gal? I think you should be doing the talking right now, don't you? We've all been worried sick about you, wondering where you were, what you were doing, whether you were safe. And now you want me to tell you a story? Please."

"Not a story," Galway insisted. "The story. Your story."

CK saw curiosity beginning to build in the eyes of her teammates. Junebug said, "You're a crazy old man, Gal, you know that, don't you?"

Rebel reached over and started to thumb through the journal. "Careful with that, young lady!" Galway said, obviously fighting the urge to snatch it back from the private detective's hands.

"Galway," CK said again. "Where have you been?"

James was reading over Rebel's shoulder now, and he pointed to a spot on the old, yellowed page. Galway seemed to be feeling protective over the book. He ignored CK and instead said, "Look, don't touch the paper if you can help it. Don't you all know anything about document preservation? The oils on your fingers can permanently stain the page, or you might cause a brittle spot to wrinkle and tear."

"Galway," CK was getting annoyed now.

"CK," he said, looking her in the eyes.

Suddenly Rebel set down the book. "I want to hear the story again, too, CK."

Galway eased the journal back toward himself. "Thank you," he said with a hint of exasperation in his voice. "So tell us already, CK. Stop keeping us in suspense."

CK threw up her hands in frustration and sank down into the soft cushions of the love seat next to her. "Galway, first, you owe me an explanation before anything. And second, I have no idea what story you are talking about. And third, even if I did, I don't feel like leading a little story-time session right now, you know what I mean?"

Galway leaned forward and looked earnest. "Celia," he said. "Tell us the story of how you got your name."

†

SEAN STEPP WAS PROUD OF THE EFFORT AND SPEED HIS TEAM had exhibited while infiltrating the Johnson mansion. But he was also extremely disgusted by the results.

He had given the all clear a few minutes ago. SWAT was making one last sweep of the premises, but now the officers who filled most of the house were the nonaction type—a few detectives like himself, a forensic team, a police photographer, a fingerprint team, and so on. He called for the ambulances and wondered how long it would take for enough of them to arrive. Then he instructed a blue nearby to call the coroner as well.

He saw Lincoln Sayles enter the front doorway and look carefully around. Sean made eye contact and motioned him over.

"We were too late," he said when the civilian arrived. "Most of the inhabitants of this house are gone already."

"Most?" Lincoln asked.

Sean nodded. "There's a dead body in the basement. Another on the second floor. There's an unconscious kid down the hallway—looks like he may be in a coma. There are two other injured gang members with various degrees of broken bones. The rest are gone. Apparently they figured it was safer to run away than it was to stay."

Lincoln nodded.

"There are still a lot of questions to be answered around here, though," Sean said. "For instance, downstairs in the basement room where one of the dead bodies is, there are also the remnants of a large wooden cross. Some binding wire. And possibly some instruments of torture."

"What about Johnson?"

Sean scratched his head. "Loftis Johnson is upstairs on the second floor, stretched out halfway in a closet and halfway out of it. He keeps drifting in and out of consciousness. It looks like his lower spine might be broken, and he's lost a lot of blood from a broken nose and cuts and scrapes all over his body."

"Wow."

"Yeah. And whoever did this appears to have known what he was doing. It looks almost surgical, like he intended to paralyze Johnson but also wanted him to live an otherwise healthy life."

"And the Sinner?"

Sean snorted. "You know the answer to that."

†

MARIA ELIZA UNLOCKED THE FRONT DOOR TO THE CENTER cottage and stepped inside. She immediately noticed the rumpled cushions on the couch and the absence of one of the chairs from the living room. She absently fluffed the cushions and peeked into the kitchen. She saw an opened can of beans with a spoon sticking out, and a half-full water glass. The perfectionist in her caused her to cluck disapprovingly while she tidied up the kitchen and wiped down the counter.

When she finished, she stood for a moment by the sink and wondered why she was avoiding the back bedroom, why she was afraid of what she might find back there. She called out gently from the kitchen, "Mr. Galway? Mr. Galway, are you still here?"

There was no response, and that made her feel just a little more uneasy. She walked slowly to the hallway and gazed down at the bedroom doors. As usual, the first room was open and lit with daylight flowing through the open curtains. The second room, the forbidden one, was closed.

Maybe it's locked again, she thought, and secretly hoped it was.

She walked down to the end of the hall and put a hand on the knob of the door. It turned easily in her grasp. She remembered the reason she had come and steeled her resolve. She opened to the door to the room.

He lay on the bed, arms folded neatly at his sides this time. Beneath his eyelids, his eyes danced with dreaming. He was breathing through his mouth, punctuated gasps as if somewhere, in the realms of dreaming, he was running. She wondered if he were running away from something or to something.

He was so bloodied, though most of that blood had dried by now. His face held pain below the scars. His body looked wrecked, like it should not function. He twitched from time to time, leg spasms that arched his back and made the bed creak beneath him.

She looked at the broken man before her and felt a sudden, otherworldly compassion.

She returned to the kitchen and gathered a bowl and cloth, filling both with cool water. She walked back into the forbidden bedroom and saw that his eyes had stilled now. His breathing was steady, shallow. His arms and legs were relaxed and uncurled.

She dabbed the cool damp cloth across his forehead, touched his cheek as if she were a mother caressing a sleeping child.

"So you are the Sinner," she said softly to the wounded, sleeping man. "My name is Maria Eliza Garces. And I will be your saint."

†

CK Ivors looked at the eager faces surrounding her in the lounge. James and Rebel both had a look of surprised wonder. Junebug was simply curious. Chance seemed slightly uncomfortable, probably because Keena was sitting next to him on the couch. The assistant appeared unsure what was going on but definitely interested to hear more.

Galway had that look he got when something was terribly important, when he wanted desperately for you to know what it was that was terribly important, but he was unwilling to tell you exactly what was so important or why.

"It's just family folklore, Gal, you know that. Just tales that parents make up to pass the minutes before their children must go to sleep."

Galway didn't respond. He just continued to look at her expectantly.

"Fine," CK said. "Fine. You all really want to waste time hearing this?"

"CK," Junebug said gently. "You're the one wasting

time. Just tell the story already. I don't remember most of it
or I'd tell it for you."

CK glared at her photographer, then softened when he
gave her a reassuring smile.

"All right," she said. "Well, it's just something my mama
used to tell me late at night when I couldn't sleep because I
was having a fight with my dad or I was mad that my little
sister got a new dress and I didn't. You know, that kind of
stuff. I don't know if it's a true story or not. Probably she just
made it up to make me grateful for all the things she and my
dad did for me.

"Anyway. A long time ago, back before the Civil War,
my great-great-great-great-grandfather, Reuben, was born a
slave down in southern Virginia. When he grew up, he married one of the other slaves on the plantation where they
lived. Her name was Caroline. They had a daughter who
they named Celia.

"Reuben was a good man, and a hardworking one, but
he strained at being a slave. Said it was unnatural and unholy.
So he tried to escape. They caught him the first time and
brought him back, beat him and Caroline just to make the
point. But a year later he ran again. He wanted to make it
north to Canada, where he was determined to earn enough
money to buy his wife and daughter out of slavery.

"They caught him again. Beat him. Raped Caroline
right in front of him—Mom didn't tell me that part until I
was in college. Told him if he ever ran again, there'd be hell
to pay. Then, apparently as punishment for him, they made
arrangements to sell Celia away from the plantation, to
some slave owner in Florida or something.

"So Grandfather Reuben did the only thing he could think to do. He ran again, and this time he took Celia with him. She was five years old. He had made a contact in Philadelphia, an abolitionist who promised that if Reuben could get that far, he would arrange his passage to Canada.

"Well, they never made it to Philadelphia. No one knows for sure what happened to them, but the rumor was that bounty hunters caught and killed them on the way.

"Caroline turned up pregnant—either from the rape or from before Reuben left, nobody knows for sure. But the fact that there are a number of people in my family with green eyes says there's some white blood in us from somewhere, so, you know, you can do the math.

"Anyway, Caroline gave birth to a second daughter in 1861. She named her Rebekah. She was born a slave, but died a free woman about forty years after the Civil War. I am descended from her."

CK paused and looked again at the faces around her. Most were grim, several nodded knowingly. Galway looked sad and happy at the same time.

"Well, to make a long story short, when Grandma Rebekah grew up and had kids of her own after the war, she named her firstborn daughter after the older sister she'd never met. And that became a tradition among the women of my family. Anytime a firstborn daughter came along, she was named after Great-Aunty Celia. And that's how I got my name. At least, that's what my mama always said."

"CK," Junebug said slowly. "That's right. Your real name is Celia Kaye Ivors. I always forget that."

Chance added, "Heck, I never even knew your name was Celia. I always thought it was just Seekay. Figured it was some special Southern thing or something."

Galway turned the journal toward CK. "I think," he said, "you'll want to read some of this. At least the first part."

CK looked puzzled. "Right now?"

Rebel reached for the book. "Don't be insensitive, Galway. She can't read this while we're all watching her."

CK felt both curiosity and fear seeding themselves within her. "Why don't you read it to me, Reb," she said. "Why don't you read it to all of us?"   †

Jennison dies like a pig, squealing in protest and flailing his legs as if doing so could make him fly. He hangs from the monstrous oak, and I watch the rope squeezing, squeezing, until it separates soul from body and Jennison is finally still.

The night is quiet. Peaceful. There is no one around for miles; I have made sure of that. I thought I would find satisfaction in watching him die. Boasted to him of it while I beat him with a horseshoe that mangled his face until it mirrored his warped spirit. When he could no longer resist, I bound him and carried him on Destine's back to this secluded place.

"I have a family," he had groaned. "A wife. A son. He's only a boy."

His voice might as well have been speaking to God, because I wasn't listening.

When we got here I strung him up and left him sitting on Destine's broad shoulders.

"I have seen you," I said to him. "You inhabit my dreams and make them all nightmares."

"Who are you?" he had croaked before he died. "I don't even know you."

I found myself disgusted that he could so easily forget me, forget my family's farm, forget my burning barn. The truth sank in quickly, though. He had made a life of this, of chasing—and killing—runaway slaves. Mine was only another helpless, faceless presence in his greedy path toward a bounty hunter's payday.

"I am just a sinner," I said finally. And then I slapped Destine's rump and sent her running, watched the noose jerk him off her back, watched the man fade and disappear before me.

Now I take the paper from my pocket, gather Destine and ride to his side. I pin the paper to his chest. It bears my mark, and a list of the crimes that Jennison has committed. I thought killing Jennison would somehow make my guilt ease, but now I realize it has only added more blood to my hands. I am damned more yet, this time by my actions rather than my inactions. I turn to ride back toward the town where I first found Jennison.

I am the judge. I am the jury. I am the executioner.

And I have two more men to murder before this week is done.

NINETEEN

HE HEARD THE TAP-TAP-TAPPING OF A COMPUTER keyboard for a full minute before he actually recognized what it was. He licked his lips and tasted the faint scent of wildflowers that so often accompanied his waking from a long sleep. He let out a deep sigh, and the typing on the keyboard stopped. He waited, forced himself to breathe shallowly and evenly, forced his face to maintain its relaxed expression. Perhaps he had dozed off again, he couldn't tell.

Eventually the clicking of fingernails on the keyboard resumed.

As was his custom, he let his senses fill in the picture

before opening his eyes. His body tingled with health and life. It had been a healing sleep.

His soul tingled with sorrow and regret. It had been a dreaming sleep, a reminder of the first of his terrible dreams. A memory of Celia.

The typist had stopped again now. He heard bare feet gently flapping against the hardwood floor, then heard the deep swoosh of curtains being swept away from the window pane. Even beneath closed eyelids he could see the light that flooded the room, feel its warmth on his bare chest and legs. He was wearing comfortable shorts, it appeared. Socks. No shirt. And handcuffs.

The bare feet stepped pleasantly across the room again and soon the typing resumed.

He carefully tested the handcuffs that kept his palms resting gently on his abdomen. They were secure but not tight. Almost like bracelets that wouldn't slip over your hands. He could move his arms, though, if he wanted to, as long as his wrists stayed about six inches apart. That could come in handy at some point. And his head was free of any restraint. Also a plus.

He heard a man's voice from the doorway. "Myers is going to grab some sandwiches," the voice said. "You want something?"

The typing continued while a woman's voice responded. "Yeah, that'd be great. Ask him to get me turkey on sourdough, hold the mayo."

"You got it."

"Thanks."

"Making progress?"

The typing stopped again. "Yeah," the voice said. "But ... well, this one is different from any of the others I've done."

He could hear a smile in the man's voice. "Keep at it," he said. "We all can't wait to read it."

She laughed then. "That's what scares me!"

"Be back in a flash with your sandwich. You want a soda with it?"

"No, thanks. Got a tall glass of iced tea around here somewhere."

"Right."

Silence returned to the room, with only the tapping of the keyboard to spread its music across the stillness.

He understood now that his legs were bound over the socks, just above the ankles. Leg irons. Too tight to slide out of, even with the socks. But again, not so tight as to be painful. He tried to pull his feet toward the edge of the bed without being noticed by the typist. He quickly ascertained that the leg irons were attached to something that must have been bolted to the floor. He would not be able to leave this bed anytime soon. That could be a problem, but he wasn't ready to deal with that yet. He still needed to discover more about the situation and about the woman who was with him in the room.

He listened again to the typing. There was something he liked about it, something comforting. He felt the sunlight warming the air in the room and breathed again the faint scent of potpourri.

He had been in worse prisons than this, he decided. He quietly drifted off to sleep once more.

When he woke next it was nighttime. He couldn't tell if he had been sleeping for a few hours or a few days. To him it didn't really matter anyway.

The sheets beneath him were fresh. A blanket was spread carefully over his torso and legs, but the room was a comfortable temperature anyway and the blanket seemed barely needed. He heard the hum of a heater blowing warm air through vents, and decided that it must now be winter. His handcuffed hands lay on top of the covers, still centered on his abdomen by the short chain that connected the two wrist cuffs together. His legs were still chained and bolted to the floor.

The woman who had been typing was apparently gone, but there were male voices talking softly outside his door.

"Strangest thing I've ever seen in my life, Sean," the first one said.

"I know what you mean."

"I mean, this guy was a bloody mess when that maid showed him to us. Just sleeping and bleeding and unaware of anything."

"And the maid acting like it was no big deal, like that kind of thing happens every day."

"Well, she was right, wasn't she? I mean sort of?"

"Yeah. Funny though. If CK hadn't called and insisted we check out the cottages back here, we might have missed this whole area."

"And that maid wouldn't have let us in, and we wouldn't have found this guy and so on. I know. Makes you almost believe in God, don't it?"

"I do believe in God."

There was an awkward silence, then the first voice resumed. "Still, I don't know what to believe about that guy in the bed there."

"Yeah."

"Think he's really the perp that ruined the priest?"

"Looks that way. And that Ackers kid, and even Loftis Johnson, too."

"You think Johnson's lawyers are going to be able to keep him out of jail this time?"

"You've seen the evidence. What do you think?"

"I think it's an open-and-shut case. Johnson's guilty, and it's obvious."

"So you think he'll get off scot-free too?"

"Yeah. He's still going to be in a hospital for some time with all the surgeries still left to do, and going to have to learn how to use a wheelchair after that. Between now and when his actual trial starts, my guess is that some technicality will surface, or some key witness from the Crux Crue will recant his testimony. Isn't that the way it always happens?"

There was a silence again. "Not always."

"You think I should go check on the prisoner again?"

"Why? He hasn't moved in forever. Just keeps sleeping. Doctors said it's not a coma, though. He goes through normal sleep cycles, just seems to skip the stage where you wake up."

"Freakiest thing, Sean. If I hadn't seen it with my own eyes, I wouldn't have believed it."

"Yeah, I'm with you. That broken nose snapping back into place is what got me."

"And those cuts closing up in a matter of seconds? Gave me chills."

"Scientists should study this guy for miracle cures."

"He's been all healed up for months now. I wonder why he doesn't wake up."

"I wonder what we're going to do when he does wake up."

The chatter turned to sports or weather or something else he wasn't interested in, so he tuned the men out and lay in the bed collecting his thoughts. So he'd been sleeping for months, but apparently not years this time. Interesting. He'd had greater wounds that had healed in less time in the past. As always, he was mildly curious about how the time for sleeping was determined.

But I can't control it, he thought. *Never could.*

He considered working up his escape plan, but his mind wandered. *Who was that typing girl?* he mused. *And when will she come back?*

A low buzz filled his ears, and even behind his closed eyelids he felt the darkness begin to swirl again. It was time for yet another sleep.

It was daytime. The light streaming through the curtains offered evidence of that. He opened his eyes and saw a woman seated in the corner of the room, a laptop computer on her table. She was peering intently into an open book beside her laptop.

He blinked. Even from here he recognized the book, the leather binding, the yellowed and aging paper. He knew that if he were to look at the cover he would find the symbol—his symbol—imprinted onto the leather.

So, he was in his own cottage. And she had found his journals. He wondered absently how far she had read, and how piteously she hated him. She must, after all. He was a sinner.

He was covered by the same blanket he'd felt last time he woke. Still bound at his hands and feet. Had he just slept overnight since his last brief period of wakefulness? No matter. It was time to go. He had seen them, and he didn't want to see them again. He had to do something to stop them, and thus to stop the dreams about them.

He breathed carefully and then sat up in the bed. The motion tickled the peripheral vision of his visitor, and she snapped her head his direction. Her emerald eyes widened slightly, striking against the cool chocolate of her skin. She looked at him without saying a word, and he felt like weeping. He couldn't maintain her gaze. He lowered his head to his chest and whispered.

"I have seen you."

She didn't respond to him, just continued staring for a full minute or two. Then she unhooked a cell phone from her belt and dialed a number. After a moment she spoke.

"Maria Eliza?" she said. "Yes. Yes. He's awake now. No, just now. Yes, Sean said you could come. All right. See you in ten. Bye."

He lifted his head, regained composure and looked at her once more. Neither of them spoke for a while. Finally she broke the silence.

"I brought your coat back," she said, motioning toward the closet. "It's in there, ready whenever you need it. I've never seen any fabric like it. Impressive."

He nodded his thanks, waiting.

"I read your books," she said after a moment. "All of them."

He nodded again. "I give them to you. Do what must be done with them."

She looked surprised. "I can't take your books. They're evidence. And they're antiques. They're heirlooms, possibly worth a million dollars or more. They belong to your family if you don't want them."

"I have no family. They're yours. Do what must be done with them."

"What must be done?"

He didn't answer.

"I can't take them. The police won't let me. They are evidence and someone else's property. It would be stealing."

"Steal them then. Either way, I give them to you."

A man walked in, a day's stubble on his chin, eyes tired.

"I heard voices," he said, then he saw the Sinner sitting up in the bed. No one spoke for a moment. "Well," he said finally. "So you've come awake after all. We had bets on whether you would." No one spoke, so the man continued. "My name is Sean Stepp. I'm a detective for the local police department."

"The journals," the Sinner said. "They are mine. I give them to this woman. To Celia."

Sean Stepp looked surprised but nodded slowly. "I'll see what I can do," he said. "But right now nobody gets them. They are evidence in a criminal case." He paused. "Against you."

The Sinner nodded without reaction or remorse, keeping his gaze focused on the woman. "I understand," he said.

"You'll be going to a real prison soon," the detective said, not unkindly. "We would have moved you before, but your, um, *condition* made the doctors unsure of what would happen if you were transported. Apparently you freaked out the paramedics just a little bit when your dislocated shoulder snapped into place all by itself. When they saw similar little miracles happening to your wounds, they recommended that you not be moved until you woke up." A pause. "Until now."

The Sinner nodded again.

"The doctors wanted to move medical equipment right in here at first," the detective continued. "The maid—the woman we found with you—she told them you wouldn't need it. They didn't listen to her, of course, and only barely listened to the paramedics who were first on scene. But it turns out the maid was right. Even while you were in a coma, with the wounds from the beating you took, your vital signs were normal." He shook his head. "No bodily functions, though. No need for food or liquid—you're organs just kept working like normal. No waste at all either. But still a normal, functioning body. The doctors and the research scientists are very interested to know how you do that. But every time they tried to hook up medical apparatuses, your body seemed to go into some kind of shock and just shut down for a while. They finally just took all their hospital equipment away and let you sleep in peace, though they did take samples of your blood and muscle tissue for further study before they left. And now that you're awake, well, they intend to run quite a few tests."

The Sinner didn't respond.

"We have a lot of questions for you," Detective Stepp said after a moment.

The Sinner remained silent, and the detective glanced over at the woman.

"Me first, Sean," she said urgently. "You promised."

The detective seemed torn, but nodded anyway. "Where's Maria Eliza?"

"On her way. Why don't you go wait for her at the front door?"

The detective looked wary.

"It's okay, Sean. He can't hurt me, not with the cuffs and chains on him like that."

The detective pressed his lips together, then finally nodded again. "Myers and Kennedy are right outside this door," he said.

"I know," she said.

The detective took a hesitant step toward the door. "Listen," he said to the Sinner, "you want some water or food or something? You need to use the bathroom?"

The Sinner shook his head. "No."

The detective looked at the woman. "I'll wait to start the clock until after Maria Eliza gets here," he said. "But remember, twenty minutes. That's all you get, and then we need to start the prisoner transport. Got it?"

"I got it, Sean. And thanks."

The detective walked slowly from the room, leaving the Sinner and the woman alone again.

They gazed at each other for a moment, then she spoke. "I'm not who you think I am," she said.

"I know," he said. "But you are her family. I see her blood in you, her face in your features."

CK nodded. "She was, well, a long-lost aunt in my family."

A look of true sorrow flashed across the Sinner's face. "I am sorry," he whispered.

"I know," she said. "You slept a long time, even after your body had healed itself."

"How long?"

"Almost ten months. It's winter now. February nineteenth."

The Sinner blinked in rapid comprehension.

She picked up the leather-bound journal from beside her laptop and opened it to the first page. "Is that you?" she asked.

"I haven't used that name in a hundred years," he said.

"But is it you? Are you Beverly Scott Thomas?"

A pause. Then, "Yes."

"But how can that be? How can you be someone who is more than a hundred fifty years old?"

"Mine has been a life marked by unique curses."

She bit her lip. "Your dreams."

The Sinner closed his eyes.

"When you dream," she continued, "do you see the future?"

A pause. Then, "Yes. And the past. Failures from my past."

She swallowed. "How many people have you killed? Or maimed?"

"More than my years."

"How many have you saved?"

Silence.

"Raven is safe. Raven Ann Rinehart. Sean out there caught the man who was hurting her."

"I know," the Sinner said. "I have not dreamed of her

anymore, so I knew you had saved her."

"I can't save anybody," CK muttered.

"Nor can I. Not even myself."

The Sinner waited, eyes closed, ready to answer any question this woman would ask. She was Celia's blood; she deserved answers.

He opened his eyes when another woman walked in. She looked at him with eyes of love. She carried a book under her arm, which she carefully placed next to him on the bed. She smiled and placed her palms on his cheeks. She pulled his face close to hers and whispered.

"*Gracias a Dios*," she said. "I am here to save you."   †

Funerals should always be in winter
when the sky spits colors of corpselike gray,
when the stale air shatters like glass on cheek,
when sepia is nature's choice of dress
and a barren country remains oblique.

Funerals should always be in this month
when the Christmas carols have long expired,
when all the lonelies curse the lovers' day,
when casket-carrying numbs the fingers
and solitude bleeds misery away.

Funerals should always be in this week
when earth itself resists the sharpened spade,
when soil groans angrily awake from sleep,
when the greatest presence is the absence
and life lies lifeless on the rubbish heap.

Funerals should always be today
when my heart lies ripped from cavity ...
when frigid sorrow beats through my veins ...
when memory blurs within my tears ...
and I long to join you in the aching, hardened ground.

TWENTY

CK IVORS DIDN'T KNOW HOW TO RESPOND WHEN Maria Eliza had come marching right up to the Sinner declaring that she was here to save the man. *He's a murderer and an immortal,* she thought to herself. *Just exactly how are you going to save him?* But she waited anyway. Maria Eliza deserved at least that much. She had, after all, been the one who led Galway—and the others eventually—to the Sinner's house and then to the Sinner.

When Sean's men had searched the cottages on that fateful day last spring, they had found Maria Eliza sitting in the Sinner's room, holding a vigil, waiting for him to awaken. She'd cleaned his wounds as best she could, but the Sinner was still a bloody mess of humanity. Sean had told CK that he actually thought the Sinner was dead at first, until Maria Eliza had informed him, "He is just sleeping. It is his healing sleep. When he wakes up, he will be healed all over."

CK and the others arrived soon after that, and there'd been a time of questions and confusion and ambulances and police cars and angry arguments over what to do with the sleeping man and more. Two of the paramedics started to administer aid, then got seriously spooked by something, and finally just stood back, refusing to touch the sleeper and arguing that no one else should touch him either. And through it all, Maria Eliza just sat quietly, watching over the Sinner as if he were her only child, as if her baby was down for the night with a fever.

Sean finally conferred with the paramedics and the police chief and even Judge Santos, and together they had decided not to move the Sinner any more than necessary, to wait for him to wake up and then start the criminal process from there. Sean had insisted on precautions, however. "If you'd seen what I saw in that main house, you'd insist on chains too," he'd said when they installed the leg irons and then bolted them to the bed and then bolted the bed to the floor. He applied the cuffs himself, wary of the Sinner waking up and reaching out to do damage with two free hands.

When everything was in place, when everyone had gone but the officers left to guard the body, CK had made her move. It had taken some convincing—and some promises of favors and testimony in the future—but Sean finally agreed to give her what she wanted most. Time alone with the Sinner. Maria Eliza had made a similar plea, so Sean decided to grant them both their wishes. After the Sinner woke up, he said, there would be some transition time while the necessary personnel got their things together in order to transport the prisoner to the high-security jail down south. They could have twenty minutes then, but only twenty minutes and then he had to kick them out and get on with what he called "real police work" surrounding the Sinner.

Twenty minutes was certainly a lot less than CK wanted, but Sean wouldn't budge on that one. "You shouldn't get any time with him at all," he pointed out. So she agreed, and she and Maria Eliza traded phone numbers so that one could call the other at a moment's notice when the Sinner finally woke up.

Then, in a fit of accommodation, Sean had actually agreed to let her set up a laptop in the Sinner's room so she could research her next book from the journals and other antique tomes collected in the cottage—and so she (hopefully) would be there when the Sinner finally woke up.

CK had taken final reports from all her team members and settled up their financial accounts. Rebel and James had gone back to Oklahoma City. Galway had melted into the world of his happy conspiracies, though he still showed up at odd times just to check in. CK knew he was waiting for the Sinner to wake up too, and gave him any information she could.

The final version of Chance's video game had released. It was not a best seller, but it had inspired a core of devoted fans who set up Web sites and ran contests online and swapped clues for cheat codes and such. Chance sometimes joined in the Internet dialogue, anonymously, and seemed to enjoy that people liked his game. It looked like that sequel would be happening after all.

Keena stayed on as CK's assistant, proving her value time and again. And Junebug, well, Junebug was always nearby, and CK kind of liked the comfortableness that he made her feel inside. Especially when she had been spending most of her days sitting in this Sinner's cottage, waiting for the prisoner to wake up. Of course, now that he had awakened, CK found herself suddenly disinterested in the long list of questions she'd written down to ask him. It was the eyes, she decided. They made everything else seem unimportant.

There was something innately desolate about the man. Something lost, which had been lost for a hundred years or more.

She found it hard to believe that he really was the Sinner of legend, that he had lived within three centuries, that he was the same nineteen-year-old boy who'd witnessed the horrible murder of her great aunty Celia as a child. And yet, she found it equally hard to disbelieve those facts, particularly after she'd seen with her own eyes the miraculous appearance and subsequent healing of the stigmata on the man while he slept.

It almost made her believe in God again.

Not that she disbelieved God, really. She just hadn't taken time to get to know him yet. Maybe she would someday. Maybe.

Meanwhile, here was Maria Eliza Garces, and next to her was Beverly Scott Thomas, and now the minutes were ticking quickly by.

"Maria Eliza," CK said, "Sean said he was sticking to his twenty-minute time limit."

The maid glanced back at CK and nodded, a happy grin on her face. "Thank you, CK," she said. Then she pulled a chair from the table and placed it close to the Sinner's bed while he watched in careful wonder.

"Sean says we should, you know, stay out of arm's reach," CK said uncomfortably. The maid ignored her.

"Beverly," Maria Eliza said. "I have seen you."

The Sinner groaned softly and dropped his head.

"I have seen you, stretched out on a cross, surrounded by wicked, hurtful men."

"I am wicked," he whispered. "I am hurtful. I am a sinner."

"Beverly," she continued, "he is the Friend of sinners."

The Sinner did not respond. Maria Eliza reached for her Book, turned to a place she'd marked and read aloud:

> One of the criminals hanging beside Jesus scoffed, "So you're the Messiah, are you? Prove it by saving yourself—and us, too, while you're at it!"
>
> But the other criminal protested, "Don't you fear God even when you are dying? We deserve to die for our evil deeds, but this man hasn't done anything wrong." Then he said, "Jesus, remember me when you come into your Kingdom."
>
> And Jesus replied, "I assure you, today you will be with me in paradise."

The Sinner sat up straight once more, his face a stone. He lifted a cuffed hand and touched the woman next to him on the cheek and gave a rueful smile. "Thank you," he said calmly. "But I am more than merely a thief on a cross. I am a murderer. I am a man of pain and violence. I am a devil. I am a Judas. I am a sinner—the Sinner. There is no forgiveness for me. There never has been, not since the day I betrayed innocent blood."

He placed a hand on her head. "But may God bless and keep you, for you are his saint."

Maria Eliza got angry then. "Who do you think you are?" she hissed at the man. CK jumped to her feet and started tugging on the maid's arm to pull her away from the prisoner. But Maria Eliza would not budge. "You are not God," she continued. "You can't choose who deserves forgiveness and who does not. You are a sinner. If God chooses to forgive you, that's his business, not yours! Why do you think he has kept you alive all these years?"

"To punish me. For my sins."

"You poor old self-centered fool," the maid said pityingly. "He gave you time, more time than anyone in the rest of the world. He gave you visions to tell you he was near. He showed you evils, terrible evils, so that you could know nothing was unforgivable, that there was always time to change. He gave you signs in your own body, symbols of the price he paid for you. What you call a curse is his mysterious blessing, his patience. The harshest, most determined display of grace. He calls you, the worst of sinners, to come to his mercy. And you still can't see that, after a hundred and fifty years? You are truly a fool."

The Sinner was visibly shaken by the little woman before him. "How could God ever forgive a devil like me?"

Maria Eliza breathed deeply. She looked at CK and then back at the Sinner. "Because he is God. He does what he wants, whether you like it or not. And I'll tell you something else. God is not the only one who forgives you. Celia forgives you. Right now. Today." She turned to CK. "Tell him," she ordered.

CK felt a sudden rush of fear. "What?" she whispered to the maid. "Are you mad? I'm not that little slave girl. I never was."

Maria Eliza smiled comfortingly. "Of course you're not," she said softly. "But you are her family. Her kin. Her blood relation. You are all that's needed."

CK felt her mouth go dry as her brain processed the maid's information. She felt the silence of the room suffocating everything, and realized it was as Maria Eliza said. "I understand," she said finally.

She looked at the Sinner, and he stared back at her, eyes hollowed, face unmoving. And behind the red flecks that speckled his eyes, CK thought she saw a candle—so small, so faint, so weak—barely light itself in his soul.

"I'm sorry," he whispered contritely. "I am so sorry. For Celia. For everything."

CK took a deep breath, then exhaled. With a trembling hand, she reached over and traced the scar on the Sinner's right palm.

"Beverly Scott Thomas," she said finally. "On behalf of my family, on behalf of my great-aunt Celia, I forgive you."

He searched her eyes then, looking deeply into them for just a glimmer of hope. She nodded quietly. "Forever," she said—and knew she meant it. "Forever."

Maria Eliza held both their hands in hers. "Beverly," she said, "if she, a sinner like you—if she can forgive you, then why couldn't God do the same?"

The man's eyes flicked around the room, first looking at CK, then taking in Maria Eliza, then landing with impact on the scars within his hands. He started to shake his head, to relax his face into a mask of resignation and calm, but his brows furrowed again and his gaze returned to CK.

"Forever," he whispered to no one. CK felt herself nodding again.

Maria Eliza brushed a hand across the Sinner's forehead. "Today in paradise," she said.

He looked at her quizzically, unsure. She smiled. He looked again at CK, a deep hungry look that found what it wanted in her face.

Then there was a moment of unexpected recognition in the eyes of the Sinner. A faint grin played at the corners of his lips. He sucked in a deep breath of air, and two shocks of hair, right above both his temples, suddenly turned cottony white. He lay back down in the bed, placing his handcuffed wrists across his abdomen.

Then a frown creased his brow. "Julian," he said. "Julian Albert Conant."

For the first time, Maria Eliza looked confused. She glanced over to CK for help. CK stepped forward and locked eyes with the graying man.

"I understand," she said. "I'll find him. Sean and I will protect him. I promise."

"Thank you," the Sinner breathed, his face relaxing into a restful gaze. He blinked once, twice. A soft, thick sigh escaped his lips.

And then he breathed his last.

The Sinner's body relaxed as the light flickered and faded in his eyes. And then his face was a mask of peace. He stared with an unblinking gaze toward the ceiling, and his chest finally lay still.

CK felt a sense of panic rising within her. "Maria Eliza," she said, "what's going on? What did we do?"

"We let him go home, CK," she said. "Where his dreams of heaven will finally come true."

✝

LOFTIS JOHNSON LAY IN THE BEST HOSPITAL BED THAT money could buy. They were telling him that the third surgery appeared to have done what the other two could not, that his hip was finally showing signs of accepting the surgeon's repairs. But Loftis couldn't feel it anyway, and thus couldn't care more than as a matter of common interest. His spine was still shattered at the base, leaving him paralyzed from the waist down. The doctors had been very clear. He would never walk again. As soon as he was willing, they would begin physical therapy to teach him how to adjust to life in a wheelchair. At present he was still unwilling.

They would not tell him what had happened to the Sinner. His sources seemed to think he was in police custody at an undisclosed location. That was fine. The Sinner was never a prisoner for very long. Soon he would break out of their grasp and then Loftis would capture him again.

It might take years to find him, but Loftis was a patient man when he needed to be. After all, Loftis was not the forgiving type, and as they said, vengeance was a dish best served cold.

He would wait, then, and watch, and when the time was right, the Sinner would suffer more than he could imagine.

Loftis Johnson died waiting.   ✝

TWENTY-ONE

CK IVORS HAD INVITED ONLY JUNEBUG TO JOIN HER for this little ceremony. They stood in CK's backyard, looking solemnly at the tarnished iron garbage can with holes poked in its sides.

"You sure you want to do this?" Junebug said. "I mean, you could probably get a lot of money on eBay for those things."

"Yeah, I know."

"Or at least donate them to the Smithsonian or something. They're history, for goodness' sake."

"I know."

"Galway will never forgive you."

"He'll get over it. Eventually."

She looked at the stacks of books on the ground beside her. There were forty-four of them. She'd been tempted to keep just the first journal, just the first book that told her own family history. But she'd remembered the Sinner's request. "Do what must be done with them."

"Light the fire, Junebug."

"What about your book, CK? Don't you need these for your research?"

She pursed her lips into a rueful smile. "I already deleted everything I wrote about the Sinner from my computer files this morning."

"Everything?"

"All four hundred and eleven pages."

Junebug shook his head. "You spent nearly a year working on that manuscript. How could you just throw it away?"

CK just shrugged. "Seemed like the right thing to do."

There was a pause. "What will your editor say?"

"I already worked it out with Corson," she said. "I told him my next book was going to be a children's picture book. About the Underground Railroad and a little slave girl named Celia."

"And he went for that?"

"Well, no, not at first. But I told him I'd buy twenty-five thousand copies out of the first print run to donate to charity, and well, he changed his mind. Money seems to do that for a publisher."

Junebug nodded. "What about me, CK? I could use the money. Why not give these journals to me and let me sell them on eBay? I promise to buy you a really neat Superman collectible out of my earnings."

CK laughed. "No, Junebug. No."

He shrugged. "I figured it was worth a try."

He sighed and took a large wad of newspaper and dropped it into the bottom of the metal garbage can. He lit a long match, let it burn for a moment, and then dropped it down the can as well. The paper quickly caught fire and began to blaze.

"Here goes nothing," CK said as she tossed in the first book. *Good-bye, Aunty Celia*, she thought.

She dropped in the second and the third journals before Junebug joined in to help. In a moment, all forty-four books were burning in the garbage can, causing the flame to rise up over the edge and spewing the smell of ash and smoke. They watched the fire burn for a few minutes, neither one saying anything, just listening to the shrill crackling of the fire's fuel and the burning oxygen hissing within the can.

"This is the last of it," CK said finally, unfolding a worn sheet of paper torn from one of the more recent books.

Junebug peeked over CK's shoulder and read the words. "Erasure?" he said.

"Just a title I gave it. Seemed to fit."

Junebug continued reading. "'*Let me be forgotten by posterity*,'" he said. "Well, I guess burning a hundred and fifty years of his journals is a big step toward accomplishing that."

CK watched the fire and didn't answer. She felt the heat fighting the cold air around her. She took one last look at the paper in her hand, then crumpled it into a ball and tossed it into the inferno.

Just as she did, she realized she couldn't remember

the Sinner's face anymore. Only his eyes. Chocolate brown, flecked behind with tiny dots of reddish gold in the pigment.

"C'mon, Junebug," she said at last. "Let's get something for dinner."   †

EPILOGUE

HECTOR GOMEZ FELT NERVOUS WALKING INTO THE EIGHTH-grade class, especially since the teacher was out of the room at that moment. But he summoned up his courage anyway and marched in among the bigger kids.

"Hey, aren't you Emilia's brother?" he heard a girl's voice calling out kindly to him. "She's not in this class right now, little bro. She's down in Gleeson's room, number 216."

Hector ignored her and walked toward the sandy-haired boy sitting in a desk at the back of the room. He was coloring his fingernails with black marker and didn't notice the younger boy making his way toward him until Hector was almost at his desk.

He looked at Hector with shallow eyes, and said nothing.

Hector stood in front of the desk for a moment while the two boys exchanged looks.

"Hey, Emilia's brother," a boy's voice called from the other side of the room, laughing. "I wouldn't mess with that kid if I were you."

Then the laughing quieted down as curiosity began to quell the noisy activity that usually accompanied the teacher's absence.

Hector felt butterflies in his stomach, and felt his fingers clenching and unclenching into fists at his side.

"You want something, kid?" the older boy said finally.

Hector nodded, and then delivered the message he had come here to give. He was careful to make his voice even, controlled. Businesslike.

"I have seen you."